CW00947084

A RUSSIAN

IN THE

AMERICAN ARMY

—WWII

The Fighting 4th Infantry

KARL THOMSON

outskirts
press

Outskirts Press, Inc.
http://www.outskirtspress.com

Paperback ISBN: 978-1-9772-2443-9
Hardback ISBN: 978-1-9772-2503-0

Outskirts Press and the "OP" logo are trademarks belonging to Outskirts Press, Inc.

PRINTED IN THE UNITED STATES OF AMERICA

1

U.S.A

I n 1936 a young Russian couple descended the gangway into Ellis Island, full of hope for a new life in America. Albevt and Svetlana Vetov were in their early thirties and had brought their ten-year-old son, Alexander, to America where he could have a good life. Both of Albevt and Svetlana parents had been White Russians. That had nothing to do with the white race. It meant that during the Communist revolution when the "reds"took control of the country, the "whites" fought the reds to stop their country from becoming a communist country. Albevt's father had been a professor at the University of Moscow. During the early years of Communist control, both of Albevt's parents were taken from their university apartment by a group of Red supporters and just vanished and were never heard from again. Albevt was with a baby-sitter at the time and she sent him into the countryside to some of her kinfolks to live on their farm. There he grew up as a fine, smart, healthy boy that did very well in school. Like most Russian farm boys, he grew up strong from the hard work on the farm even though he was never a large boy. He was also very well liked.

From the first time he saw Svetlana when he was sixteen, he vowed in his heart he was going to marry this beautiful young woman even though she was a year older than him. At that time in Russia most men married younger women than themselves.

Albevt worked hard to win Svetlana's mind and heart and in three years they were married. Life was hard in Russia in the late teens and early twenties. The fact that both families had been white Russians made it much harder than for those that embraced communism. From the first, Albevt and Svetlana had planned to leave Russia but money was very hard to come by in those years. Albevt was a hard worker and they both saved for their dream of getting to America.

Finally in the spring of 1934, when Alexander was eight, they moved to Holland. Here Albevt got a job at the shipyards at more than twice what he had been paid in Russia. It also cost more to live in Holland, but they both saved all they could and Alexander grew up speaking both Dutch and Russian. Even back in Russia Alex's parents both had studied English as their goal in life was to move to the free country of America when they could. From his earliest years Alex had learned some English. Schooling was free in Holland and Alexander did well in all his classes and in sports. There the classes were all in the Dutch language so Alexander polished up on Dutch so as to speak Dutch like the high class children did in Holland schools. A lot of people in that part of the world knew two or more languages so Alexander learned and spoke all three with ease and perfection.

Life in Holland was good and things began to look better. Both of Alex's parents worked hard and saved all they could. After all, their goal had always been to get to America and that dream never dimmed. Svetlanna had kinfolk in New York and every time she got a letter from them it renewed their drive. In 1935 she wrote that they were coming to New York and asked them for help in procuring everything needed to get into the United States and to become citizens. In 1936 they sold off almost all they possessed, said goodbye to a host of friends and boarded a steamship for America. Alexander liked the ocean but his poor mother, Svetlanna, was seasick for the first part of the trip. Entering the New York harbor, they were amazed at the skyline. In 1936, there were no super tall buildings in Holland. They unloaded onto Ellis Island and it took several days to get permission to go on into New York City.

After finally getting off Ellis Island and into New York City they sought out Svetlanna's people who stayed with the other Russians that had come to New York and were living in Hamilton Heights. This was an area just north of a large black community known as Harlem. In spite of these being hard years in America's economy, things were getting better for all. Their apartment was only a few blocks from the docks on the west side of New York. Many Russian men worked at the docks. These neighbors helped Albevt get a job unloading cargo on the docks. Both Albevt and Svetlana had studied English, mostly from books as they had always planned to come to America. So even from their first days on Ellis Island they could speak English well enough to be understood. Albevt's hard work and sharp mind paid off quickly, both on and off the job.

Albevt and Svetlanna were both Russian and were still living in a Russian community where both English and Russian were used commonly, almost interchangeably for Alexander and his parents. Albevt's impressive knowledge of Dutch, English and Russian, both written and spoken, made him an important man on the dock. This, along with his hard work, drew the attention of his supervisors. He now spent more time directing the work than just being a strong worker. He had the ability to get along well with most all men and could read and write in three languages. That made him an excellent choice to be a loading crew foreman. Within two years he was raised from loading foreman to dock foreman, and with every promotion came a pay raise. They moved into a much nicer apartment, and became well known as a very successful middle class family.

Little Alexander swapped to English in school with ease and the fact that most of his classmates and even some of his teachers also spoke Russian was a great help. Of course, Mom and Dad had tried to teach him some English even before they got to America and this also played a role. Still he was raised in a Russian community were

Russian was the everyday language so he had full command of all three languages and could move from one to the other without a moment of hesitation. Both his mother and father had never called him anything except Alexander. In an American school it was now Alex. He was always in the top ten percent in his classes except in advanced algebra. It was admittedly challenging staying near the top of the class. When Alexander entered high school it did not take him long to get more involved in sports and he even took a class in acting. There his real talent shone brightly and he was in all the plays, the leading man in most of them. He was a good-looking young man, one of the school's best actors, as well as a standout in sports. It is not hard to understand how the girls in his school thought of him. In the 1930's there were three very distinct class-es of people. Those that were very affluent, the middle class who were the working semi-wealthy and held decent jobs. But, by far, the majority were the poor working class, that was looked down on by those above.

This was where the Vetov's fit in but Albevt Vetov was well known in Hamilten Heights as a leader and spokesman. However while he worked well with the upper class he never looked down on the working poor. Even though he did not own his own business as most of the people of their group did, Albevt Vetov was a man to be respected.

There was also the plain working man and working men back then had to live on very little. Alex's parents made sure Alex treated these with respect, as his father did. Alexander Vetov had a good life in New York City and he always had a girlfriend. Some he liked, while others he thought he was madly in love with. However things were changing politically speaking. Europe was a boiling point and even the East was heating up. Mom and Dad were hanging onto every radio news broadcast and Dad studied the newspaper with great concentration. Even teenagers talked a lot about how serious things were. After the First World War most Americans swore they would never again get involved in another war.

After Hitler reneged on his supposed peaceful takeovers, the Germans became notorious for their blitzkrieg. Then a couple years into the Second World War, Hitler turned on Russia. The news at home from mother Russia was all about Hitler's invasion and what horror was taking place there. Although Alex was born in Russia, of course they'd left when he was a small boy. At that age he only remembered what young boys think and do. Those memories were good, so Alex only really knew about current Russia from his parents. Of course, all the other Russians that he lived with and went to school with also taught him much about Russia just by their everyday talk. He felt deeply involved with Russia as he watched his parents suffer with every newscast or letter they received.

He developed a deepening hatred for the Nazis. When Pearl Harbor was bombed Alex still had not even reached his sixteenth birthday, but he set his mind that the day he graduated from high school was the day he was going to enlist in the Army. The year 1942 became a year of despair, and though the newspapers tried to offer hope and promise of better times, everywhere in Europe the Nazi s were overrunning everyone and everything.

The only seemingly bright spot in Europe came when the British were able to retrieve many of their troops from Dunkirk and then stopped the Nazis in the Air Battle of Britain. Even that had not stopped Hitler because that was when he turned and attacked mother Russia. Meanwhile Hitler was still trying to bomb England into submission. In the Pacific it was no better as Japan seemed they could not be stopped as they spread out over Asia like a flood.

Here again there were just a few little bright spots: one, the word came of Dolittle's daring air raid and the bombing of Japan. Of course, the battle of Midway ended encouragingly. At great cost to America, four Japanese aircraft carriers had been sunk and the Japanese had to turn back and retreat temporarily to the homeland. While Midway did stop the Japanese from heading toward America, it did not stop their drive on the other side of the Pacific where their land forces were pushing forward everywhere they went. In the battle of the Coral Sea neither the Allied navies nor the

Japanese navy really won as both fought hard and both took heavy losses before withdrawing. This made Alex start thinking about joining the Navy and fighting the Japs. This did not last long as it had always been in his head to fight the Nazis. He really wanted to become an officer so he studied hard. He read books on becoming an officer and was disappointed to find out that to even have a shot at becoming an officer he needed to be a college graduate. This is what the prewar books told him, so now he set his sights on becoming a master sergeant. He followed the news and read about heroic actions, looking forward to the day he could join up himself.

Almost all the rest was bad news in 1942, even though everywhere people were trying to encourage each other. America was now wide awake and was cranking up her entire resources. Americans were mad as hell and working with all their might and ability. Factories had converted from making things for the good life into factories of wartime production. Every ship and dock in America was loading war materials for use by the desperate Allied forces. Not just the American military, but every Ally that could hold a gun against the Nazis or the Japs needed help and America did her best to provide it. Albevt Vetov was now working double shifts to get ships loaded and off to Britain from New York.

By 1943 and Alex's last year in high school, America had poured men and material over both oceans and had Germany, Japan, and Italy occupied on all fronts. This was not to say America and her Allies were always winning. But now they were winning more often than they were losing. It was far from over but things had made a major turn-around. As tens of thousands of young men and women graduated in the summer of 1943 it was now their turn to take on their share in this worldwide war. Graduation was on a weekend so it was Monday before Alex signed his papers. In 1943 America was in full swing, using every fiber of its being to win WWII. Every factory was straining to produce the vast array of material needed to be ready to win and American youth were joining the armed forces by the thousands. Many thousands of young men just like

Alex finished high school and signed up for the military the following week.

Even though many Americans had been fighting in Africa and now in Italy for two years, most everyone knew the next big step was going to be the invasion of Europe, taking it back from Hitler. Basic training for Alexander was what every person that has ever gone through it well knows and understands. It was no different for Alex and his brightest moment came when most of his instructors thought he was a good candidate for Officers Candidate School. However, he was only seventeen and did not have any college so that was out. The second best advantage he had was, of course, his ability to speak, read and write in three languages. The third good thing in Basic was the fact that, not only he was an excellent soldier, he was he an excellent shot. From Basic Alex was sent to the swamps of Louisiana in the heat of August for training with the 4th Motorized Division in what was known as the Louisiana Maneuvers. He wondered if the heat and humidity was going to kill him, as this was so different from living in New York City. Still he made private first class while in Louisiana. There, he was assigned to be a driver of an American half-track and did not even have a driver's license. What does a boy in New York City need to drive for? You take the subway. Alex really enjoyed driving his half-track and took to it like a fish to water.

Then a month later the whole division was transferred to Camp Gordian in Georgia for training in the Carolina Maneuvers. Here he drove everything including an old WW1 tank.

With his M1,he was one of the top three shots of his company on the rifle range. After receiving expert marksman for his shooting, he was recommended for a promotion to corporal. Again his age shot him down but the recommendation was on his record. After the Carolina maneuvers the 4th was sent to Fort Dix in New Jersey where they were changed from a Motorized Division into an Infantry Division. Alexander hated giving up his half-track, but no more than the men of the 4th liked having to walk everywhere they went, but they were no longer motorized.

While there he made corporal and was again recommended for Officers Candidate School. The same old thing, too young and no college, shot him down again. Men of the 4th began to wonder if they were going to spend their entire enlistment in the States training. After this, the 4th was on the move again and sent to Camp Gordon Johnson in Florida.

Here they started their training with the famous Higgins landing craft, making amphibious landings on Florida beaches. Everyone knew by now they were soon to be invading Hitler's Europe even though no one ever told them that was going to happen. The 4th was very proud to be considered probably the best trained assault troops in the American army. In spite of his youth, his great record and proven ability to be a leader allowed the young man to be promoted to sergeant. Landing his squad on the Florida beach from a Higgins boat, Alex was determined his squad was going to be the best it could be. Of course the Higgins was not his but he felt like it was. Even though he pushed his squad hard he never asked them to do anything he would not do. In every way he worked as hard or harder than any man in his platoon. His men liked him for this and the fact that, unlike some sergeants they knew, he cared about every man in the squad. When other squads asked the men of Alexander's squad about their "kid" sergeant the men always said Alex was tough but fair. They said there was not a man in the army that would be any better at taking them ashore in Europe and leading them into combat than Sergeant Vetov.

The day Alex walked up that gangway to board the troop ship to England he was so full of excitement. He had made corporal before finishing training and was promoted to sergeant before being sent to England. He was very proud of those three stripes on his sleeves. The second day out in the Atlantic the roiling of the troop ship brought many men to the rails to discharge their breakfast. Alex was in the lead to the rail and seemed to live there. In fact, though most men got used to the rolling of the ship, Alex was still sick when the ship docked in merry old England. Alex told his lieutenant about his mother's trip across the Atlantic and said he must have more of her blood in him than he thought. He said, "I thought about joining the navy, some sailor I would have made."

It seemed all of England was one huge military base, there was miles and miles of trucks, tanks and artillery everywhere. Even that did not match the miles of hastily constructed warehouses and even huge piles of crates covered with tarps. Then it was back to training and military exercises in England in preparation for D day. One thing seemed for sure—it appeared that for every English girl between the age of eighteen and sixty there were twenty Americans and that did not even count the British males. The Brits were nice enough and treated the American servicemen well enough, but could not resist saying Americans are overpaid, over-sexed and over here.

Being a typical young man with relatively few young British women around, they all looked wonderful. Somehow their British use of the English language made it sound wonderful and very sexy. The troops had very little time off but when they did, they all headed for town and 99.99% were hoping to pick up a girl or woman as long as she was of legal age. In town it seemed to Alex that there were hundreds of Americans everywhere he looked and among the many Americans he seldom even saw a woman. When he did she was so surrounded by men he could only get a glimpse of her.

By his third liberty Alex had decided that girls were out of the question. And he really wanted to see some British countryside, since there was nothing else to do while on leave but get drunk and that was not Alex's thing. So he rented a bicycle and peddled off down the road and into the countryside. This was a world totally strange to him but wonderful. He had lived in New York City most of his life, and he could remember little of Russia. What he could remember was of the crowded streets and buildings of Moscow the one time his father had taken him back for his grandmother's funeral when he was eight.

While riding the British train from one camp to another he had seen a fairyland from books while looking through the train windows. Now he could see, smell and almost taste it all, and it was beyond belief. This beautiful open green British countryside with fresh air like none Alex had ever breathed in his life. He had lived in large cities all his life and, once in the army, it had been army camps. Even on maneuvers in the woods of Louisiana and the other maneuvers none of the air had smelled like this British air. He was so captivated by it all that he just keep going and going.

All of a sudden he felt like it had been a week since he had last tasted water. About a mile down the road there was a small thatched roof cottage with a white picket fence around it with flowers and shrubs. As Alex rode toward it he thought it was a scene right out of a book. A place like this could not be real, the world just didn't contain places like this in real life. Arriving at the picket fence in front of the cottage, he looked at the strange British front door to the cottage. It was made in two pieces where the top half can be opened while the bottom half stays shut. The latch on the inside of the picket fence seemed strange to him, but he figured it out, opened it, walked to the door and knocked on the top half.

The top half opened and there stood a very beautiful teenage girl, who smiled and said, "May I be of service to you, sir?"

Who on earth says things like that, and Alex was speechless as he looked at the most beautiful creature he had ever seen. His tongue was welded tight in his mouth and this beautiful girl just stood there looking at him as he fought to get his mouth to work again. Finally it broke loose enough to murmur "Water, please." She smiled and said, "Certainly sir," turned and walked back into the cottage. She was wearing a soft blue blouse with flower prints on the front and the back was the same soft blue. Her skirt was a darker blue and full flowing. Her body was perfect in every way and, as she returned, her light brown hair softly brushed her shoulders as she walked. As Alex reached for the glass of water he was not sure he could even hold on to it. He must drink it with spilling it all over himself. With a thank you he reached for it and he did hold onto it with an effort. As he drank, a look of concern came over the girl's face and she asked "Sir, are you alright? You look shaky."

Alex's voice was somewhat back to normal as he said, "I'll be fine now, thanks so much for the water." What he wanted to say was he was "you're the most beautiful girl in the world and that would make any man on earth shaky." But he said, "By the way my name is Alex and 'Sir' is my father."

With a big smile and a wonderful laugh the girl said, "Glad to meet you, Alex, I'm Becky." Then she said, "Maybe you're just hot and tired; we have a bench over under that shade tree on the side of our house. Why not rest a while before starting back to camp?" Without waiting for an answer she opened the bottom of the door and walked out. She took his hand and led him to the bench where they both sat down. Alex's mind shouted there was never a story-book ever written this great. He had died and gone to heaven.

For the next hour they talked. Alex wanted to know everything about her and she in turn had many questions about Alex. Finally it dawned on Alex it was going to be hard for him to get back into town in time to catch the last bus to camp and told Becky as much. He said, "Becky, this has been the greatest day of my life. May I come back to see you again? Please say yes, as I will just die if you say no."

Becky smiled and said, "I don't want you to die so I guess I'd better say yes."

Alex said, "We never know if some jerk might mess up in training this week and keep us from getting liberty next weekend. We never know until the last minute. If I do get liberty, may I come then?"

Becky blushed a little and said all right. "May I have your address so I might at least post you if I am denied liberty this next weekend?"

Becky said, "I will go inside and get something to write it down for you." In a short time, she returned and handed Alex a piece of paper. "My address is on it, and if you're here next weekend I will be here also."

Alex wanted to ask Becky if he could kiss her as he wanted to do so very much. But this was 1943 and he knew this kind of thing just did not happen in these days. Alex was scared he might offend her if he asked, so he kissed her hand, got on his rented bicycle and peddled hard to get back in time as he knew that a late arrival might mean being restricted to camp.

Back in camp even the five mile forced marches and calisthenics did not bother him. It just helped pass the time until he could see Becky again. If he was not allowed to go back to see her, he just might as well shoot himself. Alex did not dare to mention her to his buddies, he would fight and die for them, but he sure did not want them to know about the most beautiful girl in England. It was a slow week in many ways. He had never experienced anything like this before in his life. He had liked girls from early in life, it must have been well before the other boys his age started talking about girls. Even then, when they started talking about girls, what they were really talking about was sex. It was not about just being around them; it was having sex with them. Yes, Alex had sex several times already and had been in love more than once. Now he doubted if he had ever been in love before and it sure was nothing like this. Becky was more beautiful by far than any girl he had ever dated. Of all the women he had seen in movies or been around in his life, Becky still was the best. None had ever been as attractive to him as Becky was. This was not saying that every man on earth would call her the prettiest woman on earth, although only an idiot would not put her in the top ten percent.

Thinking about it Alex decided that if he could marry Becky and never even have sex with her in his whole life he would do it in a heartbeat. Such a thought had never crossed his mind before. How could this be? Everything was all mixed up in his head, and Alex knew he had never really been in love before in his entire life. He even came to the conclusion that few people on earth had ever had this thing as bad as he had it. There were no words on earth to explain that wonderful weekend. When he started back to town to return to camp he knew he was going to marry Becky, though he realized that within days he would be in France. Nonetheless, if he survived the war and Becky would have him he was going to marry her.

He had spent only a little time with Becky and here he was so mixed up, messed up, and so unexplainably happy he could not think straight. Finally it was announced that his group was going to be allowed liberty again the next weekend. Here he was with no way to contact her; she had no phone since a German bombing raid. That raid had been trying to take out an air drone not too far from her home. It missed the airfield but totally destroyed the local phone exchange. It might be repaired by now but Alex had been so busy just being with Becky that after she told him the exchange had been bombed out he had not even searched for a way of reaching her. How on earth could he have been so stupid? He could write as he had already done every day, but a letter or post, as the British called them now, would never reach her in time. Alex had received a wonderful post from her that day that was in his pocket over his heart. There was no way the British could get a letter back to her before the weekend. He was going to have to hope and pray that she would be there to welcome him again as she had done the last time. He started asking his buddies if they knew where a flower shop was in town and soon realized he had just made a big mistake. They all wanted to know about Alex's girl. He was flooded with questions about her. A bunk mate asked if they had sex yet and Alex bloodied his nose. The whole barracks jumped in to stop the fight before they all got their leave canceled. This did help matters, but now everyone knew this was not a booty call for Alex. No, it was plain to see Alex was in love and that explained a lot about why he'd been acting as he did the past week. He was even told where a flower shop was in town without any sneering remark at all.

The bus taking the men into town had a terrible driver that day. Alex was sure he never took the bus out of low gear. Finally when Alex got off the bus, he headed straight for the flower shop. Then to the shop that rented bicycles. The six miles to Becky's house took a long time using pedal power. As he drew close he saw the most beautiful seventeen-year-old woman on earth come out to meet him. He handed her the flowers and put the kick stand down and turned to face her. She stepped close and kissed him softly but full on the lips. Alex thought he was going to melt down right into his shoes as a wax candle does when left in front of a fireplace with a roaring fire. Becky took Alex's hand and led him into the cottage where she introduced him to her aunt and uncle with whom she was living and then put the flowers in water. After this she picked up a picnic basket and handed it to Alex. Then she turned and picked up a folded tablecloth. Out the back door of the cottage they went hand in hand and up the small hill to a very large, very old tree. Then Becky spread the tablecloth on the ground as Alex helped. Then she sett the basket on the edge of the cloth. When Alex looked up Becky had gone to the tree and placed one hand on it with her back to Alex. When he placed his hand on her shoulder she turned to look at him and tears were streaming down her cheeks. Alex pulled her close and just held her. Becky said, "I am sorry. I wanted to bring you here as this is my most favorite place. I never thought I would cry but I just broke under the memories."

Alex continued holding her for a while and finally said, "You want to talk about it?"

At this Becky again took Alex's hand and said, "Let's sit down." Becky said, "This has always been my happy spot and I wanted to share it with you, as being with you has made me happy again. But now that we're here, the last years have broken through and ruined it all. I am so sorry it happened as I wanted this to be a great weekend together. Becky started crying again and Alex softly pulled Becky's head over on his shoulder and said, "Tell me about it, I want to know and help if there is any way I can."

Becky started, "Aunt Lizzie was my mother's sister and we lived in Coventry. We came often to visit and we all loved it here. I had an older brother and a younger brother that loved this tree as much as I did. My older brother, Edward, climbed all over this tree and I was right behind him—a bit of a tomboy. We both had to keep a watch on Jimmy, our little brother, as he was too young to do much climbing. Papa would have to come up here and make us get out of the tree to go eat our supper and we would be right back the next morning unless it was raining. The whole place was like heaven to us who lived in the big city of Coventry. Then the war came and Edward joined the Royal Air Force and his Spitfire was shot down in the Battle of Britain and he was killed. Edward had been shot down before but he bailed out and went up the very next day and shot down another German109. The last time he was shot down he went down with his Spitfire."

Alex pulled her a little closer and Becky kept on going. "I was away at boarding school when the Germans came at night in a mass formation and bombed Coventry. They bombed and bombed until there was little left. My home was completely gone and they only found pieces of bodies that could not be recognized." Now Becky broke into hard sobbing as Alex held her. Finally the weeping slowed and Becky looked up into Alex's face with swollen red eyes and face. To Alex she was as beautiful as ever and feminine enough to need to be held and taken care of. He leaned over and softly kissed her on her lips, not to be romantic but to show her he cared. She kissed Alex back and hung on to him like a person that was drowning. In a way she was, drowning in sorrow and the embrace and kisses were reassurance of the sharing and bonding of two souls, nothing more. And yet can there be any more of an external help that a man and a woman can have in life than this? After a long while Becky pulled herself back and announced, "I am not going to let myself break down and totally deprive us of our picnic."

They ate their cold chicken and had a bottle of wine as they tried to bring their conversation back to lighter things. There was another cousin that was also living at the cottage with them, a boy of twelve from London. During the war thousands of children were sent away to safer places so they would live and not die or be wounded in the intensive bombings.

When Alex was invited to stay in the boy's room for the night, he was very grateful. This way he could be there for another day. The next day was a good day even if there was still a strain in the air. Becky showed Alex every part of the little farm and it was a wonderful time of bonding with a little romance thrown in. As the time of Alex's departure approached he made sure he had every way possible of contacting her in the future. As time was running short, Alex wanted so much to tell Becky he loved her and wanted to marry her. But he was held back by the knowledge of the war. He also knew that many men were using the war to get what they wanted without regard for the pain and suffering that this could cause. Alex loved Becky far too much to cause her any more suffering in her life. As he got his bicycle ready Becky pulled him close and kissed him hard and long then said, "Alexander Vetov, I love you."

That did it. Alex pulled her back close and said, "Becky Johnson, I love you with every fiber of my being." Taking her in his arms, he kissed her long and hard. Riding to town to catch the bus back to the base, Alex's mind was full but he knew that if he survived the war he was going to marry Becky Johnson.

As the days turned into weeks, Alex spent every moment he could with Becky. One weekend as he went to rent a bicycle there was only one left out front of the store. A great dread gripped Alex as he walked over to it and glimpsed a sign on it. With relief he read, "Reserved for Sergeant Alex Vetov."

It was another wonderful weekend, as Becky had her own bicycle and they rode about a mile into the next small British village. They spent a good part the day going from store to store just looking, talking and laughing. The day was a wonderful day except Becky would not let Alex kiss her as this was her home village. Here everyone knew everyone and they knew not to let these Americans get too close to their daughters. Europeans also believed these Americans were overpaid, over-sexed, and over here, while so many of their own men were gone. Though the townspeople were nice, Alex still felt like he was under a magnifying glass and Becky was every family's own personal daughter.

In a way she was. Everyone knew her story—that she was the last of her family—they had all been killed by the Nazis and the village had all taken her in, just like her aunt and uncle had done. They were there to protect her, and all these Americans made it a hard job.

Alex understood and actually appreciated it. His buddies were great guys and he would trust them with his life. But he would not trust them even seeing Becky if she drove through town in a Sherman tank. As long as he could hold her hand and just be with her and talk to her he could not be more happy.

When they got back to the cottage they went in and greeted her aunt, got a drink of cool water, and went back to the outside bench. There he kissed her softly even if her aunt was looking. In fact, they did a lot of kissing but kept things under control. Even though this was not the first time Alex had told her this, he told her again. "Becky, you know how much I love you, you also know that the army may be called any moment. When the time comes for the army to leave, all communications will be blocked. I will write to you every day as I can; however, it may be days or weeks before you receive these postings."

They talked some more and Alex had to go catch the last bus out. He got on the rented bike, kissed her one last time and rode hard for town.

That week the base was closed to all outside communications. The men were told to get things ready, they could write letters but the letters would be held on base until a future date. No one had to be told anything; this was why they were here. Every one was ready to get on with it, and the necessary items used in combat were separated from the collection of personal itemsthey'd gathered up til now. Alex kept telling his squad that everything they carried was going to get heavy before they reached Germany. Private Johnson, who was still overweight after Basic and all their training, had a very heavy backpack. Sergeant Vetov demanded to be shown its contents, dumping it on Private Johnson's bunk. Private Johnson must have had three pounds of candy in that pack along with other snacks. He was not the only one; most all of the squad had unnecessary items. One private had two books he said he wanted to read. Every other day Alex wrote Becky, even though he knew she was going to get them all at one time.

Then one day they were all transported to the ships and loaded aboard. There the ship just sat, and sat; it was so crowded there was little room to move around. Finally in the early morning hours the ship moved away from the dock and out into the harbor where it anchored again and sat. A long, hot sweaty night came and they felt enclosed in one huge sardine can. The next day it just sat and nerves were growing very frayed in that overcrowded ship as they went into another night on board.

In the very early hours of the next morning the engines cranked and the ship began to move. The unit was scheduled for the second loading and landing of assault craft onto Utah Beach. This meant that Alex was going to be on the beach only ten minutes after the first G.I. went ashore. Again the ship stopped, only this time it was somewhere in the English Channel and was being surrounded by hundreds of ships. They were all blacked out and men were not even allowed to smoke or show any kind of light. At least there was a pretty stiff breeze blowing and that helped. Even June in England is not too hot; but on that super overcrowded ship in the harbor with the June sun shining down had been boiling.

Out in the English Channel with the cold water of the channel and wind blowing, troops pressed to the windward side where Alex and his squad were. Then suddenly it grew cold during the night.

The great number of ships could not even come close to the number of airplanes flying overhead. They flew overhead all night.

It was strange to see all these airplanes approaching, then turning off their lights so the Germans could not see. Somehow it bothered Alex that all those airplanes were turning their lights off except for small red lights on the tail of each aircraft so they wouldn't run into each other. The muffled sounds of untold numbers of bombs exploding on the French coast sounded like the world's worst thunderstorm and it never ended. When the very first streaks of light started showing from the east the Navy opened up with everything they had, and they had a lot. The ships' amplified speakers came on with a prerecorded message from our Supreme Commander General Eisenhower with a message about our mission and wishing every man good luck and God's blessing.

There were so many ships Alex thought that if one ship was tied to the side of the next it would make a huge bridge from England to France. Then it was not long until the ships started moving again. There were no battleships or cruisers close to the transport; they were out front. When those big boys opened up with their huge guns, Alex wondered if they could be heard in Paris. It was getting lighter with every minute as thousands of airplanes kept passing overhead. Then the transports slipped past the big battle wagons and stopped again. It is not long until "prepare to embark" came over those speakers. On the deck, officers were calling out unit names and telling them to go over the side. Alex was reminding his men to make sure all the equipment was secure and tight, so that nothing would get caught in those cargo nets. The rope net they would be going down would be swaying with the movement of the waves, making the transports roll from side to side. He told his men to make sure each had put a condom over the muzzle of his rifle to keep the salt water out. Those rifles were hopefully going to keep them alive in France. Last, Alex told each man to also check out his buddy standing next to him to make sure nothing was loose that could get caught in the cargo net. As the first landing craft pulled away, more men were called to go over the side, even while the second Higgins boat had not yet pulled in or secured to the transport ship. It was amazing how fast the men were going over the side and down the net. In minutes "Assigned section two, on rail," was called and Sergeant Vetov made sure all his men were there to go over on that wet net rope ladder.

They had climbed these so-called rope ladders hundreds of times and Alex knew these were nothing more than huge cargo nets like his dad had used all Alex's life. Now it was time for his squad to go, and over the side they went. The little Higgins boat was lumberinging up and down in the waves while the transport ship roiled from side to side. This much movement had never be done in practice and one man fell but he was right over the landing craft and wasn't hurt badly. He was not a part of Alex's squad and all of his men made it fine.

There were so many men on that little Higgins that they could not fall down, but the men shifted back and forth like a wave. Once released from the transport and starting forward, things settled down a little. As the Higgins pulled away from the transports, they moved into an assault line so they would all hit the beach at the same time. This was so the Germans would have too many targets. If they had come in a few at a time the machine gunners could change from one to another and shoot at them all. Headed in to shore they were going with the waves and the shifting of the men almost stopped. As they approached the sand enemy cannon fire started hitting all around the little Higgins boats. Every once in a while, one of the Higgins was hit and it was no more. As they got closer, machine gun fire was added to the cannon fire. The steel front ramp stopped most of this fire until the ramp was lowered to allow the troops to depart the Higgins and make a mad dash for the beach. This is when German rifle and machine guns rained their fire into the open boats. If this was not enough, German mortars and small artillery had that shoreline pre-sighted in and the whole shoreline and beach was one long explosion.

The men that got off their Higgins and through that line of fire still faced a beach with no protection other than their GI shirts. Any Higgins that was right in front of a MG 42 lost a lot of men before they even got off their boat. Alex's boat was one of the lucky ones; it did not land right in front of a machine gun. Still the rifle fire and explosions took their toll. Stepping over their fallen fellow soldiers, they rushed to the front. They quickly spread out in the shallow water to avoid making themselves easy targets for the Germans and rushed for the dry beach.

2

FRANCE

This beach was not at all like what they'd trained on in Florida. It was covered in rocks, some as large as tennis balls and millions as small as marbles. There was a lot of driftwood large and small with tons of trash. Even though they faced German resistance, the 4th Division pushed inland taking on everything they faced. When Alex's squad ran right into an MG 42 machine gun nest about forty yards right behind the beach, that held them up. They tried different ruses to get close enough to take it out, but the rapid fire of that 42 held them off. Finally Alex was able to work his way over to the side and get a clean shot at the re-loader. He took the shot and the re-loader fell over dead. It was not long until a new belt of ammo was needed and the gunner turned to get one as his loader was dead. That was the gunner's big mistake as his head was exposed for a moment. Alex only needed a second and the German had just given him one. Now that the machine was stopped, the squad could advance foot by foot, yard by yard and nothing else held them up for too long, even though many German riflemen tried. The 4th was taking out Germans all right but they were also losing too many men while doing it. Most were to minor wounds from bullets, flying shrapnel and even twisted ankles in all those rocks and trash. To Alex it was not nearly as bad as he had been made to believe. Others felt they had just arrived in hell as they saw so many men go down. Most just kept going as their squads got smaller. Alex still had all twelve of his men and they all kept moving though some had minor wounds.

Behind the beach there was miles and miles of flooded land. The so-called roads on his map were nothing more than narrow little dikes between the fields that the Germans had flooded by opening the dikes. Anyone that got onto one of these "roads" were going to draw German fire as they were standing out in the open. There was no choice; it was *take to the water regardless or die*. Sloshing through deep mud and water was slow and hard, it also made one feel naked and pinned down. They tried staying close to the dikes, but that still opened them up to enemy fire. Moving out away from the dikes was worse; as soon as they were spotted, they drew fire and there was nowhere to hide. Hearing a lot of firing from an area of high ground. Alex's squad knew that it was German as the sound of the MG 42 could not be mistaken. They slipped close to a little patch of trees on dry ground that was not much larger than an average house. It had a very small storage building on it that shielded the squad somewhat. It was apparent that the Germans were pouring a withering fire somewhere else. This turned out to be into the waters of the field across the dike from his squad. This dike separated them from the other field that was receiving all that MG 42 fire. The machine gun crew was only paying attention to the Americans that they were firing at. Staying low and moving slowly Alex's squad got close enough to lob two grenades into the machine gun nest. As the grenades went off the squad charged the spot where they found four wounded Germans and three dead ones. The MG 42 was so hot it was smoking as it lay on the ground.

A voice called out, "Coming out 82nd" and slowly several men appeared from a dike so small it was less than a foot above the water. The 4th infantry had just met up with the 82nd airborne. The 82nd guys were coming across the field when the Germans opened up on them. The only place they could go was behind that small patch of dirt. The Germans did not approach as they could have easily done. They had just stayed in their position and kept up a steady fire. To say the 82nd boys were glad for the help would have been putting it very mildly. Within another hour they'd met up with more men of both the 82nd and 101st airborne. It seems the paratroopers had been mis-dropped all over the place. Now there were three sergeants in the group, but Alex just kept going in the same direction with his two squads while the paratroopers followed. It was not long until they approached another patch of high ground. There was nothing growing on it, but it looked like it was covered by a large camouflage net.

They had passed a large shell or a bomb crater a short way back that had blasted the dike all to pieces. Alex and the two other sergeants talked about going through the hole to the other side of the dike. Now a force of 48 men, they decided to stay together and on this side. This was a force large enough to be a platoon and strong enough to take most enemy positions. Of course, it was not a normal position, as they were all in waist deep mud and water. Their best speed in that mess was six feet in four minutes, and at times it took ten minutes to cover the same ground. The three sergeants together slipped back to the bomb crater and talked things over. Alex said he thought that it was an anti-aircraft gun and the 82nd sergeant was sure it was an anti-tank gun. They decided to split the group and attack the gun regardless. The sergeant that thought it was an anti-tank gun agreed to lead the 82nd airborne troops to the other side and went through the hole in the dike to try to reach the big gun from that side. They all agreed that it was going to be necessary to move slowly and use the dike for cover as much as possible.

The third sergeant said it was impossible unless they waited for dark to cover themselves. He would have no part of a suicide try and as no one outranked him he was not going to die for nothing. He was going to take the five men under him and leave, which he did. Nine more men that were not directly under anyone left with them. So 48 was down to 33 men. While they were dividing the men a group of American bombers came overhead and, sure enough, it was an anti-aircraft gun that fired away at the American aircraft. Alex hoped all the gunners were watching the planes and pushed forward, still slow with every boot stuck in that mud. As the airplanes flew out of their range the gun crew swung their long barreled gun around to get ready for another flight of American planes. Alex watched the long barrel swing back around and he squatted down with only his head and M1 out of water. At a distance Alex hoped the M1 would look like the other thousands of floating sticks and trash they were going through. In a few minutes, another flight came over and the long barrel started to swing around following the aircraft. Alex stood up into a hunkered over position and pushed forward as fast as the mud would allow. When the gun stopped firing Alex went back down into hiding as much as possible in the water. Another flight, another small advance, back down again, even when in a squat he was inching forward through the mud.

Three more flights and they were close enough to see each German very clearly. The anti-aircraft crew was paying no attention to anything other than their gun and the Allied aircraft. There were at least six infantry and a two man crew with a MG42. The water is starting to get too shallow to hide in and Alex softly said, "Next flight, spread out and fire on my first shot."

Alex shot the two men he believed were the MG42's crew and kept his eye on the 42 as all the men from both sides of the dike opened fire. The "impossible to win" fight had been won without the loss of a single American solder. The firepower of that many American men on two sides of that anti-aircraft battery, literally chewed that position up. Alex's little group of men were on the move again after a short rest. The 4th Division pushed on until they got the best foothold on any of the five landing beaches. Being the most successful did not mean it was easy in any way. Sergeant Alex Vetov's squad and the lieutenant had been seen as successful in taking out that MG42 machine gun behind the beach emplacement.

The platoon lieutenant told Alex he had done a great job, and Alex's squad was now very sure they had a top notch sergeant leading them.

When another squad's sergeant was wounded, that squad's corporal looked for Alex to lead them and Alex did a great job. That evening the lieutenant told what was left of all three squads that he wanted Alex to take over them all until things could get reorganized again. The company had lost too many sergeants and there were not enough to go around, so some were going to have to double up--at least until a new sergeant could be found or their old sergeant could return, as his wound was not too bad.

There were no longer enough men to form three squads. They were made into two squads and Alex had them both. The second day was a rough one as much of the 4th advanced right through many German units and gun emplacements. There were places bypassed so the whole division could move faster and still stay together. The goal had always been to penetrate inland as far as possible and the overall orders were to continue to do the same. Just the same, it was necessary to clean up the mess that was all around and behind them. The front line had to be held against German counter attacks. It was also necessary to keep the Germans that were behind and still all around them in check and rounded up. There was even German artillery in different pockets behind their lines that had to be taken care of and American artillery was just now being brought ashore in large enough amounts to get set up and help. As great as American air power was, there was very little it could do against targets behind American lines as the chance of killing Americans was just too great. There were still not enough American tanks ashore to take on such a challenge. Even though they did a great job when they could, tanks also faced the most danger. Sending tanks against German artillery in emplaced and well-camouflaged positions allowed the German artillery to knock out tanks before the Americans even found the enemy.

As so often occurred, it was up to the boots on the ground to find and most often to finish off the enemy. The front line had to hold so a squad here and there was pulled from the line and sent to clear the mess still behind the line. The lieutenant had seen Alex and the other members of his squad fight so well the first day that he sent them out on a mop-up detail. With the other squad attached to his, Alex now had 24 men. During the night Alex had heard the sound of more than one German 88 going off somewhere behind them. He well knew what this artillery was doing to the troops coming in and the wounded being returned to the beach. When his squad was given the job of cleaning house behind them, Alex headed for the sound of the 88's. Having been ambushed at every turn the day before, they moved with care. The squad looked for the enemy everywhere, and all too often they found them. Most of the time they were in small groups and some were ready to surrender. Others fought to the death, but the ones that surrendered were also a great problem.

Before noon Alex had more prisoners than he had men in his squads, and four of his men were now wounded. They were walking wounded and only one needed help in walking. So he had to send his wounded back with a man to help the badly wounded one. Sixteen prisoners required at least four men to guard them, along with two of the walking wounded to help guard them. Alex now only had nineteen men, but there those 88's were firing again and Alex knew the hell that they were causing back on the beach. The 88's would fire four fast shots and then not fire again for a half hour or so, then four more quick shots and dead silence. Thinking it over, Alex decided that the Germans may be about out of ammunition and were waiting until everything was moving again on the beach. But he thought the real reason was that they knew they were behind enemy lines and would fire to cause as much damage as possible, then shut down so they would not be found.

Carefully heading in the direction of the last firings Alex looked through the trees with the binoculars the lieutenant had given him. He saw nothing, then as he continued to look he saw a German officer coming out of a ditch or some low ground. He stood there holding a pistol in his hand pointed toward the ground. Then Alex glimpsed several German helmets that appeared to be lying on the ground. No, the helmets were moving, so there had to be men in a trench or hole hiding all but the top of their heads. The officer was about 150 yards off, but for Alex that was an easy shot. He had taken become excellent at shooting his M1 Garand in basic training. It had just come as natural to him as eating his lunch. Early on in basic training at the rifle range he had achieved his marksman rating and in England had placed in the top fifty of the whole division. When he earned his sergeant's stripes they had tried to give him one of those little carbines. No way, he kept his Garand and now he settled down on the ground. Using a fallen tree as a brace, he checked out the soft wind and lightly squeezed his trigger. The M1 kicked with the full power of its 30-06 round, but Alex paid that no attention as he watched the German officer crumple like a sack of wet washcloths.

He and the whole squad just stayed where they were as they knew there was well over a dozen Germans in that trench—now down to nineteen total. After just watching for a few minutes a white cloth tied to a bayonet that is fixed to the barrel of a Mauser rifle came up in a slow waving motion. Alex said, "Stay down," as he stood and called out in as loud a voice as he could muster: "Lay your rifles and belts down and come out."

Within a few minutes sixteen Germans were standing alongside the trench, with their hands on the tops of their heads. Telling the squad to keep him covered, Alex walked out of the line of fire and toward the Germans. At about fifty yards, he called out again, "Keep both of those 30s on them, boys, and if any move cut that whole line down."

One of the Germans interpreted and the rest stiffened and froze as Alex approached. Looking for any sign of rank and seeing none,

Alex called out, "Who is in command here?"

No one moved but several of the Germans looked at a middle aged man close to the center of the line. There were no markings of rank on his uniform but it was different from most German soldiers' uniforms. Walking up to that man, again Alex asked, "Are you the ranking man here, soldier?

The man said in broken English, "No sir, I am Dimity Zoliff, former captain in the Russian army. Forced slave and private in the German army." At that moment a strong gust of wind almost knocked Alex over. All that could come out was "Russian Army?"

Yes sir, all but three of us are Russian, the other three are Czechoslovakian. The only German here is now dead, thanks to one of your American sharpshooters." Now Alex was even more shocked than before, he had heard stories of how the Nazis had taken prisoners from other countries and forced them into their armies to beef up their forces. Without turning his back, Alex waved his men in while calling out, "You men on the wings stay put and keep those thirtys ready."

Two of the squad members were carrying Thompson sub-machine guns that were held on the prisoners while the others checked out each prisoner for weapons. Now it was the Russians that were shocked as Alex told them in Russian that if they were truly surrendering and would behave themselves that he, Alexander Vetov would do his best to make sure they were fairly treated. Upon hearing this, several of the Russians started taking off their hated Nazi uniforms. Alex demanded they stop as they were not allowed to move regardless.

As each prisoner was checked out, he was told to be seated on the ground, to keep his hands in front of him and no sudden moves. While this was happening Alex and a Russian named Dimitry were in deep discussion. Dimitry explained how as prisoners of war the Germans had learned they were "white" Russians that did not like communism. The white Russians had the choice of joining the greater German army of corroborating nations to protect the borders of the greater Germany or going into the concentration camps. When Alex told Dimitry his squad was here to find and destroy the two Germans 88s, Dimitry told him that it was going to take a hundred men to do this job and asked Alex if he had that many men. First there were four 88s that were well protected by six machine guns and about 50 troops. Well, now about 35 troops as this group that had just surrendered was part of the protection detail. Asking if Dimitry would give up information about the fortification of the 88s, Dimitry said the German officer that Alex had killed, had all the information in his officers' personnel items below in the trench. He also had some information in his own pack in the trench. Alex made one of the biggest risks of his life and said, "Will you help me find it?" Dimitry said yes and they both went into the trench, Alex with his Colt 45 1911 on him. Dimitry gathered up several of the officer's things and then he got his own pack and they came out of the trench together.

Seeing the German officers P-38 pistol on the ground Alex picked it up, holstered his 45 and checked the chamber of the P-38 to make sure it was loaded. Then Alex carried the P-38 as they all started back toward the American C.P. As Alex and Dimitry walked behind the others, they talked like old friends until all of a sudden Dimitry pulled a Walter pistol, stuck it into Alex's ribs and said, Please do not move, my friend, I would not like to kill you."

Then he let out a shrill whistle and within seconds the Russians had over-powered the whole American squad. Disarmed, the Americans were marched back to the trench where all the Russians quickly rearmed themselves with their own weapons. Speaking in English, Dimitry told everyone that if they were good tonight that tomorrow they would all be allowed to return to the American lines unharmed. It was just that the Russians had something they must do tonight. The Russians prepared food and shared it with the Americans. About 8:00 p.m. Dimitry and several of the other Russians slipped away into the night, leaving four to guard the Americans. About midnight there was a huge explosion that shook the ground for miles around. It was about 2:00 a.m. when Dimitry and twenty more white Russians showed up at the trench. They had with them a German general and six other German officers. It must be admitted that some of the Germans looked a little worse for wear. Dimitry said in pretty good English, "We better get the hell out of here while we can, but before we go I have something I want to give each of our new American friends to make up for the way we treated them this night."

He opened a large leather bag and started taking out pistols and dress Nazi daggers. Dimitry said, "I understand that Americans like German war souvenirs and I have three German Lugers with holsters and some German officers I.D. cards. Also I have six P-38s with holsters that have extra magazines and German officer I.D. cards. Sorry we were in too big a rush to keep up with which cards go with which guns. We were a little busy while we were blowing up an ammo dump, a half-track, and a fuel depot along with four 88s and several machine guns. Now let us go surrender to the Americans before the Germans come looking for us."

That was quite a sight: a squad of the 4th Division followed by 49 armed men in German uniforms marching toward the American Command Post. When Alex guessed they were getting close to other Americans he halted them all and made his way into the command center. Once there he asked to see his captain and had a hell of a time getting permission to let the Russians come in with German rifles on their shoulders, but that is what the Russians wanted to do and after all the explanations were made to the general himself, this would be allowed as long as every rifle and solder had been checked to make sure there was no ammunition in or on any of them. As it turned out, the location that the German 88s were in was a location that the German high command had planned on using to make a major counter attack to kick the 4th Division back into the English Channel.

Dimitry had some plans of his own. First, he wanted to let all his men make their own decision if they wanted the war to be over for them. Or if the Americans would allow them to return into occupied Europe and work among the millions that the Nazis had enslaved so the Allies could have better information and help from the people themselves on winning this war. Even the general could not make that decision; it had to go to the top. Saying goodbye to the Russians was hard but Alex had to get back to the war.

The captain gave the squad an overnight leave to stay at the command compound, get some hot food, and some needed rest without the worry of the enemy coming in and killing them in their sleep. Tonight the letter to Becky was a long one, telling her everything that had happened, though he tried to make it sound as if things had been somewhat under control.

Next morning Alex started out again to run down enemy troops behind the lines with his squad until they ran into a few 101 boys doing the same thing. Remembering how it felt to try to take on an enemy that outnumbered them many times over, they all agreed to stick together. Hearing gunfire they all headed for the sound of a zipper. The very rapid sound of a MG 42 sounds like a super loud zipper being closed, so Hitler's zipper was the term American troops used when they heard that sound. In no way could it be confused with any other machine gun except a German gun. Following the sound they came up behind the MG and were able to toss a couple of hand grenades in. Three more German riflemen were shot and five gave up. Lo and behold five 82th boys were very grateful their brothers had shown up and stopped that MG 42. They also thought it a great idea to stick with this group. The group was growing but the 4th had a problem, one of the 82nd boys was a shave tail second lieutenant in his second day of combat. There was no question that he was very unsure of himself. As an officer, he was in charge. Still things worked pretty well until he stuck his head over a stone fence at a French farmhouse and a German sniper took the top of his head off. Alex looked at the hole through the lieutenant's helmet and head. Alex had a good idea from what direction the bullet had come. The men carefully spread out to make it harder for the sniper to keep track of them all.

Alex crawled around the corner, staying well below the stone wall until he was protected by the French house. Now it was over the wall and up to the house that gave him cover from the sniper. On the other side of the house and about thirty or forty yards away was an old barn with portions of its shingles missing. Thinking of the hole in the lieutenant's helmet and knowing where the lieutenant was looking when the shot rang out Alex was pretty sure it had come from that barn. There was a bush on the corner of the farmhouse so Alex lay down and carefully pushed the muzzle of his rifle into the bush and waited for the sniper to fire another shot. While looking down his M1 sights, he saw movement and instantly fired at it. Alex quickly rolled back around to the protection of the farmhouse and used the butt of his rifle to shake the bush. He was hoping the sniper would think that is where the shot had come from. Nothing happened, but that location had been given away so it was back to the stone fence. Finding another location was not going to be easy.

Alex heard a rifle shot from the direction of the barn and a distant "all clear" coming from the barn. Every man came slowly out of his hiding place while Alex made his way to the barn. There in the barn was one of the 101 men holding a scoped Mauser sniper rifle and wiping blood off the stock of the Mauser. Over his shoulder he had the sniper's ammo belt and under the GI's ammo belt he had a P-38 pistol. The 101 man said, "Sarge, you got him right through the neck and I thought you might like this sniper rifle as you are such a damn good shot. I got his pistol and I'm keeping it, being first on the scene and all. If you want to play with that Mauser to see how good it is, here is his ammo belt." He continued, "I understand German snipers are only issued the very best in ammo as well as in all their equipment. Alex took the rifle and ammunition as he did want to check it all out. Looking at the 101 man Alex could easily see where stripes had been removed from his shirt sleeve. It was a large enough area that it had to have been at least a staff sergeant. Alex wondered what offense a ranking man had committed that got him busted back to a buck private.

Church bells sounded in the distance and everyone wanted to go check it out as church bells meant there was a town and it had to be close, so off they went. No one said anything but everyone knew what was on most of the men's minds. A French town always had French wine and, who knows, maybe French women as well. If Germans were there in force they could slip off without getting into a fire fight. If there were only a few, well, that is what they set out to find. If there were no Germans there, fine. There would still be wine, French food, and well whatever. They approached slowly and carefully until they saw an American jeep driving fast directly into town. Now they all just walked out onto the road and into town. This was where the 101 had set up headquarters and, looking around, they realized the 101 ex-sergeant had disappeared like a puff of smoke. Alex walked into the command center, saluted and asked the lieutenant where he and his men could resupply themselves. They were low on ammo and everything else Alex explained.

The lieutenant said, "You will have to get the major's approval and pointed him in that direction. Once there, the major wanted detailed information on why they were not with their unit and where they'd been. Giving the major a brief idea about their trip he called in an orderly and sent Alex to see the colonel. Being questioned again, Alex was informed that he and his men were now under the colonel's command and he and his men were a part of the 101 until they were returned to the 4th. The colonel had orders to take and hold two bridges against a counter attack and he did not have nearly enough men to hold one, much less both. He said he was very short on non-commissioned officers and Vetov's ass was his until he decided to let him go back to his old unit. Turning to his orderly he said, "Take this man to Major Dodd and tell him he has a few more men."

The conversation with the major was even briefer, but Alex was told where to take his men to get resupplied. As soon as they got resupplied they were to meet the colonel at the church. They headed for the bridge as soon as possible with every man they could get.

The men needed everything, but the fact that most all the squad was wearing German sidearms drew a lot of attention. At the church it was the same and when Private Wilson from the squad was asked about it, he answered, "Every time we killed or captured a German officer we took his sidearm and dress dagger."

As almost every member of the squad had a German pistol, the 101 man asked, "How many German officers have you killed or captured?"

Wilson took a bite of his Hershey bar, paused a moment and said, "I really don't know; we did so many we didn't have time to count and after the first dozen or so officers, we did not pay any attention."

The 101 man looked at all these new men with their German pistols and daggers and just walked away. Whatever, Alex's little group was shown respect by the others as long as they were with them. When the major showed up with two lieutenants, everyone got their packs and gear and Alex swung the Mauser over his shoulder on one side and his M1 on the other. One of the 101 lieutenants looked at Alex and asked, "What the hell are you doing with a German sniper rifle?"

Alex answered, "I shot the sniper and took this rifle."

"Well, get rid of it." At that point the whole squad stepped forward and several of the 82nd and 101 boys did also. One of the 101 boys said, "With all due respect, sir, when that sniper killed our 101 lieutenant, This 4th Division Sergeant shot and killed that sniper at over two hundred yards with his M1. In appreciation for what he had done we gave the sergeant that sniper rifle as we had no other thing to show our appreciation of that marvelous shot he made to revenge our 101 Lieutenant." The lieutenant stood for a moment and said, "So what the hell?" and walked off. It was all a matter of principle and besides it was only a little over forty yards. While the 4th was still a motorized division when Alex first joined it, they had studied a lot on how not to get stopped by an enemy. Now Alexander was going to use everything he had learned about how to get through a defensive army to stop the advancing Germans.

They had to walk most of the night to get to the bridge and they had three fire fights on the way. They were there before daylight. When the two dozen men that were already there at the bridge saw them coming, they thought a relief party had come; and they sent up a cheer. When they learned they had to stay and were expected to have to fight off a German counter attack, it was a different story, as there was no way less than a hundred men were going to hold off a major German counter attack.

The new men rested until daybreak and started trying to plan for the known counter attack. Tanks and armor against M1s just did not make any sense at all. When the 4th was a motorized division and Alex was first assigned to it, they studied a lot on how their enemy would try to stop their motorized units so they could best get around them. Looking at the problem in reverse, Alex sucked it up, went to the major, and said, "Sir, I was with the 4th when it was a mobilized division. We studied how to attack a place just like the Germans are going to attack us here, and sir, we cannot stop them unless we use the weapon that we have that is greater than anything they have, sir."

The major said, "Alright son, what do we have that is greater than a German army has?"

"Sir, we have short range walkie-talkies that are only good up close, but here at the bridge we have a long range SR-30. My squad can walk to the top of that hill with a couple of those walkie-talkies and extra batteries and we can see what is coming and how many. We can call back down here and you, sir, can call in what the Germans no longer have, and that is the most powerful air force in the world.

The Germans cannot send their armor through the hedgerows. They will have to stay on the roads or close to them. Between the river and the road our pilots will not have a problem finding them. Low flying medium bombers and fighter aircraft can give them hell. This will give you more time to prepare and will cut their number down to make the fight more even. Sir, our aircraft are already in the air and will be all day. When I report the Germans to you, then you can give them time, location, and number. Sir, if the Germans can be held back a day it will give you time to prepare to defend this bridgemaybe even get some artillery that will give you the advantage, sir. Turning to the first lieutenant the major said, "Give the sergeant anything he wants while I call division." Within fifteen minutes there were twelve men walking down the road again.

Private Kirkpatrick said, "We walked all day, all night, and now we're walking again."

Alex answered, "If German tanks start over that road before we get to the hilltop, we will not be walking; we'll be running."

After an hour of walking, Alex heard the sound of a fast approaching aircraft and looked back. Coming in low, a P-51 Mustang passed right over their heads and wiggled his wings as he flew on, following the road. The guys returned to talking and it was not long until they heard a couple of distant explosions. Nearing the high ground, five Thunderbolts came in on the same path the P-51 had taken and again it was not long until there was a whole series of explosions several miles away. The ground was mostly flat with a slight upgrade from the river behind them. The hill was not much of a hill, just a patch of ground higher than the surrounding ground. It did have a bunch of trees with shade that looked good on this hot June day. Once on top they could see smoke that had to have been at least fifteen miles away. Alex took out his binoculars and looked down the road. He could not see far as the road curved into the farmland that was covered with hedgerows.

That was a disappointment, as he had told the major he

would be able to see the German counter attack a long way off. Still he could see for about three miles and also knew he could hear German tanks coming for several miles before ever seeing them. Urging his men to get some rest, he told Kelley to go to the north side of the trees and look out for Germans coming from that direction. Then he told Brown to do the same on the south side as he surveyed all the ground around looking for any movement. Looking to the south it was all farmland and hedge-rows were everywhere. East was the same so the German armor could only use the road, as they could never get through those hedgerows. German infantry could, but armor never; and infantry against infantry was an even fight. After an hour of surveying the ground and road, Alex decided to check on his men. Every man he had told to get some rest was sound asleep, after all it had been over forty hours since any had slept for more than an hour or two. Brown was awake but having a hard time staying awake and Alex told him to stay awake one more hour and he would be relieved. Kinney was even worse. He was biting his thumb to stay awake and Alex told him to go get Rhoads to take his place.

Just before sundown, Alex heard more airplanes coming and looking back toward the bridge he saw several C-47s coming over and three of them released three Waco gliders that made a swing and came in, landing in a field not far from the bridge. About fifteen minutes later three more C47s approached and this time white parachutes spilled out from all three. As the C-47s headed back to England a flight of Mitchell twin engine medium bombers flew over and in a few minutes the roar of hundreds of bombs went off ten or more miles away. Right at dark a German motorcycle with a side car without lights slowly pulled up. When it reached the point in the road where someone could just barely see over the crest of the road and look down upon the bridge it stopped. A German officer got out of the side car, took out his binoculars and slowly surveyed the bridge. He took his time and remained there for fifteen or twenty minutes. Several of the men wanted to shoot them both, but Alex said they must keep their position hidden.

As it grew dark, Alex woke up half his men to stand watch the first half the night, reminding them not to smoke or show any light for any reason. Then he and his other men lay down. They were out like someone had turned off their switch. At 0100 he was shaken awake and the other half of his men took over. A little after two, Alex heard the unmistakable clacking sound of a half-track coming very slowly. It was a cloudy night and there was very little light, but it was a sure thing that half track was full of infantry. This spoiled everything, Alex knew those solders were going to spread out and would soon come and check out the bunch of trees where he and his squad was. Alex said, "Let's get the hell out of here."

Going to the north side of the trees away from that half-track they continued north, stumbling in the dark but continually moving north for at least a half hour. Now they slowly began to turn a little west and continued to circle until they were headed toward the bridge. The first gray streaks of dawn were just starting to appear when Alex and his squad called out the call sign and were recognized by the guards. The major was awakened and Alex was presented to him. With a salute Alex said, "Sorry, sir, the Nazis run us off and they now have possession of our observation station."

The major said, "That's alright, son, that was a hell of a plan and the Air Force reports that most of the enemy force has been annihilated."

Alex's response was, "Sir, we were run off the hill by a half-track before 0300 and while we were getting away I heard without question the approach of several German heavy tanks, half-tracks, and trucks."

The major turned to his staff and said, "They are still coming; get the Air Force and get our men ready. Sergeant, you are with me," and they moved out to get things prepared. The major asked if Alex could tell exactly what he had seen and what he thought about what he'd heard. The Waco gliders had brought in two M3

105 howitzers and a jeep with one of the new MW 44 jeep-mounted radio sets. This offered much better and more powerful communications. The new paratroopers had more than doubled the force and they'd also brought in heavy fifties machine guns and more thirtys as well.

Yesterday and last night hundreds of anti-tank mines had been planted in and alongside the road. Many more anti-personnel mines had been placed any place that was thought to be an approach field for troops. Looking at the mine field Alex turned cold; his squad had come through a part of that field. Both 105s had been dug in so as not to appear like artillery from long range and to offer some protection at the same time. The Germans needed that bridge to drive the Americans out of France so it was not in danger of heavy artillery from the Germans. The Germans had the high ground which gave them the advantage. When it was just light enough to barely see, here came German tanks over the rise. At two to three miles the German tanks opened up with their big guns on all the surrounding ground up to about twenty yards of the bridge itself. They sure did not want to damage that bridge, but they wanted to destroy everything except the precocious bridge. Alex was sent back to his men. The 105s could hit targets five miles away but kept quiet as their job was to stop those tanks.

The first tank was a Panzer and it was in front of the first Tiger tank by about fifty yards. It was the bait tank to see what the Americans had and it stayed on the road. The other Tigers and Panzers spread out, along with a dozen half tracks. These, along with assorted armored vehicles, attempted to approach the bridge from all the flat land along the river. There was a lot more than thought after the pasting the Air Force had given the Germans yesterday. Another Panzer hit an anti-tank mine, but all it did was to blow a track off one side which made the Panzer turn sideways on the road and stop. Its cannon was still very much in operation until a 105 put an anti-tank shell into its poorly protected side. The firing of the 105 immediately brought a round from the closest Tiger tank but it over-shot giving the 105 crew time to reload and fire again. They fired this shot at the Tiger that had fired at them. It was a dead center perfect shot, but the Tiger might as well have been hit with a tennis ball. The Tiger did not miss and the 105 exploded like a large bomb had hit it. The second 105 on the other side of the road also fired at its closest Tiger and they hit it just where the turret and tank body come together. That shell knocked the entire turret off the Tiger killing the entire crew.

That second 105 now fired a third round at a Panzer, setting it on fire. The third and last Tiger was on the other side of the road and could not get a shot at the 105 as both the burning Panzer and the killed Tiger were in the way. The 105 made another quick shot at a German self-propelled cannon and it also burst into flame. The Tiger came around its dead sister tank with its gun swung to the side for a quick death to the American 105. The Tiger tank just exploded and in one second a P -51 passed not more than twenty feet over it. It was followed by a whole flight of P-51s along with Panzers, half-tracks, self-propelled guns--blowing up, burning or just stopped in their tracks. The P -51s had come in from the side from down river so they could attack the Germans in such a way as to make sure their fire would never enter the American lines. After making two more strafing runs, their rockets and bombs had been used. All five planes came over wiggling their wings and headed elsewhere. A year later when the war was over the 101 adopted this flight of five and called them "their air cavalry" as they had come in at the last second and saved so many as Western movies showed the American cavalry had done for the early settlers. The sad part of this was that only two of the five pilots were still alive.

As the fighters flew away, German rifle and machine gun fire started peppering the American troops. As great as the air power was, the German counter attack was not wiped out, but most of their armor was. Charging German troops were greatly hindered by all those mines that had been planted. They still out-numbered the Americans and their orders were to get that bridge, intact at all cost. Alex moved his squad forward and used that knocked-out Tiger tank as protection. In the first part of the fighting Alex's precious M1 had been hit and it stopped a bullet that could have easily killed him. The only weapons he had now was his two pistols and the German sniper rifle, so he used the sniper rifle. If Alex had tried he could have found another M1; instead he just grabbed the Mauser and the Mauser's ammo belt and ran for the dead tank. Like a baseball player he dove for the tank and when he looked up he was looking right between the tank's treads underneath the Tiger tank's belly. It looked like the whole German army was running right for him. Directly in the center was a German officer in a Black SS uniform. The Mauser came up instantly and the cross-hairs were right on a big black Nazi Iron cross hanging from that Nazi's neck so Alex pulled the trigger.

That big eight millimeter bullet hit so hard it literally knocked the Nazi backward. At the same time Alex heard both Thompsons from his squad start their chatter along with M1s, carbines and who knows what else. The wave of Germans that were also running to get behind that dead tank just melted away. Alex simply stayed where he was as he could still see over the bodies that could protect him from German fire and there were Germans everywhere. Not only that, it seemed that several were officers and some officers and men were in black. All the men in black melted under Alex's fire so he started in on the officers, some out three to five hundred yards. Man, that Mauser with its Ziess Scope could hit anything. Alex figured if he could just get within a thousand yards of Hitler this war would be over. After all the German ammunition was gone and Alex backed out from under the back of the tank, he found another M1. He still had plenty of M1 ammunition for that rifle and he kept up the fight. In a couple of hours the firing began to slow down and more and more Americans were coming forward. One American ran forward toward one of the destroyed half-tracks and all of a sudden with a big boom he was blown into the air and fell back to earth in pieces. He had just stepped on one of our own mines and had lost his life for no reason. The cost of the battle for the bridge was very high both in German and American lives but the Germans never got the bridge.

There were 36 American dead and about 100 wounded. Four of Alex's men were wounded, two needed medical help big time, and two were minor; but his number of effectives was dropping fast. The big brass in the 101 had called for ambulances and trucks to take the wounded away. Alex and his men started looking for replacement ammunition and water. There was very little of either, so the men were relieved in small parties to go down to the river. There they got water while the remainder stayed in place to take on the next attack from the Germans. Alex's men had been on the spear point of the fight and had just about used up all their ammunition. Alex got permission for his men to go back and get ammunition. There was very little to find, a few magazines here and there and only four banderillas of Garand clips. Hawkins went and started taking ammunition off the dead G.I.s and some of their buddies got mad at him, but he had been doing it with respect. As things calmed down Sergeant Vitov looked through several of the discarded M1s and picked one he liked over the one he had picked up at the tank.

This was considered a great victory for the 101, and it was. However it was not just 101 boys that fought to hold that bridge. Before that last load of paratroopers came down, there were more men from scattered troops than the 101.

Coming out from under the Tiger and still seeing Americans coming forward, Alex and his men started shouting, "Stay back, mines!"

This was picked up by others until all stopped and retreated. Getting back to the bridge the first lieutenant said, "I don't know if you guys are really brave or just downright stupid."

Matthews said, "Just tired, boss, just tired."

The squad got some water, then realized they were missing Mueller, they found him covered under a half tent tarp. That night they all slept under that bridge, and Alex started a letter to Becky that he was too tired to finish. It really did not matter; there was no way of knowing when he could send it off any way.

The next day, elements of the 4th arrived and they rejoined their outfit. When reporting in at HQ, Alex was told he was now a staff sergeant but it might be a month or so before he got his fourth stripe. Food, showers, and sleep for sixteen wonderful hours then it was time to head west while the 101 went north to hook up with Omaha Beach forces.

New divisions were coming ashore all the time and headed out to cut the Cotentin Peninsula off from all Nazi control. Some of the German army was a scattering of too old or too young, then mixed in with the conscripted of Europe. There were enough hardened war veterans in the German army to keep the rest under control. There were SS units that were all hard as rocks and many common German soldiers that had already been fighting for years. Every day no one knew who, when or where the 4th was going to face, fight and possibly die in combat. Army life was army life and everyone had to take it as it came.

Back on the road again the next day, the platoon was all loaded in trucks and started west. They had not gone five miles when a jeep cut them off and brought them to a stop. The company captain talked to the platoon lieutenants for awhile, then got in his jeep and left. Alex's lieutenant walked to the back of the first truck behind him and asked if Sergeant Vetov was aboard. Then the same thing happened at the second, then the third truck Vetov was riding. Vetov was to get out and the drivers of the third and fourth were told to pull out of line and wait while the convoy went on west. The lieutenant explained that a small pocket of Germans were still holding a small French town off to the left. Half of the platoon was going to go clear it out under Vetov. While the lieutenant continued on with the other half and the company.

When they came to the next road to the left Alex's two trucks turned off and went hunting for the town in question. Alex had moved up into the truck cab with the driver and was studying a map when the driver slammed on his brakes and threw the truck into reverse as a stream of 8mm bullets slammed into the motor of the truck. Alex looked up in time to see a German motorcycle that had a machine gun mounted side car firing at them. The truck motor only ran the few moments it took to get the truck back out of the line of fire. The lead truck was out of the war for good but not one American had gotten a scratch except the driver got some glass splinters in his face when the windshield was shot out. Including the truck drivers, Alex had 28 men with him including a medic and aid helper.

Being afoot again was what the 4th men were used to anyway as they all dismounted the trucks and looked for an ambush. There were no Germans around and Alex quickly concluded the motorcycle was only a lookout. Alex left the two drivers and six men behind to guard the remaining truck. He also instructed the medic to pick out the glass and bandage the first driver's face—then to follow the other men into town as they might be needed to take care of wounded men. Alex also left two to stay with his two medical men. Now he had 18 men and this is about what Alex was used to anyway. Intelligence reported there were only a few Germans ahead in the town. Alex sent out four point men. As they approached the town there was little cover in the last mile. Taking his Ziess binoculars, Alex carefully searched the town and he saw no movement. This was not good at all, French, Germans or whatever...someone or something should be moving. Not even a dog or a cat. Alex had never seen anyplace in war or peace that had no movement observable. Telling his men to just stay put, he moved forward about four hundred feet with a radio man to a small farmhouse. Nothing happened when he reached the house and there was no one inside. In fact, it looked like no one had lived there in years. Using his walkie talkie he called the other walkie talkie and asked for three more men to come to the house one at a time, moving with the house between them and the town as much as possible.

While Alex was watching, a German motorcycle with the machine gun side car rode out of the town. It slowly made its way down the road toward where it had been when it machine-gunned the first truck. From the first sight of the motorcycle Alex was back on the walkie talkie, telling his men to stay back. It was too late— two men had already started, while the third was held back.

On the walkie talkie Alex said, "Send a runner back to the trucks. If he can make it before that motorcycle does, tell them all to get in the second truck and get the hell out of there back to the main road and if they can get to a radio powerful enough to call company, let them know we are badly outnumbered. The rest of you hide if you can and let them think we have run off after our truck was shot up."

As the two men coming toward Alex spotted the approaching motorcycle they lay down in the field. The two Germans driving the motorcycle with the side car came slowly, watching along the road very carefully. They did not seem to pay much if any attention to the old farmhouse off in the field or the field itself. After a while it returned, driving at a moderate speed on into town. The two men in the field made it to Alex and now there were four of them in the farmhouse.

It was not long until a German half-track moved out of the town, approaching pretty fast for a half-track. Like tanks, they did not move quickly and speeds over twenty miles an hour were very hard on their moving tank-like tracks. A German soldier was sitting above the armored front with a machine gun at the ready. The back of the half-track was full of German soldiers all standing up with their heads and shoulders above the top and rifles at the ready. It was plain to see they were going out to hunt the fleeing Americans. The steel shield covered the front windshield except for small slits to see through when it was down. Now it was up for the driver to see clearly as it approached the crippled

American truck. A rifle shot smashed the front glass and the half track driver fell over dead. As he fell he mashed the gas pedal and the half- track jumped forward, sending the troops sprawling in the back. Off the road it went and right into a tree with a jolt that took care of any German trying to get up. If it did not, the hand grenade that was tossed into the back did. Then for good measure two more were tossed in. An American private opened the front door of the half-track and turned the motor off. He pulled the dead German driver out, wiped some of the blood off the front seat and climbed in, looking things over. While he was doing this, other Americans had gotten the large back gates open and were pulling German bodies out the back.

Still watching the town with his Ziess binoculars, Alex saw many Germans moving around in the town. Then he glimpsed a troop truck coming out of the town just like the half-track had done except much faster. After it passed Alex, his three men rushed back across the open field to join the rest of his men. He had no idea what had been happening but was fearful for his men with that half-track and now a truckload of German troops going after them. Then he heard a German MG 43 open up and lots of M1 rifle fire. His heart was in his throat as he sprinted toward the battle.

When he arrived there all he saw was his men walking around a German half-track and a shot up German army truck. After the Americans had taken down the German half-track and cleaned out the back a little they thought it would help take that French town back as they had no armor of their own. They had put on German helmets as they didn't want to be recognized as Americans until they got close enough to fight. They had no idea they were going to run into the truck load of German troops. When they did they just played the cards they had been dealt. As the half-track got close to the truck, the American behind that MG 43 opened fire on the truck. First across the windshield and then across the troops in back. The first shots across the windshield killed the driver and he ran off the road turning the truck over onto its side spilling the

German troops out, which the German MG42 machine gun and M1 rifles made short order of.

It was growing dark and one of his sergeants said, "Staff sergeant, what we did worked just fine so far. Let's load up and take it on in and get that French town back for the French., I think you have the right idea."

The German truck was on its side and the sun had gone down. The German radio in the half-track was requesting information and Alex took the mike. He told the German on the other end in broken German he was a Dutchman in the German army and went on in the Dutch language. After a minute the German on the other end gave up, simply saying to have a German officer call him back.

Now Alex called for a German-speaking American because though he could speak some German, he could never get away with playing the part of a German officer or radio operator. Within minutes a German-speaking American was found and they went through the pockets of a German colonel and pulled out all his papers. It was twenty minutes later when the radio came back to life and the American speaking perfect German said that Colonel Werner was leading the search for the Americans hiding in the foliage all around and would do so all night until every last American dog was rounded up. It would take all night and probably be daylight before the job was finished. The colonel had sent word he would call when he was finished and not before. They used the half-track to right the German truck and they used mud to cover the bullet holes. Not one American had been killed and only five wounded.

Talking to the other two sergeants, Alex said they needed daylight to attack the town so get everything ready and get some rest. A little after midnight the entire other half of the company showed up and Alex explained everything to the captain and lieutenants. One lieutenant declared that Alex's plan to use the German half-track and truck was against the rules of war.. They should wait until morning and attack the town with American flags flying. Alexander asked to talk to the captain in private and they walked off a ways.

Alex opened with, "Captain, sir, many men's lives were saved today and even more can be saved tomorrow."

Here the captain stopped him and said, "Staff Sergeant Vetov, the lieutenant is right. We cannot plan a battle using German colors, as I understand it you did not plan the fight to happen this way. Your men acted upon their own intuition to capture the German half-track, without you being present. Then they brought it back to protect the rest of their fellow soldiers. Running into the German troop truck was totally unplanned and your men fought bravely and defeated the enemy all before you rejoined them. This action today was a great victory for the 4th and it seems that tomorrow will be a continuation of your original orders. I am taking Lieutenant Morris and his platoon back to HQ with me tonight. As a German truck is not an armed weapon, as such and your lieutenant might use it to back up a part of his platoon. He will not use it except to follow and relieve a part of his command. If follow up troops rushed in to help other American troops 'with American flags flying that would be nothing more than what Americans have always done.' I feel that if your men were in actual battle before a call for help was made, that would be the army way."

The captain and Lieutenant Morris with his platoon headed back to HQ that night. Two other lieutenants were simply told to stay on location until the area was cleared. The German half-track was filled with all the men it could carry before dawn and headed back for the town. It was just turning daylight in the morning and the armor shield was lowered over the windshield. This was used to hide the shot out windshield and also to give protection from enemy fire. The headlights were turned on like the German troops were returning in complete victory. Approaching the German roadblock, the half-track opened fire. Alex's radio man sent this signal: "In combat with superior enemy forces. Request help from all local U.S forces."

Turned out the Germans had an under-strength battalion of less than 300 men. This was still enough to put up a three day fight. Alex would have to bring in the whole company and another American Company as well. So much for the Intelligence idea of a small mop up for two squads.

This little town had been a town where the Germans removed every working man from thirteen to sixty or so to do slave labor to build defenses against the Allied invasion. Then they had moved in this under-strength battalion just returned from the Russian front to rest, refit and refill ranks. A hard experienced German fighting battalion took over the town. They had several German soldiers moving into each house and turning every person there into their personal slaves. With the men gone, the rest need not be explained.

3

HEADED WEST

A lex's platoon had four squads with 53 men, counting replacements. The limit was supposed to be 50 riflemen plus all the other machine gun groups, mortar teams and so on, but in battle the number would soon drop below fifty. There were three sergeants that had come ashore at Utah including Vetov and one replacement. They still had the same second lieutenant and company captain with about 200 men altogether. This company was to go up the northwest side highway and then head for the port city of Cherbourg, clearing out the Germans as they went. Cherbourg was one of France's best ports and therefore the Americans needed it in the worst way and as soon as possible. Still there was a lot of real estate and Germans between Utah Beach and Cherbourg. While the division now had a few trucks, they were used for supplies. Infantry means walk and that is what they did. As this was D company also known as Delta company and always called Dog company by the men in it.

Alex always thought it had been appropriately named by the men. Today it was his platoon that was in front when they received the first fire. It was an MG 42 and every man in the platoon hit the ground. Damn it all, those Germans must have been making MG 42s by the trainload and passing them out to every fourth German soldier, was Alex's thought as he tried to scrabble deeper into the ground. Everyone was trying to get some cover and there just was not much cover to be had. Alex lay still so as not to draw fire as he very slowly pulled the newly issued M1 up to where he could quickly bring it up into firing position. Alex did not typically cuss but right now he did, even if it was only in his head. Damn it, he now had a newly issued battle rifle that was surely taken off a dead soldier or at least a badly wounded one that was not going to need it again. He had looked it over but he had not been allowed to fire it in the camp because of the short time they had before starting out again. He did not know if it would even shoot. He had checked the barrel to make sure it was clean, but that was all.

He quickly raised the rifle and fired at the muzzle flash of that MG 42. The only thing that happened was a string of German bullets swept past him and his left arm hurt like hell. Next it was a company bazooka man that sent his round right through that window. No more MG 42 but rifle fire was still coming from that house. Alex lay still again as every man in the company opened up on that house. Within two minutes a white cloth was in a different window and six Germans came out. Briggs came over and hollered "Medic, medic," and in short order a medic was there. The medic cut Alex's sleeve open and poured some sulpha powder into his wound and then cut his sleeve off at the shoulder and started wrapping Alex's arm. He was a guy Alex had known in England, the medic grinned and said, "This might get you off KP but this scratch is not going to get you off the line."

Then he tossed Alex the bloody sleeve. The sergeant's patch that Alex was so proud of was hanging, a bloody mess.

Alex's squad was standing around him and it was easy to tell they were all re-lieved until one of the men said, "Gillespie got it, right in the head."

Brown said, "Man, he just joined us yesterday straight off the boat."

Alex said, "I'm sorry it happened but keep his new M1 for me, and turn in this piece of junk with him. I never want to see it again."

It may have been a scratch but it sure felt like a whole lot more to Alex.. Six platoon men were down wounded and two were dead. So men went into the house to wait while an ambulance was called. One look around at what our bazooka had done and the men walked right back out. When the ambulance did arrive three of the wounded were put inside and the two dead were placed on a jeep. The one that stayed with the platoon looked a lot worse to Alex than his wound was said to be by the medic. The man had said he wanted to stay with his platoon so he was allowed to do so. Alex decided right then he was not going to complain about his wound, he did complain about everything else—that arm sure hurt.

By the time they bivouacked for the night his arm was worse, not better. Still that was nothing like it felt the next morning when he thought his arm was going to fall off. Then when the medic changed out the bandage, Alex was thinking hard about what he'd ever done to the medic to get treated this way. Alex had to give permission for Private Bender to try out the new M1 the next morning before catching up to the platoon. Alex had to *get* permission from his lieutenant to stay behind and test-fire the new M1. Alex knew he would not be able to test that hard-kicking rifle with his wounded arm. He also knew what a great shot Bender was so he got permission to stay and do it for him. Bender fired three rounds and Alex said, "Left and low." He twisted the sight adjustment and fired three more rounds and said, "Perfect."

Then he fired the last two and put in a new clip. Since they were following the whole platoon, they were paying no attention to the farmhouse in the field as they walked down the road. A shot rang out and Alex's arm no longer seemed to hurt as he put his rifle to his shoulder and pumped eight rounds into different parts of that house. Bender was carrying a Thompson and he emptied a magazine into the house. Alex had reloaded and was looking for signs of movement as they both hunkered down behind the usual stone fence that most farmhouses had in that part of France. As Bender finished putting a new magazine in his Thompson he said, "Cover me," and rushed the front door. Nothing happened and Bender came back out to the door and stopped, he said, "Sarge, come see this."

Alex approached the door and followed Bender inside.

There on the floor was a young very pretty French girl in her early twenties holding a German rifle. She was dead with a bullet hole in her chest. Walking down the road the two men discussed why this had happened. Together they guessed that the young French woman had fallen in love with a German soldier during the years of German occupation. That may be the German who'd been killed in the invasion of American troops and she wanted revenge. They talked about how many different ways it could have come about, but one thing was sure—she did not want to live without her German lover.

Alex asked Bender how he could control his Thompson so well as most soldiers just sprayed an area when shooting a Thompson. Bill Bender just grinned and said, "Sarge, it's just like sex—the more you practice it, the better you get." He continued, "Have you ever watched Brown with his Thompson? I tell you he can make his Thompson do anything he wants. That man could get his Thompson to grill steaks for lunch if he wanted it to."

It took a little explaining as to why they'd taken so long to catch up, but within a day everyone in the platoon knew the story and most had their own ideas of what had happened to cause the death of a lovely young French woman. As it turned out, this was the only fight that the platoon had that day and it was very rare indeed. That night Alex got four letters from his Becky and he wrote her a long one after rereading each one over again.

The next day made up for one easy day in buckets as they entered a small village full of Germans. A point squad from Fox Company had been sent ahead to scout out the route. Things seemed pretty clear until a little after 0900 when a German artillery barrage started hitting deep into the division. Men scattered so they wouldn't be bunched up and tried to find places that gave some protection. The general had always tried to be fair in having different companies take point and today it was Fox.

Being point, Fox was pretty well spread out and the artillery shot over them and was really pounding Able and Charlie, which were more bunched up. This meant that the Germans had an observation post somewhere from which they could see the U.S. Division. In turn, this meant that O.P.s were always on high ground so they could see. Or aircraft were used and the Germans had few aircraft anymore. There sure wasn't one overhead right then. None had even come over that day so it was a ground O.P. Scouts were sent in all directions as this was very flat countryside with little high ground. Wherever it was, it had to be knocked out quickly. Scouting squads headed for anyplace that had any height at all. One place that looked promising was a dairy farm that had a tall barn and a silo beside it. Alex's squad was not picked to go out but he could see the barn in the distance. Such an obvious place was not a good choice for any German simply because it would be the first place the Americans would look. What the Germans liked was a wooded hill or some place that allowed observation and also escape. That farm and barn was a death trap and an O.P. there would not have a chance of getting away. A little after 0930 the artillery started spreading out in an ever-widening circle. Alex guessed the O.P. had been taken out and the German artillery no longer had pinpoint instructions.

Alex never passed a building again without watching it with care. It did not matter if the whole company had just passed it.

As Alex walked beside his squad the very next day, they received fire from a barn about a hundred yards into a field. To get to the barn the men had to pass a house a good thirty yards off to the side of the line of fire. After the incident with the French girl, Alex kept his eyes on the house. Everyone else, it seemed, was only concerned with the barn. After the second shot from the barn someone called out, "Sniper."

Most of the men close to the sniper found cover and those that had not were doing their best to find some. About twenty men started working their way forward to take out the sniper. Alex's squad was further off down the line and the men were getting behind trucks or trees for cover. Alex said, "Let's go," and he and his squad ran forward toward the house. Once they got the house between them and the barn, Alex turned his men and ran straight for the house. Just as in most other farms, there were several small buildings around the house. Stopping in a ditch to catch their breath, Alex told his men that there may be Germans in the house too. "If there are, we are going to clear them out; if not, we're going to use it for covering fire for the men that are going straight in."

Alex explained to his group of twelve that half of them were going to rush the building close to the house. The other half would give covering fire for the first half. Then the first group would do the same as the last half came over.

Alex led the first group and as they were running a German Schmeisser opened up on them. A Shmeisser is a German 9mm sub-machine gun that holds either a 25 round magazine or a longer one that holds 32 rounds. When a magazine is empty then it must be replaced with a full one. Unlike the much more powerful MG 42 that fires from a continuous belt of the much more powerful 8mm round, the Shmeisser has to change magazines often in a fight. Two of Alex's men fell before getting to where Alex was. Alex waved to his other men to stay put and took a quick look with his mirror. As soon as the German glimpsed the mirror, he sprayed the little building again. The men that were still behind the first building returned the German's fire with rifle and Thompson fire. Alex and three of his men charged the house, firing as they came forward. From the moment the Shmeisser opened up on Alex and his men Alex heard the unmistakable sound of a MG 42 firing as well. He knew that this fire was not hitting his hiding place so he put two and two together and realized the whole thing was a trap. The sniper was the bait to draw troops into the open field where the Americans had no protection and the hidden MG 42 could kill many. As Alex ran, he pulled a hand grenade from his belt, pulled the safety pin with his teeth and hurled it through the open window. The grenade detonated but the MG42 did not stop--too many rooms, too many walls. All the squad was at the house now except for the two wounded men.

Alex tossed in a second grenade and then headed around the house to the right. Every time he came to what may be another room he smashed the window and in went another grenade He could hear the same thing happening on the other side of the house. In short order Alex was in front of the house and there were two MG 42 barrels with their muzzles still hidden inside the house throwing a steady stream of fire into the Americans in the open field. He saw Brown lofting a grenade through a last window. Alex grabbed for another grenade but he had no more. One of his men handed him one and it too landed in the house. No more resistance from the house or the barn as the Germans in the barn made a quick getaway out the back side. There were no live Germans in the house except two badly wounded ones.

The trap worked too well, and the dead and wounded were brought to the trucks. There were nine dead Germans in the house, but the sniper got away. Alex had two severely wounded men but none dead. The regiment was far worse off, and Alex did not want to know the losses. That night the lieutenant colonel came to congratulate Alex on taking out the two German MG 42s. When his captain came by they talked a long while.

Before the captain left Alex asked, "Sir, may I speak freely?"

The captain stared for a long moment, then said, "Alright sergeant."

"Sir, where are our promised Shermans?"

He said, "Sergeant, I have asked that same question repeatedly and have not been given an answer."

The next morning they were off again and Alex's squad was getting smaller and smaller. Of course, after yesterday the whole company had taken a bad hit. They had been moved way back in the marching order for more protection—right in the big middle of the whole division so their chance of getting into a firefight was very small. So as they marched they relaxed as much as possible and tried not to worry too much about what would happen next. Alex urged them not to bunch up so as to avoid a whipping if caught in another artillery barrage.

Intelligence had informed the captain that there was a small communicant center three or four miles off to the left. Normally these small centers were just relay stations with only a few soldiers to guard against local resistance fighters. So the captain called in Alex's lieutenant to pick a squad to go find it and blow it up. He was also told that there might be a small security detail there, so he promised to get him some replacements. The lieutenant picked Alex's squad to lead two intelligence officers to check it out and gather all information about the building. To this group was added a three man demolition team to blow the center up after the intelligence boys had finished their job. Then as an afterthought he noted some green replacements that had just come from the transport ship off shore. As there had not been time to assign them out, the captain thought this was a good way to give them the feel of a little combat. More important it gave him time to get around to reassigning these men. Last but not least, they could carry all the stuff the intelligence officers gathered up back to base. Then there was the need for strong backs to carry the demolition supplies to the sight. Twenty-four green as grass replacements were handed over to Alex for this simple and easy job.

Alex went off with what looked like a full platoon. In reality, Alex only had 14 men that had a single day in combat, including himself. This was hostile territory that a single American soldier had yet to set foot on. It had to be alright as Intelligence had claimed that all belligerents had moved out of the area. When they reached the location there was not a thing there.

The two intelligence officers outranked Alex and one of the demolition crew was a sergeant so Alex could not tell them anything. His squad and the 24 replacements were all he could command. Alex put four replacements with one experienced squad man, and sent them out in six different directions to locate the German communication center. He reminded the new recruits to obey the experienced man and stay quiet as they were behind enemy lines. Then he told them all to be back before dark. All the men unloaded their equipment and packs When one of the replacements turned his canteen up high to get a drink Alex knew he was emptying his canteen. Alex said, "Private, it may be three days before you get to fill that canteen again. You're going to get mighty thirsty before you get the chance." Speaking to all, Alex said, "If any man gives this man or any other man a drink of water from his own canteen, be it tonight or tomorrow, he will be on point until he learns to conserve his water."

In the entire group there were only four compasses, so Alex found two landmarks and sent two of the groups toward them. He gave the other four each a compass and dispersed them all.

A little over an hour later a rifle shot rang out and again it was quiet for about thirty minutes. This time there were several rifle shots and much closer than the first shot. Alex looked at his five last men and the other five as well. He said, "One of my squad match up with one of the other men. You go about thirty yards into the trees to look for Germans coming our way. You shoot the first German and then get back here as fast as you can. The rest of you, when you hear that warning shot get back here fast."

The first lieutenant stood and said, "I am the ranking officer here and no one is going anywhere; we will make our stand right here."

Alex said, "Sir, the reason I have assigned one of my men to you is for your own protection. This little space of open ground will have us all dead or much worse in short order. Lieutenant, do you have any idea what the Gestapo will do if they get their hands on an American intelligence officer? You will be praying for death this time next week, and before they finish burning off your feet, you will be begging for death."

Turning back to his men, Alex continued as though the lieutenant had never opened his mouth. "My squad, fan out in a circle and take your man with you. If we get taken prisoner, "Shoot the lieutenants before they are captured, America cannot afford for the Gestapo to get their hands on them. This time the lieutenant didn't say anything.

One by one the scout groups came in except for two--then the last two came in together but there were only six left of the ten. Alex spread all his men out with half facing the direction from which the last group came. The others formed a semi-circle around the center of open ground, but among the trees. It was not a long wait. Fifteen or so German soldiers approached the Americans. As always, Alex had instructed all to hold their fire until he fired the first shot. The Germans were coming briskly as they imagined they had a small patrol on the run. Alex intended for the men to wait until the Germans were within ten yards and cut them all down. At about thirty yards a replacement soldier started shooting and so did everyone else on the defensive side of the circle. Within seconds the Germans were gone and Alex heard an M1 firing from the other side as well. He rushed over, thinking that side was being attacked as well. There was a replacement yanking on the trigger of an empty M1. Alex reached down and grabbed both soldiers of the replacement and pulled the shooter up. The soldier wiggled and jerked like a snagged rabbit until he realized it was the sergeant in command. Alex took the bayonet off the M1 rifle, handed it to the teenage soldier, then ordered him to surrender his rifle ammunition belt. He told the teenager that when he learned how to fight he would get his rifle and ammunition back. Until then he was expected to get close enough to the enemy to kill them with his bayonet. He walked over to the second lieutenant and handed him the rifle and ammunition belt, saying, "You are going to need this."

Calling to everyone he said, "Now that we have told the Germans where we are and about how many of us there are. This means we are going to have to fight our way to our assignment, fight to take it and destroy it, then fight our way back out. Listen to me good and get this. You are not going to pull a single trigger until you're dead sure you are going to kill a German. Pull another stunt like what just happened and I will take your rifle away, unload it and give you one cartridge. When you show me one dead German, then and only then will I will give you one clip for your Garand."

This is when a replacement walked over, saluted the lieutenant, but turned to Alex and said, "I know where the communications building is, sir. It is about two miles from here. He pointed in the direction. "About fifty yards from it there was a group of Germans. It did not appear to be many more than we have with us, about thirty or so men."

Alex said, "Remember basic training, private. You do not salute sergeants, nor call us 'sir,' only commissioned officers. If you have it right, we can still get in there and complete our mission."

The first lieutenant again spoke up and said, "We need to get out of here right now. As ranking officer I order us out while we can still get out."

Alex spun toward the lieutenant and said, "We have an order from our colonel—to gather information from that communications station and if it can be done we are going to do it. I was given an assignment and come hell or high water I am going to complete it, sir."

Turning back to the private Alex said, "The men that were shot—show me exactly where that occurred. No man here is to fire a gun unless the Germans shoot first. Even then, do not pull a trigger unless you know exactly where that bullet is going. With that the whole group moved into the forest, carefully moving forward. Surprisingly, they did not meet a single German soldier. Alex decided that they thought they'd run off the American patrol, but he did not count on it. They reached a place where they found a dead

American and a little farther, a bloody spot. There were signs that a body had been dragged off the trail. There was an occasional drop of blood along with the drag marks.

Then about fifty yards through the trees a cottage became visible. Behind the cottage was a tall antenna tower with multi-antennas attached. Several German soldiers milled around. Alex motioned for all his men to get down and stay back. Taking the private that had been leading them, Alex slipped back into the forest a little ways and had the private show him the German camp. Looking the Germans over, he guessed there were only about thirty or so showing themselves. Then back to his own men, he explained the situation to all. Then he added that if he were the Germans he would have brought his men back and left a few at the communications building as bait. Then he would have left a few more at the camp as a second bait. Then he'd take the bulk of his force and hide them in the woods, upon command to charge out and destroy all the Americans. As Alex finished, again the lieutenant said, "It's hopeless; let's get back to our own lines."

Alex states that this would be disobeying orders. "Our orders are to find, inspect, and gather all internal information, then destroy the building and equipment. That is exactly what we are going to do today."

Taking his time, he moved his force back into the woods a little farther, placed them in defensive positions and went back to watch for a while with the private that had led them in. As they watched and waited he told the private, "I believe that if we wait a while, if the Germans have set up a trap for us, they'll decide we are not here and go on about their business--besides, we need darkness to fulfill my plan."

As the sun set, several of the German soldiers were walking around while others were sitting at their camp. All but three of the soldiers had returned to the camp, where they were bait in a trap—or not, no one knew. These Germans were not solely what Alex was after. They were after the communications center. Alex slowly spread out all his riflemen to take on the camp when the first shots were fired.

To the rest Alex said, "Stay back until it is full dark. Then we're going in silently and take those guards. The soldier that had led them in said, "Sergeant, let me and my two friends take those guards. We three are Apache Indians from New Mexico and we know how to do it."

Alex said, "Go get 'em," wondering if he had done the right thing or not. When the three showed up, all three were holding large hunting knives. Alex didn't want to know how they'd been able to get those knives from America to France. The three Apaches spoke very softly, made signs to each other, and disappeared into the darkness. In less than thirty minutes the two patroling sentries just disappeared. And then one reappeared wearing a German helmet and jacket but American army pants. The Apache came around the corner of the house to the front door. When the German sentry realized something wasn't right he tried to take his rifle off his shoulder. A big hunting knife flew through the air into the neck of the sentry. The only sound was the sentry falling.

While the knife was being recovered the other two Indians arrived—one dressed in full German uniform. The knife thrower calmly wiped the blade off on the dead German as the other Apache pulled him away. Now they gathered at the front door, and the one in the German uniform entered first with the other two right on his heels. Other than a tinkling sound of breaking glass no noise came from the building. In a moment a back door opened and Alexander and the two intelligence officers went into the building. In less than a minute the back door opened and an arm waved for help. Several men went in and came out with arms loaded with file boxes and radio equipment. More men filed in as others came back out. The demolition men stepped in as still others are brought out the last of it. Finally they all came back out and the first lieutenant ordered the demolition men to blow the building. Alex said, "Not yet," and he and the first lieutenant got into a mumbled argument. The lieutenant said, "We have finished our mission; let's go."

Alex said, "That camp may have two of my wounded. We're going to retrieve them."

The lieutenant said, "Over my dead body." At that, four rifles pointed toward him and one private said, "That can be arranged."

All the men slipped down and partially surrounded the German camp in a one-third circle. The three Apaches and three of Alex's squad took out all the guards. The sound of a single rifle shot coming from the communications building alerted the Germans. Within fifteen minutes it was all over and Alex walked over to a German half-track and a German army truck. Alex said, "Let's ride a while."

The two wounded were put in the truck with all the stuff from the communications building. It was a tight squeeze but everything and everyone got in the half-track or truck. Alex climbed into the German half-track driver's seat and looked it over. All writing was in German but most things were the same as the one he'd driven in America. After trying the gears and levers he took off down the road. After a mile there was an explosion but they kept going. They were sure they passed Germans that night but no one paid any attention to German trucks on German real estate. Once back, close to American lines, everyone got out and hauled into camp all the confiscated things. The demolition men took care of the truck and half-track with timers. The longest that they had were one-hour delayed fuses so that is what they were set for.

When Alex made his report he only wrote the bare facts, and mentioned nothing about the differences he and the lieutenant had. When he got to his tent there were two MPs waiting for him. He was arrested for disobeying a direct order given to him by a superior officer in combat. This was a very serious charge; he was loaded into a jeep and taken directly to battalion headquarters. He was put in a fenced-in area next to the stockade housing German prisoners. Alex was a mild-mannered man but he did have a temper, and that temper was boiling over.

The next day he was brought in for a pre-trial hearing, before having to face a court martial. His JAG lawyer was a young second lieutenant. He asked if he was Sergeant Alexander Vetov and other questions to establish exactly who he was. Then he asked the big one, "Did you disobey a first lieutenant while in combat? Alex answered, "Yes, but..."

There he was cut off and his defense JAG lawyer said, "There are no buts in this army; you did or did not. There is never a time when a sergeant has the right to disobey a first lieutenant, and that doubles when in combat. You are guilty or not guilty and your so-called reasons can be presented after the verdict in regard to your sentence. You will be notified as to your trial date." The lawyer stood and walked out, not allowing Alexander to make any more comments at all.

The next day, Alex's lieutenant colonel was at the gate of the stockade and called for Alexander. "Sergeant, what is this I hear about your disobeying the first lieutenant?"

Through the fence Alex said, "No sir, I followed your orders to the letter and my men succeeded in following them."

"What did the lieutenant order you to do?" the colonel repeated.

"Sir, he ordered us to disobey the regimental orders and return to base without even trying to obey regimental orders as were given to me personally by my company captain, sir."

"Son, this was not mentioned in your written report. Why was it not mentioned?"

"Sir, I had no desire to disgrace an Army First Lieutenant intelligence officer. He was there to get intelligence and I and my men were ordered to lead him and a demolition crew into a combat zone, sir."

"Sergeant, are you accusing the first lieutenant of cowardice under fire?"

"No sir, it is not my wish to accuse the lieutenant then or now of anything. But my job was to follow my orders and that is what I did. With the exception of trying to override a direct order from regiment, I tried to show the non-combat lieutenant respect, sir."

"That is not how the first lieutenant tells it, sergeant, in his report, but I will look into it."

Alex snapped to attention, saluted, and said, "Thank you, sir."

The lieutenant colonel walked to his jeep and was driven off.

The next day Alex and four other Army prisoners were driven back to division headquarters. There they were issued new uniforms, told to clean up, get shaved, and be ready to appear before the court martial board.

Alex was not called that day, but he was called first the next morning. At the prosecution table sat a JAG colonel and two other officers. Across the aisle Alex was seated with his JAG attorney whom he had only spoken to twice before. However in the back of the court were several familiar faces. There sat his regiment commander, a brigadier general, his lieutenant colonel from battalion, his company captain, his platoon lieutenant along with several other faces he knew.

Everything was called to order and all formalities are read. The first lieutenant was called first and told to recount the day when Sergeant Alexander Vetov disobeyed a superior officer. The lieutenant related how he arrived at the base camp and took command of the platoon. Then he led them into enemy territory to get information and destroy enemy communications. All the while Sergeant Vetov was holding back and trying to give orders. Arriving at the supposed location, as the commanding officer he ordered out patrols to search for the enemy. When one patrol got into a firefight he ordered all troops into the fight and again the sergeant protested. When they got to the fight, there was the supposed building. After the fight was won he ordered the platoon to guard the area. Then he went in and cleared the building while Sergeant Vetov was determined to leave the area of the building. As he was the ranking of the only two officers on the field, his orders should have been carried out without question. He and his second in command, a second lieutenant, calmly checked everything out. Gathering up all useful papers and equipment they left the building and ordered it to be blown up. Outside, Sergeant Vetov wanted to go down to where the defeated enemy camp was to see if his captured men might be there. As ranking lieutenant he allowed the platoon to go over to the enemy camp where they did find two missing men. Then he led the platoon back to American lines.

Alex could not believe what he'd just heard. As his JAG attorney questioned the lieutenant, he was thinking, How can this be happening? Alex well knew that enlisted men and commissioned officers live in two different worlds. It was also a fact that officers stood together most all the time when it came to any enlisted man. But this was just so far out of line, how could this be? Alex knew this lieutenant was trying to protect himself from what he knew was the real story. The truth could destroy the lieutenant, while the huge success of the mission could make him. So he had just gone for the glory that he might get if he could rewrite what happened.

The lieutenant's report was read in open court and then Alex's report was read. The lieutenant's report was eighteen pages long, Alex's was only two pages. The orders for the mission were read and there was no mention of who made up the platoon mentioned anywhere. The report said that a squad under Sergeant Alexander Vetov was sent out to lead his squad on a patrol to guide and protect two intelligence officers and a three-man demodulation crew. There was nothing about the replacements mentioned at all. More reports and information were introduced and after a noon break the court came back into order.

Now Alex was called to tell his side and he did without saying much one way or the other about the first lieutenant. He was questioned repeatedly in different ways as to what happened that day and Alex told it as it happened. Every time Alex was questioned on disobeying the lieutenant's orders Alex responded by saying he was following regiment's orders to the letter as he had been ordered to do. These orders were signed by his lieutenant colonel and therefore superseded an order from an unknown non-combat lieutenant that he was guiding. He had always shown respect to the first lieutenant except when ordered to disobey direct regimental orders.

Finally Alex was re-seated beside his stone-faced JAG lawyer. Others were called to the stand to give their statements. During a short break, Alex's colonel talked quietly with Alex's Jag lawyer. When the court was called back into session Alex's JAG lawyer asked to call a new witness that was there from day one. This witness was one of the replacements that went with Sergeant Vetov that day. This man had never met either Sergeant Vetov or Lieutenant Scott until that day. Therefore he had no private knowledge or opinion of either man to affect his answers. The judge said, "Call your witness," and Alex's JAG lawyer called Private Goyethey to be the next witness. "For the court's information you are Private White Owl Goyethey, an Apache private from New Mexico." He went on giving date of induction to when he came to Delta Company. "Private Goyethey, tell us in detail what happened that day as you witnessed it."

The private gave all the pertinent details as Lieutenant Scott's face became redder and redder. He went into moment by moment as he told of how he and two other Apaches took out the Germans at the house. The fight to rescue the captured Americans and defeat the Germans. He finished with the wild ride back in the confiscated half-track and German truck. The prosecuting attorney started in trying to discount his testimony. He made a big mistake in asking if there were others that would back up his story. Private Goyethey said, "There were thirty other men there, pick any one you want and they will tell you the same thing."

The major general said, "We will retire to consider all the testimony and this court will reconvene tomorrow morning at 0900."

Alex's captain came to see him at the compound and they talked through the fence. The captain told Alex there was no doubt that after Private Goyethey's testimony Alex would be found not guilty. However this had created a huge problem for the U.S. Army. They had accepted Lieutenant Scott's report and it had been reported back home and everyone thought he was the latest great hero. They had put him in for the Silver Star and he was on the cover of Stars and Stripes. To announce he was a coward, a liar, and whatever else would give the Army a huge black eye. Even worse, it may do damage to the Army's ability to enforce rank and necessary obedience to orders from commissioned offices and even non-coms. If the true story ever got out the damage it may do is beyond imagination. The Silver Star would never be approved for the lieutenant and the Army would take care of the rest in a quiet manner. Alex agreed wholeheartedly and said the incident was closed as far as he was concerned. Then he added, "Sir, I have one request, if I may be so bold. May I have those three Apaches in my squad? I need replacements and those three would be perfect."

It took two more days but Alex was released and returned to his squad to find out that now three Apachesw had been added to his squad. These three never gave Alex any problem except two of them liked to drink. All three could disappear at night in combat and do more damage to the enemy in one night than most squads could do in several days. This also had its down side; every time some night dirty work was needed in the whole company, guess who got called? Besides the Apaches' skills, the whole squad became well known as to what it could do behind enemy lines. The three Apaches fit in well with the rest of the men and also taught them how to work well at night. Alex was given another stripe and his squad was jumped up to eighteen men for special operations. Yes, the Apaches helped make this squad what they were to become, but Alex had other fine, well-trained men that worked together like a smooth machine. Even his platoon was jumped up to five squads instead of four, like other platoons. The whole company called on Vetov's squad for special night work. The captain called them Vetov's night fighters, and every man in it was proud to be a part.

In fact Alex's men were out so often it was not unusual to be gone before dark and return two or three days later. Thus it became necessary for them to get some sleep while other men were marching. Sometimes they slept in the trucks while moving with the division. In fact it wasn't uncommon to see a truck loaded with supplies and the "night boys" on top sound asleep. Somewhere along the way their nickname got changed to the "bats." Even the German Army heard of them and tales were told that the American "bats" were all trained Indians that could disappear like ghosts in the night. These men preferred their knives to guns. And German sentries were told that the "bats" were in their area to keep them on their toes at night. Within reason, the bats got special treatment in some ways and there were always some men that wanted to be transferred into the bats. On the down side the bats lost 38 men killed or missing including two of his three Indians, and 61 wounded in twenty weeks.

As the "bats" were always out to get information, and army intelligence was always demanding that their agents be allowed to work with this group. After Alex's last experience with army intelligence, he wanted nothing to do with them. So a compromise was reached totally outside of army rules, and it was never admitted to by the army. A new spy system was set up in which the intelligence corps worked with the bats but did not order them around. Men came and went as Alex's men remained between 15 and 30. Half of Alex's men could speak French or German and some both, and that helped make them very good at the night work. Alex now let his men carry nine mm pistols over the forty-five. Even though the forty-five's had much better knock down power, the sound when fired was distinctly different from the nine the Germans carried. When behind the lines a nine mm going off attracted little attention. They also carried four special .45 caliber bolt action rifles that had large, long and heavy silencer barrels. These had been obtained from the British with the help of the intelligence corp. To keep the Germans from killing Frenchmen and women for sabotage, they would leave an American paratrooper helmet or something else behind to show that the French Resistance did not do whatever the bats or intelligence had done. The French loved the bats for this and worked closer and closer with them in every way possible.

When Alex's men could get good information about where the Germans were, and how many there were, that helped the Americans to no end. One night a twelve-year-old French boy ran into some of Alex's men and they were afraid to let him go as he might tell the Germans where they were. They decided to just keep him until their mission was over and then release him. Alex did not speak French, even though he knew enough that he could get bits and pieces of a French conversation.

The boy was talking to two of his men in French when the name Gestapo was mentioned twice. Alex wanted to know all about the Gestapo and he got the story translated into English. There was a Gestapo headquarters in Deauvill and something big was going on, the boy did not know what it was but many were coming and going. Getting all the details about where they were located, Alex wanted to blow them up but knew there would be many Frenchmen and women killed if he did. Alex decided to finish getting information regarding a German supply dump, and he spoke as much as he could to the French boy. As this trip was only to get information for the Air Force the boy was told to not tell anyone they were ever here and they let him go after they started back to the American lines.

Once back and giving the information to the Intelligence officer that stayed with the division, the intelligence colonel offered Alex a cup of hot coffee and they talked for a long time. The subject of the French boy came up and the colonel really got excited about it and wanted the whole story. The officer made lots of notes and asked many questions; then he said, "Do you think your group could go back in and kidnap one or two of these Gestapo agents?"

Alex said, "I could have blown them all up yesterday, but I did not because the Germans would have killed many French men, women and children in retaliation. In fact, they night have killed the whole town as they have done in the past."

Then the colonel said, "Yes, you are right, the cost would be too high." They said good night and exchanged salutes, then the colonel said, "Alex, my boy, I consider you a good friend. When we are by ourselves call me John."

Alex slept most of the day, as he and his men had been out for so long. When he finally walked out of his tent there sat the colonel's jeep and an MP that said, "Sergeant, the colonel wants you at operations."

Arriving at operations, Alex walked into the tent and snapped to a salute in front of a sea of brass. There was his regiment's brigadier general and several other officers.

After the salutes Alex was told to take a seat and one was pointed to. The Intelligence colonel sat beside him and all the others took a chair.

A man in civilian clothes said, "Colonel John Thorson called me from London yesterday with the best idea to hurt Nazi Germany to date or the craziest idea to ever come out of Intelligence before. He wants to have the Sergeant Alexander Vetov to take a group of men into occupied Deauvill, kidnap a group of high ranking Gestapo agents, and bring them out. But here is the kicker, he wants to pretend that these Gestapo agents have turned tail and have asked the Allies for political asylum to get away from an unbalanced dictator, Hitler himself. If this can be done, we may be able to shorten this war, avoid having Hitler kill hundreds of Frenchmen, and simultaneously pull some of the rug from under Hitler's feet. He is losing some of the backing of his own. We know that some of his own officers have tried to assassinate him, so this is the time to act. The overall plan is to get men into Deauvill and kidnap five Gestapo head men—three of the higher ranking German officers, have them driven out of town and back toward our lines in front of their own soldiers, where they will be met by a powerful force of our American officers like it is a parade. This sounds impossible but we have been working on this plan in London for a while. We just were going to use it outside Paris when we get there. Here and now is even better if we can pull it off. We have most of their doubles already in London and can have them here in twenty hours ready to go. Sergeant, we have twenty-four men who speak perfect German with Nazi SS uniforms and twelve in German army uniforms. We have a full convoy of German vehicles in which to bring them out but they must be captured or killed quietly before we can put on our little show for all the German troops in Deauvill, Now let's get into details and pull all the kinks out of our performance."

While Alex stayed for the planning session--other than being asked a few questions here and there—the ranking officers made all the plans. After a couple of hours Alex was dismissed while the rest were still at it. Laying on his half tent tarp that night Alex thought a lot. This could never work, mainly because everything was changing every day. Anything this big would take at least several days to get set up and by then the men that were at the Gestapo local headquarters would be gone with different people there. Also, the American army might have advanced enough to scare them off. Big operations like this would take days to put together. Like other big operations there was just too much that could go wrong. Most days, if the bats had not been out for a few days, all NCOs met with their lieutenants to get their assignments. Today the company captain was there with all the lieutenants and NCOs. He informed all his men that most of the company and most of the battalion were going to make a sharp left turn and go deeper inland. "Be ready to move out by one thousand hour. Charlie Company will lead out followed by Bravo, then Delta and Alpha. Delta's "bats" will remain behind to hold this section of the line against counter attacks. Each company in the entire battalion will leave one squad behind to hold this line."

These were very unusual orders indeed. Alex had never heard of taking one squad from each company in the entire battalion. This meant that nearly 90% of the men of Delta were going elsewhere to fight, leaving behind only 10% to hold a line that a battalion had held before. One of the battalion majors and three lieutenants stayed behind and directed the remaining squads to take the place of their whole battalion. After the last trucks of the battalion had disappeared, the remaining lieutenants and sergeants were walking back to their men in the line. A convoy of trucks then drove into camp. No one thought anything about it as trucks came and went all the time. Once the convoy started unloading men the lieutenants and sergeants were called back. As the first truck started unloading, someone called out, "They are rangers."

Army rangers had been trained to be the best of the best for D-day and had been trained very hard to get that ranger patch on their sleeve. Only the first six trucks were rangers, however, as the remainder was a mixture of new recruits and men from mixed units.

One of the majors called out, "Vetov with me; the rest of you sergeants go pick out eight replacements from the new recruits and leave the veterans alone." Taking Alex to the gathered rangers, his major called out, "Where is your major, lieutenant?"

The ranger lieutenant turned and saw the major's oak leaves and snapped to attention, saluted and said, "This way, sir." Alex followed along like a good puppy and also did the attention and salute thing when introduced to the rangers' major.

Introducing Alex to the ranger major, Alex's Major stated, "This is Sergeant Alexander Vetov. He is the leader of a special squad of men that are best known as 'the Bats.' They operate mostly at night behind enemy lines, and continually bring us information that has saved many American lives. He and his men are the reason you are here, so I know you will want to talk."

The two majors saluted each other and Alex stayed with the rangers as his major turned back to the new men. Ranger Major Hinderson was perhaps in his mid to late twenties, and showed signs of first hand combat. The major unfolded a map across the hood of his jeep and the major wanted Alex to explain every yard of ground between them and their target. Finally the major said, "You have been very helpful."

Alex snapped to attention and said, "Sir, are you saying I and my men are not going with you?".

Major Henderson looked up and said, "That will not be necessary, sergeant."

Alex said, "Sir, there is no one that knows that place as well as my men and I do. If you just want to kill Germans you do not need me and my men, sir. If you want to make it look like they are defecting you need us. Even German defectors do not kill their own men without great necessity. We know which French are in the resistance, sir. We know where the whore house is that the German officers use, sir. We have seen it all in the daylight and night."

"All right, sergeant," he said. "You have convinced me, get your men together. We are going in tonight."

Alex wanted to ask questions about the raid but thought it best to just keep quiet. That ranger major might change his mind again and not let Alex and his men go in.

Within an hour more vehicles came in, led by a U.S. Army truck. There were three big Mercedes marked with Nazi and generals insignias. These were followed by two large German staff cars and three German half-tracks, with four German motorcycles. Alex -was asked by a ranger sergeant if he knew where the German lines are. Could he and some of his men get through somewhere without being seen? Would it be possible to slip a motorcycle with a side car past the German lines?

Alex was not sure but he would talk to his men. Alex gathered all fourteen of them together, and they came up with a plan. Every evening, just as it was getting dark, a German soldier on a motorcycle with a side car attached brought a big container of coffee to the German outpost. As Alex and his men had planned on taking this strong roadblock and outpost already, they knew all about it. The rangers also knew it was there but had no details or plans on how to take it out.

Alex suggested that the German bringing the coffee be taken out instead and the coffee be laced with morphine from the medical supply post. Then the guards could be taken out the way real defectors would do it. His plan was approved and the rangers showed up with lots of morphine. As they needed every moment of darkness to get everything done, Alex sent four of his men with four rangers across into German lines three miles off from where the real action was going to occur so it would look like an American patrol had come in. As this happened very often, it would raise no suspicion nor be connected to what was really happening. When this group opened up a good-sized path through German lines, 22 rangers wearing Nazi SS and German army uniforms would follow them through.

Having watched the German deliver his coffee on several nights, Alex's men knew the German had always done the same thing every night. He stopped at every picket stop and gave the Germans their coffee. At the first stop, four silenced .45 bolt action British rifles took out all three guards and the motorcycle driver as well. A German-speaking American ranger got on the motorcycle that had the large container of coffee in the attached side car. The morphine was added to the coffee and well mixed. Then the ranger in the German uniform delivered the doped coffee to the next stop. At every stop the coffee was passed out and then the next until the last German post and roadblock. The eight men that had opened the way for the other 22 rangers worked their way back to the road. Every time they came upon a German soldier that they had to take out they left a pamphlet written in German telling all readers that the war was now lost for all those German soldiers caught in the surrounded pocket. Sometimes they put one in a dead soldier's pocket or in his hand like he was reading it. The pamphlet said they were cut off and could never get away alive. They were cut off from the rest of France and would die without cause if they resisted. "Lay down your arms and come to the American lines and you will be treated fairly. Then as soon as Hitler is forced from power, a true government will take over Germany and the war will be over. Then they will be released to return to their families and a normal life.

In fact they left many of these surrender pamphlet scattered in the woods as they walked into town just like they had been dropped from airplanes. The German-speaking motorcycle driver told the other rangers when he met up with them that there was a German patrol out that would be coming back down the road. So, with a laugh like he was making a joke he said, "I'm going to give them some coffee also so do not shoot me when I come back."

He made three more stops to give German soldiers a shot of coffee. With the last two he used his knife quickly and deadly, then rode back into the American lines.

There he made a quick report and joined the entire convoy of captured German vehicles as they started toward Deauvill. Enough Germans had been taken out from both sides of the road to make the trip to the roadblock easy. After the roadblock, every time they passed a German soldier, either one or twenty, they all snapped to attention and gave the Hitler salute. The rangers and bats had arrived on the outskirts of Deauvill much earlier than expected and there they stopped and talked things over. The major said, "Let's do this," and they all cranked up and headed for town except one half-track stayed back to come in as a rescue in case things went wrong. In the Mercedes were men dressed in typical suits with jackets like the Gestapo wore. Each man had very official-looking credentials and all kinds of papers to arrest agents, soldiers and others that were plotting against Hitler. Other rangers dressed as soldiers had the same papers for the arrest of German officers for the same crime. Then the American/Gestapo agents spread out over the town, making arrests right and left. They had so many, in fact, that they had to get real German soldiers to hold them under arrest while they went and got others.

Alex and his men had to watch this from miles away as they could not play the part of Gestapo. In reality, Alex said that waiting the five hours for everyone to return from Deauvill was the hardest five hours he had ever spent waiting up to that time. While in Deauvill, the Americans gathered over a hundred men, all pleading their loyalty to Hitler, and were told they would get a hearing in Berlin.

Real German soldiers were required to carefully search every prisoner as one German officer had shot himself rather than be questioned by the Gestapo. Then eight German troop trucks were commandeered and all prisoners were loaded in and started south. A few German solders tried jumping from the trucks and they were shot at and some got away, but the Americans had to make it look good or they all would have run away. When they reached the German roadblock they were all surrounded by American troops and then the real Germans knew they'd been taken and there was not a thing that could be done about it. Most of the German troops went into prisoner stockades. Officers and all SS men went into a separate stockade. All Gestapo agents were flown to England, and everything was kept as hush hush as possible. Alex and his men went right back to being "Bats, the word that large numbers of high ranking Nazi's had defected to the Americans." This sent a shock wave throughout the ranks of the German army and the Gestapo. Hitler and the Nazi party said it was all an American lie. Who believed what will never be known, but it didn't help the Nazi cause though many Nazis already knew there were men in their ranks that wanted Hitler gone.

4

SLUGGING IT OUT IN FRANCE

Alexander had read a lot about France, but seeing its hedgerows was something he just could not imagine. Somewhere in ancient history the French farmers left two or three yards between their fields and let Mother nature grow her own fences. In hundreds of years of growth these fence rows had not only grown up in to a near solid wall—the bigger trees formed fence posts and between smaller trees and brush the obstructions were so thick one had to see it to believe it. This growth was to a point where it would have been hard for a man to get through to the next farm without cutting his way through. Even that would have been a very long, tiring job. Either the hedgerows had caught enough dirt or dead vegetation in all the years of growing or the farmers had piled it up. Without being cut back but allowed to pile up, their bases were now well above the fields. This made a dam of dirt several feet high with trees and brush on top to protect a defending army as good or better than those old ancient forts of hundreds of years ago. Some believe that the non-stop plowing, planting, and harvesting had actually lowered the fields while leaving the hedgerows up high. Who really knew? Maybe some of both, but this was something the Allies had not counted on when planning the invasion.

The Germans used the hedgerows like the walls of an ancient fort in every way except standing on top of these old walls. While it was hard to find a spot an adult could get through, it was not hard to find a spot that a soldier could push his rifle barrel through. There was enough space to fire at a man on the other side while remaining hidden himself. The roots of all that vegetation held everything together like bars of steel. This dam of dirt completely protected a man behind it. So the Germans had a million miles of pre-grown fort walls to protect themselves. To win this war the American army had to conquer these hedgerows one at a time. The first time the 4th Division hit these hedgerows, it quickly decided that there had to be a better way to fight nature than this. They tried to use a bulldozer to push through by raising the blade enough to make a shield to protect the driver. At long distances the blade did stop rifle bullets that hit them. A rifle shot coming from the side was always deadly, as only the blade was there to protect the driver. Even the blade only worked until the bulldozer started getting close to the enemy. Americans even tried putting steel plates welded around the driver. Even the biggest D7 bulldozers came to a sudden stop when their blades hit most of the hedgerows. That was also when the Germans turned their Panzerfaust on the bulldozers. Even the strongest steel on bulldozer blades was like a sheet of paper trying to stop a Panzerfaust 100. The Panzerfaust at close range could turn a bulldozer into scrap metal.

Now it was WW1 all over again, to send more men than the enemy had bullets to stop them. In fact, storming a hedge row was even worse than storming the trenches in WWI. To continue to lose six to ten Americans for every German would mean the Germans would win the war. As great as our air power was, bombs hit all over the field, occasionally killing our own troops. Low flying fighters coming in to try to do the job allowed the German air defense of machine guns. Even the rifles all pointed right at a fighter coming in very low often shot the plane down. Then even if the American aircraft got away, the fighter was most always badly damaged. The Air Force often hit the wrong hedgerow, killing both Americans and Germans. The Air Force and high command said *no more* to this practice. It was back to hacking through or blowing a hole in the hedgerow while under tremendous enemy fire. Either way of getting through the hedgerow showed the enemy exactly where the Americans were going to come through and allowed their entire fire to concentrate on that spot. The Americans that did get through had to charge across open ground to attack the next hedgerow. When they were successful and took it away from the German defenders, the Germans simply pulled back to the next hedgerow and started the fight all over again. Fighting this way did not require the Germans to have a lot of men; it only required them to have a lot of bullets, machine guns, Panzerfaust, artillery and supplies.

The 4th Division was called upon to take the hedgerows and they brought in all the Sherman tanks they could get. A Sherman is armored far better than any bulldozer could ever be. The hope was the Shermans could run right through the hedgerows. In the few places the Shermans could break through by charging forward and backing up and trying again until they got through. This showed the Germans just where the Americans were going to come through and gave them time to prepare for the Sherman to break through. This also required the Shermans to climb up the mound of dirt from which the hedgerow was growing. This exposed the soft belly of the Sherman and the belly was lightly armored. The exposed belly allowed the Germans the perfect target. The Sherman can be equipped with a bulldozer like blade however. The blade on the Sherman was about half as wide as the bulldozer blade, it was also much thicker steel and harder to be penetrated by rifle bullets. Still not even a fraction enough to turn the Panzerfaust or cannon fire. This blade did put all the power of the Sherman motor on a smaller spot and this worked a lot better to break through. Even here, it had to find a weak spot in the hedgerow and pound it over and over to get through.

A farm boy from New Mexico told the engineers how they cleared mesquite trees on their ranches. They used the bulldozers with narrow blades just like the ones on the Shermans. However they welded sharpened pointed teeth on the bottom of the blade. Then they ran the blade down into the dirt a few inches below the surface where the roots were not as strong as at ground level. Then the sharp teeth on the blade could cut the softer roots rather than trying to push over a tree and all that brush. The army welded teeth on the blade of a Sherman and tried it and it worked. It not only went through the hedgerows but could take out enough dirt to not make the Shermans climb so high to expose their soft belly nearly as much.

This became the main hedgerow buster of the American army. Even this resulted in heavy losses in American armor, as often the Germans were just waiting for a tank to break through. If it was a small field and the next hedgerow was close, they were waiting with a Panzerfaust to destroy the first tank through. If it was a big field and the Panzerfaust did not have the ability to shoot across it with accuracy, the Germans then had dug out a spot on the back side of the next hedgerow and placed an anti-tank cannon there. So the foot soldier still took the worst of it in hedgerow fighting and this was slow, hard, and very costly. Even the few roads in this part of France had the hedgerows on both sides and no one knew where or when the enemy was going to open up on them. The army's advance was now measured in the taking of hedgerows or casualties. Of course, to high command it was reported in yards and casualties. As they were never going to admit that a bunch of trees was what was holding up the advancement of the American army.

Regardless of the number of casualties required to defeat the German army, the hedgerows had to be taken. Most squads preferred to try to follow a Sherman through, then try to rush the enemy. Alex preferred to take the end of the field where two or more hedgerows met, then work their way down through it when passable or right beside it. Then they would go on down to where another hedgerow joined it, and start all over again. Still this was better than trying to run over an open field into machine gun emplacements. This was slow tricky work but his men always worked with another squad on the other side of the hedgerow. These two squads worked together and were very good at cleaning out any Germans in the vertical hedgerows. This job brought the Americans and the Germans close together. In that context, pistols and short sub-machine guns like the M3 grease gun, the Thompson and the M1 carbines worked better. Sometimes men shot each other at only six feet and a shot of over thirty feet was rare inside the hedgerows. Trying to throw a hand grenade into the tangle of brush and trees was rarely tried as it could not get through and often bounced back killing or wounding the man that had tried it.

By now most of Alex's squad had a mixture of hand guns they had collected as they moved inland. Some officers discouraged their men from having or using hand guns. Alex kept quiet about it but secretly encouraged it for places just like this. When they were in tight places like they were now the handguns could be used much faster than a long heavy M1. When Alex was not at the very front of his men he was studying the hedgerow yard by yard. When he was the lead man in this jungle of brush and trees he used his Luger to clear the brush and had his .45 as back up. The sound of the 9mm Luger did not alert the Germans as much as the louder different sound of the 45. He and his men were extremely good at clearing out the vertical hedgerows. Most of their casualties came from the enemy firing at them from the horizontal hedgerows. The men in back were responsible for protecting the squad in front as they fired backward at the enemy in the horizontal hedgerows. When it was possible Alex tried to keep a few yards between the men in front and those in the rear. This was designed to keep the enemies' sight and mind on the back forces that were firing at them. It is just natural to shoot back at those trying to shoot you, rather than shoot at an enemy that is elsewhere.

The big push came when a company rushed across the field. When these charging men came alongside, Alex's squad joined them but kept up clearing out the vertical hedgerow. Sometimes the Germans had set up an MG42 in the corner of the field so they could get a crossfire on the Americans. If the Germans MG42 crews were giving their attention to the troops coming across an open field, then they were easy pickings for Alex's squad. If they were looking down the hedgerow, Alex was coming up the opposite way. Then the squad tried to get as deep into all that mess of brush and trees as they could get. Practice may or may not make perfect, but with Alex's squad inside, and the other squad on the outside, they became very good at it. Like all the men working the hedgerows in France there was a large loss in casualties. While deaths were about twenty five percent of the casualties, the wounded made up the other seventy five percent. Taking care of the wounded and getting them out and back for medical help was the job of the medics and their helpers. However in a big fight the medics could not start to get this all done immediately and it was often the wounded man's buddies that did the job as efficiently as they could. Even then it had to be done when most of the hard fighting was over. Therefore the bravery of the medics that rushed into the fight and took care of wounded men while under fire themselves earned them the nickname of the "angels of the battlefield." Any soldier that has ever been under live fire from an enemy that is trying to kill him knows how well deserved this title is.

When a hedgerow was the protection for a very large field, the minute one of our dozer Shermans broke through, it was stopped by an artillery shell. The damage it did to a Sherman proved it to be one of Germany's new high powered cannons. As the new Russian T 34 tanks appeared on the Russian front, the smaller German anti-tank guns could not stop them. So the German army had increased production of both self-propelled guns and truck-pulled guns. Along with these, they had also developed the new Panzerfaust 100. These not only were much more powerful, they had much greater range. The Panzerfaust 100 could also be reloaded whereas the early models of Panzerfaust had cheap throwaway tubes. The 100's were well made and the sighting systems were far better. These changes included new anti-personnel charges, so now these were truly handheld cannon. This one hedgerow that Dog company had to take had an anti-tank cannon, with several of the new Panzerfaust 100s. Add to this more soldiers than normal and plenty of MG42s. The first charge of American troops was a disaster with many casualties.

The captain called his lieutenants together and gave them one of his longer speeches. "Our company has been ordered to try to flank the cannon and put it out of commission. We are going back to the road, resupply and follow Alpha company in a breakthrough. Our orders are not to stop until we get through all three hedgerows on the other side of the road. This is going to be a night attack so be sure of where you are firing. We do not want to kill our own men tonight so go in with fixed bayonets. Remember Alpha Company is in front of you. Tell your sergeants this, so they will tell their men. Also no hand grenades except on machine guns." The lieutenants gathered their sergeants and the sergeants their squads and they all moved out.

The plan was to attack the first hedgerow with only half of the company, then be reinforced by the other half as soon as needed. This meant that late that afternoon the hedgerow was going to be taken regardless of cost. So soldiers moved back out of the fighting line, filed by the ammunition truck, then on to get water and what they would need for three days.

The company started the four mile hike to their new battle line knowing well that this time tomorrow there would be less of them. Still two miles away, they could hear the sounds of battle and knew that Alpha had started the penetration. While marching to their destination they had to move to the side of the road to allow a convoy to pass. There were nine Sherman tanks, three had the new hedgerow cutter blades in them. Two more had blades without the teeth, while the other four were just Shermans. All were driving with their hatches open and every face had the look of awareness—they recognized what was ahead.

There were several supply trucks and a whole lot of army ambulances. Before the convoy had fully passed the company a first lieutenant said, "Take ten. This is the last you will get for a while, check your equipment, in an hour you are going to be using it."

It was not long before three of the ambulances came back by. It was already getting late in the day when the men turned off the road onto a newly made one which cut through a hedgerow into a field that had been turned into a base camp. The company never slowed down even though close range battle was going on. All the Shermans but one had already passed through and the last one was widening the opening through the second hedgerow. Again the company never slowed down as they marched right through the widened hole. While marching forward the squads started peeling off to both sides. Alex's platoon lieutenant sent Alex's squad to the far right. As they approached the corner where two hedgerows came together a piece of white cloth was stuck out on a stick. In German, Alex called out, "Come out with your hands above your heads."

Alex did not know much German but he had been taught that much in England. Alex sent his prisoners back while he and his twelve remaining men went into the brush. When they recovered the German rifles that had been left behind, to their surprise, they found a MG42. If those Germans had opened up on them from that distance with that 42 the whole squad would have been cut down.

Alexander did lose one man in taking the next hedgerow when it turned parallel to the other three they had come through. With Americans on one side and more Americans coming through and around the hedgerow they were in, several more Germans gave up. Most of these Germans were extra old or young, including a lot of foreign forced troops. Even so, this fourth hedgerow was thinly defended compared to the last three. Half of Alpha company dug in for the night while the other half turned to the left and started down that hedgerow. When they cleared it they dug in for the night also and let Easy Company come up and take over. Shifting clouds allowed some light, just enough to see where to walk. Then when they parted and allowed the half moon to shine, it was easy to see the hedgerows around them. Third squad got into a firefight as soon as they approached the next hedgerow. The lieutenant asked Alex if he thought he might be able to get around the third squad. Then flank the fight to come in from the other side. Alex told his squad they were going to try to angle across the field when it was the darkest. When the clouds parted and allowed light to come through, they were going to lie down flat and not move at all.

When it grew dark again they were going to come back into the lines and kill the Germans. If it worked they were going to do it all night. *It's the darkest just before dawn* is an old saying about life but that night it was really true. They had been able to take over a mile of hedgerows by coming in from behind the Germans. Full sunup, Alex left his men on point and made his way back to his lieutenant and reported. Then he asked if his men could get some sleep as they had been up for over twenty hours without a real break. The lieutenant said, "Fine you can pull your men back," to which Alex responded, "With your permission, sir, they would like to sleep right where they are."

By mid-afternoon the battle had passed them by as when the Germans realized they had been flanked they withdrew about a mile. Unfortunately, that had allowed them to move their cannon and all their equipment with them. After the next big push, the Americans began to experience the receiving end of German artillery.

Delta company had slipped into the woods for some protection and this was both bad and good. The bad side was when artillery exploded in woods it would bring down trees and huge limbs that did damage like shrapnel. The good side was that these same trees blunted the explosive force and also caught some of the shrapnel so the destroyed area was smaller. Regardless, that was where the captain had brought them and today it had worked out well as only a few shells landed there. When the barrage stopped and the division started to regroup, another twenty or so shells landed where the first pattern had hit. Word came for the companies to remain spread out but to return to the march west. Now an occasional shell would land on or near the road and the German gunners were also moving west with their cannon fire. As the road was no longer a healthy place to be, most of the division's foot soldiers stayed well away from the road when they could.

Now the road was only used for vehicle traffic and even then they were spread out so one shell could not take out more than one vehicle. As Fox Company approached the village, they did it in textbook order and that saved lives. As Able and Charlie came up, they spread to both sides of the village as 105 were brought up and started taking out houses in rapid order. Able Company totally went around the village and covered the back side while Easy Company took Able's place. The village was not that large and could not have much more than a platoon of Germans. Now the Germans were totally surrounded by four full companies of Americans with Sherman tanks and artillery. Before 1100 hours white flags began appearing all over the place.

Six miles down the road was a town that had a population of over 5000 before the war and no one knew how many French civilians lived there now. The place had been bombed more than once as it was known to house a German garrison. It also had coastal batteries that photo resonance had shown to have been very badly damaged if not destroyed by American bombers. These batteries posed no danger to the 4th as they could only fire out to sea. Orders to the 4th were to make sure these batteries were no longer a threat to American shipping, then to overwhelm all German resistance in the area. Army intelligence had estimated anywhere from 5000 to 10,000 German troops in the area. This was going to be a hard fight and everyone knew it. Even before the village surrendered, part of Able Company had to turn around and fight off German reinforcements. These had been sent to defend the village from the Americans but had arrived too late. At six miles out a running battle ensued and there was sniping against the 4th as it proceeded toward the town. Orders had stated that all American forces were to capture Cherbourg as quickly as possible. This meant that every place between had to be taken as quickly as possible, then the whole peninsula of all German forces must be cleared. The general ordered that the town be surrounded so no Germans could escape to fight another day. All night Americans worked to surround the town. The next morning a jeep with a flag of truce and an American major was sent in to demand the surrender of the town. This was to save the lives of French civilians as well as the lives of the German garrison. When Major Holster was ushered into the Nazi command center and met the German officer in charge he knew his request was going to be denied. This German officer was dressed in an all black uniform showing he was an SS officer. After numerous insults to Major Holster, the Nazi said that all Americans and British forces were going to be wiped off the face of the earth. In fact, it should have been the Americans who came to surrender to him, and not the other way around.

As American artillery was being set up to start the bombardment of the town. A long line of French men, women and many children were marched out and made a line over a hundred yards long in front of the town. Behind them stood about eighty German guards with about a third in black. When the line was formed, a German staff car drove to the American lines. All four men inside were dressed in black and three disembarked. One was a German major with two lesser German officers and even their driver was SS. The American captain in charge was not sure what rank they held, if any. Speaking British type English the SS Major demanded to be taken to the American general. The captain said, "I am in charge here; if you talk to anyone you will talk to me."

The SS major face registered nearly uncontrollable anger. When he got himself back under control, he said, "Tell your general that if one shot is fired toward a single German soldier these two hundred fifty French will be shot and every hour after that another two hundred and fifty will be shot until your dirty unkempt army leaves this town. If your general refuses to obey our orders, we will kill every Frenchman here. Then our German forces will kill every American here."

Then with a red face and fire in his eyes he said, "In all civilized armies ranking officers are never spoken to by enemy combatants of lower rank--never again speak to an SS officer without respect. The Nazi stormed off to his staff car and headed back into the town at a very fast pace.

The captain got into his jeep and told his driver, "Take me to the General." It was a short trip and the general's response to the captain was, "This is what the Nazis have been using from day one of their existence."

At 1300 every American tank and piece of artillery opened fire. Of course, the American artillery in front of the hostages fired well over the their heads. That didn't change the fact that as the first American cannons fired, the Nazi soldiers started killing the hostages. As the hostages fell to the ground the Nazis that were doing the killing were now exposed. American riflemen that were expert marksmen killed most of the executioners. Then heavy machine gun and rifle fire covered that whole side of the town. After several minutes of this heavy fire it stopped and hundreds of American soldiers rushed into that part of town, followed by medics and others that tried to help. Unfortunately the Nazis were very good at their jobs, and most of the French were dead or dying.

The Americans that stormed the town went in like mad dogs, to make every German pay for the horror of their actions. Alex's battalion was sent to the beach to accomplish the orders of making sure those fortifications could never be used against American shipping or American landing forces. The Germans had also well-fortified the beach with concrete pill box fortifications, trenches, barbed wire and machine gun nests. That beach was well protected against landing forces from the sea. Unfortunately for the Germans, the big guns were all pointed toward the sea. Unfortunately for the Americans machine guns and rifles could be pointed backward to take on Americans coming from behind. Still, all the preparation had been for seaward assault and that helped the Americans a great deal.

What did not help was the vast stockpiles of all types of ammunition, machine guns, weapons and supplies that were there for the defending German army. The battalion was now well experienced in fighting the German army and approached their objective with the perfect mixture of fury and care. With the help of three Sherman tanks and a lot of bazookas and hand grenades they approached the beach defenses. Most of the 4th Division was employed in taking the town while Alex's whole regiment was sent to the beach defenses. The American bazooka had been much improved since the beginning of the war, but not near as much as the Germans had. The Germans had improved the fire power and now had the Panzerfaust 100, a handheld bazooka type weapon that one man could use to take out a Sherman tank with one shot. So now the troops had to protect the Shermans, where the Shermans used to protect the troops. This is a much simplified statement and not totally true but it makes its point. Tanks could no longer just rush in with the knowledge that their armor was going to protect them from everything but the big guns. First, the barracks behind beaches and close to the town had to be cleared of enemy troops. They were large enough to house several hundred men to man the big guns and coastal defenses. There were two very large three story barracks right behind the town. There were more smaller barracks up and down the beach spread out in both directions. Easy Company got the job of clearing all these barracks.

Here the Shermans could stand off at a distance too far for a

Panzerfaust to be a great danger to them. Then still put their rounds into those barracks, but first the escape route of fleeing soldiers had to be blocked. Three machine gun squads and five rifle squids were sent to get between the two big barracks and the beach defenses. Once in place, the Shermans and four 105s started knocking the barracks into pieces. When this happened, Germans emerged by the hundreds to head for the beach. The fire power of three thirty caliber machine guns and over fifty riflemen with semi-auto fire can stop far more than the few hundred trying to get away. Well, over a hundred enemies surrendered and now it was time for the buildings to be cleared. Nothing but boots on the ground could do this job, and it was going to be a dangerous one. Not just because of enemy troops inside the building but much of the buildings had been destroyed by cannon fire. Any part could collapse or all of it at any time. It also provided excellent defense for the enemy in its wreckage.

So many big shells had exploded in the barracks no one knew when parts would cave in, as it was part two story and part three story. Major Carlton decided to send two squads into the west end of each of the two biggest barracks. Then with men on each floor they'd all move together down the full length of the barracks so they would not shoot each other. Alex was told to take the top floor with six of his men. The other sergeant was told to take six of his men to clear the second floor. A lieutenant was assigned to oversee the whole operation and he took the rest of both squads with him to clear the bottom floor. As much as Alex loved his M1, crawling through a wrecked three story barracks was no place for a large heavy rifle. Two of his men had Thompsons, while one had an M3. There was one select fire-folding stock carbine that a wounded paratrooper had given to the squad. Two others decided to use their captured German pistols or their 1911s and one still wanted his M1. Alex had his Colt 1911 45 pistol and his Luger for back up so that was the way they went in. All the floors were badly damaged and moving around in them was sticky to say the least. It took

Alex and his squad a while to even get up to the third floor. They had to go a little to the west to make sure it was clear then back to the starting point. There were huge holes in the walls and floors so there was no problem in talking from floor to floor. Alex called down to the second floor saying they were ready to start clearing the floor. The second floor relayed the message to the first floor, and they all started forward. One area had already been checked before starting forward with the other men on the two lower floors. It was a large shower and restroom. Next they had several small officers' quarters with closets that all had to be checked out. Alex was right; this was a job for hand guns, not large rifles. Long, nine pound M1 rifles did not move easily through a semi-destroyed building, even if for no other reason than the necessity of having a free hand to hold on with.

One of the officers' quarters did not even have a door and not much of a wall either. Taking a quick look, Alex then returned for a sure look inside. He saw that an artillery shell had exploded inside the room. The whole outside wall of this and the next room was gone as were most of the ceilings and floors of both rooms.

On what was left of the room floor was the remains of what had been a human but it was hard to tell for sure. After the eight officer's rooms, there was a huge barracks room full of what had been bunk beds. Exploding cannon fire had turned them into match sticks and rubble that was well nigh impossible to get through. It was a huge room that must have held a couple hundred men. Other than the one body, there was no one else. Next was a massive stairway leading down to the second floor. Then it was a repeat of the other end in reverse, another huge barracks but this room only had two holes in the walls so there was not near as much damage except a large section of the roof was gone. The squad got through this much faster than the other end, and again they found officers' quarters.

The first room after the barracks room was a large office. This was intact with desk, filing cabinets, and all the things that made for an office. Looking at it Alex thought that perhaps the other one was an office also, there was not enough remaining to be sure one way or the other. The sound of a couple of pistol shots came up from below, then the chatter of a Thompson. It was quiet again but only for a moment as more shots rang out These shots sounded like they might have been outside of the barracks and Alex guessed that some diehard Germans were holed up somewhere, but they were not on his third floor. The rest of the rooms were clear until the squad passed a small stairway just like the one on the other end. There were still shots coming up from below but gunfire to Alex was as common as breathing when on a battlefield. Then they entered the shower area, another big section of wall, floor and roof was gone and there were eight or nine bodies scattered around the room. Most were naked, some had remnants of cloth on them, and again it was hard to tell where one body stopped and another started. Those cannon shells sure made a mess of things. Some genius in the squad said, "Those bastards must have been taking a shower when that shell hit."

Alex said, "I might feel sorry for them if I had not seen their buddies machine gun those French this morning."

Calling down the small stairway, at first they got no answer. On the second try, a distant voice said, "Stay put, we're coming." Alex stood waiting while the others went back into the shower dressing room. After waiting a few minutes, Alex walked back into the dressing room next to the showers. His men were passing a bottle of wine back and forth while they all pulled German uniforms and stuff from the lockers. A couple of the men had German pistol belts with holsters hanging around their necks. A couple more were holding unopened wine bottles and all had their hands full of stuff they were going through. Alex walked back to the stairway and called again. This time a close voice said, "Nearly there," so they waited again. After a few minutes a voice called up, "We're here and we're going into the bath to check it out. Come on down."

Back to the lockers again, this time Alex said, "Let's go," in a sergeant's bark. All six men grabbed what they could and came.

Some had their hands so full they could hardly cross the damaged floor. Alex and his squad descended the small stairway and the whole second floor squad looked up at what Alex's squad was carrying. A voice said, "Where in Hell--?"

Brown said, "Shower room lockers." Every member of the second floor squad disappeared faster than a dropped five dollar bill. Alex walked on down to the second floor and it now seemed every man in Alex's squad had at least one wine bottle. Add to that, most had German pistol belts with full holsters, parts of German uniforms and their pockets were bulging with loot from those lockers. Again Alex called down to the first floor. Instead of an answer he heard gunfire and it was close. He turned to his squad and said, "Stay here and get rid of some of that stuff. If the lieutenant sees it he will make you get rid of all of it and you know it."

More gunfire from below. Alex said, "I'll be back. I have to find what is going on. Stay here and stay on your toes; they're fighting downstairs. Take care of anyone that tries to come out the back of the first floor but, be careful, it might be our own men."

Running down the second floor hall, he found it an exact copy of the third floor. Some places he had to climb over debris while in other sections he could move fast. Reaching the huge center hall, he stopped and listened. He heard English. He called out, "This is Sergeant Vetov." Coming out he stepped onto the stairway landing. Below him was the rest of his squad, along with more of his platoon.

"Where is Lieutenant Kelley?" he asked. Many hands pointed down the hall and said, "He is in the kitchen, we were ambushed and they got him. "It's a stand off. If we force our way in they say they will kill him."

Alex said, "Show me," and they made their way forward into a large dining hall. Several Americans were in the hall occasionally exchanging shots with Germans on the other end of the dining hall. As he came through the doorway several German bullets tried to get him, but they all missed. Asking questions of the men and studying the room, Alex lunged back through the doorway to safety. Another spattering of bullets but none hit him. He called out, "My squad, upstairs with me now, the rest of you stay put." When the men reached the top of the stairs, Alex told them, "If they hear us coming on the second floor the lieutenant is dead so we're going to the third floor and are going to stay quiet as we make our way down to the other end.

Up the stairs and down the third floor hall they went—then back to the second floor landing. There was Sergeant Fry and his squad and they had more loot than Alex's men did. Alex murmured, "Drop the loot; we are back in the war."

Then he explained the situation. Alex said, "Fry, take your squad and go downstairs and go outside. Creep along the beach side of the barracks until you can see the small windows of the kitchen, then stop. Beyond them are the large windows of the dining room. If you can slip some of your men beneath the small windows without being seen, go on to the large windows. If you are seen the lieutenant will be killed. Stay hidden until you hear gunfire inside the kitchen. Then stand up and shoot those windows out on the kitchen and dining room. Kill as many Germans as you can, but be careful and do not use grenades as there are Americans in both rooms as well as Germans.

"Brown, you do the same on the other side and every one keep quiet until I open fire. Davis, give me that carbine. Let's go." And down the stairs they went.

Alex tried to open the end door into the first floor of the barracks, and it was locked. Both teams went out their side doors as Alex tried to see if he could get the door to move.

Then he heard Brown, "Here, sergeant here," and Alex rushed for the door following Brown down the outside wall to a large service door. This door was on the side of the barracks that was facing town. Here there was a large paved parking lot where the Germans came to unload the trucks for the barracks. Brown grabbed this door and it swung up and open. Brown had seen Alex struggling with the first door and as he passed the truck door he'd pulled on it and it moved so he returned and got sergeant. "Get the rest of the squad that I left in the building," Alex said as he slipped inside. This was a large storeroom where the food trucks unloaded and someone had overlooked locking it. Holding the paratrooper carbine Alex pulled the bolt back enough to make sure there was a round in the chamber. He glanced at the select fire switch and moved it to single fire.

Carefully slipping into the hallway Alex saw a door with a large glass window in it and was sure it led into the kitchen. He knew most service doors in commercial buildings with kitchens have windows so kitchen employees don't run into each other while carrying food stuff. Staying to the side so he would not be seen, Alex slipped to the door and sneaked a look. There, less than twenty feet in front of him, was Lieutenant Kelley with a bloody head. Standing behind him and a little to the side was a SS officer with a P-38 to Kelly's head. Alex also saw a dozen or so black uniforms behind overturned tables and other things. They were all looking the other way. He tried the door and it was locked. Stepping back just a little, he lowered the carbine and pointed the barrel up at an angle so the bullets he was going to fire through the glass would not hit Kelley. Two quick shots and that window flew into many pieces. In another second the carbine was up and a third quick shot went through the Nazi's head. The SS officer that had the pistol to Kelley's head was trying to look back toward the sound of the shots that broke the window. Lieutenant Kelley was falling to the floor and Alex did not have time to think about Kelley.

He pushed the select fire switch and sprayed the Nazis in the room. From the first shot, bullets came through the windows on both sides of the kitchen. On full auto, the carbine was empty in seconds and Alex knew the Nazis were going to be returning fire through that door so the second the carbine ran out of ammunition he jumped to the side. However right behind him a private stepped up and put a burst from his Thompson through the lock on the door, pushed the door open and again sprayed the room. Kelly had not moved a muscle since he fell and the private that sprayed the room with his Thompson, grabbed Kelley's feet and pulled him back through the doorway into the storeroom. Kelly's hands were tied behind his back and his eyes were closed. The private pulled him partly over to the side and said, "I think he is dead."

At that Kelley twisted, opened his eyes and said, "Thank God, you men came, I thought I was a goner."

Lieutenant Kelley looked terrible, with lots of blood and bruising, but he was moving. The lieutenant had been badly beaten up but thankfully there didn't appear to be any gunshot wounds. Later when asked about why he fell and just lay there he said, "Every boy in Georgia knows that when a possum gets caught it plays dead so its attackers will leave it alone. If it is good enough for a Georgia possum it's good enough for this Georgia boy."

To finish the final mop up in the barracks, Lieutenant Kelley told Alex to take over the platoon until he could return or until reassignment by the captain. Then Kelley was taken to the aid station to get checked out and patched up. The kitchen fight had finished the resistance in both the large barracks. Taking the barracks fulfilled only half the orders so Alex had both squads make sure they were ready for the assault on the beach. Rifles replaced handguns, ammo was checked, and canteens were filled.

From the barracks to the beach is one quick step, not in distance or in time, but is the next part of the orders. Fox, Able, Charlie, and Dog companies were assigned the job of taking the beach defenses directly behind the town. Men spread out and studied the ground in front of them. There was a lot of open ground and lots of German troops in those trenches. Every Sherman tank commander knew those trenches were full of German anti-tank Panzerfausts, so they had to stay back. They also knew they could sure help with their big fifty caliber machine guns and cannons. They sprayed those trenches anywhere there were not Americans rushing in. Alex had never liked the little carbine; he'd always called it a pop gun. After today in the tight confines of the barracks he'd decided it is not a bad toy to have after all. Still he returned the carbine and retrieved his M1 to storm the beach. Right in front of his platoon was the back of one of the big gun concrete bunkers with a concrete pill box on each side. A series of trenches connected all three along with trenches running the full length of the beach. This was to the advantage of the Americans as the Germans never expected to be attacked from behind on the land side. As stated, all defenses were pointed toward the sea to defend the beaches from invasion. The big disadvantage was those trenches were full of German troops and were very well-equipped.

There was one row of trenches for the fighters to battle a landing. A second row to run supplies through and be a place for troops to fall back to if the front line was overrun. If someone was high overhead and looking down on the defenses it would look a very twisted crazy ladder with all the short trenches running from the front trench to the back trench. It wiggled and twisted so when a shell exploded in one section the shrapnel could not fly far and kill too many men. After a good pounding by the Sherman's cannon and fifties the Shermans had to stop firing to allow the troops to charge in to take the trenches and defenses. Charging machine guns over open ground was like the scenes from WW1. It had to be done and once the rear line was breached, men spread out in both directions. Alex with his platoon was now without their lieutenant so Alex, as staff sergeant and under the direction of his lieutenant, took over and led all five squads in the assault. The big gun bunker had a larger network of trenches around it that connected to the two line trenches. This was necessary to allow the flow of German soldiers and materials to and around this large installation. This also made it harder to take it away from the German troops in this mess of trenches.

The big bunker had one weak spot and that was the service road leading up to it. With much use the road had cut into the sand and soft earth of the beach. There were places where the road had been graded by machine or slave labor. This had left piles of beach sand and dirt in many places that allowed men some cover in spots while charging across sixty yards of open flat land. When they got close enough to see the back door of the bunker was already blown partly off its hinges, the men threw hand grenades into the trenches then instantly rushed forward and used their rifles to finish the job. This trench ran about ten yards and made a sharp turn. The troops repeated the use of hand grenades and rifle fire and followed the trench in both directions. Being behind the bunker, this trench was not dug to fight from, but rather for men and materials to move with better protection from exploding cannon fire. It was too deep for the Germans to stand up and fire over the edges. Other than a few places cut into the sides that allowed a few German soldiers to step up and fight from a higher position. This gave the platoon the advantage and many Germans were caught like rats in a trap. Some surrendered, some ran, some fought on, but the platoon kept advancing around both ends of the bunker.

A soldier would open the rear door of the bunker enough to throw in a hand grenade. One was tossed in and after it exploded, two men from the squad went inside. It seemed as if a large Air Force bomb had exploded right inside the open front, or just outside. Regardless, it really messed things up inside. Both of the huge Navy cannon had been derailed and it had made some of the in-house German cannon powder and shells explode as well. There was no sign of bodies so the two men went back outside and rejoined the fight. Two squads headed west, and two squads headed east, cleaning out the ladder-like trenches as they went. The pill boxes were a different matter as the defenders had removed their two machine guns. The Germans had set them up on both sides of the concrete pill box to defend against beachside attack. Charging rapid fire machine guns over sand beaches was worse than suicide.

So the platoon kept up a steady pace of firing while more men came down the trenches from both sides until they got close enough to use hand grenades. Within three hours Delta Company or dog company, as the men called themselves, met Fox Company on the east side and it only took another hour longer to meet Able and Easy on the west side.

As darkness came the 4th had all but quashed the resistance on the beach and Alex requested that his and Sergeant Fry's squads be allowed to stay at the beach in the old barracks until morning to rest. The major was happy to grant such a simple request. Alex went and talked to Sergeant Fry, then they went together and talked to both their squads. He told two different lieutenants that the major himself had given these two squads permission to stay in the old German barracks that night so no one should be surprised at lights moving around in there that night. Once in the barracks, Alex went to the storeroom and pulled out a bunch of empty burlap sacks that he saw there. Every man in both squads received a bag and Alex told them all to go get their goodies if they would follow the rules. They all had just left their stuff on the floor when asked to go save their lieutenant, so Alex warned against fighting over who owned what souvenirs.

Anyone that indulged in fighting would lose his right to any of it. Second, lights out were at 1100 as it would attract too much attention after that. Third, each one had to put his name on his own sack and leave it in the storage room until Alex could make arrangements to get them moved. Fourth, this would cost as Alex was going to have to make arrangements to get the stuff stored and then back to England, so Alex had the right to get into any bag and take out bribe payments to get things taken care of. He promised to do it in a manner which was fair and equitable to all. Fifth, no wine, glass, or perishables, but each man could take one bottle now if he could do so and not get caught. The same was true of small items that could be carried on their person or gear from tonight on.

Forget bulky items as they simply would not pass muster, so they had to use their heads and go get their stuff. Last thing, neither Sergeant Fry or Alex had anything to do with this or even knew it happened. Right!

The next day the battalion pulled out and headed west again. Every time they ran into German resistance, a company or two was assigned to take care of it. The rest of the battalion marched on in the rush to capture that all-important port for supplies to come ashore. At 1300 the last company ran into stiff resistance that was more than 300 or so men could handle, so they formed a defensive line for the night and waited for daylight. The attack that the colonel had expected did not come, so word was sent to Alex to come to command center. Once there, Alex was told that whereas it would be a few days before Lieutenant Kelley could rejoin D Company that he, Alex Vetov, as staff sergeant would remain in charge of the platoon. Next he was told he wanted Alex to split the platoon in half to do reconnaissance on both sides of the road in the area of their line of march. Then they looked at the colonel's maps and discussed the terrain and possible problems to be faced. As they finished perusing the maps, the colonel said, "Vetov, you have done a great job and I've recommended you to the general to be given a battlefield commission to the rank of second lieutenant. Alex was not expecting this and stood still for a moment; then he saluted his colonel and said, "Thank you, sir."

The next morning Alex simply told the platoon that until Lieutenant Kelley returned that he was in command and briefly explained the job that had been ordered of them. Pack up for a three day patrol and I'll be back in thirty minutes. That was the start of one of the longest three days of his life. Alex put Corporal Campbell in charge of his old squad and sent them to the left side of the road. He had Private Brown with his Thompson remain with him—sending 1st squad to the right side, and 3rd squad to the left. Then he said' "Second squad is to follow first squad about thirty yards back. Go about another fifteen yards outside of first squad, and the 4th squad is to do the same on the other side."

Alex walked in the roadside ditch with the fifth squad. He could see better from the road. That put him in the front middle and very exposed. Glancing at Brown, Alex could see that he was not happy about the exposed position.

They had not gone two hundred feet when off to the left there was a single rifle shot. The ditch was a couple of feet deep so he and Brown instantly dove down into it. After thirty seconds Alex tried to look over the ditch and there was another rifle shot. This shot was followed by the chatter of a Thompson. Alex carefully slipped into the woods and was soon met by two of his men. One man's bloody arm was hanging down and the other man was helping him. This pair never slowed as they passed Alex. The helper merely said, "Sniper, we got him," and kept walking. Continuing toward the sound of American voices, Alex walked into a small group of men gathered around a body on the ground. It was Greenwood, a replacement, on his third day ashore. By the time Alex, Brown, and the four men carrying the body got back to the road a jeep was there to carry the wounded and dead men back to camp. Fifty or more men from the camp had come running. Being so close to camp they'd heard the gunfire. Even less than a hundred yards and Alex had lost two men—and one was gone for good. This was not a smooth start, and Alex knew he could not let the men think about it. So he ordered the men to get their rifles, return to their assigned positions, be careful and move out.

After dispersing the men, he waited fifteen minutes to let them get back to their assigned positions, then moved his fifth squad out also. Before nightfall the platoon had been fired on nine more times, though no one else was hit. They did not they find any of the shooters, it was only harassment fire but it was sure working. It was a no smoking, no light, no talking camp that night. They were moving at first light and Alex had shifted the squads around so no one would be on point all the time. At 0710 a German group of about twenty men were found and the patrol took them out without another loss. Alex decided the German officers' Ziess binoculars were better than the U.S. issue and gave his old ones to Brown. He also took the officers' Luger as he'd sent the one Demetry had given him back to England and had been using a P-38. Besides, this one looked brand new, even though it was dated 1939. Alex missed his old Luger; it just felt better in his hand. Now he had a new one. They were already out of range with their little two-way radio when he spotted a German unit of several hundred men so Alex sent two with a marked map back to find the 4th. Minutes passed and he didn't hear anything on his radio about them making it back. His radio was admittedly short range and could not broadcast back to command, but that did not mean the command's high powered radio could not send word back to Alex. First thing the next morning Alex sent six men back, as this was too important to take a chance. Now he was down eight more men and had worked his way around the German force to check out the planned route.

The third day out came—the day they were supposed to turn around and head back. They heard a half track on the road and wondered why it was moving during daylight hours as the American Air Force patroled the roads during daylight hours. It was not long until the half track and a German staff car pulled into some woods and drove between the trees. They seemed to be coming right at the Americans as they held their ground in the thick woods. The German half-track and staff car stopped and five German officers got out, along with half a dozen German soldiers from the half track. The five German officers had uniforms that indicated their high ranking. These and three soldiers walked out of the woods glancing up for American airplanes. They then walked a short distance to a little French farmhouse. They never slowed down as they opened the door and went in, leaving the three soldiers outside to stand guard. The back of the house was even closer to the woods than the front. However the woods were not nearly as thick there in the back of the house, making it harder to hide. Alex's curiosity bubbled over. Whatever could five ranking German officers be doing in that house? Two of those officers had red stripes on their slacks and that meant they were generals. The chance to take two German generals was worth any risk. Taking twelve of his men, Alex explained how important it was to get rid of two German generals. He sent two of his men back to the platoon and told them to surround that half track and when they heard gunfire coming from the farmhouse to make sure not a single German got away. Being generals, these probably would not stay anywhere very long, but Alex still had to wait for his platoon to surround the half-track.

Checking his watch Alex gave his men thirty minutes to surround the German troops at the half track. He told six of his little group of men that he knew they were expert shots and to stay where they were. If those Nazis made a break for their staff car, to shoot them. Shoot whoever came out of that door, but make sure they first shot the ones with the red stripes and then the rest as they could. If five officers went in, there had to be even more Nazis inside that house. There were two French cars in front of it. That meant to Alex that more Nazis had taken those French cars and driven here. After all, the Nazis had taken everything in France that they wanted. That left ten men plus Alex and he knew that front door was covered by six great American shots with M1 rifles, and a Thompson. Trying to take their time and move carefully, Alex and his four remaining men made their way to the back of the cottage. There was a chicken coop right behind the house so they didn't leave the woods until the chicken coop was between them and the back door. They looked things over and then, one at a time, made their way to the back of the chicken coop.

They were nearly ready to rush the house when the back door opened and a Nazi officer strode out, into the backyard and on into an outhouse. Brown handed Alex his Thompson and said, "One less Nazi son of a bitch," as he pulled out his combat knife. Brown moved without a sound over to the outhouse and stepped around front. He yanked the door open and literally jumped inside. There was still no noise as the German officer was killed. The outhouse door reopened and Brown stepped out with a bloody knife in his hand. A window broke as the sound of a German Schmeisser sub machine gun sprayed 9 mm bullets into Brown's body. Alex was holding Brown's Thompson and he emptied that forty five caliber Thompson into that back window. While Alex was shooting into that back window, the front door of the farm house flew open and men start pouring out. As they raced out five M1s and a Thompson started a stream of well-aimed 30-06 and 45 rounds into German bodies. In the back of the house four GIs rushed the back of the house. One went down as another window was shot out. Alex dropped the empty smoking Thompson, pulled his Colt 45 and rushed the back window into which he'd just emptied the Thompson. He and his two remaining men each threw a grenade into the house simultaneously and heard them explode. Then there was another explosion and the last three Americans, including Alex, went down.

Alex awoke in an aid station with a doctor working on him and he passed out again. The next time he awoke he felt things shaking and he hurt like he was in hell. An Army nurse said, "I cannot give you anymore morphine until you get to the hospital. You are in a C-47 and we will be landing in England in about thirty minutes."

That nurse had the slowest watch on earth. Alex knew it would be a couple of hours before they landed even though he couldn't look at his watch. Upon landing, Alex was loaded in an ambulance and taken to a base hospital. As soon as he was in the hospital, he was wheeled into the surgery wing but there he stayed in the hallway nonetheless. After another long wait he grabbed an orderly's arm and asked, "Why am I out here in the hall?" The orderly peeled Alex's fingers away and answered, "There are guys in worse shape that must be helped. Your wounds are not life-threatening. We will get to you later, but no more morphine for now."

Alex did not remember much of the next couple of days, but on the third day a two star general walked in and asked how he was doing. Alex was lying on his stomach and it felt as if his entire back was bandaged from his butt to his neck. Trying to be brave and respectful, Alex answered, "They tell me I am going to be all right, sir."

The general said, "Well, lieutenant, when you get well enough, you are going to get the Bronze Star. You are the kind of man we need right now so get well soon."

It turned out Davis was in the same hospital ward and he had been with Alex at the back of that house when the grenade went off. They were the only two men from the back of the house still alive. So only Davis knew what had happened that day.

Davis said, "After Brown was killed, the other four of us rushed the house to immediately follow up the grenades exploding inside. Clancy got shot before he got near the window in which he was going to throw his grenade. Dominguez was shot and killed after he got his grenade inside."

Davis wasn't crystal clear about the rest of what happened out back, but he told Alex he thought he'd figured things out. "All four men had pulled their safety pins at the same time and run to the house together. All three grenades inside went off together. Clancy must have been holding the firing lever down in his hand as he lay on the ground badly wounded. Then Jordan went over to check Clancy, and maybe the moment Clancy died he released the firing lever. Jordan was standing right over him when the grenade went off, killing him instantly. Sarge, you got all kinds of shrapnel in your back and burns from the explosion. I was farther away but I got a piece in my shoulder that really fixed me up big time. Got a few other pieces but they will all heal.

"It's what happened next that really got interesting. That house was full of Nazis meeting with a bunch of leading French collaborators. They were afraid for their lives, as our American forces were taking France back. Officials are still talking about what might have happened if our little raid had not stopped it. The three grenades killed some in the house and wounded others. As the Germans and French collaborators ran out the front door to get to their cars, our men cut them all down. This is still not the most important part. Our boys attacked that half-track, but the Germans had also heard the gunfire and were alert. Trying to take a half-track with only rifles is no easy task, we lost four boys dead and six wounded. That made a total of eight wounded and we were behind enemy lines. Four of our boys put on SS uniforms and two of them got in the staff car while two more put on the generals uniforms. Those uniforms were all bloody and everyone was scared to death of getting caught. More men put on German uniforms except for the pants while others put on German helmets. All the badly wounded went into the back of the half-track, and we put enough men in to make it look like a full guard for the generals. Our boys got the half-track, the Nazi staff car, and those two French cars. We filled up the two French cars with our walking wounded wearing German jackets and helmets and, of course, one driver. The staff car went first, then the French cars, with the half-track last.

Davis paused for a moment, as if in memory of the dead. "We went flying down the road for the American lines. All those Nazis are so well-trained that as soon as they saw the general pennants on the front fenders of that staff car they jumped out of the way and snapped to attention, giving the Hitler salute. When we approached the American lines we did not know what the hell to do. We stopped to discuss getting out and going in on foot. Jones said, 'Hell no!' and he pulled out that American flag he always carries and tied it on the half-track radio mask. While he was tying the flag on he said, 'Get rid of the German uniforms quick—some of these injured are dying. Our boys won't shoot when they see our flag.' Well, they shed the German uniforms, and put all the wounded in the half-track. Knowing the cars didn't stand a chance of getting through our lines, they left them behind. Then the half-track headed on in. For the first time in their lives the guys were glad the Germans made such good half-tracks.

Our boys did shoot a barrage before they recognized the American flag. As only small arms were used, that half-track turned every bullet and even a bazooka shell. The men that rode in the cars walked in late that day and the rest of the outfit got back to the company a couple days later as they had to fight their way back."

Later that afternoon, Alex was taken by ambulance to a small landing strip, placed on a DC3 and flown back to a recovery center, along with a full plane load of wounded men. London was being targeted by Hitler's flying rocket bombs and anything within fifty miles was in danger of those bombs. Next Alex was sent to another recovery center by train partway to Scotland. As soon as he could Alex wrote Becky and told her where he was. He started the letter with, "I am wounded but it is not so bad." Then he went on to tell her how much he loved her and was sure the war would be over soon and he wanted to marry her as soon as he got back from the war.

That weekend Becky Johnson and her aunt walked into the hospital. It was a wonderful visit but the hospital was very strict about visiting hours. Becky and her aunt spent the night in town and stayed as long as allowed the second day. Then they had to depart, but now Alex and Becky were talking about getting married. Within another week Alex was walking and healing up well. On his fifth day there, Alex was told he was going back to the English base of the American 4th Division to finish healing as his bed was much needed.

To Alex that was great news as that meant he would be much closer to his beloved Becky. The very next day he was on the train heading south again. He was surprised to find that the 4th was now sharing the base with Patton's Third Army. In fact the 4th Division now had just a little corner of what it had before D-day. In fact it was now a replacement training center and building after building of business offices. Alex called the whole thing a "paper work factory."

Every day Alex asked the doctors when he would be released as he had a better place to finish his recovery. The doctors told him that his wounds were healing nicely and soon he would be allowed to take short leaves from the camp if he would take care of himself. Inside the replacement assignment center was a smaller section for returning recovered soldiers. This was where Alex was informed that his battlefield commission to second lieutenant would be presented to him along with the two prestigious medals. They said they did not have the exact date but it would only be a few days.

5

THE BRONZE STAR

The doctors were right and in a week Alexander Vetov stood before an honor parade along with others and received the Bronze Star along with the Purple Heart. This was also the time when Alexander Vetov was given the official battlefield promotion to second lieutenant. He had received his field promotion after it was determined that Lieutenant Kelley was not going to be able to return to duty for some time. In the audience was a beautiful and proud Becky Johnson.

Given another two weeks leave for full recovery, Alex spent time with Becky as much as he could. Alex told her the camp gossip claimed the war would be over by Christmas and he said they could get married. The next thing Alex said was a big mistake. "After the war is over and we get married we'll head for New York, you will love it."

Becky froze, looking like someone had just thrown a bucket of ice water in her face. "New York, I thought…" and that was all that came out, as Becky just stared at Alex. They talked a lot the next three days, about their hopes, plans and expectations. Alex apologized profusely for just blurting it out and assured her they would make up their minds together. After all, it was all about how much he loved her and wanted to make her happy. Becky said that she'd somehow never even thought about leaving her beloved home. Yes, she loved Alex with all her heart, but this was just so hard. Alex was now careful about what he said to Becky, but in his mind the way of life before WWII dictated that when women got married they went with their husbands, and not the other way around. Both Alex and Becky told each other they were going to work it all out. Winning the war came first, as there was no choice there.

Then the doctors said that Alexander was fit for duty and the same day he was ordered to report for the return to France. Alex once again walked ashore in France and rejoined his 4th Division, – this time coming ashore as a second lieutenant. He was assigned a new company, as is the army way, and it was about seventy/thirty in its make-up. That is, seventy percent were vets and thirty percent replacements. These replacements were from other platoons that had been broken up as men and officers were killed or wounded. Some were in fresh from America and had never faced combat. Then there were others who had caused trouble in other units and were undesirables. After the final capture of Cherbourg, the 4th had to do some re-organizing, replacing, and were re-supplied with equipment. They were even given three days to eat, sleep, bathe and wash their clothes.

Vetov's new platoon's name was quickly reduced to, V's Platoon, or VP. The army called it Fox Company Platoon 4. In actuality, Alex had more men than he was supposed to have. He had four squads of twelve men each, not including the four sergeants. Then the platoon had a machine gun squad with two thirty calibers, –three-man teams in each There were two bazookas with two-man teams for each and last a four-man medic team.

Alex himself had a staff sergeant, a driver and a radio man. He was assigned a brand new Ford-made jeep. The wonderful thing was a small supply trailer came with the jeep. In the back of the jeep was the very latest in radio communication. There was also a rack over the hood of the jeep to transport wounded. The radio was big and bulky but it was much more powerful than the old equipment had been. Alex began getting to know his men. Every man in the outfit hoped that he was going to put some of his personal load in that trailer. It would have taken two deuce and a half trucks to have carried all their stuff plus the necessary command supplies.

Somewhere down the line some machine gun crew had learned to make another rack that would fit over the stretcher rack. This held the two thirties, their tri-pod bases and six cans of belt fed 30-06 ammunition. Since it could be quickly removed, Alex had allowed the machine gunners to use this rack until they reached a combat area. The machine gun crews were informed that the first time it slowed them down in combat that rack was going to be left behind. One thing Alex did allow was for the entire floor of the little trailer to be filled with cans full of belts of 30's ammunition. There were two full cases of grenades and two cases of bazooka rounds. The machine guns used the same ammo as the M1 did and Alex had already seen his men scramble for ammunition in a firefight. His men were going to have lots of ammo anywhere they went. Alex also recommended for his men to pick up a few of their fired and empty M1 clips when it was practical since they could be reloaded with eight cartridges from the machine gun belts if needed as he had seen men do when they ran short on ammunition.

He warned his men that they would sure feel naked without ammunition for their rifles and loaded clips were not always available. The army supply trucks always had plenty of cases of loaded M1 clips. All too often the trucks were not where the men needed them. How many actually carried empty clips Alex never knew. One thing was for sure, if any man ever ran out of rifle ammunition one time, he made sure it never happened again. Alex saw a lot of his men carrying extra cloth bandoliers full of ammunition. Having a lieutenant that had come up through the ranks and even winning the Bronze Star in combat sure made his new men feel a lot better about their commanding officer.

For now Alex looked over the division map to locate where his new platoon was, and where he could pick up his new weapons and supplies. As always when a new or returning officer entered the front he was issued a new .45 and a carbine. Alex frowned on carbines but took it without complaint. Hitching his new pistol belts, he pulled out a new Remington Rand 1911 and rounds. He wished he had his tried and true Colt back, but it was gone forever. They were really the same and he felt silly for his feelings, but that Colt had gotten him through some sticky situations and he missed it. Looking at his new carbine, he noted it had a full stock, not like the folding stock on the paratrooper model he'd used before. That was fine; he liked the full stock better. Turning it on its side he looked at the safe/fire switch and he didn't like that. The paratrooper model had a full auto switch on it, but life was life, and Alex knew he would be able to soon find another tried and true M1. Before facing his new command, Alex needed to find his new staff sergeant. When he did lo and behold there were not four stripes on his sleeve, but the six stripes of a master sergeant. By his very looks Alex knew this was an old line, well-experienced sergeant from the old army. This sergeant looked like he could have been carved from solid ironwood and could not have been more stiff as he snapped to attention with Alex's approach.

The sergeant smartly saluted and Alex returned the salute. "At ease, sergeant," Alex said, and the man relaxed just a little. Alex saw the sergeant's eyes drop to his service ribbons, medals and bronze star before the eyes instantly returned and held steady. Action and reaction: Alex looked at the sergeant's chest full of four rows of service ribbons. As Alex looked up, the master sergeant had a perplexed look on his face. He was still stiff and Alex asked, "Is there a problem, master sergeant?"

"Sir, no sir," barked out like a machine gun.

"Relax, sergeant, something is not right. Tell me."

After a brief pause, the man said: "Sir, permission to speak freely, sir."

Alex said, "Speak up, master sergeant."

"Sir, I thought I was going to get a shave tail lieutenant right out of O.C.S. a green platoon full of newbies, leftovers, and discards, and I am glad as hell that I have an experienced officer, sir."

Alex responded, "And I am glad to have an experienced master sergeant as my right hand man. Now sergeant, let's go have a look at our new platoon.

Sergeant Harman said, "I just got here. Let me get the men ready first, sir."

Alex responded, "I think I will see the men now, master sergeant."

Even with Master Sergeant Harman at his side, Alex still felt out of place approaching his new command. The platoon was scattered and in various stages of dress in the July heat. When a solid deep voice roared out, "Front and center," It was amazing how fast over fifty men formed ranks. Even before they all reached their places, that same voice said A-t-t-e-n-shon."

Men snapped to as the last ones filled in the ranks and stiffened to attention. That voice started again, "This is your new commanding officer, Second Lieutenant Alexander Vetov. On his chest he wears a Bronze Star. That is the second highest medal for bravery our government offers her greatest heroes. He also wears a Purple Heart. Scars on his neck and face prove he did not get a paper cut at O.C.S. I am Master Sergeant Harman, I am not your babysitter, I am your ass kicker. Your C.O. and I will be back here in one hour and every man will look like a United States soldier of the Fourth Infantry Division. This camp will be in perfect dress condition or every man here will think he has just arrived in Hell." Turning to Alex he said, "Sorry sir, I could not introduce you properly to that bunch until they are presentable as members of the Fourth."

The sergeant continued, "I only arrived on base minutes before you did, sir, or you would have never seen this mess.".

Alex said, "That is OK, sergeant. Let's go and find our quarters and come back here in one hour for the rest of the introductions."

Alex found his command tent, and beside it sat his jeep with a

Private D. Walls sound asleep behind the wheel. Walking inside his tent, he was pleasantly surprised to see it in perfect order. His cot was made up to basic training order with his foot locker at the foot of the cot. His duffle bag was laid over the footlocker, and even his folding desk was set up, clean and neat. Not too far away he could hear Sergeant Harman's voice and he thought of some G.I. being chewed up and spit out. Laying his map case on his new desk he sat down in his new folding chair.

Outside a light rain began to fall as Alex slipped out some papers and an area map. He looked at the map and then started studying the listing of his new platoon personnel. He was still doing this when he heard Sergeant Harmon, "Permission to enter, sir."

"Come in, Master Sergeant Harmon," Alex called as he stood up and reached for his pistol belt. There stood Sergeant Harman dripping and at full attention. The sergeant paid no attention to the wetness whatsoever.

"At ease, master sargeant, and your first order is-in a combat zone, as we will be in a day or so. You will not salute me or come to attention in my presence. And, second, wherever we are, unless you are bringing someone else in with you, you will simply say 'incoming' and come on in. Well, maybe when in a base camp you can add the sir."

Taking his cue from the master sergeant, Alex walked out into the light rain without his GI rain poncho. Side by side they walked to the small staging area and there stood the entire platoon. They were in dress ranks and most were wearing their rain gear, though about a dozen were not. They now looked and acted like an experienced army platoon. Alex made a short speech and the sergeant dismissed them. The two men walked back to the command tent and Alex was surprised at how wet he had become it such a short while. His sergeant, however, looked like he had fallen into a lake, as he had been out forcing men into proper attire and getting in proper order during the entire rainstorm. "Permission to leave and get into a dry uniform!"

"Permission granted, but sergeant, remember, when it is just the two of us drop the sir."

"Yes Si--." He turned and as he left Alex was already discarding his wet uniform as well. Once in a dry uniform, Alex pulled back the tent door flap and saw the rain had stopped.

He walked back to his folding desk, put his papers back into his map case and went to his jeep. He saw that the side curtains had been replaced to keep the jeep dry inside. Alex spotted his driver through the clear plastic in the door and he was sitting in the driver's seat wearing a rain poncho and helmet. The helmet was pulled as far down in the front as possible and his driver was asleep again. It was only about a hundred yards to H.Q. but why get his boots muddy? Opening his passenger door, he he said, "Private, H.Q."

In one second there came a Yes Sir and the jeep roared to life.

Mud flew as the jeep leaped onto the road and up to H.Q. Major Harris was there talking to a new captain Alex had never met before. Seeing Alex, Major Harris smiled and turned to greet him. "Good to see you back, son," He shook Alex's hand, then turned back to the captain. "Lieutenant Vetov, this your new captain; Captain Rhodes this is one of your new lieutenants--Second Lieutenant Alexander Vetov. Lieutenant Vetov landed on Utah Beach with us on 6th June and has a fine record. He was wounded a few weeks back and was sent to England to recover."

All three men returned to a large wall map and started going over plans for their part of the whole division's next move--showing battalion's place and last to Fox Company's position. Then they started laying out plans for the order of march.

While his Platoon was eating their breakfast, speakers all over the camp came to life. "Attention, Attention," and then the division general came on and said, "Men, the German 7th army has just broken our lines and are headed our way. At 1100 our division will start east to stop this German counter attack and recapture Cherbourg.

Then another voice said, "All battalion commanders report to H.Q." Alex started going through the things he would need for the battlefield. Master Sergeant Harman rushed in, stiffened into a salute and said, "The men are in preparation, sir." He turned to leave and ran into Private Walls.

Walls said, "Sergeant, I cannot get the trailer hooked up to the lieutenant's jeep; it's just too damn heavy."

Both men disappeared as Alex continued to prepare. Then he headed for Captain Rhodes C.P. [command post] with his map case. He was the third outside staff man there but the C.P. was soon filled. Captain Rhodes was giving orders right and left and, gradually men were departing to get their platoons ready to move out. Alex was ready to move out with his men. Then Private Walls came to the door of the tent saluted and said, "The jeep's out front, lieutenant. May I help put your things in the jeep, sir?"

"Come in, private, all the things in the middle go," Alex said as he continued to get things ready. His experience had taught him what he needed and what was not necessary. In the jeep on the way to the staging grounds Alex said, "Private Walls, in combat areas do not ever salute me or come to attention in front of me. In fact, do not even call me sir when we are in open areas. These German snipers are good and I do not want to get shot, understood?"

"Yes sir. Done, sir."

The platoon was still gathering when Alex arrived and a deuce and a half truck was headed toward the staging area while men were throwing their duffle bags onboard. It pulled up directly behind the jeep and trailer and a huge man disembarked. He was well over six foot tall and looked more like a guerrilla than a man. He was a two striper. He walked up and saluted asking, "Sir, is there anything you want on the 6x6? Alex shook his head no, then turned to face his new platoon who were all standing at attention. He said, "At ease." Then as there were now many men that were not at his first meeting with the platoon he said, "I am Lieutenant Alexander

Vetov. I came ashore in the first wave second row on June 6th. I am not new at this job. Every man in this platoon will obey orders at all times.

He stopped, took off his helmet and rubbed some mud over the lieutenant bar painted on the back and held it high for all to see. German snipers are good and they always shoot officers first, I have one Purple Heart; I do not want a second one or a White Cross. When you show deference to officers, commissioned or not, while in combat situations, you place a target on them. Do not do so. In a short time this company will be in combat which will demand that each man have both freedom of movement and the necessity of carrying all that he will need to sustain himself for days at a time. Therefore carefully go over all that you are carrying in. At the same time, a full canteen is a necessity not an accessory. The issued medical pack is already stripped to a minimum; keep it as issued. When used up, replenish it as soon as practical. A full ammunition belt is also a requirement..."

As the 4th started out some lieutenants climbed into their jeeps or supply trucks, Alex did not. He led his men out of camp on foot just like he did as a sergeant. In fact, Vetov's jeep was slow getting started, as his machine gun squad was busy tying their machine guns onto the hood. On the fifth of July the lead elements of the 4th Division ran into the seventh German army.

By the 6th there was a thirty-mile-wide battle going on. The 7th German army was no soft touch, they were a hardened, tough bunch that had already been fighting for years. Some things had changed since Alex had led men in D Company ashore. In weapons Thompsons were being replaced by M3 grease guns and many more carbines and M3s were flooding into companies. Many things were now lighter and or easier to use. It seemed any soldier that worked mortar, machine gun crew and many others were now being issued the new, much lighter and smaller carbines or M3s. Most of the men that had Thompsons and fought on the front line refused to trade their Thompsons for M3s. The light weight was nice but the performace of the Thompson was much better. Their rations had been changed up some and all medical packs contained an extra morphine and dressings.

Now there were many extra M1s, as all the new troops were equipped with new weapons. All returned weapons from wounded men were placed in a storage tent for later pick up. Lieutenant Vetov took one that looked good and when he had a chance, he was going to shoot it to make sure it was all he wanted. While there he picked up a handful of 1911 .45 magazines as well. Last, he found a folding stock carbine with a select fire switch. He called Walls in and handed him the carbine and the .45 magazines to put into the jeep. Next he went to a rack where he picked up a Thompson that was holding a fifty round drum magazine. These drum magazine were very rare indeed and Alex could not resist—he took it also. Most of Alex's new confiscated items were kept in his jeep wrapped in a tarp. As he was now directing over sixty men, he seldom got to shoot at the enemy himself. The little full stock carbine was much lighter and smaller than his M1, so most of the time he carried the carbine and left the M1 in the jeep. Every time he heard close range rifle fire he swapped the carbine for his M1. At 1500 21th July Alex was called back to the C.P. where he met Captain Rhodes and Major Harris.

Major Harris said, "Lieutenant Vetov, you have had pretty good luck at scouting and turning flanks. We're locked down tight here and are getting nowhere. The German 7th army and other German units have a line from the coast to here across most of the Cotentin Peninsula in the St-Lo area.

"Over here in section G12 on our map we have only a few troops but the Germans have not made a push in that area. Battalion wants you to pull your platoon out and go over to G12 and find out what's going on over there. If the Germans are planning to come through, we must know about it. We want you to send your men in and scout the area and find out what the Germans are up to. There is a chance that they also have thin lines and that is why they haven't tried a push in that area. The Germans have a strong defensive line through St. Lo. And for the moment have gone over to defense rather than continuing to try to take Cherbourg back. We know that the German 34th is strong in G11 and it extends into G12. The German 9th is in G13 and extended into G12 from the other side. Your job is to find where the two meet and hopefully find a weak spot where they meet. From there, try to work your way around the enemy's flank, if you can find it. Thus far everywhere we've tried we have hit a brick wall. It's rough country that only infantry can get through so maybe the Germans will not have it too strongly defended for a good platoon to break through. If you can get a spearhead in, we will send as many men as you need for a breakthrough. We're sending your boys by truck down this small twisting road." He pointed to the map. "We're including two 105s for back-up if you need them. Draw enough supplies for a week."

They studied the maps and army intelligence reports until Major Harris had to leave. After Major Harris left, Captain Rhodes did not seem to show a great deal of interest, but told Vetov that he was sending the first platoon to back up the fourth, Alex's Platoon. That was nearly half of the company that Vetov was either leading or was backing him up. The first road into G12 was best called a farm trail twisting among the trees. Alex stopped his trucks and said, "This is it so let us try it and see what we run into."

They started in, following the little trail and when they'd traveled about a mile the trail ended in a fairly large field compared to the size of French farms as a whole. Alex knew that if there where Germans here that walking through that open field would mean dead soldiers so he pulled back into the woods. Alex led his platoon around through the woods that skirted the field, and started through the forest on the side. About a hundred yards in, an MG 42 opened up and it sounded like it was on or near the other end of the field. No bullets were coming toward him so Alex pushed forward until he could see the German machine gun nest. He was wondering what would be the best way to take it when a burst of fire came from not far in front of him. There was another very well hidden MG 42 firing into the open field. Looking back, Alex could see that both MG 42s were firing into the First Platoon that had walked out into the open field. They'd hit the ground for protection and were an open target. The machine gun crew that was so close was not paying attention to anything but those unprotected U.S. Troops. That German MG42 was so close it was easy for Alex's riflemen to cut them all down quickly. But some German troops were crossing the field to finish off the Americans who were pinned down.

Alex pushed a dead German off the MG 42 and he lay down like the German had been. The 42 was designed to be fired from ground level. Alex sprayed the advancing Germans with the rapid firing MG 42. All Alex's men joined in firing at the advancing Germans that were now the ones out in the open. It took the German army a little while to realize that their own gun was cutting into their ranks. They ran back to the woods for cover but many of their number never made it.. If Alex had not run out of MG 42 ammunition he could have done much more damage to the fleeing Germans. There was more German ammunition but no one close by knew how to open and reload the German machine gun.

The men of Alex's platoon, however, were very busy with their rifles and many Germans fell. Of course, by now the operators of the other MG 42 had discovered what happened and trained their fire on the Fourth Platoon. To get a good shot many of Alex's men had moved partly out of the protecting trees and now the other MG 42 opened up on them. Three were wounded but none badly and none were killed as they rushed back under cover themselves.

Alex knew that his men were too few in number to rush that other German machine gun without the loss of many of his men so he called for a bazooka team to come forward on the double. Before the bazooka could get there the other machine gun nest blew up.

Someone had gotten close enough to toss in a hand grenade. It was now a yard by yard advancement, with rifleman against rifleman. By the time they reached the corner and around into where the other MG 42 had been, Alex had one dead and several wounded.

It was much worse for First Platoon as they had been in the open field. Alex went and talked to the lieutenant of First Platoon and told him to take care of his men—that the fourth was going to scout around to see if this was their only line of defense. Staying in the trees, Alex's Fourth Platoon worked its way forward slowly and carefully. The firefight that had just taken place would have made every German within many miles very aware that the Americans were close. They had not gone a mile when Alex spotted movement with his Ziess binoculars. This time it was a full-fledged hedgerow and Alex could clearly see it would take an army with armor or artillery to get through so this was not the end of the German 7th.

Alex knew his platoon and the First Platoon could never break that line of Germans so he backtracked all the way to the trucks and returned to the road they had turned off of to take the farm trail. They went another three miles and tried going in again, this time with not even a path to fallow. Walking into the forest again, he noted the shadows already getting long. Then they spotted some German troops moving in the woods. These troops were coming straight toward them so Alex motioned for his men to hide and at about thirty yards the Americans opened fire. The Germans did a fighting retreat, but they did end up in a strong defensive position and dug in. In the fading light Alex searched for a weak place that he might break through but found none. Twice during the night Alex sent a squad of men forward to look for a place that could be broken. None was found. The Germans tried the same thing three times that night. So off and on all night there were small firefights going on. Sometime after midnight, Alex could hear German trucks behind the German lines and he figured that reinforcements were arriving for the Germans. At 0100 Alex ordered a withdrawal and they returned to their trucks a second time. This time he told his men to get some rest if they could. After posting a strong guard, Alex returned partway to their old position with an artillery man and four others. The first rays of sunlight revealed German infantry coming in strength. Calling back to his two 105,s Alex started sending shells into the German positions. As Alex could see the Germans very well, he ordered each barrage to move to exactly where the most Germans were.

The Germans pulled back and Alex had two of his men stand watch while the rest ate and grabbed a little sleep. When it became light enough, the First Platoon started back to rejoin the fourth. At 0700 in the morning, here the Germans came again. The shelling started and the Germans seemed more determined this time.

Alex ordered the artillery to bring their fire just as close to his own men as they could. When the First Platoon rejoined the fourth, they brought all four 30 caliber guns with them and now had four mortar squads. At maximum range, all four mortars opened fire, along with the 105s, and four 30 caliber machine guns. About sixty M1s and other small arms, turned the German charge back in full retreat. Alex thought the Germans may now try to outflank the Americans. He hurried to the other lieutenant and they talked things over, noting that now the Germans had hit such a strong center they would not try again but might hit both flanks at the same time. Since the First Platoon had already lost so many men, Alex would move all his men to the right, leaving one of his two 30s where it could cover the left end of First Platoon and could swing around while staying in the same position for covering fire into their former field of fire. One bazooka team would remain with them for the same reason.

Alex knew he was really sticking his neck out, but he knew the Germans had more men than he did. He'd studied how the Germans operate and he really believed that the Germans would try to outflank him. Which end, or both, he had no idea but tried to prepare for both by splitting his force to cover both. Leaving one machine gun crew and one mortar team just like he did with the First Platoon now Alex left fifteen men to cover the 75 yards that had been covered by fifty men. For two hours nothing happened, then German artillery opened up on their old position. Watching it all, Alex well knew what it is like being under a heavy artillery bombardment, but the choice had been made and there was no going back. Then the German artillery started spreading out to both sides and going back behind the former American line. Alex was very pleased about this eventuation. This proved the Germans were convinced that there was a larger force of Americans than there was. Or that they imagined the Americans were moving back to get away. Either way, right now the Germans were wasting their artillery on empty ground. The artillery stopped and Alex could hear a firefight start on the other end and he feared that all the German force had struck the other end. This did not last long, as his own men opened fire. He heard rifle shot, machine gun, the softer pop of carbines, the rapid chatter of .45 caliber American sub-machine guns along with the roar of hand grenades going off. It told Alex he was right; they'd hit him on both sides at once. The charging Germans outnumbered the Americans at least three to one. As many Germans fell, there always seemed to be another to take his place.

Then it was over. There was still an occasional firing but the assault had been turned. Alex hurried to the old line to make sure that the Germans had not attacked it also. The only signs here were the damage done by German artillery. Alex rushed to his men. There were two dead and nine wounded but they had held every inch of their line. Dead and wounded Germans were everywhere and Alex's men were checking them out. As Alex was checking things out, Master Sergeant Harmon walked over, holding his 1911 pistol in his left hand, and Alex knew he was right handed. There was blood seeping from his right shoulder, and his right arm seemed to be just hanging and useless. His helmet was missing and there was blood coming from his head. He blurted, "We held them, sir," then collapsed.

It was amazing but twelve of the fifteen men that were ordered to stay in the center were still alive. Eight more were wounded from a minor few scratches to two that the medics feared may die. What had been a farmers' field two days ago now looked liked a volcano had erupted on one end of it. How anyone survived that bombardment, Alex was not sure. First Platoon had the same fight, just like the fourth. The two platoons, together with their support force of machine gun men, bazooka men, artillery and others had numbered well over a hundred men to start this assignment. They now had 23 dead, and 61 wounded. Thirty two were slight wounds and only twelve of these required more than just a patch-up and staying on the line. Alex gave a full report by radio back to battalion and asked for new orders.

When orders came it was to leave his command under the other platoon's control. He would return with the wounded convoy. The rest of his company was coming forward to keep the Germans from counterattacking through that area. His orders were for him to come directly to battalion HQ. When Alex got to HQ he was asked in detail about what he'd found. Then he was asked why he had not gone farther before trying to break through.

Alex said, "I didn't want to drive past a place that might be open so I was taking places that looked good as I came to them. Once engaged, I thought it best not to leave a place open for our troops to be flanked.

The 1st and 4th had stopped a strong advance with consistent artillery attack—then two determined assaults from the Germans had not penetrated his defense line at all. There was no way the enemy was going to believe this was a patrol with the limited men and equipment Alex had Therefore the Germans must think that it was a strongly defended part of that section.

Alex's company captain had to leave at that point as his last two platoons had been ordered up to join the other two. The lieutenant colonel who was the commander of the battalion took Alex over to the map table and they reviewed where the last fight was. Then he asked Alex why he thought the Germans had that particular area so heavily armed.

Alex said, "Sir, since you have asked my opinion, may I speak freely?"

The colonel stared at the second lieutenant for a long moment, then said, "Yes, what do you think, lieutenant?"

"Sir, I believe if I was a ranking German officer and my orders to recapture Cheroourg had been impossible to complete. And then I was faced with an army that was getting stronger every day while my army was not being reinforced, my thought would turn to saving my army. That would mean my evacuating before it was surrounded on this peninsula. I would run for the open country in the main body of France. There his army could maneuver as it needed to and he could choose the best locations from which to fight. Here on this peninsula, with his enemy on two sides and the ocean on the other side, there's no chance for him to win. His only chance is to get off this peninsula. To do this he would have to control all the main roads east into the main body of France. The north side of the Cotentin Peninsula is where the Allies have landed and we totally own it. So the southeast side is the only way to get out."

Pointing to the map, Alex added, "These roads back down the peninsula into the main body of France is the only way to move a whole Army out. That would be greatly hindered if the Americans could control these two coastal roads so they could fight the German Army on three sides instead of only two. My thought is that this group of Germans, whom we know have a lot of heavy German artillery, is going to use it to help escape. They may hide it in this heavy forested area here." pointing to the map, "by day and move it by night as they well know we control the skies during daylight hours.

"Or they could well use it to keep our men and equipment off the coastal roads, or to protect their troops if they decide to take the coast to cover their retreat. Regardless, that artillery could have a powerful effect either way the Germans go. A second thought is that this is the tail end of the 34th German and they want to keep it strong regardless, as well as to protect their artillery. Just maybe, the German 9th well knows our awareness of his position. So this is not as strong as the end of the 34th is. That connection point is what I was hunting for when we hit this point," again pointing to the map.

"Sir, I would like to go back down there, and if there is a soft spot, I and my men can find it. This will not stop the whole German force but it just might put a pretty big bump in the road for them."

The battalion colonel looked impressed. "What do you need?"

"Sir, I need what's left of my platoon and we will just scout it out and avoid taking on the entire German army again.

"Lieutenant, you got it and I am going to send First Company. They will stay on the road until they hear from you. I am also go-ing to send Major Sloane with First Company and you will report directly to him. He is well experienced in combat--he landed with me in North Africa, then Italy. While you are being taken back to your platoon, think about what you might need and tell Major Sloan."

When Lieutenant Vetov got back with his men and looked them over, he realized how beat up and tired they were. He even hated the fact that he was going to ask them to move out again, but he was not going to trust men he did not know. Looking at them as they got in line, he walked by each man and spoke to them individ-ually. Six men had wounds that Alex knew should have kept them off the line. He made them stay behind and heal up before another patrol. Going to his jeep, he took the Thompson that was wrapped in a tarp and inserted the fifty round drum. He dug deeper and took out a five set of Thompson thirty round stick magazines. The nor-mal issued Thompson magazine was only twenty rounds and came eight to a canvas pouch. As the thirty round was much longer and heavier, they came five to a pouch. Putting his prized M1 Garand in the jeep, he spoke to the rifle, like it was an old friend. "This trip is close range work, I will be back for you." Alex, and what was left of his platoon, got resupplied and back into their trucks.

Every man appeared tired as he climbed into the back of an army truck. Even counting himself there were only 29 in the back of the trucks as they started down the road. Alex smiled as he looked at what the men had brought with them. These men were veterans. There was an unopened case of hand grenades, a steel five gallon water can, and a medic pack that only certified medics were supposed to have and he guessed the other truck had the same They had enough ammunition to start a war, and that just might have been in the back of their minds. When they got near the area where the big fight had occurred they were stopped by some men from the Bravo Company. A master sergeant walked to the back of the truck and asked, "Lieutenant, we would like to ask permission to come with you."

This man knew not to salute officers in combat, but he was still respectful. Alex said, "This is just a patrol; too many men will make things worse, not better. Why do you want to come anyway?"

Without any hesitation the sergeant said, "Master Sergeant Harman was my best friend. We have our own trucks and we will stay on the road if that is what you want. We'll just back you up in any way you choose. Our captain has given us permission and we are all volunteers and experienced in combat."

"If you men will take orders, come on," Alex said and he told his driver to go. It was a bright night and they were driving without lights so often they hit bumps. In spite of the rough road it was not long until the Bravo company trucks caught up. The next path heading out through forest, Alex stopped both the trucks and men started spilling out. It turned out there were 32 men from Bravo Company and Alex wondered how that many got into two trucks.

Whether he wanted to or not, Vetov now had a full platoon; and Alex and the sergeant talked things over. The sergeant convinced him that some of his men ought to go in, along with Alex's men and some of Alex's guys needed to stay behind until they renewed their strength. Men needed to be at the top of their game when on patrol. Alex agreed and he selected twelve of his men and the master sergeant took twelve of his own. Here again Alex wanted the sergeant to stay behind and be in charge of all the other men. Plans were made and the patrol of 24 plus Alex and the master sergeant would go in with another 14 following them at a distance to back them up. The rest would remain with the trucks, but spread out over a hundred foot circle. Alex took his Thompson with the one 30-magazine round pouch on his belt.

One case of hand grenades was emptied by the 24 men who were going in first. The front patrol started down a path that had probably only been used by cows. Then following at a distance the second group went in. They had not traveled far when Alex smelled the strong odor of German cigarettes. A little farther they could see a small campfire. They stood still and watched the German soldiers appearing and disappearing. Alex motioned his men to go back as he knew this was not the place he was looking for. After withdrawing several hundred yards Alex changed his plans and started cross country through the forest parallel to the German lines. This going in and out seemed to be taking far too long. He left one of his men to tell the following group what he had decided and how to follow the patrol. The German line seemed to be solid and more than once everyone had to take cover as a German patrol passed them. After playing cat and mouse all night, Alex let his follow up group catch up and they turned back toward the trucks as it would soon be daylight. When they reached the road Alex called the trucks on the radio and had them come to him.

Alex had to pull his men back over two miles to a road that headed in the right direction. Once there, waiting for them were another ten Army trucks. With two more full platoons, now Alex had most of a full company. Plus there were two army half tracks pulling two 105 howitzers, and of course there was Walls with the platoon jeep and that powerful radio. Alex called in and reported that thus far it was all negative.

They were going to get some sleep and pull an afternoon patrol in full strength. It was already 12:32 when the trucks stopped again. When Alex found a small road heading west by northwest to his objective point he stopped the column. He appointed two fresh squads to start the penetrations, but he required both to stay at least thirty yards away from the small road itself. If there was going to be any German outpost it would be on or near that road. Each squad carried a hand-held short range walkie-talkie Alex also brought up a SCR radio in a 35 pound backpack with better range. The two squads that flanked the small road were to go in about a quarter mile and come back close enough to see up and down the road for any sign of Germans. The squad on the other side was to do the same to make sure the road was clear. Then they were to go back out and do it all over again until they made contact. After the first two squads started in, Alex had all the 105s set up to give reinforcement fire if needed Then if the first men in ran into trouble or might need help to cover a quick withdrawal, the 105s could do the job.

After all, no one knew precisely where the German line stopped. The half tracks were pointed into the woods with their machine guns ready. When they arrived, Alex gave orders for the first platoon to follow the fourth in on and around the road. After twenty minutes Alex took his other two platoons with him and started into the woods on both sides of the road but close to it. By 1610 Alex and his men came upon a MG 42 machine gun nest and all the German soldiers were dead from knife wounds. By 1730 they had found thirteen dead on both sides of the road. Then an MG 42 opened up somewhere in the distance and its sound was soon followed by the sound of a hand grenade exploding, maybe more than one. Regardless, the 42 was no longer in operation, but rifle fire was intense. Taking the telephone type handset of the SCR he said, "This is Lieutenant Vetov, everybody get up here. Call battalion, tell them 'Open Door' I repeat 'Open Door.'

"Open Door" was not quite right, as one half of Fox Company had hit the tail end of the German 7th Army between their 9th and 34th regiments. Then it was a hell of a fight to hold on until the battalion showed up to take over. When the battalion did arrive, it flooded up that same little road and snaked around the end of the German 7th until the 7th saw this was now a losing position and made a hasty retreat. They did not go far until they dug in again. Fox Company had gone about two miles when they came under heavy artillery until after dark. The only thing they could do was dig in and wait it out. At 2130 it stopped like someone had thrown a switch and the wounded were taken to the rear. Alex had one dead and three wounded and as heavy as that artillery had been it was a miracle that he had not lost more. Making his rounds of all his men, Alex had them all dig in and made sure his sergeants set up their watches on three hour shifts so his men could get some sleep.

Each squad was assigned a point team of two men to go forward twenty yards and dig in to guard against German penetration during the night. Sure enough, at a little after 0300, rifle fire broke out but it only lasted for seconds. When daylight came, there was one dead German and at two more locations there were blood trails. At 0400 it started again and kept up, so Alex's point men slipped back into the defense line. There they held their ground during several fairly strong probes by the Germans. This lasted less than an hour and they only received five slightly wounded men with no other casualties. When the company was ordered forward early that morning it had gone less than 100 yards when machine guns and mortars opened up on them. Fox tried pushing forward at different spots all morning before Alex was sent for again.

Again Major Harris said, "Son, I need you to take two platoons to drop south and see if you can find a way through to get behind the German 7th."

The platoons were off again to learn if the Germans could be flanked. Try as they may, they found a solid wall of Germans at every point. Alex kept up with reports on his SCR until 1800 when he was told to hold his position until notified. His men dug in as they heard the sounds of firefights coming from a distance. As it grew dark Alex turned the volume down on his SCR radio so that any German that got close in the dark could not hear it, regardless of whether the operator was wearing headsets or not.

The men took turns getting rest and being on watch until 0400 when the radio came alive again and Alex was called for. He was told that the whole German 7th was withdrawing and the entire 4th Division was following the retreating Germans. Alex was told to take his men, pull back and regroup until he could be informed as to how best to move his men back into the main body of the 4th. When Alex got back with his men, it was well into the morning and he discussed the situation over with the other lieutenant and sergeants. They formed as good a defense perimeter as possible, knowing that if they were hit with a much larger force of retreating enemy troops they did not have much of a chance.

Food, water and supplies were spread out among the men, and all heavy weapons were placed for the best possible defense. Orders were orders so they now waited for new orders to arrive by radio. They were about a half mile from the road that led back to the 4th so they could move their trucks and half track quickly to it when they received orders. The 105's were hooked up to the trucks for fast withdrawal but the 105s crews were assigned to the truck that their 105 was hooked up to so the 105 could be quickly unhooked and put into operation when needed. The combination of preparation to fight at any moment and still be prepared to move just as quickly took a great deal of planning and work.

The first Germans down the road were a two-man motorcycle team that were scouting ahead. Alex watched them with his Ziess binoculars as they passed, knowing they were the scouts with more to follow. If a single shot was fired the whole 7th German army would descend upon them. If the Germans were in full retreat and using this road to do part of their retreating, then there was no way it would be possible to get back to the 4th from here. A better location had to be found. Alex went to his jeep and used his powerful radio to contact battalion. He explained his situation to a major and asked for permission to find a better place to hide his men in the hope of getting it by past the road or at least far enough away from it to fight without facing vast numbers of German troops in one battle.

The major said he would talk to the colonel and get back as soon as he could. The afternoon dragged on as distant sounds of battle could be heard. Several American fighter planes flew down the road and returned and finally the motorcycle team returned and passed by. Alex put two and two together and decided that the aircraft had detected nothing or there would have been the sound of bombs or at least aircraft machine-gun fire, so for now things were clear. Finally the radio came alive and Alex was instructed to hold his position until he could be relieved by advancing American forces. If a better defensive position could be achieved, he must do his best to save his men.

6

GETTING OUT ALIVE

"Hold your position with a handful of men while a whole German army is coming to run right over you."

How can this be done? Well, first of all, finding a very good place to hide is the only answer, other than getting killed or captured. These last two are not good options so hunt for that hiding place and do it quickly. Thinking back to where he and his men had been, Alex remembered not one good place. So it was time to drive east by southeast along the road and hunt for a good spot. What would a good place require to hide his trucks and his men? Being set up on the only good road in the area with the entire German 7th army pulling a retreat. The alternative would be to stay in an unprotected place and get run over and killed. Alex knew a retreating army was going to take the path of least resistance so he wanted to locate a place that was not good traveling ground. In a couple of miles there was a small road that headed west; this was not the direction the Germans were going, so maybe it was safe. After several miles the road became nothing more than a trail and the ground grew rougher and rougher.

Tucking his trucks into a low forested cove Alex left them there, took his jeep and scouted ahead. Looking everything over, he located a high spot in the forest a mile or so off the road. The north side was very rough while the south side was a wooded but smooth side, leading away from the hill. Driving toward the hill Alex heard the sound of clanking German armor. He left the jeep and walked to the top of the hill overlooking another small road. Small or not, there was a German column moving down it. There was no longer a choice. Now portions of the German army stood on both sides of him. The hill was not high but was large enough to hide the trucks and men from the approaching enemy. Besides, Alex knew the Air Force was going to be chasing the Germans and he had to remember this. He went back to his jeep and hunted the best places to hide each truck.

He left orders for everyone to pack up and took his jeep to check out the small patch of forest. It was even better than he'd hoped for. There was open ground that the trucks could drive on which was too low to be seen a couple miles behind the hill. The ground was rough but Alex was sure the trucks could get through. Back he went to his men. "Let's get out of here; there are thousands of Germans headed this way." He led out and after turning off the trail he found the ground rougher than he thought. But those big Dodge Army trucks were tough and could go to lots of places other trucks could not begin to go. Every time one hit a rut too deep to get itself out, the men piled out and a half-track or another truck hooked on and pulled it on through. By the time the next bunch of German tanks started arriving on the road below the hill all the American trucks, artillery and men were in low places and could not be seen from the road. Naturally, Alex and his SR radio went to the top of the hill to report on what he'd seen and would be seeing.

Fearful of the retreating German army running over his platoon like a tidal wave, Alex also set up his men in defensive positions. He sent back to have his 30-caliber machine guns brought up along with his mortar men with every mortar shell they still had left. They set up a U-faced defense just spread out enough so one mortar or artillery shell would not take out several men with one shell. Alex requested the First Platoon to stay with the trucks and wounded men to protect them. They hoped with all their might that any pilots could see the big white stars on their trucks if they saw them at all. They sat waiting and watching as they glimpsed German troops passing below them less than one mile away. There seemed to be endless bombing by the American Air Force. Most of these air strikes were many, many miles away and could only be heard as a very slight rumbling. Every once in a while a fighter would come closer. Again it was a long watchful night but nothing at all occurred to harm Alex's men that night. The nearly continuous sound of German troops moving on the road below was still intimidating.

The next morning Alex was watching the Germans below as a strange small German truck drove toward him on the road below. It was one like those that merchants use and are not seen in an army. Then Alex saw a metal disk on a short pole mounted on the roof of the truck, making a circle around as it slowly drove by. Alex had been broadcasting to inform H.Q. about what was coming down the road. He knew it was a German radio direction finder which could find the source of radio waves. He quickly said, "All radios off," turned his off and sent one of his men running down the back of the hill telling everyone to turn all radios off. The small truck stopped right in front of Alex and the little circle moved back and forth searching for a signal. As Alex turned his radio off the truck started up again, moving very slowly and the metal circle was making another rotation. The problem was: how long was it going to take the sergeant to run a mile and get all the radios below turned off? The little truck drove on for less than a mile and stopped again. The antenna was circling again and then it stopped. Within a minute a troop truck stopped behind it and German troops unloaded. They started straight for the hidden Americans. It would be easy for the Americans to take care of the one truckload of German troops but that meant they were found. Alex did not know what to do so he decided it was all or nothing.

He and four of his men went through the brush toward the

little truck. The Germans were now coming in small groups, hitting the ground as Allied aircraft occasionally came closer. Alex and his men made their way close and waited for a slow-down in passing Germans. When they could see nothing coming, they rushed the two trucks. The troop truck driver was just leaning against his truck when one of the Americans killed him with a knife and started dragging the body away. The metal antenna was moving back and forth searching when Alex yanked the back door of the small truck open and sprayed the inside of the truck with his Thompson. One of his other men jumped inside the radio finder truck, pulled the driver out, then started the truck and headed off down the road. Alex pulled the dead driver off the road as the German troop truck cranked and took off after the radio truck. The fourth man finished pulling the dead German off the road into the woods. While they were ambushing the German trucks, Alex could hear gunfire as his men took care of the searching troops. Alex had just gotten himself and the dead driver off the road and into the brush when the clack of a German Panther tank was heard coming. While this group of Germans were passing, a flight of American Thunderbolts came down and made a mess of that German column. Then it continued on down the road taking out more German troops.

After this, it was time to get back to the hilltop, grab all their stuff and go back to their hiding place as the road was blocked by burning German tanks and trucks. Alex knew that more Germans would be coming to clear the road and who knew whether some of them might come up into the woods where Alex had been hiding if more American planes came. It was very doubtful that there might be more direction finder trucks on the road, but if that first one had reported that he'd found an American observation post, there might be more coming. After all these reports were called in, more American air strikes took place. So Alex and all his men just hid while Germans cleared the road. Then when the enemy moved on, they went out and hid the German bodies they'd killed defending themselves.

In the middle of the night Alex took a chance and called H.Q. to find out where the German and American troops were so he could decide what to do. When he found out the American army was getting close he made his decision. At daybreak they all loaded up and started back up the trail to reach the main road which the Americans would be coming down. All the while, they hoped and prayed that the white stars on their trucks would be seen and recognized by Allied pilots. When they got close to the big main road they could still hear the distinct sound of German armor so they again found a good hiding place.

The sound of the American Sherman tank was vastly different from anything the German army had. As five Sherman tanks passed down below, right where the Germans had passed yesterday, Alex's platoon packed up and drove down into the tracks of the Shermans, turned and followed the tanks.

This was when Lieutenant Vetov did something he very seldom ever did. With the protection of the tanks in front and the battalion around him, Alex got into his jeep and went to sleep as they drove after the German army. That evening he radioed in a full report and sat down to write Becky again, as it had been over a week since he'd had time to do so.

When he reported into H.Q. again, he filled out all the written reports and took on the job of writing letters to the families of all the men whom he had lost or was missing. The list seemed to be getting longer every time he had to do this. Some lieutenants did not write these letters, but Alexander thought it was the least he could do for these men that had paid for this war with their lives. Next he tried to check up on all the men that had been wounded under his command in recent weeks. Then it was time to get his men resupplied and give the new recruits the information and advice that the local training had not covered. Alex thought that if he was back in the States training men, there was a lot that he was never taught in America or England that these guys needed to know.

For the next week it was one battle after another. The German 7th would only move back far enough to find another section of ground to give them the advantage. They dug in and held it as long as possible, then retreated to the next line. Different platoons were used as point to scout or lead. These charges were made to make the risk equal for all, and Fox Company lost far too many men. Replacements were coming in all the time to refill the ranks. It was common practice for platoons to be led into battle by their COs. This also led to the loss of many lieutenants and captains. Now so many of the new officers were fresh from the States and were ninety-day wonders who had no combat experience. As a lieutenant Alex felt it his duty to try to help all the new officers and men to learn how to stay alive. They desperately needed to understand how to be up front and still stay alive, as this was not taught back home in the States.

It was in one such charge that Alex took a bullet in his side that only glanced off a rib. It never entered his chest but did bust up the rib so he had to be operated on to remove bone splinters and set the bone. This time he was not sent back to England and was back on his feet in a few days. Being on his feet was still a far cry from being able to go back on the line. On the fifth day after being shot he returned to HQ and was given a desk. In another three days he was checking on his troops but forbidden to return to the front lines until released by the doctors. Even when he was released for combat his side was still giving him trouble. This, Alex would never admit to anyone, but it slowed him down and he spent more time in his jeep than he'd ever done in the past.

Moving HQ forward again, Lieutenant Vetov closed his eyes "to rest them" as the jeep moved forward very slowly and the column was paced by walking men. The jarring of the jeep woke Alex up and he saw Walls was off the road. At the same time there was the very loud sound of many Shermans. Alex twisted his head and could see a long line of Sherman tanks coming up the road. Alex and his jeep were no longer on the road. This was a large clearing extending up to the road. Well, in reality they were sitting beside the road as they had been forced to get out of the way. Alex looked at his driver and said "What the Hell?"

Private Walls looked back and said with a big smile, "It's Patton's Third Army, sir, and he's pushing his Armor through our front. He's not stopping for anyone, sir. I had to get off the road and picked this clearing to do so."

After somewhere between fifteen to twenty Shermans passed, Army troop trucks came with all kinds of supply trucks. The entire 4th Army had to move over to let Patton's 3rd Army get past. Patton had no time to waste and he had the equipment to do it as he had trucks enough to haul everything to move his army. Most of the 4th simply moved on boot leather and felt they were lucky if they had enough trucks to carry a portion of their supplies rather than make their own packs even heavier.

Alex and Walls had gotten out of their jeep and just stood watching as they were being passed by elements of the 3rd Army. Then there was the sound of a police siren and occasional blast of air horns getting closer. All the vehicles started moving to the roadside and here came a 3/4 ton Dodge command car flying up the road. Alex had seen lots of command cars but he had never seen one just like this one. The Dodge slowed down but not too much as it veered off the road and headed straight for Alex and his jeep. On the front of the Dodge was a plate with three bright white stars. Looking at this, Alex knew who was coming straight at him, He and Walls both snapped to attention and saluted. General Patton's command car was within four feet of them when his driver finally got the big command car stopped. General Patton returned the salute, not with his hand, but with a quick move of a cavalry riding crop in his hand moving up to his helmet and quickly back down. Who are you, lieutenant, and why are you up front?" said the general.

"Lieutenant Vetov, 4th Infantry, sir. I was sent to scout the area and then to spearhead the breakthrough. Very good, lieutenant, very good indeed. Keep up the good work."

With that the command car was thrown in reverse and backed up in a turning move. The siren came back on as the command car darted for the road again and soon disappeared toward the front of the tank column. That was how Lieutenant Alexander Vetov first met General Patton.

The rest of the day there was a line off and on as some of the 3rd Army passed on the road. At about 1400 a jeep with Major Harris made its way around the 3rd Army that all but had the road blocked. Again Alex and Walls saluted as Major Harris pulled up and parked just as General Patton had done several miles back. The major and lieutenant started a long conversation and after an hour or so several 4th Infantry trucks made their way around the now-stalled 3rd Army trucks. The place Walls had pulled over was the open field of a French farm. Major Harris got on his radio with division and after a while walked back to the jeeps. There he talked with three captains and several others. Finally returning to Alex he simply said, "Battalion is making this our H.Q. for now."

As a light rain started falling at sundown, Alex got into his jeep and spent the night there catching up on a little of his lost sleep.

By daylight the sun was shining and trucks were pulling onto the farm. By noon a field kitchen had been set up and command tents became operational. Even Alex's officers' tent had been set up and Alex had a chance to use the company showers before calling it a night. Next morning it was full army life as all first lieutenants and captains were called in for Major Harris to go over plans for future movements. As it turned out, these plans had to change regularly as Patton did not play by the rules. In fact, Patton only had one rule, "advance, advance, and let nothing slow me down." Pushing his tanks, men and equipment, he advanced more in four days than the Allies in central France had moved since D-Day. This was not true of the Americans that had fought up and down the peninsula. While Patton was covering vast amounts of ground he was also leaving vast numbers of German troops behind him.

It was army practice to protect American tanks from German heavy artillery and even much more so the hand-held Panzerfaust 100. It seemed Patton believed his tanks moved fast enough to keep the artillery from hitting them. The tanks were equipped with fifty caliber machine guns and could spray every place a German soldier could stand with a Panzerfaust. That kept the danger under control at least in part. Now, in some ways the tanks could go back to protecting the men more than the men protecting the tanks.

If the army took one mile of ground in a day, most of their officers were happy. If Patton's tanks moved twenty miles, Patton was furious it was not thirty. It was Patton's plan to rush around large bodies of German troops with all possible speed—then cut them off and destroy or force surrender with as much speed as possible. Unfortunately, in his haste to get on with the war and his impatience with slow moving army commanders, Patton would often get things started and then turn things over to boots on the ground to do most of the work. If he waited even an hour, some opportunity to bag another German army might get away. Like a teenaged boy driving a car, the faster the better seemed to be his plan and goal.

On the other side of the story, Patton's supplies could not keep up with him and his tanks. Often his tanks trundled off and left his fuel and ammunition far behind. A big part of this was the fact that passing large numbers of enemy troops made it easy for the enemy to fall in behind the American armor. The supply trucks were then not protected by armor, and many fell prey to German troops. The Panzerfaust designed to destroy heavy armored tanks could do tremendous damage to trucks and troops trying to keep up. While the Third Army was supposed to protect its own, it was so spread out over France, there was no way it could protect Patton's tanks, as they were moving too fast for others to keep up. This was especially difficult for the fuel trucks to keep up as German soldiers had instructions to use every effort to stop the fuel from reaching the Shermans. On one occasion, five tanks began to run out of fuel and they backed up into a five-pointed star formation with their cannon and machine guns pointed out to defend themselves while they called for help. If their call was picked up by the Germans or the Germans just found them, it really did not matter. It was not long until German infantry had surrounded them and the Americans were fighting for their lives. A Panzerfaust hit one Sherman and set it on fire and the other four tanks were counting down the last minutes of their lives. As they were running out of ammunition heavy machine gun and rifle fire suddenly started cutting into the German troops. Able Company from the 4th American Division had shown up and the four Shermans and their crews were saved. Later in the war when a ranking officer of the Third Army wanted to know why a Sherman had a small 4th Division insignia below the 3rd Division patch, he was told the story. The questioning officer climbed off the tank and said no more about it.

It was not unusual for trucks to pull up to Shermans and unload fuel and ammunition into almost empty tanks. The American Air Force had destroyed so much of the motorized German equipment that Germans were headed east on foot, bicycle, or any motorized French vehicle or farm tractor they could confiscate. It was not uncommon to see a French tractor pulling a farm trailer headed east and packed with men and their things. This became a problem for the Air Force as they were very hesitant to open fire. They knew there were fleeing German troops, but how many French, men , women, and children were also in that mass of people. As people always run away from a battle, they do not know or care if they're among enemy or not, if only they can get away. It was also a fact that many German soldiers hid among the refugees for protection. For the American 4th Division and all American servicemen, the job now was to separate the enemy from the French and it was no longer involving a few acres; it was now thousands of square miles. As always, the 4th inherited the job of taking care of all the problems that Patton's 3rd left behind.

Sometimes when they were marching, the 4th would chant Hi Ho, Hi Ho it's off to war we go – We are the 4th Infantry – and proud as hell to be – The Air Force has clean sheets – it's in the mud the 4th sleeps – The navy gets eggs and bacon – the 4th gets k-ration. Hi Ho, Hi Ho it's off to war we go – We are the 4th infantry – and proud as hell to be – Patton's third army gets the tanks - while the 4th gets no thanks – while the 3rd gets the trucks – It is the 4th that protects their butts. Hi Ho, Hi Ho it's off to war we go – We are the 4th infantry - and proud as hell to be – Hitler heard the 4th was coming - He pissed his pants – and started running – the Nazis said we are the best – the 4th said you ain't met us yet. Hi Ho, Hi Ho, it's off to war we go – We are the 4th infantry and proud as hell to be – Across France we march – to the Nazi's tails – we hold a torch – on to Paris here we come – The 4th will get this war done.

The 4th Infantry had a few other verses to their chant they should not be put into print. Some might not think they formed an appropriate commentary.

As Fox Company moved forward, they were back to the same old job, but one they were very good at. To seek, find, destroy or capture and do it all over again and again. Major Harris liked to do this in a systematic way, but every day the radio was listing "hot" spots here and there that Harris was ordered to go take care of.

One day it was an easy round-up of tired, hungry, discouraged German soldiers. The next was a hard-fought battle of diehard holdouts. A two day fight ended only when the Germans ran out of ammunition and were forced to surrender. Orders are orders so Harris' system was only used when his men were not already deployed elsewhere. The truth of the matter was that a perpetual list of these hot spots waited for any platoon that needed action. Every day wrote a new chapter in the book of war and any mission that Alex completed and brought back all his men safe and sound was a good mission regardless.

As the 4th got closer to Paris, Major Harris was promoted to lieutenant colonel and moved up to battalion. Captain Rhodes made major and as the ladder moved Second Lieutenant Vetov was made First Lieutenant Vetov. The two company captains had far less combat experience and one relied heavily on Alex while the other did the company paperwork. Captain Billings was a good man, but unfortunately as with many good men in war, his jeep was struck by a German 88. As the other captain was a paperwork man, this left the field work to Lieutenant Vetov. Although he was not the ranking officer in reality, Alex became second in command of Fox Company. As the acting second in command he stayed in the field while Major Rhodes seldom left H.Q.

In the field Alex stayed in close proximity to his four platoons and in reality all 238 of his men. In fact, this was only an average number, as dead and wounded men were subtracted from the company and replacements were added. By this time, Lieutenant Vetov knew his men like a mother knows her children. He knew his real killers, those that would take on the hardest jobs and treat them like another day at the office. Unfortunately, he had to keep replacing these men since their bravery all too often got them killed or wounded. These were also the best men to train new men, as they knew what it took to win at war. When new recruits arrived no one knew which ones would become great, good, fair, or failures in battle—least of all the men themselves. They thought they knew, but they did not. It was amazing how things changed in men minds when other men began trying to kill them. Sometimes there were men that really believed they were brave yet ended up hiding when bullets began flying. And again there were some quiet fellows that seemed out of place in an army uniform that would charge a machine gun with a hand grenade. There was no way but time and battle for an officer to find out which was which. While training is good, it takes real battles to bring out the best and worst in men. As bad as it sounds, in some ways it took the worst, most hateful things in a man for him to be a good front-line soldier.

On August 18th H.Q. got a call that Platoon Leader Walker had been killed and the platoon was under heavy fire. Typically Alex called for support and then got in his jeep and told Walls to head for the location. Once there Alex saw his men facing two MG 42s and a large number of riflemen. One of the 42s was in the corner of a hedgerow and the other in a small farm house across the road. This was no longer heavy hedgerow country but there were still a lot of them around. Going back to his jeep, Alex said to his radio-man, "Go wide," and he went on the air in the open warning all approaching troops to come in carefully and gave them details. As he finished a voice broke in and said, "This is P185 Third Armored. I have a Sherman about four miles away, might I be of help?"

If it had been an angel from heaven calling down it could not have sounded any better. "Yes, you can," Alex called back on the radio. "Do you need our location."

"Already got it from your first broadcast; just stay back and let this little pea shooter take care of those 42s," came the return voice.

Back on the radio, Alex commanded all units to hold, do not approach. In fifteen minutes the sound of the coming Sherman could be heard and Alex walked out into the road. As it approached, the hatch on the top of the Sherman flipped open and a sergeant popped his head through. The Sherman was loud so Alex shouted, "Phone" while pointing to the back of the Sherman. The Sherman slowed down but did not even stop and as it went by the sergeant disappeared and the hatch has closed. As the tank passed by, Alex stepped behind it, opened the metal box enclosing the phone hand-set that was connected to the sergeant. Alex explained the whole setup with details of where both 42s were and where all the rifle fire was coming from. The voice on the phone said, "Stick to the back of my little pea shooter like glue as none of those 8 mms are going to get through this armor. That does not keep one from com-ing from the side and spoiling your day. Alex snuggled up against the back of that Sherman and as it came around the slight curve in the road German bullets started bouncing off the armor plate. For a minute nothing happened other than those bouncing bullets. Then the sound of the thirty caliber machine gun mounted on the front of the Sherman began to rattle right back. Then the roar of the tank cannon and Alex thought he would never hear again. Putting both hands over his ears he stopped and just held them until a German bullet nicked his shoulder. This quickly reminded him how badly he needed that Sherman between him and the Germans. He knew better than to uncover his ears. How could he have been so stupid? The Sherman stopped and the phone was swinging back and forth against the back of the tank. Alex heard a strange sound far off over the huge roaring in his ears. He knew it was still the tank's thirty caliber firing. It sounded so different now, as though it was a mile away or at least a long way off. He let go of his right ear long enough to grab the swinging phone and hang it up but he could hear something coming from the phone. Alex put the phone to his ear and heard the sergeant's voice but could not make it out so he hung the phone up.

Bullets were still bouncing off the tank as Alex dropped to his knees and re-grabbed his right ear. The Sherman lurched forward and Alex jumped up and quickly snuggled up against it but did not let go of his ears. As the Sherman moved forward the turret turning to the right. Bullets were still hitting the tank armor but not with the rapidity of a 42. The Sherman fired its cannon again, then just stopped while still firing its thirty. Americans were now firing at both the house and the hedgerow. Alex was just leaning back against the Sherman when there was another explosion somewhere out in front of the Sherman. The tank just sat as men from the 4th rushed the house and the hedgerow. Without the two 42s the Germans no longer had the advantage. It was still a hard fight and the Germans had better cover than the Americans, except for that Sherman tank. Then again the Sherman hung back in order to avoid getting hit by a Panzerfaust and put another cannon shell into both the house and hedgerow.

The M1 rifle had a great advantage in firepower over the German bolt action rifle, as it was an eight shot semi-automatic. But as far as bolt actions go, the Mauser was the best bolt action rifle in its class. The Americans also had a very good select-fire Browning twenty round magazine that had been used in WWI. But it was not even in the same ball game as the MG 42 or the Panzerfaust.

After most of the firing had died down or moved off, Wall and three other men rushed up to Alex and asked if he was hit. By this time Alex had removed his hands from his ears and the roaring was not as bad. Wall's mouth was moving but nothing was coming out other than some strange minor sound from a mile away. By this time the sergeant from the Sherman was out talking to the men, but Alex had no idea what was being said. As it turned out, Alex's men were asking if he'd been hit by enemy bullets, as he acted just like it when the cannon fired. The sergeant knew just exactly what had happened and he was trying to apologize to Alex for not telling him to hang up and hold his ears. In as nice a way as he could, he did not understand how anyone could have just stood there while a cannon went off without protecting their ears. Walls led Alex back to his jeep and returned him to the medical tent. The 4th told the 3rd boys they and their Sherman were god-sent. Gathering up their three dead and eleven wounded they returned to camp. The Sherman took off fast, hoping to get back before it was missed.

The company doctor gave Alex aspirin and sent him to his tent. The doctor told his men there was no way of telling how bad it was. It would take a few days... Both ears were bleeding and that had to heal. The next day Alex could hear some but it was like everyone was talking while eating a mouthful of oatmeal. His head and eyes hurt and Alex couldn't understand why his eyes hurt. The second morning he woke up it was not nearly as bad and he could hear some, just not nearly as good as normal. The doctor said Alex needed a specialist and should see one when he could. That day the battalion broke camp and that was the day he was informed he would be awarded his third Purple Heart.

Alexander tried his best to see if he could get it stopped but it was already in the works. When Colonel Harris asked Alex why he was trying so hard to get the presentation stopped, Alex confessed. The bullet was only a scratch and who wants to be reminded of being so stupid as to not hold his ears while standing right behind a live cannon.

While the men were packing up there was a different attitude in camp. Alex turned to Corporal Walls for information as he always did when he wanted to know what the men were talking about. "Scuttlebutt has it we are going in to take Paris back," Walls said.

Well, they were headed in the right direction but in the army that did not mean a whole lot. Alex wanted to ask Major Rhodes if he suspected anything, but he knew better. He and Captain Eaton got along fine as Eaton handled all the company paperwork and Alex handled the men. Alex often wondered what Major Rhodes did, but he'd wondered the same thing when Rhodes had been his captain.

As Alex was still on restricted duty he walked in one day and handed Eaton a mortar shell tube with paper shoved into both ends. They had been friends in an informal way for some time as it was the two of them that really ran things in Fox Company. Alex said, "Take it to your tent tonight and open it there." It contained a fine bottle of French wine and Alex knew Eaton had a great fondness for fine wine. Besides, he really owed Eaton. A couple weeks earlier Captain Eaton had called Alex in and handed him a box. On the lid of the box it simply said "Lieutenant Vetov; Fox Company." No other information at all. It turned out to be from his old D Company and inside was his German Luger, the Ziess binoculars and several other things. These were things Alex had collected along the way. When Alex had found himself back in England and recovering, he'd wondered about his "stuff." Even though Alex had obtained another Luger and even another pair of Ziess binoculars, it was nice to get the old ones back. But he knew the army and he never expected to see any of it again. Now here it was and from that day forward the two men became even closer. There was never a time in history when two friends were more different. They were like the front and back of a dollar bill. Exact opposites but closely connected, as it took the two of them to really be any good for Fox Company.

Alex also knew better than to ask Eaton any questions about things concerning his paperwork that did not concern him. Eaton was a man of very strict principles. He was also a man with few if any friends except Alex. As he was a captain he was respected, his work was respected, but that did not allow him to have anyone close, except Alex. The next day they went to mess together as they often did and Eaton said, "We need to talk. Can you come to my tent tonight?"

Alex said sure and he was there as soon as he was sure Fox Company was taken care of. When Alex got to Eaton's tent, Eaton said, "Let's take a walk."

The conversation started about Fox Company in general. When they reached the firing range it was dusk and it was deserted. Eaton said, "We might not have to fight for Paris after all. It is super hush hush, but super secret talks have been going on between German big brass and our big boys. A lot of Germans do not want to see Paris turned into another Warsaw just like our Air Force has not been bombing Paris. If Hitler was to find out he would have every last one of them executed. Even a rumor about this would turn Paris into dust. Us paper-pushers stick together and I got this from division intelligence code." That was it, the conversation turned back to order of movement for the morrow as they walked back to their tents.

In three days they could hear the church bells in Paris, but there they just stopped. On August the 24th all ranking officers of the 4th Division were called together and informed that although the 4th was in front of everyone else, it was going to be the Free French army that would be the first into Paris and the 4th was going to be the first American Division in. Then the bombshell was dropped. "We are not going to invade Paris; the German Army is withdrawing as we speak. We will march in as liberators and we will look the part. Every man in the 4th is going to look like he was on parade in Washington D.C. Now go to your units and get every man, truck, and bootlace ready. As word spread, the 4th went crazy but did so in the biggest rush ever to look good. On the 25th the French marched into Paris with the tri-colors flying, followed by the 4th with the stars and stripes. After the last four years of Nazi domination only those Frenchmen could express how everyone felt and reacted.

Being the first Americans into Paris the French greeted the 4th with open arms to say the very least. There were hugs, kisses, wine, food and shall we say other things. Keeping the American soldiers in marching order was hard but that night it was impossible as American soldiers seemed to melt into the night. The next day was not much better, and in truth some men should have been court martialed but what could be done when whole squads of good men were AWOL. Officers knew these men had marched from Utah Beach, fought bravely across France, leaving behind many of their buddies buried in French soil. They deserved a night on the town in Paris and Paris had opened its doors to these men. Still discipline had to be maintained or that army would have never left Paris. However, it looked a lot more military when it marched into Paris than when it left.

7

BACK TO JUNE 1944

The White Russians were kept separated from the other prisoners–even other Russian prisoners. The high ranking American and British officers talked about what Dimitry had proposed. There was much discussion, but word was sent to combined intelligence in England. After a while it reached General Eisenhower and Winston Churchill and there was again much discussion. When Eisenhower and the general staff put their stamp of approval on this plan, Dimitry asked for two things. He wanted Alexander Vetov to be the main man between himself and the U. S. army and the British. He wanted no contact with the Communist party or any involvement with them. He was still a white Russian. The Reds had destroyed most of his family, along with white Russians and most anyone they even thought might be in disagreement with Communism. Destroying the Nazis was his number one goal and he'd gladly lay down his life to destroy this hell on earth. But he loved his Russia and would do nothing to hurt her, and he hated those that were holding her in the clutches of Communism.

Every man that Dimitry had with him, and they were not all Russian, stayed with him except six whose health was too precarious to take on this very dangerous mission. They were all trained and prepared in England for their service against the Nazis. They needed to learn other languages and many things, and on the funny side, it was amazing what these men were able to teach their trainers and other trainees. The current need was so great that it was not long before some of these men were slipped back into European countries and sparks of freedom began showing up in new locations. The biggest thing was that these men had developed a sense of understanding about how to read people. Even staying alive under Nazi officers had taught them much—when and where to do things and when to wait. In other words they were some of the best. Information began flowing into England from the first week. Plans for a new underground factory to develop and manufacture new German fighter planes became known and as Hitler now used slave labor for everything, this opened the door. Two Russian engineers were brought in with hundreds of other laborers that could remember the smallest details. Natalia was a worker on the kitchen crew and every day she looked for the best way of picking up information from other men and women. A well-cleaned food pail meant the work for the project was progressing on time. A dirty pail said it was having its problems. An uneaten bean or any scrap of food left behind when the workers were all hungry was a statement that outside help was needed to slow or damage the progress the Nazis were making. A very small Bangalore, a few grains of sand or dirt, showed where sabotage could be done without the Nazi leaders knowing whether it was sabotage or just bad luck. Scraps of trash could contain coded messages and always slowed things down without the leaders knowing why. A broken twig in one's food meant a wooden brace was going to break. A small piece of uncooked food meant that a drive rod would not be properly lubricated.

Then of course there had to be those bad accidents and major failures that sometimes brought executions. Some were actually willing to give their lives to stop the Nazis. When the resistance received a request from London to have a train derailed or a bridge blown up it was time to plan how to do this without too many innocent people having to give their lives in the Nazi retaliation. The

Nazi rarely believed bad things just happened. It really did not matter who was at fault, as long as someone suffered really bad. The Nazis loved their train system and believed it perfect so when the order came

for a certain train to be derailed much thought was put into it. It was decided that they would use an old switching tie rod that had been discarded as being too worn—to pose no danger. It could be placed in a vice and bent back and forth until it was very weak, then painted to look brand new.

With all the slave labor it was easy to slip it into the warehouse as brand new. As all rail traffic was so well organized and all train movements were recorded to the moment they traveled over any spot, timing was no problem at all. Loosening the tie rod nut just a little the day before made the nut move and shake with every train that passed over. With Nazi proficiency the rod was inspected right on schedule and the order went out to maintenance for an instant repair. The maintenance was very careful to get just the right rod and replaces the brand new rod with the bad one. Now a small stone from the road bed was placed between the moving rails so tremendous pressure would be needed to bring the turning rails into line. When the line switch was made, the new rod failed and the rail switch was half open and half closed. Before that day no one had ever thought a train could fly all by itself. The Gestapo and engineers pored over that disaster and there could be no doubt about it; the rod had failed. The wreck had crushed or sent the stone flying and it was no longer in evidence. Inspection had called for a new rod and one had been installed. The final report said that the fault lay in the poor grade of steel being turned out in a time that Allied air forces were continually bombing the steel plants. This had resulted in a defective part and it was not sabotage or the railroad's fault. In spite of the report, the maintenance director was fired, along with the sectional superintendent and less proficient employees were given their jobs. In Nazi Germany someone always had to pay.

How do you blow up a bridge without someone seeing a bomb fall from a plane? In Belgium when an act of sabotage was committed the whole town where it happened was made to pay big time. Sometimes the entire populations were all killed and the town burned. If it happened between two towns, both paid the price. Orders were orders so the bridge had to go. Studying the problem, Dimitry and his crew made an adjustment. It was thirty miles from Belgium into Germany and forty miles into Germany was a beautiful little bridge over the same road that would stop the same traffic. So guess what? One night a barge was under that bridge loaded with explosives. Even the Gestapo could not kill and burn down two German towns. Then as a side note, when military traffic tried to use the small sideroads to get into Belgium, American P-51s had a field day, knowing just where they would be and how slowly they would be moving. By now the German troops were rushing back to Germany as fast as they could reasonably do so and the Allies needed to know how, when and where. So now spies were needed by the thousands, kids on bicycles made great spies, as well as housewives that could count while washing the dinner dishes. However, now the Gestapo and the German army no longer even made an excuse. It used to be said shoot first and ask questions later; now it was just shoot now and shoot again later.

It's a shame that sometimes we human beings just think that smart people cannot be wrong. Much information that came through Paris was rejected by London as their analysis of what it is possible for the German army to do cannot be wrong. They said, "Our figures show us that Hitler now is down to only so many men here and so many tanks there. This war is nearly over, it is nearly Christmas and we need to get started on planning to send men home. Let's all go have a good Christmas. Farmers along rural roads were hearing hundreds of tanks and trucks moving at night. Paris got the word and sent it to London, London said hog wash. Germany no longer has any to send. But just to be sure, we will send a few planes over to check things out. Sure enough, with the bright sun shining there was not a truck on the roads. When Hitler started his push into Belgium in what became known the Battle of the Bulge, many American and British high-ranking officers were making plans for Christmas. When mid-ranking officers were rushed to the front and saw thousands of American troops fleeing, they said, "I cannot believe our men are running away from a few old men and young boys. Our intelligence says this cannot happen."

When a few saw German Tiger tanks they changed their minds but it took days for people to believe that intelligence was wrong. Many times Dimitry had asked for Alexander Vetov to work with him but was always put off. As weeks passed, more and more of Dimitry's men were killed or captured. In spite of the torturers of the Nazis not one ever turned Dimitry in.

To help control things, Dimitry's men were scattered among different groups in several occupied countries and Dimitry agreed that this was best for all. Most were sent to countries bordering Russia where they could use their Russian to help get information to help the Russian Army as it was now beginning to come back into the previously conquered countries. After all, Russia was one of the big three. Every time a man was moved to another place, all contact was lost for one another's protection. All that was ever said as each departed was a promise to get together in mother Russia after the war. Dimitry himself was so fluent in German and experienced in the German army, he blended into the fleeing German army. Many times, he pretended to be a disabled German soldier with papers supplied from captured or dead German soldiers. The normal precision of the German army could not be proficient with thousands of their troops fleeing back to Germany. And as disabled German soldiers were of no use to the German army, they were tolerated but otherwise useless. So Dimitry was able to gather mountains of information as to where, when and how things were going with the fleeing troops. With every move, he reported on fresh troop movements to the front along with very accurate counts of equipment. After all, no one paid any attention to a disabled German soldier as there were thousands everywhere. Even when he had outdated papers, Dimitry could talk his way out; being disabled he was no longer able to get his papers updated. In fact he often went into a German army station and asked for new papers to get back to Germany and the overworked clerks stamped approval or even issued new papers to a disabled German sergeant with several medals and honor notes in his papers or on his uniform. He ate, lived, and traveled with other disabled Germans.

Staying in one spot just long enough to gather information, he would move on to another so as to not attract attention to himself. Sometimes Dimitry would disappear for weeks at a time and no one knew if he was alive or dead. This made his handlers very unhappy, but Demetry played by his own rules. When he did show up, he brought in vast amounts of information. Information is the grease that keeps the wheel rolling and few other agents even came close to providing the information Dimitry did. While the gathering was his most important job, it was not the only one he took on. While remaining aloof from most all other spy cells, he continually supplied them with plans to sabotage or destroy German war efforts. He was responsible for starting many of these spy cells while remaining unknown to all but a very few leaders. The Gestapo knew that there were people out there delivering much information to the Allies. Out of the thousands that were, very few people even on the Allied side knew how much of it was coming from Dimitry. The amazing fact is that a large part of it consisted of little bits and pieces that Dimitry had put together like pieces of a gigantic jigsaw puzzle. He correctly informed the Allies about strengths that the German army had in tanks and where they were being built. The entire Allied intelligence laughed at his report of the sum of new Tiger tanks and said that the Germans could not have one tenth of what Dimitry said they had until the Battle of the Bulge was fought. Some American and British intelligence officers laughed out loud at the thought that Germany was manufacturing their new jet fighters in caves in different parts of the country and putting them together in separate locations. American experts said that was something even they could not do

If the Americans could not do it, it was a sure thing that the Germans could never do such a thing. It was just some rumor Dimitry had heard and reported it as fact.

Gathering information was just one part of what Alex himself was doing. He also was gathering information to make plans that would hurt the Nazis in their war production. In gathering information Alex had come across members of the French underground that were out to hurt the Germans by killing them when they could. They destroyed German installation's, derailing troop trains, and any other thing they could do to hinder the Nazis. Alex appreciated this. However he thought that they were going about it wrong. Every time they killed a German the Germans killed ten or more Frenchmen. Why not kill Germans without reprisals when they could? The resistance said they were doing what the Allies were asking them to do. Alex said he understood but if there was a way to get the job done in a way that did not cause the killing of mass numbers of French men, women, and children why not do it as well? The resistance listened but said they were not going to stop doing what the Allies wanted them to do as they were at war and war brought on death. Again Alex agreed but still said when there is a way to slow down the Germans from killing their countrymen would they try it? The resistance agreed to this so Alex said, "Let us make some plans of our own."

The Germans had taken over all the industry and most businesses in France. Alex looked first at a large French plant that was making ball bearings for the German army. All ball bearings are very important, as any type of machinery cannot function without them. So quality control is very important in their production. One bad ball bearing in a Me109 motor can cause the motor to freeze up in flight and bring that plane down. In the wheel of the same plane one bad bearing can cause the plane to crash on take off or landing. One hundred bad bearings could slow down a whole German Division when trucks and tanks had to stop for repairs. And as long as the Germans thought that it was just maintenance, no French would suffer. The French had to still make high quality bearings. If somehow just an occasional reject got into an already-approved shipment this would do more good than killing a hundred German soldiers. After all, it was the French that were making these bearings. Now the production was carefully watched and bearings were carefully checked for size and quality. There were always some that did not pass quality control and they were removed and dropped in a five gallon bucket. At the end of the day the rejects were weighed and if there were too many the workers were shorted on their food as punishment for their poor work. If only two to four bad bearings were sent out in a shipment that would mean that two to four pieces of German equipment would have to be stopped and worked on and who knows what damage that could do to the German army. When one bad bearing was found by a German mechanic in making a repair it is doubtful he would do anything about it unless it became repetitious. Still, bringing down a 109 fighter or even jamming the gears of an 88 cannon would help the war effort.

Finding a way to get a few bad bearings from the reject buckets into the shipping containers could be worked out. Besides, even a few less rejects in the reject bucket helped keep the food flowing to the workers. In the same plant there was a woman that worked in the kitchen. She would go out any night and risk her life to cut telephone wires. She often made plans now on how to communicate with fellow workers in the plant that were true Frenchmen on how to slow down the plant's production. Even the German inspectors would hurry things up when production numbers started to fall. It was a very bad thing even for the German overseers when a production quota was not reached. This meant cutting corners and making it easier to put bad bearings into shipments. She developed ways to get things done. A clean pan meant that things were on schedule for the Germans. A dirty pan meant that someone had slowed things down. A very small twig in someone's food told them to cause a problem with their piece of equipment. A raw bean or small raw piece of food in one's meal meant a meeting of the workers that were working together to fight the Germans. A extra large helping or a piece of meat in their food meant to be careful as they were being watched. This and many other such things created a communications system to which the Germans never caught on. How much these bad bearings did to the German war effort no one knows but the failure rate in all German equipment went up a great deal. These French were never caught by the Gestapo even when many that continued to kill soldiers were killed.

Dimitry helped start plans like this all over France and moved on into Belgium as a wounded German conscript. There the local resistance was ordered to blow up a bridge over a river close to the German border. Dimitry knew it was a standing order of the local German forces to round up and kill the inhabitants of villages where sabotage took place. When it was between two villages both villages were killed. This was just too high a price to pay for blowing up this bridge.

Alex simply moved the plan across the border into Germany even though it was a lot harder to do the job in Germany. There was another bridge on the same road that the German army was using and in truth it was not as heavily guarded as the Belgium side was. A heavily loaded barge was floated down the river loaded with stolen German explosives and that bridge went sky high. Even the Gestapo was not going to kill a German village. Killing entire villages was not uncommon in WWII and in a few cases it was not always the Germans that did it.

The Germans did their fair share. Howeverl in Poland it became common practice for any plant that produced for Germany and most all did. When that plant was found to be sabotaging production, many or even all the workers and their families were shot to show the locals they would not allow for anyone that stood against Germany to live.

One of the worst cases was a fish canning plant in Norway that canned sardines for the German Navy. Someone in the plant put something in the sardine prep huge cooking vat that poisoned the sardines. When the cans were traced back to the plant the entire town that the plant was located in was burned to the ground with all the people inside. Any one that tried to get out was shot. Then to prove their point, every fishing town within miles was raided and groups of inhabitants were rounded up and shot to show the people of Norway what the Germans would do to anyone that did not instantly obey any German's order.

The greatest planned sabotage was one that helped the Allies a lot and was never discovered by the Germans. One such plan was accomplished mostly by one man. This man was a Belgian engineer that was also a leader of a resistance group. He was the main man in helping Dimitry blow up that bridge in Germany. The Germans had turned the factory that the engineer worked for into a producer of fuel systems for German tanks. When the Germans had started production of the Tiger tanks, they needed to design a stronger fuel pump and system. The Tiger was so much bigger and heavier, it had required a larger motor to power it and it used gas at an unbelievable rate. The German design that was sent to the factory was good but was very complicated and slow to build The Belgian engineer studying the plans saw a couple of weaknesses that could lead to the collapse of the system when under stress. So he began to study how to make the weaknesses disable the tank when it was under combat stress. Considering hard use, the recoil of the monster cannon and other things worked in his favor. This had to be done in such a way that it would not be caught by the German designers. So he went to work on a design to do what he wanted it to do, while still being good enough to fool the original designers. When he finished he presented his design changes to the German designers saying two changes made his design stronger and much easier to manufacture and therefore faster and cheaper to manufacture. The Germans built and tested his design under laboratory conditions and declare it superior to their own. They presented this to the German army study board as their own, and never mentioned the Belgian engineer. The German army studied and approved it and immediately ordered the new type to be made and installed in all Tiger tanks. Under hard use the pump started leaking gas that spilled into the engine compartment. This stopped Tiger tanks in their tracks. These had to be repaired in the field and even made some to catch on fire. When tank commanders complained, the only names on the conversion were German engineers and designers so guess who got blamed? This problem was never solved by Germany until near the end of the war and by then it was too late to matter.

While Dimitry was doing his work of setting up plans to slow the German production, he never slowed up in gathering information. He had informed the Allies about the German build-up before the Battle for the Hurtgen Forest. Intelligence said the Germans no longer had the men and equipment to pull it off. Even though Dimitry was not the only one to report the huge German build up. When the Hurtgen Forest fight was over, Intelligence and the army said, "Well, Vetov and the others were right but now Germany has used up everything they have and will give up. Let us rest our troops and get ready to pack up and go home. We did not get to Berlin before Christmas but it is now over except the surrender, and our troops need the rest anyway."

Word came from Dimitry again that said the Germans still had a full army ready to come in again just like they did to start WWI and they did to start WWII. "This man has been in the war too long," they said. "Our army could walk into Germany with BB guns after their Christmas rest and take Germany's surrender like they did at the end of WWI.

Let us go back to when the Russians were first approaching

Germany. As the Russian armies came rushing back toward Germany and the German army fell apart in many places, Dimitry found a dead prisoner of war, took his clothing and made his way to the outskirts of a German POW camp and as the Red Army approached, stumbled into Russian lines, and declared he was Dimitry Zoliff, a Russian officer that had been captured by the German army. This was all true. The Russian army halfway believed his story and definitely believed the old prisoner number tattooed on his arm. He was given food and put in a stockade with hundreds of other prisoners from the German prison camp. There he learned all about the prison camp and how the Germans had recently brought in hundreds of new prisoners to lay mine fields to hold back the Russian army. Getting all the information on the mine field he could get, he went to the gate and told the guard that he was a captured Russian officer and he had knowledge of the mine field. He was taken to a Russian officer and Dimitry saluted him in the Russian manner and gave great detail of the mine field and how he'd been forced to help lay it. He also told the Russian officer how he had spent his nights breaking off small pieces of wire from the barracks to use to disable the mines as they were laid so his comrades would not die in that field. As he rose to leave, he again saluted and turned to go back into the camp. The Russian officer stopped him and said, "Comrade, I see no reason for a fellow Russian officer to stay with those other prisoners." Then he was taken to a place where he could get himself cleaned up and was given an old Russian officer's uniform and a place to sleep.

Four days later a Captain Dimitry Zoliff was determined by the Russian government to have been a real officer in the Russian army. Dimitry was questioned in great detail about his history and there was no problem at all, as it was all fact. The next week he was welcomed back into the Russian army, reinstated to his old rank and placed over a company of Russian troops to push into Germany and destroy it. He was back in a Russian uniform and he still had the opportunity to kill Germans. He went after them like a hungry dog.

Being a survivor of the hated Germans made him a hero in the eyes of his men. The way he led his men in combat and the fact that he was well educated caught the eyes of his superior officers and he was promoted to the rank of major.

From the day Demetry put on that prisoner's uniform and walked toward the Russian lines was the last day the Allies heard from him. He was just one of many hundreds that had worked behind the lines to defeat the Nazis. Stalin had been so afraid that the officers in the old Russian army might betray or at least not obey him without question he decimated the ranks of officers. When Germany invaded Russia, the number and quality of Russian officers were not able to properly lead the Russian army. Once the tide of war started turning and Russia was able to start pulling together millions for its new armies, there were not nearly enough officers to go around. The education of the bulk of these new soldiers was very low indeed. Even the ability to read and write was enough to make privates into sergeants. The newly made Major Zoliff stood out like a shining star as a well-educated man. He was good with his men, and well-liked by his fellow officers. At the planning tables his advice was solid and strong and everybody was sure this major was going places in the Russian army. Military rank in the Russian army is different from most other armies but Major Zoliff was soon the equivalent of an American colonel as his section of the Russian army pushed into Poland. To the Germans that faced Zoliff's Regiment, he was known as Zoliff the Terrible. This was because Dimitry planned all attacks with such perfection and his men carried them out with fear.

After what the Germans had done to the Russian people, German soldiers were afraid of the advancing Russian armies. Dimitry Zoliff was made a general and part of his army included over two hundred Russian T-34 tanks. Dimitry used these tanks to defeat the Germans in every battle he headed into and Russian newspapers and radio broadcasts proclaimed his mighty deeds. With every battle won he also became more of a politician in the ranks of the Russian army, but a very smart politician, very careful of showing anything but a worshipful attitude toward Stalin. He did not try to climb up in the Communist Party and even refused to join it, saying he was a military man and did not want to be a part in the government of the people. He said he did not know or understand politics but declares himself to be a man of the people. He said that a good military man knows his place and he lives for the defeat of Germany. He leaves the government in the hands of the party. Military men are those who obey the government and stay out of politics he declared. The more he talked this talk the faster he advanced upward in the military and henceforth the government itself.

Then he was called back to Moscow and met Stalin himself. There he said the same things but very carefully and let Stalin and other leaders draw his words and spoken feeling out of him. When asked political questions he skillfully turned the conversation back to military matters and the soon-to-be victory over the Germans. When asked about what his plans for after the war, he went into a well-rehearsed speech to the affect that he hoped Russia will maintain a strong army. If it did he hoped to remain at least a small part of it. This was where his mind and heart was. He went back to his army with the assurance that he would always not only have a place but have an important place in the Russian military.

8

CAPTAIN ALEXANDER VETOV

The liberation of Paris was celebrated in all the Allied countries as well as in the streets of Paris. How the French people had kept all that wine hidden from the Germans was not known, but now there seemed to be a million bottles in Paris streets. Getting the 4th out of Paris was hard enough, but getting the Paris wine out of the soldiers of the 4th was much harder. As the 4th turned to the north to cut off fleeing German troops the party was over and it was time to get back into the war. It was not a long wait but they were now being moved in troop trucks as intelligence knows just where the fleeing Germans are. At least they thought they knew where they were. On the second day the entire Fourth Division was unloaded along an eleven mile stretch of road. With all the support groups, there were over 20,000 men and their equipment, making a fair-sized little city. Here Alexander Vetov was promoted to captain but in the process, transferred back to the 22nd regiment of the 4th Division pointed toward Belgium. Alex was very proud of his promotion but in some ways it was very difficult to leave his men and start all over again. Now he had to learn exactly who was who in his new H or Hotel Company. Rank means a lot but it still does not tell a company commander who is good at his job. The more he can know about his 200+ men, the better he was going to be able to lead these men into battle.

It was not long until his company was chosen to round up and clean up a bypassed area. This was something he'd been doing ever since his second day on Utah Beach, so he knew what to do. Only now he did not know the men assigned under him. He didn't know who could get a precarious job done without losing too many men. When soldiers advance into a prepared defensive position, the cost can be high. There must be very good leadership in lieutenants and sergeants as well as experienced men in the line itself. So many things could go wrong so fast that only experience could succeed. Then he received orders to move out in only two days. Then they were to go into battle on the fourth day. Alex had to solely depend on rank and his own experience. He sized up the best way to fulfill the orders. He called in his lieutenants and gave them their assignments, and then gave and received questions and answers. Looking the ground over, Alex saw that the Germans had moved into a medium-sized French town. They had barricaded the roads into the town, which meant they were going to make their stand right there. The ground was mostly flat with a slight roiling surface like an ocean makes without too much wind. Using his Ziess binoculars, he saw a Tiger tank flying a Black SS pennant. Where it had been hidden back in the town was anyone's guess. Alex had hoped to save another French town but when he saw that Tiger tank with the Black SS pennant the hope melted away. It was very rare for SS troops to surrender at least without facing a brutal fight first.

That sloping ground was as high as any. Alex had all his trucks and armor drive to the highest point and spread out to look like he'd brought a battalion rather than just a company. All the artillery he had was his eight 105s and he also spread them out. Alex sent word to six of his 105 operators to try their best to hit that Tiger tank with armor piercing rounds, then to make range corrections until they got a perfect hit. The other two were given the same orders, except they were to use fire shells. They would fire at his command and after the first round hit, they must make corrections, as the other 105 were prepared to fire.

"Take your time and get it right from the start," said Alex. "Do not count on just shooting and then walking your follow up shells in." Alex assigned three platoons to move to within a mile of the town and set up all six of their thirty caliber machine guns. His lieutenants were instructed not to open fire until the first 105 went off, then spray everything with rifle and machine gun fire.

The first 105 shell landed about twenty feet behind the Tiger and the second 105 was right in front of the Tiger. The tiger instantly responded, firing over a 105 and doing little damage where the shell hit. The third was a fire shell and it hit the Tiger right on the tank's cannon, sending fire in all directions. This blinded the Tiger tank operators and when they tried to back up, they backed right into a building. On about the tenth 105 shell, the Tiger exploded, damaging houses on both sides. By now all three platoons were advancing and the six machine guns were being moved forward.

In the town there was some fierce fighting, but most of the Germans were not fighting very viciously. Only about a hundred yards into the town, a white flag appeared in a window and one of Alex's new sergeants thought it was another German. It was not; it was a Frenchman holding a French flag and carrying an English sub-machine gun. He was quickly followed by three other French men and a woman. The woman spoke English and quickly told the sergeant she and her people knew just where every German was and asked if they could lead the Americans there. She and her companions were led to the lieutenant, and he called Captain Vetov. Alex did not wait; he climbed into one of his two half tracks and headed into town to meet the French. What Alex learned changed his plans. He was told that most of the hard line German fighters were located in the very center of town. The French believed that at least three quarters of the German forces in town were sick and tired of the war and would surrender if given a chance. In fact, many of those in German uniforms were from conquered countries and had only served in the German army at gun point. If the Americans would allow the French to assist, there were whole sections of the town that would likely submit to the American Army without any fighting. \

Slowly but surely, rifle fire began dying out and French men were leading German soldiers to the American lines with their arms raised. Now Alexander had to crack down on his own men as too many were now paying more attention to French wine and women than to the fight.

By late afternoon the center of town was surrounded by Alex's men and equipment. Alex sent a request for all Germans to surrender and let the remainder of the town be saved from destruction. The Germans had until midnight to make their decision. Any German that came out to the American lines before daylight, his life will be spared. Captain Vetov went back to his half track and called his CO at battalion. When he got through to his lieutenant colonel he explained how they had taken most of the city with few casualties. This could not have been done without the French help. Most of the surrendered Germans had been brought out by the French and most of the Germans had surrendered first to the French and not to the Americans.

Now Alexander made the big request. "Sir, I have a plan to save the rest of this wonderful town. If you will allow me to, I'd like to leave the east road open for the rest of the hard line German troops to break out on so we do not need to destroy this French town with hard fighting. This will not be an agreement with the SS officers as to not bind any American to an agreed escape of the Germans, but rather I want the Germans to think they have pulled a fast one on us and have gotten away on their own. I know much of our battalion is already on that road about ten miles from here. If this plan works and battalion just stops and waits, these SS troops will come running right to you, and if it does not work, nothing will change. We will whip them tomorrow but with the loss of all the business district in Cheriva—plus the loss of many American and French lives."

The Colonel said, "I'll have to run this by the general, but I can't see that you are doing anything different from your orders, "to kill or capture the German resistance at Cheriva."

When Alex was called back to his radio, and he reviewed his strategy to allow the Germans to to break out and get trapped in open country rather than destroy another French town. The general agreed adding that they must make the Germans think they're using brilliant trickery.

Alex asked the lieutenant whose platoon was covering the west road. Together they discussed how they can make it look authentic without losing American lives. They were going to set up a simple road block whose personnelwere going to run away when attacked. Alexander ordered his troops on the main east road out of town to pull backd. That was the road to Germany and the perfect choice for escaping Germans.

Midnight came and went with no movement from the SS of any kind. Then a little after 0230 the radio stuttered to life and a voice said, "They have taken the bait, sir.

Then it wasn't long before all kinds of German motors were cranked, and the voice on the radio stated, "Here comes their armor."

Counting it down, the voice said slowly, two Tiger tanks, followed by two, no three, Panzers. In another thirty seconds the voice stated, "German half-tracks, looks like three…"

Now the radio is quite for several minutes before it return's, We have had three staff cars, nine trucks and maybe twenty civilian cars followed by more foot troops. Mixed in among them all were three or four motorcycles. Come full daylight the only Germans left in Chervia were sixteen badly wounded and nine dead. The Germans had been using the large Church that was in the very center of the town as a hospital. Hotel Company had to get right behind those fleeing Germans to to slam the back door shut when those Germans ran into the open country.

Many of the German troops were afoot so they couldn't move too fast. So Hotel Company did not rush after them but took a half-track for a scouting car and followed about an hour after they left.

While it was still dark they followed very slowly without any lights until the very first rays of dawn gave them enough light to see better. They'd hardly quickening their pace than there was a group of Germans just sitting in the road. They had a white bed sheet stretched across the road with a pile of German rifles holding it down on each end. Fifty yards on down the road there was a group of Germans all sitting down and many were holding or waving white cloth. By now Hotel Company on the move after the German army. Alex's Jeep was with the third Platoon on the road following H company's armor. Alex had been chewed out too many times by senior officers for being out front, a perfect target for German snipers. The radio in the back came on again with the scout car announcing the large number of surrendered Germans.

Alex ordered his driver to pass the Armor and catch up to the scout car. When they reached the scout car they saw the mass of Germans. There was an old German sergeant that was standing with one American sergeant from the half-track scout car. When Alex stepped out of his jeep this old German soldier came to perfect attention and saluted Alex with a British style salute. Alex returned the salute and noticed a large number of WWI German medals. This was what was called a re-tread, a soldier that had served in WW1 and now in WWII. By his manner he acted like a German officer and not a sergeant and Alex wondered if he was hiding the fact that he was a ranking German officer. This was not uncommon so they would not be questioned as an officer. Some men thought it better to be treated as a common soldier.

In a perfect British accent this German said, "Sir, I and these soldiers would like to surrender to the American army. Sir, we have a number of walking wounded that need medical attention. Sir, as per the articles of war, we have removed from our persons all items of combat, and have all our I.D.s out for inspection. There were over a hundred men sitting on the sides of the road. They were divided into smaller groups, not just jumbled up like most prisoner groups. There was no question about it; these Germans all knew and respected this old man. It would make him very helpful in handling these prisoners.

Captain Vetov said, "Come with me," and calling his master sergeant to follow, walked in among the prisoners. As they approached each group the old sergeant called out their regiment or other pertinent facts. As they walked, Alex asked different questions about their needs and why they were from so many different units. As the conversations became more comfortable between them, Alex sprang the big one, "What rank were you in World War One?" They had been walking and now the old sergeant stopped, looked at Alex and pulled himself up, "I was a colonel in the Kaiser's army, sir."

"Why are you wearing a sergeant's uniform?? Alex asked.

"That is what I am in today's German army, sir."

Alex gave him a curious glance, and the old man understood.

"I refused to acknowledge the Nazi party."

Alex said, "I have personally met commissioned officers in the German army that are not wearing the Nazi Party button."

The old sergeant said, "I was imprisoned in 1937 for publicly speaking out against the Nazi Party. In 1940 I was released upon agreeing to rejoin the army as a captain. Three months later I was busted back to a lieutenant for the same reason. By '42 I was cut again to sergeant and told that the next time it would be the firing squad and the only reason that I had remained alive this long was the German army needed officers and at least sergeants that could lead men in battle."

Alex changed the subject, "Why were so many soldiers left behind?"

"While loading up in trucks to pull out, it was all done by SS officers. If you were not a Nazi or were too wounded to fight, you were left to walk. We were told to stay up with the army but as soon as we got out of town the trucks revved up and left us, so we stopped and sat down. We knew you would be coming after us and we knew we could not fight the whole American army. The Nazis did not even have enough space to load all the soldiers claiming to be Nazis. We separated them into the group that is on the left side of the road, but I doubt if any are real Nazis. They just joined the party to get the benefits, as being a Nazi in the army had more."

By now the old sergeant was having a hard time keeping up and Alex asked, "How old are you, colonel?"

The old man stopped and tried to hide a smile, but could not hold back the pride of having his old rank recognized by Alex. Trying to straighten up as tall as he could he said, "A young 79, captain."

"Well, colonel," Alex said, "if I may be so bold I can see where you have removed metals from your uniform. May I ask why?"

The old man said, "I see no honor in this war and pulled them off and threw them away when I no longer had SS officers over me. I wear the ones given to me in World War One for there was some honor back then."

By now, the sound of distant battle was heard and Alex assigned his first platoon to take charge of the prisoners. All the rest of his company except the platoon and one armored half track, were ordered to take charge of the prisoners. The rest headed east. They had not gone far until here came the German –army that had just left last night, right back at them again. This time British Spitfires were giving them hell out in the open. Alex was still in the open as well and he was not sure about what the Germans had in artillery. How Alex wished he still had the old German beside him to tell him what the Nazis had. It works both ways, however. The Germans also stopped to review this new enemy. The first thing Alex called for was to get his eight 105s spread out. While this was happening, he summoned his battalion colonel to coordinate his actions with what his C.O. wanted him to do. He described his position and was told to hold his line right where it was. There was no cover whatsoever and no time to dig in, with a larger force coming right at him. By now his 105s had opened up and were tearing holes in the approaching army. This is when a German Tiger tank pulled to the front of the German force and landed a shell off to the side of one of Alex's 105s. Alex's 105s could kill a Tiger if it could get a shell in just right, but all a Tiger had to do is get a shell close enough to kill the crew, which was totally exposed. The Tiger fired again and this time it hit close to one of his Shermans but caused no damage. If any of his infantry was hit Alex had no idea at this time.

Three British Spitfires came in from the side and the Tiger went up in a cloud of fire and smoke, as well as a Panzer tank. Strafing and explosions were destroying the advancing German army, as well as a steady stream of fire from Alex's 105.

The whole German division now turned south to try to make a run for it. Alex grabbed his map case to look to the south and see what the country there looked like. In this case the map did him no good whatsoever so he returned it to his map case. Back to his radio he inquired what battalion wanted him to do. Alex was told to hold his ground as G Company had been sent to round up the remains of the German army. Then he headed to the new Regiment H.Q. in front of him while his platoon delivered the German prisoners to designated RC-27.

They instructed, "Fill out all reports, get them to battalion along with a requisition for supplies. All company commanders would meet at 0700, and at that time all recommendations for advancement in rank should be delivered to Staff Section 14 before noon."

Alex murmured to himself, "Fine, this is going to take all night again."

On the first of September the 22nd crossed the corner of Belgium toward Germany and was reported to be the first Americans to set foot into Germany. As they approached the Siegfried line on September 14th they were surprised at the small amount of opposition they were facing. This did not take long to rapidly change, and the 22nd retreated as they did not have forces to push the issue at that time. For two weeks it was a full time battle in pockets up and down the line. On the 4th of November the entire 4th Division was ordered to prepare to move into the Hurtgen Forest, along with several other units. Operation Market Garden in September, aimed to punch into Germany with parachute troops to spearhead the drive. It was stopped in its tracks. So now the military minds decided to punch their way in with brute force. A large portion of the ground the Allies decided must be taken was this huge forest with trees at the unbelievable height of one hundred fifty feet, the height of ten to twelve-story buildings. This was Germany and this forest had been defended in WWI. It was part of the forest that Caesar with the might of Rome declared was a most terrible place while trying to conquer the wild German hordes that refused to surrender.

On the 4th of November 1944 the 22nd Regiment of the 4th prepared to push into the forest and Captain Vetov stared at it with dread. His experience in fighting the Germans in hedgerows and other much smaller batches of forest in France had well taught him how tough it could be to advance into strongly -defended forested lands.

On the 6th the 22nd started into the forest and for the first little while they met very little resistance. In a strange way it was like the height of the trees was a measure of how much resistance was to be met. Less than a mile in, the trees were already reaching into the heavens a hundred feet high. Here German troops were as thick as the trees were and German artillery was already coming down at an alarming rate. In basic training American troops had been taught to hit the ground so most of the shrapnel would fly over their bodies. Here, two things worked against the Americans as German artillery was exploding high in the trees. This tore apart treetops so branches, whole tree tops, as well as German shrapnel rained down on the troops. An American soldier lying flat on the ground was ten times more likely to get hit than if he was standing up. Standing next to a tree might protect in some ways but it also increased the odds of broken off treetops falling straight down to hit them. Fox holes were of no value during an artillery barrage as most of the danger was coming down from above. After the barrage was over, there was no time to dig a fox hole before German bullets or even charging German soldiers tore into them. Even then, the mass of roots of those fir and pine trees were so thick that digging into the ground was like digging through a pile of twisted lumber buried in the ground. Armor was of little use as it could not get through that mass of trees. When they tried the Panzerfaust 100s, they stopped the Shermans in their tracks. Time had reversed itself and had returned to the early days of trench warfare of WWI—only the trenches and barbed wire of WWI were now the trees and shattered treetops slowing the advancing troops. But the German machine guns were now even many times more deadly. They fired several times more rapidly and were much more reliable. The German machine guns of WWI were big, heavy and hard to move. The MG 42 could be moved in seconds by one man, and be easily hidden and with 9mm MP 40s sub machine guns were common. Most G.Is called all German sub machine guns Schmesser's.

American High Command also made the same mistake they'd made in WWI. *If we push enough troops fast enough we will run over the enemy.* Unlike WWI high command said, "We have more troops than the enemy does so we will win." They should have looked at the ability of the enemy having more bullets than Americans did soldiers. The enemy had the equipment and ability to put those bullets to great effect exactly where they wanted them to go. As great as Allied air power was, it was of little use in 150 foot tall trees between armies fighting within yards of each other. The American artillery was in the same spot as the Air Force and was never sure where they were shelling German or American lines. There was one more very important fact and that was the mindset of the average German soldier. Most German soldiers were drafted into their army. Many were not Nazis and many had joined the party for its benefits, not because of its beliefs. High Command had now watched these Germans flee across France and thought of them as a beaten demoralized enemy. This was true to a point. So what had changed and changed so much? The Germans were now standing on German soil. To the average German soldier, France really did not mean much other than his team had won. While there he had witnessed what the German Army did to the people of France and all the other countries they had passed through. Whether he had personally been a part of these atrocities or not he knew about them. Now the German soldier was in his own country that was being invaded by foreign troops. It was now his wife and children that were going to face what the women and children of all the conquered countries had faced. It was now his fight for what was his and no longer a fight just for Hitler and Nazism. Maybe, just maybe, if he fought hard enough, both sides just might stop and call it enough, as they did in WWI. Maybe they would not destroy Germany with fighting on the ground in Germany itself. The thinking on the Allied side was just the opposite.

The British and the Americans had gotten whipped in the Market Garden fight. Now they said, "We will not be stopped." They tried advancing in several places and hit hard resistance. American and British intelligence said our air power had destroyed most of German's ability to produce. Their people were hungry, we had cut up most of their armies, and destroyed their air force. They were determined: We will pick a spot and push through without stopping like we have the last two months, we will enter Germany and win this war. They pulled together a huge force, pointed it at the Hurtgen Forest, and said "Go take it."

The 4th division was one of the first thrown into the fight. Captain Vetov in the 22nd led his men into that meat grinder. From past experience, he told all this platoon leaders to tell their men to avoid going flat on the ground during an artillery attack in a forest. When artillery started in heavy forest they must use their heads when going for cover. Next, they were warned, do not pull the trigger unless you know what you are shooting at and, above all things, always protect the next man's back. The third day in, his company was locked down and had lost far too many men.

Alex hurried to the front to study the situation and using his

Ziess binoculars he spotted the muzzle flash of an MG42. It was coming from under a large tree top that was leaning against another tree trunk. The branches of this downed treetop were hiding everything except that muzzle flash. Captain Alex called for a bazooka team and pointed to the spot, telling the man to locate and fire.

After a moment the bazooka man said, "I don't see anything."

Alex said, "Give me that thing." He lined it up and fired. There was an explosion behind the treetop and Alex saw men around him begin to move and he called "Hold." He stayed put while telling the loader to reload. After a minute Alex sent another bazooka shell into the exact same spot. After the second explosion, he said to his men, "Pepper that area and lay down the bazooka."

He grabbed his binoculars and looked around. As his men were firing, about ten yards to the right Alex saw another MG 42 open up and again he called, "Reload!" as he picked up the bazooka again. Another MG 42 disappeared as again Alex called, loaded and swung the bazooka to the other side of the first one he'd taken out. Sure enough, there is another MG 42 and Alex took it out as well. He handed the bazooka back to the bazooka man, pulled his .45 and called, "Let's go."

Three squads rushed forward and now it was basically a rifle against rifle fight. Yes, both sides had sub-machine guns but no more MG42s. It was still a tough fight but they took the former German position.

Even while taking that German strong spot, they were receiving rifle fire from other positions and Alex dropped down in front of the place he had stopped the first MG 42. Using his Ziess binoculars Alex was looking around when another body slid in beside him. Looking up, Alex saw one of his new lieutenants beside him. "How did you know, sir?" This was all he said.

Alex answered, "Once bitten lieutenant, once bitten. You will see it again; it's a trap where the first MG is the bait and when your men think they have knocked out the 42 they rush right into a cross fire from the other one or two. It has worked far too many times. Where is that bazooka man?"

And Alex delivered bazooka fire until they ran out of ammunition. They advanced about ten yards from where they had started early that morning. Alex told the lieutenant to hold his ground but not to try to proceed any further until both sides could catch up.

"We want their flanks, we do not want them to take ours." With that, Alex worked his way back, then to the left to locate his next platoon. After explaining what he wanted he brought one squad back with him. Even though only a few yards, there was a small German flank and with only eight men Alex came in from the enemy's side and forced them to retreat. The Germans actually retreated about fifteen yards this time, freeing up six more men that had been defending the old line to move to the new front. The second try did not do so well and only bent the Germans back to an angle, holding their front line to their old position while rejoining the new line they had retreated to. That had worked well so Alex turned around and did it again on the other end. It did not work as well this time, but still made a nice little bulge in the German line before they ran out of daylight.

The next morning Alex was back, knowing the German way, he realized that they had reinforced their line that broke yesterday. Today he had 46 men with three bazookas and lots of bazooka rounds. He was also carrying an M1. It frosted all night and now there was a sheet of ice on everything. It was just thick enough to make a loud crunch when stepped on. Four of his men were carrying BARs (Browning Automatic Rifles) that have full automatic fire ability. These are also full powered rifles but only have limited twenty round magazines. About a mile from where they'd made their little breakthrough the day before, Alex spotted a little puff of smoke behind the German lines and knew some Germans had started a small fire. He also knew that this was against orders on the German side just like it was on the American side.

There was a slight slope in the ground and a very small shallow trickle of water running down it into the German lines. It was far too small to be called a stream, but the running water had kept the water from freezing. While less than a foot wide, nonetheless those few inches were not frozen. Alex took five men and all six walked very carefully one foot in front of the other, down the little flow of water. They walked slow and easy, being very careful to look at everything. Once they had moved about twenty yards, another did the same and then the third. The farther the water went the more of it there was, and the unfrozen area grew larger making the walking easier.

Alex held up his hand and gave his M1 to the next man, pulled out his bayonet and slipped forward. It was a long five minutes before Alex returned. Without comment he took his M1and continued his walk. No one said a word as they passed two German bodies on the icy ground. They had not made ten yards when they ran headlong into another German. His rifle was slung over his shoulder and he quickly tries to pull it off when the sergeant behind Alex dropped the German with the butt of his M1.

They were drawing close to the occasional small puffs of smoke when an M1 went off and a German with a rifle pointed right at them dropped to the ground. That's it, there were now Germans everywhere and men in both uniforms were trying their best to kill the enemy before the enemy killed them. Even though Alex's men had been strung out behind him, they were all rushing forward to help. The 25 or so Germans were definitely outnumbered by Alex's men. As the fight slowed Alex's men quickly formed a circle of defense. Now it was the Germans rushing forward while the Americans stood behind trees for protection. They were behind enemy lines and the enemy knew just where they were. As the Germans closed in, the American bazookas opened up with everything they had. Those BARs did a great job as well and every M1 did its part. It was not long until a lot of gunfire was coming from the direction of the American lines but not far away. Then it tapered off and a voice called out "Twenty-second coming in."

Man, those boys looked good, but they did not stop. Some went forward, some turned to the right, and some to the left. But on both sides the German army could not stand while the Americans came at them from both the front and from the side at the same time.

In most times and battles it would not be considered much of a breakthrough. It was less than fifty yards, but in the Hurtgen Forest it was a good advance. However, it was a very costly advance for the 22nd as they lost 27 dead and 76 wounded. They were pulled back to base camp for three days for refit and replacements.

As another division took their place on the front line, Captain Vetov was called into Regimental HQ for a full report and he never knew whether he was being reprimanded or thanked for his service that day of battle. He was told that a captain's job was to direct his men and not get shot. Alex decided that since he had not been shot maybe he had directed his men correctly after all. On the third day the 22nd was returned to the forest and the engineers had cut at least three roads into the trees up nearly to the front lines. Now it was the same old fight that was nearly hand to hand. There were dead and wounded being taken to the rear every day, and nearly every day replacements were coming in. These replacements were mostly teenagers with a few in their twenties returning to the front line. These had recovered from wounds that had healed enough for them to return. It was colder most of the time now and snow stayed on the ground longer. Thank goodness, better winter clothing and gear was arriving and this helped a lot.

At a little over ten miles into the Forest the 22nd hit another solid wall that seemed to be impossible to break through. The Air Force had tried to bomb the enemy but one stick of bombs hit the American forward position. That day the 22nd lost 11 dead and 48 wounded by our own bombs. Enough trees were cleared to bring in a lot of artillery, mostly 105s and they started an around-the-clock blasting of the German-held ground. After four days of 24 hours of non-stop firing Alex looked out on a very strange sight with his Ziess binoculars. Now there were still a lot of naked tree trunks standing with only their trunks left. It was rare to see one with even part of a limb on it.

The ground was totally covered with a thick build-up of the busted up timber and the general in charge sent in three bulldozers to plow it out of the way. They had not progressed ten feet into that mess when several far off rifle shots rang out and all three drivers fell off their bulldozers. Did that general not remember the early hedgerows and what happened to bulldozer drivers? Fresh troops were sent into that mess, and while they were trying to get over and through it, snipers at two to three hundred yards picked them off. Then German MG 42s opened up followed by German mortars and even German 20mms. The Air Force was called in and while the 22nd was waiting Alex tried to find someone that would listen to him. Alex wanted to bring the hedgerow tanks back in that had bull dozer blades on their front and the bottom of those blades had been equipped with huge teeth that could cut through even the heaviest brush. When that idea was discarded then Alex suggested that the fighters bring in fire bombs and burn up the brush on the German side of the forest. This idea was quickly kicked out as artillery had already started many fires in the pine and fir forest and had made our own boys run for their lives. So the artillery started up again, but this had given Alex time to ask his commanding officer if they might take his Company back to resupply. They had been on the line for nine days straight and needed to get some hot food. They needed it in that freezing weather, along with a night's rest. They could be back before the artillery barrage was over. He was given permission and he pulled his company out. Back behind the lines Alex saw to his men, got into his jeep, and headed to Regimental HQ.

As Alex pulled up to HQ with the intent to see the colonel he saw a jeep out front with a one star plank on it denoting it belonged to a general. Going in, Alex asked for permission to see the colonel, and he was told to wait as the colonel was in conference. Waiting was hard but the warm fire at HQ felt real good, so he planned what to say over and over in his head. It was over an hour before a general and the colonel came out of the office. The general looked at Alex, recognized him, and smiled as he walked over. Now Alexander recognized his old major, now General Harris.

Alex snapped a salute and General Harris saluted back, then took Alex's hand and said, "Lieutenant Vetov, so good to see you again. How are you, son?"

After a few more words General Harris said, "I see you're now Captain Vetov, good."

The general turned to the colonel and said, "I see you have a good man here in Captain Vetov. We came ashore at Utah Beach together and he was under me when I commanded Delta Company. He had to transfer out when he received his Bronze Star and was given a battlefield commission."

Like Alex had done so many times in the past and gotten into lots of trouble, he blurted out, "General Sir, are any of the old hedgerow tanks still around; we really need them in the Hurtgen Forest."

The general frowned and said, "I'm not sure, but you know we cann't send tanks into a forest. They get knocked out every time we've tried it. Tanks have to have room to maneuver and troops to protect them and neither can be done in a forest."

"Yes sir, I know sir, but where we need them they have room to maneuver and have no need of getting closer than thirty yards from German troops."

"OK, son, tell me what is going on," and the three men walked back into the colonel's office.

There Alexander explained the whole situation, along with the losses he had been taking and he was sure that the hedgerow tanks could get his men through the brush with his men to protect the tanks from Panzarfaust. This would allow the 22nd to move forward much faster and with much smaller loss of GIs. The general looked at the colonel and asked, "Well, colonel, what do you think?"

The colonel who had just been listening to the conversation, said, "It might work but where the hell are we going to find some hedgerow Shermans?"

"We have tried everything else; if I can get some we'll see what will happen. They cannot be used in thick forest but they might work in semi-cleared areas."

General Harris opened the door and spoke to the colonel's desk sergeant, "Get me General Patton at the third." Then he walked back in and said if that SOB doesn't have any he should know where some are. He grabs every running Sherman he can get his hands on. The problem is he strips them apart to keep his third Army Shermans up and running."

Turning back to Alexander he said, "Good to see you again, son, keep yourself alive." He turned and left as Alex turned and faced his colonel, he had improperly followed the chain of command and he knew it. A stern-faced colonel looked back at him, sat down in his chair and said, "You and the general go way back. Well, we will see, stay here tonight and I'll let you know what we find out, captain."

Alex snapped to attention and said, "Sir, I have orders to be back on the front line in sixteen hours."

With a smirk on his face, the colonel said, "Yes, orders are orders and procedure is important also, captain. Dismissed." With a sharp salute and a Sir, yes Sir, Alex was out of there for the night—at dawn he began the long drive back.

On the front line again, more 105s had been brought in and the bulldozers had cleared some space around them and the men as well. They had not ventured into the "mess" more than twenty yards. Some infantry had slowly advanced about sixty yards in but it had cost them four days and lots of casualties to do it. When Alex reports to his major, the major just stared at him for a long time and Alex knew the colonel had been talking to him. Finally the major gave the orders and Alex was glad to be out of there. The next three days were a repetition of every other since entering this forest. Thousands of rounds of artillery, then the smoke color of the day was fired into the enemy lines so the Air Force could get their licks in without endangering the American troops.

This third day brought a clanking as three Sherman tanks with bulldozer blades came into view. Alex ran for the back of the first Sherman and as he got there a German sniper bullet bounced off the Sherman. That was close, those German snipers were good, but even they missed on occasion, and this was one of those occasions. Taking the phone from the steel box, Alex explained they were facing a large number of snipers and MG 42s that were killing his men as they tried to get through or over that mess of downed timber. Alex suggested that a few of his men might follow the Shermans into the destroyed forest to get in deeper. The sergeant said, "Captain, I don't think that is a good idea as we will be backing up and turning as much as going forward. This will leave your men open to the machine gun fire and sniper fire and the Germans will know right where to shoot. After only going forward a few feet there will be so many branches and brush on our blades we will have to turn and push it off to the side. Just let us know where any German artillery might be and look out for Panzerfaust as well as you can. You see, we are trapped in this mess of fallen timber just like you guys are."

Alex agreed and told them to try to cut more than one lane into that mess of tree trunks. The sergeant said, "We'll do our best, captain, but first let me back up and get you safe behind that half track. Bullets are bouncing off our armor faster than raindrops. Alex was glad of the cover. The Sherman jerked into reverse and slowly backed up until Alex could step behind the armored half track. For the rest of the day, three Shermans pushed up logs and branches along with huge mounds of dirt. About every ten yards there would be a big pile and the next ten yards another pile on the other side of the path they were clearing. While there was a lot of long range rifle fire that second day and two men were wounded slightly, that was the first day since entering that damn forest that Alex did not have a single man killed. At night Alex had men slip forward into those little cup-shaped mounds of wood and dirt. During the day the Shermans would make a large mound, then add trees, brush and dirt on both sides to make the mound into a curved line so his men could go in and be protected from enemy fire while getting closer to the enemy with every new mound.

Now they started something new. Alex had his half track pull a 105 howitzer out to a mound. No men, just the 105, as eight millimeter German rounds could do no harm to the 105. At night or during the day with armor protection the 105 gun crews and ammunition could be moved behind the forts of wood and dirt and set up to fight. Now the howitzer was close enough to the German lines it could shoot a high explosive round into any target just like shooting a rifle. The difference was artillery normally fires at a target from long distance up and over, and the shell comes down and explodes with a large circle of destruction. With the barrel shooting level with the ground it could be aimed at a specific spot and take out that whole area. Several German snipers and MG 42s had been spotted in specific spots. The first day of firing that first and second 105, the Germans moved back over a hundred yards. When the Germans moved in one sector the next sector had to move also, so as not to leave a flanking spot open for the Americans. So a large part of the entire German line stretched for over a mile at the most, then tapering back to where it did not move at all. This allowed a large part of the American Army to move forward a hundred yards in one day. These mounds were also small forts where the Americans slowly got closer. From these they could return more accurate fire, had places to protect wounded, and even had protected stocks of ammunition and supplies. Regardless, this created a pocket in the German line that got larger every day. As American artillery had been used so much in this part of the forest the trees were stripped of branches so much German artillery could not be brought forward to use against the approaching American armor as when there were no branches the Air Force could see anything large.

One foot or one hundred yards, every inch of ground in this battle was bought by American blood and every inch lost was paid for in German blood. There were few days Allied aircraft could fly in to help as most days were typically cloud covered. Then of course it was very hard to find the right target among trees as tall as a ten story building.

This battle started in a very cold rain and finished in days that seldom rose to freezing and often dropped to numbers close to zero. The Americans knew they needed cold weather clothing but never expected to need it so quick or need so much. After all, everyone knew the war was going to be over by Christmas. The now much-widened road into the area, that had been so devastated by artillery, was now the main highway into the forest and each side could be worked on separately. This allowed Americans to come from the bottom of the battle and from the side at the same time, giving the advantage back to the Americans again. These first three Shermans equipped with hedgerow blades spread out about thirty yards apart and started pushing through the devastated forest. At the beginning of their push into the remains of the forest, the sergeant commanding each tank stood up, directing the driver just where to go. This quickly stopped as German snipers were just too good at their work. When a tank turned to push the build-up on the blade to the side making huge piles of broken trees, they were very exposed to the full destructive power of the German Panzerfaust, so American troops had to move in and slowly follow the Shermans in while the artillery, now firing very slowly, still laid down a rolling barrage against German troops. In five days they had reached three miles deeper in and had spread out into the forest on both sides for a width of seven miles. There was still a lot of hard fighting on both sides but there was no longer a wall of German resistance.

The Germans had changed their war plan as they could not stand hard against the power of the American combined might. It was more like a guerrilla war but spread all over the Hurtgen Forest. It was still one big bloody mess, what some historians described as the worst battlefield faced in Europe by American forces up to that time. The reason for this was a continuous battle that lasted for a full month in the terrible winter weather. Some units lost up to 150% of their number as replacements were rushed in only to be killed or wounded. More replacements had to replace those and this went on and on. Even though the battle was officially over in December, there were hold outs still fighting in February and another flare up in March. As the biggest month long battle in Europe to that date came to a close, the 4th was moved out and up into Luxembourg to recover, retrain, rest and resupply.

The next super big battle that was fought was much better known. As it was so well reported and shocked the Allied nations. But ask the men of the 4th infantry Division who fought in both of these battles. They will tell you that the Battle of Hurtgen forest was every bit as hard and many will say harder fought than the much more famous Battle of the Bulge.

9

THE BATTLE OF THE BULGE

Scuttlebutt had it that they would have two or even three weeks before being returned to the front. On December the fifth their trucks began to pass back into Luxembourg. When they reached their new camp the work of setting up a new division camp had hardly started so it was the job of the 4th to set up their own camp. By the eleventh most of the work had been done and men were eating hot meals in large company tents that keep part of the cold outside. They were all sleeping in squad tents and most had small stoves for heat. Maybe best of all there were hot showers and new uniforms and cold weather gear. Well, that was not quite true--some had new uniforms, but best of all it was a strong rumor that the war was soon to be over. The battle for the forest was supposed to be the last big fight. The Germans were low on men and out of equipment. On the 12th of December it was the first day of full unit training again and everyone slept well, knowing they were well behind the lines and had days to relax and enjoy peace for a while. That the next day's food was going to be hot and served in a warm tent, not cold and out of a box.

The 16th brought some rumors into camp of a possible German counterattack. Well, before daylight on the 17th all the loudspeakers in camp started blaring at full volume. "This is not an exercise. All troops are to be in full battle equipment and be at the staging area as called by battalion. This is not an exercise."

The 12th regiment was to be there to load up in trucks at 1100, the 9th at 1200 will march out, the 22nd at 1300 and the list went on. This was not an exercise. German troops had broken through and the 4th was going to stop them. The 22nd Regiment at least had a little more time, being on the third call-up but that still was short notice to move out.

When Alex reached the staging area it was 1244 and he passed the last of the 9th as they were marching out. All of the 22nd was on the ground before 1300. The general told them that he had little information other than the German army had broken through and the 4th was going to do its part in finishing this war. At 1305 company by company started marching out, at 1700 the men were given a ten minute break but everything was covered with a wet snow so most men remained on their feet. They did not stop again until sundown and had to spend the night beside the road in a snowstorm. Two-man pup tents were quickly set up and these helped keep the snow off.

With a cold breakfast, they formed ranks and were on the road again. The colonel came by and told Alex that the division did not have many trucks as they were camped in what was thought to be a rest area well behind the lines. What they did have had been used to rush the 12th Company forward to set up a defense. Then they used what was left to get a few of the 9th up as well. Today they would be returning to base to get the medical units and necessary supplies for the front. He knew that the men would want to know why they were not being trucked to the front, so Alex had to tell them it is not going to happen. There were just not enough trucks. The first regiments there were going to have to hold out until others could get there.

By the nineteenth the first sounds of battle reached the marching army, and the trucks were now coming back loaded with wounded. The 22nd Regiment moved into the battle line that same afternoon where the 12th had been. More than 80% of the 12th had been annihilated by the overwhelming force of Tiger tanks, German armor and artillery. Then the nearly one half a million German soldiers came. The 4th and 5th divisions were fighting side by side to hold the German tide back. Alex's company was placed on the north side of the main road through Berdort and tried to find shelter while under fire from the German forces. It was a heavy snowstorm and close to ten degrees in a fight where the Germans were better equipped for super cold weather than the Americans were. What really made it hard was all the Germans were wearing white clothing over their uniforms or their uniforms themselves were white. In a strong snowstorm they often were not seen until right upon the Americans. The Americans, of course, were all in military green and easy to see. Defense lines were set up as quickly as possible with machine gun positions established. Alex had ordered all his bazooka teams to concentrate on the road as Alex had been informed the Germans were pushing forward their heavy armor.

In less than a minute after his first troops had started to fight, the roar of big German motors was followed by three Tiger tanks rushing up the road. As silly as it sounds, Alex was thinking: How on earth can they see where they're going in this snowstorm?" Of course it looked like they were going much faster than they actually were. As the first Tiger rushed by, several bazooka shells hit the front and sides. They all exploded with as little effect as throwing snowballs would have had. As it passed, Alex could see the top hatch was open and just the top of a German helmet was sticking up. The second Tiger was only a few feet behind the first and this time an American soldier ran for the back of the tank with a hand grenade in his hand. German machine guns cut him down before he got five feet--so brave but also so useless. There were three Tigers all told, then six Panzers, followed by two half-tracks. The tops of half-tracks are open while every other part is armored. Neither half-track made it more than fifty yards as scores of Americans tossed in hand grenades. The only problem was some of these grenades bounced off or were thrown back out by the Germans. Several American soldiers were wounded by their own grenades. The grenades still did the work and one half-track ran into a large tree and its tracks started digging holes under their moving treads. The other just ran off the road for a short while and its motor died.

Nevertheless, that meant that nine German tanks had broken through their lines and were now behind them. This was a very dangerous situation to have so many enemy tanks behind them. Right now it was German infantry trying to run over them and they just kept coming. The Americans held their own until it was dark, and even then there was still occasional rifle fire from both sides. It was too cold to get wet as even lying on the snow it was still too cold to thaw. Still it was very hard to warm up by kinetic activity, as any movement brought an enemy shot. Daylight brought a little relief as the pressure that been applied all night seemed to relax a little. Many of the Americans were suffering from frost bite, but there were enough on the line now to rotate many men. They still could not just stand up and walk off as even the raising of the head brought a rifle bullet.

Alex had brought six of his 105s and hid them well so any enemy armor that tried to pass them would have their weaker sides exposed. Hitting a Tiger tank in its front was useless as it was just too well armored. Anywhere on the turret could not be penetrated unless a large high powered cannon shell hit exactly where the turret and body were connected. This would work but was nearly impossible to do. Unless it hit an exact place, the shell would just bounce off. The sides were always thinner armor and the tank tracks and driving wheels could be put out of action. Both sides of the rear of a Tiger tank contained a gas tank, and, while well armored, an American 105 at reasonable range could set the Tiger on fire. Alex and the company commander on the other side of the road had agreed to do the same thing. These two commanders were reasonably sure that no more German tanks were going to get through their section of road. Even though a Sherman tank can easily be destroyed by a Tiger tank or even a Panzerfaust, some were moved close to cover the American troops as they made their positions stronger or were replaced by fresh men.

If only this pea soup weather they were fighting in would clear, it would make things much better, but only God could change the weather. During the night both companies had brought their mortars forward enough that they were able to lay down a steady mortar fire into the German lines. This was doing a pretty good job of plowing up all the territory out in front. The steady mortar explosions totally hid the arrival of more German armor. This time it is a mixture of all types of German tanks and other armor. This time the Germans had their big self propelled 88s that could take out anything the Americans had and our Shermans had to make a run for it. The Americans had to retreat to better places to fight from, including the town of Berdort itself. Some wooded areas where the trees were thick and the trees were large enough that armor could not get through became strong points. In the town itself the houses and other buildings became places of defense. The wooded areas that protected the Americans were pretty much bypassed by the Germans. In the town itself their heavy artillery did a terrific amount of destruction. Even here the Germans were more interested in getting through in their mad rush to the west, than to finish off the Americans.

Some German armor had got through Berdor and the area around the town. The 40,000 Americans of the 4th and 5th Regiments fought hard and long to stem the flow. The 12th had been the first to block the German onslaught but now there was less than 1000 of the over 5000 men of the 12th still able to fight. The main road went right through Berdort and a column of Tiger tanks had come right through town. The few Shermans the 12th had with them were no match at all for the Tigers. The Shermans' cannon shells just bounced off the super thick and strong Tigers while one shell could hit a Sherman and blow it all to pieces. It was the same for the

American bazookas--some bazooka teams were able to damage a Tiger by hitting it in the steel treads. This was like a small pup biting the hind leg of a big bulldog. The Tiger still had all its fire power and could retaliate in an instant. The skies were so overcast that Allied aircraft could not get through. In fact, for eleven days there was such a heavy blanket of clouds over that whole part of Europe that not one aircraft could fly. Only a very few holes opened up during the weeks of the battle and Allied fighters jumped through everyone that did. Even then, most of the time the ground fog made it impossible for them to help. Once the German heavy equipment got through, the 4th and 5th closed in tight behind it, leaving it out there by itself. Isolated, and with little fuel, it could not go much farther and therefore Hitler's plan to make it back to the ocean fell apart. Intentional or not, chopping up the German army into smaller pieces made it easier to wipe them out.

A new problem arose as the Nazis sent out troops dressed in American uniforms. They were equipped with American weapons and spoke English. Some were equipped as MPs and took over intersections and misdirected traffic, sending men and equipment in all the wrong directions. Allied troops also fell to well laid ambushes by German troops that knew they were coming. They cut into communication lines and intercepted orders and then incorrect communication and wrong orders were sent out by these English-speaking Germans. This caused great problems among Allied troops as they did not know who to believe. How do you operate an army when it is the enemy giving your troops whatever orders they want to? Being in U.S. Army uniforms, they ambushed troops by walking right in among them and then turning their machine guns on the unsuspecting Americans. As word spread about these infiltrators, Americans no longer trusted other soldiers in American uniforms unless they knew them personally. Men were questioning other men about American life and if you did not know who won the last World Series you just might have a big problem. Papers did not carry much authority, as the Germans had all the right papers, many obtained from captured GIs. Even officers were questioned at gunpoint and when an officer was asked who Mickey Mouse was and he did not know, the whole squad was captured. This did not always work, as an American officer at a checkpoint asked what the capitals of different states were and he himself was wrong as he thought the capital of Illinois was Chicago. Still, different questionss about American life worked well in separating the real Americans from the German infiltrators.

Without supply trucks, the Tigers began to run out of gas and ammunition Even though Peiper's SS tank column was able to capture a large U.S. gas depot it still was not enough and some German troops walked off and left their empty tanks and trucks to walk back to Germany. That is not to say this armor and German troops behind the American troops did not cause a tremendous amount of damage before they ran out of gas and other supplies when they popped up in places they were not supposed to be with armor that the Americans were not equipped to handle. In the early days it was a one-sided battle and on the side of the Germans and not the Americans.

The massive German Tiger tank was so very heavy with all its very thick armor, it guzzled gas at an alarming rate. The even heaver King Tiger used over a hundred gallons to go fifty miles. The German plans had always been to rush forward and quickly capture as much of the Americans' gas as possible. They had planned to move so fast that the Americans could not protect their own gas depots. However their main plan was to capture so many American trucks and all other vehicles that they had trucks full of empty barrels and had issued thousands of rubber hoses to their troops to siphon gas out of everything they captured. When a man of any army is fighting for his life he is not quick to stop and steal gas.

The 22th went in to plug the hole left by the decimated 12th but still faced German armor, just not as powerful as those Tigers had been, Even so, fighting Panthers, Panzers, half-tracks, mounted 20

MMs, Panzerfaust and first line well-equipped German troops posed a great threat against M1s and hand grenades. Even the Germans that got through were no longer strong enough to go much farther. The battalion that Alex was a part of was now down to about 500 men still able to fight. But fight they did and for all practical purposes this is where the push called the Battle of the Bulge was stopped. As more and more troops came in to help fight the Germans, the Germans had no backups to even help them hold on, must less to strengthen them. Now like all tides when they reach their strongest, the next thing is the start of a tide's recession.

Some of the German armor began to run low on fuel and turned around and started back through Bedort. These Tigers could only pass through one at a time on the narrow two-lane streets of Bedort. Three Tigers were in the lead and the first one was nearly all the way through, when a bazooka team that was hiding in the remains of a house only ten yards away fired into the side of the tank. It did not penetrate the thick armor, but it did blow the tank's tread off. The bazooka team, knowing there was no place to hide from the second tank, fled as fast as they could. It happened so fast that they actually got away. The Tiger only went a few feet until it ran out of tread. This made the right side stop while the left side tank continued its turn quickly to the right. With the one tank out of commission, it just sat there trying to turn its long barrel. The barrel only moved enough to come in contact with the remains of the house.

German soldiers came forward like ants to protect their disabled Tiger. The second Tiger came forward enough to try to smash through the building across the street from the disabled Tiger. Tiger could easily crash through houses, but this was a two story commercial building and simply caved in on top of the tank with so much rubble that this Tiger tank was also trapped and could not get out. Even its crew could not get out of the trapped tank. Now there was not even room between the tails of the two tanks to drive a jeep through. The third Tiger tried to back up but a German half-track blocked it. This half-track was pulling a trailer full of empty fuel barrels. When it did try to back up the trailer jackknifed to the right. The rest of the German army tried backing the remainder of the column out. They had to fight for every foot it moved. Once the German troops got out of Berdort, they did not make it to the bridge. With the loss of two of their Tigers blocking the main road their smaller armor and most of their trucks did finally get out of Berdort.

Once out of town they decided to go another direction and started north. It was less than twenty miles across country to another bridge crossing the river. Traveling with heavy loaded trucks and armor across farmland is slow work, while on the American side of the bridge there was a road headed north right along the river. A dozen army explosive men piled into a jeep and a deuce and a half truck. The road gave them a definite advantage and they had plenty of time to rig the bridge to blow it up. Then most of the men headed back to Berdort. Three hid their jeep, hid their wire and waited. Their plan was to wait until the first tank was on the bridge and then blow it. Great idea but it did not work, as the Germans always sent troops out to inspect for explosives. Knowing the troops would find the explosives and cut their wire they went ahead and blew the bridge as soon as the first German boots stepped onto it. This blocked the Germans from crossing the bridge and returning to help their army trapped on the other side of the river. Some of the German troops ran across the thick frozen river to escape but when a German staff car tried it, the ice broke and it fell into the river. That and the fact that many of the fleeing Germans were cut down while running for the other side made many decide to surrender rather than try it.

After rounding up prisoners and taking care of diehard hold outs, Alex's colonel told him to take his company and scout the countryside to capture or kill any remaining German troops still behind the American lines. He reminded him to be very aware that there were probably infiltrators still there. Also there was no telling how many SS troops, as a whole battalion of SS troops had broken through.

Berdort had been a part of Peiper's command. Even most German soldiers wanted nothing to do with Peiper's command. Everyone on both sides of this war agreed that Peiper was a latter day general as Rommel had been in his cleverness and cunning. He was the opposite of Rommel in most everything else. He was as cruel as Attila the Hun, even toward his own men, if they did not live up to expectations. Prisoners were executed, and towns were burned when occupants did not instantly obey him. It was even rumored that he had shot his own men when he was displeased with them. No one was sure where he was, or what he had left. It was certain that he had made the biggest haul of gasoline when he captured a thousand, 52-gallon barrels of American gas at a depot.

Alex was given the challenge of going after the remains of Peiper's command. He was given six jeeps, three half-tracks, and two tank destroyers housing ninety MM high velocity cannon that could kill a Tiger tank. These were great weapons except, compared to most tanks, it was not heavy in armor. He was given the latest thing in American bazookas and mortars. Four extra 105s totalled twelve and he was loaned four Shermans. With the extra equipment came extra men and what would normally be less than 200 men became over four hundred. But Alex was going to have to split up his command to search over such a vast amount of land and do it in a hurry. Knowing Peiper was totally an armor man, he would need the best roads for his armor. Even though all the ground was frozen, Alex still believed that Peiper would stick to the main roads when possible and still need towns. These towns must be large enough to help supply him with food for his men as they had been away from all German supplies for a long time. Peiper was also hoping that in larger towns he might be able to find some gasoline. Alex studied his maps and made his decisions. Then he called in his lieutenants, explained his plans, then got some sleep in his jeep while Walls drove. The next morning, Alex sent out five of his jeeps on five of the major roads with lots of instructions. They were scouts instructed contact locals only and get information. They were not to trust information from any one in an American uniform, as Peiper's command had used infiltrators by the hundreds.

"Be very careful," admonished Alex, "as a hidden tank can kill you a mile away, and the Germans are very good at hiding their tanks. Report in at least three times each hour regardless of what you may or may not have to report." Now they loaded up and started down the main road heading west.

Alex picked one of the half-tracks to be his command car as he had lots of room for his chosen staff to travel with him. The half-track had a very good and powerful radio to take and send reports. While the half-track was an open top vehicle, the army had devised some bent staves to cover it with a tarp in wet or snow. The town they were headed for was three times the size of Bedort and had roads going from it like a spider's web. From there, Alex could get to any part of the area in short order. Now he just needed information and the first hour there was nothing but rumor that the locals had heard, Alex paid little attention to these until the same thing began coming from several sources at the same time. Still rumors were only rumors and Alex wanted firsthand proof. From the bits and pieces, Alex started plotting everywhere Peiper had been so he could see if there is a plan involved. Then jeep three called in; they had seen a German motorcycle coming their way until the motorcycle rider saw. Then the rider quickly turned and got out of there as fast as it could go on the icy road. Alex told his men to continue on down the road but to go slowly and carefully after they passed the place where the motorcycle turned around. Alex said, "Remember, a German 88 can shoot farther than the eye can see. Watch the road for any sign that a tracked vehicle has been there." The company was nearly in Amorvil before any bona fide information came in.

Jeep three stopped at a farmhouse and they said that German trucks had been going in and out on the road in front of the house yesterday and today. Bringing his convoy to a halt at another farmhouse a few miles out of Amorvil, Alex sent one of his multi-language men to talk to the people inside. The sergeant returned and said as of yesterday morning there were Germans in Amorvil. They had no information about how many, or what equipment they had or anything. The farmer had started into town and a German truck had stopped and questioned him. He came back home but three days ago they'd come and drained his tractor and car of gas. That was why he was riding his bicycle yesterday. It seems the Germans were gathering up gas and food from all over, and he had not left his house since yesterday morning.

Looking through his Ziess binoculars, Alex could not see any movement in the town. That was not good, there should always be movement in any town from daylight till dark. Alex got into his last jeep and tied a large white pillowcase to the radio aerial and slowly drove into Amorvil. He was well into the town before anyone stirred. Then in the middle of the street was an older man wearing the customary sash across his chest declaring he was the mayor of the town. The jeep stopped, Alex got out, and the mayor rushed up to him and nearly fell down on the ice. The mayor grabbed Alex and hugged him and in very broken English said, "My God, you have returned."

In the perfect Dutch language of his youth, Alex said, "I am sorry we had to drive the Germans out the second time but it will not happen again."

A big smile broke across the old gentleman's face and he changed to the Dutch language himself. "Oh, you are an American and a Dutchman all in one. Come into my home, it is too cold out here for an old man, and we will talk."

"Are there Germans here?" Alexander asked.

"I think they are all gone," the mayor answered. "They were here, three times in the last week, they come, they go and they come again. It sounded this morning like they were going again but no one comes outside, who knows when the Germans will come again?"

"I know," Alex answered, "We have come to make sure the Germans never come back again. I would love to come into your home, sir, but right now I must find out just where the Germans are so we can capture them and never let them come out of Germany again."

The old man said, "I will tell you just where the Germans are, let me get a heavier coat and we will go to the city hall. There I will tell you where every German within fifty kilometers is and if he has clean socks or not. My people have been watching their every move so you will have all the information when you return, and now you have... Oh happy day, the Americans are back and he is a Dutch boy."

While the old man disappeared into his home Alex called the half-track on his jeep radio and told them to come on into town but to be careful as he was not sure the Germans were all gone as yet. As the mayor came outside again he said he was sorry he could not take Alex to the city hall in his car. As stated, the Germans had taken all his gas. Then he added, "They did not just take my gas; they took a bayonet and shoved it in the bottom of my gas tank."

Alex had to help the mayor into the jeep and Alex got into the back. Off to the city hall they went, with the mayor trying to explain in English to the driver how to get there. Once inside, the mayor turned on the lights and got on the phones and started calling numbers. He started every call with, "The Americans are back," and within fifteen minutes people started coming in. Within the hour there were thirty people in the building and everyone came to thank Alex for coming back as though he had run the Germans off personally. The city hall was full of phones, most in different rooms but they were all in service. As the old man spread out his military map on a large table, there were many people talking to him. They were explaining that they had called all over to ask if there were any Germans and now things began to come clear. The Germans had been spread out all over, mainly getting every gallon of gas they could. Now they were all rushing together about twenty kilometers south of Armovil. It seemed that was where the tanks and large German equipment had been for several days. As hours passed, the local people delivered bits and pieces of information which indicated that for three days the Germans had spread out in an ever-widening circle gathering mainly gas and, earlier that day, had started calling everyone to come back into their main camp.

Knowing how he now needed to put this information together, Alex excused himself. He finally broke away from a very appreciative people to get back to his own command. His command was set up just outside town in a church and he relayed all information to his officers as they began planning for the next day. A little after midnight a young man rode up on a bicycle to let the Americans know the Germans had not moved. He handed the guard several pieces of paper. Then he apologized that it had taken him so long but there was not a single liter of gasoline left in Armovil and bicycles were slow. Alex looked at the papers and was astonished at what he saw. There was a long list of the gasoline the Germans had taken in both liters and gallons. A list also totalled German troops, and when and where they were seen. Three Tigers, five Panthers, four Panzers, seven half-tracks, seventeen quad twenty MM, seventeen heavy trucks, four staff cars, six scout cars, fourteen motorcycles, six with side cars. Besides, there was a list of all stolen foodstuffs including the number of wine bottles and other things.

Alex also made sure that the German camp would be watched all night and all information would be brought to the American camp as quickly as possible. Telephones over a seven-parish district would call into the city hall any information that might be useful. If and when the Germans moved, the Americans would be notified and that included the direction they went. Any farm that had a phone would call in if the Germans passed that way in an area of over fifty miles in any direction. Alex thought he had the greatest spy network anyone had ever had in all history. Turning to one of his sergeants he said, "Get two radio men and get an SR to the city hall pronto and take four full five gallon cans of gas to the mayor as well. Tell him to find a car or motorcycle that does not have a hole in the gas tank so his people have some transportation. He will understand. I want that radio manned twenty-four hours. Any information on movement of that German army I want to know it instantly."

At 0600 all commissioned officers including armor and medical came together for a briefing. "If the Germans stay still this morning, we are going to hit them here and here." He pointed to the map. "We are about even in man power but we are out gunned in the Armor department, so we will use what we have and we will win. If the Germans start moving, I think it will be east, as they have been trying to get enough gas to make a break for it. Thus, we are going to send our strongest armor down here where I've been told the creek that runs through this cut has a high east bank and just a sloping bank on the west side. That does not show up on any map so it will be our advantage. Our high bank has a good stand of trees but not so thick we cannot put eight of our 105s in those trees. Hill's platoon is going with the armor and if for any reason any of their armor gets over that creek, I want every man to leave the 105s and all get on our trucks and get the hell out of there. That sloping west side, sirs, will be our killing ground for any German armor that makes it that far. These Germans are all hard core SS killers in one of the most radical divisions in the SS, but it is not going to be their killing ground, it will be ours. We win, or we get out, clear? They are the ones trapped. If we do not get them today, we will get them tomorrow. It is going to take three hours to get our 105s there and another hour to get set up and those 105s camouflaged. Here are eight bed sheets and some choice line to hide those 105s in the snow. So get on your way, we cannot do anything else until you get set up. I want my eight 105s to take this job and you other four that have been loaned to us will stay two each with our other two striking forces. One tank destroyer 90 will be with each striking force." Alex turned to another group, "You ninety boys, your first job is the Tigers if you get a shot. Next is the Panthers. Then it is any armor you can get. Try not to get caught in the open; you do not have much armor yourselves. Two Shermans with each striking force and you guys know your machines, so do not try to take on more than you should. At least you all have the new 75s and that will help a lot. Get something to eat and we'll be on our way at daylight. Get some rest; tomorrow will be a long day."

At 0700 the radio squawked on and someone said, "It looks like the Germans are getting ready to move." Alex had hoped it would take a little longer, but life was what it was. Then at 0730 the radio came on again and the word was the Tigers had shut down again.

Alex smiled and said, "That's standard German practice to warm up a Tiger tank and then let it rest a little before re-cranking it in cold weather. Those Tigers will be moving in less than thirty minutes so let's get on the road. Before they had cleared the town the word came that the entire German camp was coming alive. Calling back on the radio, Alex said, "Just as soon as those tanks start moving, I need to know in what direction."

It was after 8:00 a.m. when the radio came on again and Alex was told they were moving south. That was not what he wanted to hear. Why was Peiper going south? That didn't make any sense. Now he was going to have to chase him and Peiper could choose the battleground. Alex studied the maps, then he called his new friends at city hall and asked questions about the ground to the south. Nothing he heard was any good; this was going to be a game of chase. Alex was about to call Hill and tell him to pack up and follow the chase when the radio came on and said, "They are now turning east, they are turning east."

Another quick look at the map and Alex said, "Everything will still work—just take a little longer to catch them." Back on the radio Alex said, "Intersection point is D-17 at the railroad bridge." There were only three bridges in fifty miles that were strong enough to hold Tiger tanks. One the Americans came in on and Peiper would have to turn around and come back. That he was not going to do. One was Garvell Road and he had already passed that road. The other was the railroad bridge; it was plenty strong to take the weight of Tigers so that was where he was headed.

Alex said, "Get there as fast as you can but be careful of the icy roads; we need all of you to arrive. This morning the ground fog is so bad they can hardly see the road in front of them. Well, the Germans can't move any faster than we can." O900 came and went and visibility was no better. About 9:30 it was plain to see where the Germans had turned off the road and headed due east without the benefit of a road. Alex looked and looked at his map but he saw nothing but flat land. He did not understand Peiper's plan but the only way across to the other side of that river was that railroad bridge so that surely was the intersection point. Peiper had to have something in mind. What was it?

Then a cold chill grabbed at Alex's heart. What if Peiper knew or suspected he was being chased. Everyone believed the fog would disappear as the day went on--it always does, well most always. There was nothing but open ground all the way to that railroad bridge. With the Americans on open ground, Peiper's superior armor could chew up Alex's whole command and spit it out. What if Peiper had been listening to Alex's radio and knew just where he was and he was setting a trap? Right now, Alex wished he was still a sergeant taking orders rather than being responsible for four hundred men. After all, only majors were supposed to command 300 men. If Alex just stopped and waited for the fog to clear, all his 105s and the men with them would be overrun and killed before he could get there. He had to just push on and hope and pray for the best. But, at this point he did not even know what was the best. Peiper's tracks in the snow began a slow turn a little to the north. Again Alex grabbed his map and looked. This was like piloting an airplane in clouds, but as far as Alex could tell they were headed for the railroad bridge over the small river not fifty yards from where Alex's 105s sat waiting.. The choice of that bridge did not make good sense either for a smart man like Peiper as German tanks often went over railroad bridges as their tracks had no problem with gaps between railroad ties. The half tracks would not have a problem as their tracks would push their tires over anyway. The tires on trucks and the twenty mm's would have a hard time but they could make it. Troops could cross if they were careful. Small wheels on light artillery and scout vehicles could never cross on their own. Alex knew Peiper would never leave part of his equipment behind. Maybe Pieper had been carrying planking to help him get over things on his way to the ocean port he'd been ordered to reach. That must be it--he was carrying his own flooring for that bridge. The driver of Alex's half-track slammed his brakes on. Both the American and Germans had been driving without lights. Now through the fog one could see the dim smoky glow of a number of brake lights in front of them.

Everyone became deathly silent and in the distance you could hear German voices. Softly Alex said, "Kill all motors and keep quiet." That was one of the longest thirty minutes in Alex's life, just sitting there. Alex was sure that Pieper was waiting for the fog to clear. Finally German motors started up again and began moving. Not Alex, that was just too close for battle distance--maybe okay for knife fighting. As long as he could see the German tracks in the snow he knew he could follow them anywhere. Things began to lighten up a little and again occasionally a red light appeared but now it was over a hundred yards ahead or so. If the fog suddenly lifted they would be much too close so again Alex called for all to slow and stay with him. Now the fog was getting spotty, some places you could see for a hundred yards and others it still hung on the ground. As group commander it was now time to call for battle formation. As the men and machines spread out, suddenly there were explosions as Alex's 105s on the opposite bank opened up on Peiper's army.

Alex was closer now to Peiper's force and the explosions just seemed to evaporate the fog for a much clearer view of the battlefield. The sound of a 90 MM high velocity tank destroyer roared and a German Panther tank exploded. Within a few seconds a second

90 went off and a Panzer did the same. Now American artillery was one long continuous roar. All four Shermans got into the action and it did not take long before the four 105s that had come with Alex were set and joined in. It seemed everyone wanted to get in on the fight and riflemen poured rifle and machine gun fire into the mass of German men and machines. Then the mortar crews got involved and Alex saw two King Tiger tanks make a break for the bridge and right over it they went, turning directly away from the battle and taking off at their fastest speed. This was no time to get involved with two escaping King Tiger tanks, even if Peiper was in one of them.

This was the time to finish a battle and permanently destroy one of the Nazi's most notorious army units, and that was just what was happening. The Germans were on open ground and were fighting a partly hidden enemy that had a lot of heavy fire power and theirs was being wiped out with every minute of battle. In spite of the fact they had no chance at all, that once super proud all-SS Nazi battalion had been cut down to a few hundred men. Even now as it was being annihilated, the men kept fighting as though they no longer wanted to live without Hitler as the victor.

A few badly wounded were taken prisoner but most had been killed. Some of the bodies were holding their SS badges in their hands where they had taken them off their uniforms and held them while they died. Alex had three men killed and over thirty wounded. Making his way to the bridge he was shocked to see that this railroad bridge was covered over on both sides of the railway with wood bridging. This made it a roadway so farm equipment, cattle and such could cross the river and connect the two large farmlands. So Peiper had known all his equipment could have gotten across if only he had not been defeated by the 4th Infantry Division that at one time he had called "that mixture of all the lowest of mankind." By that Peiper meant that the American 4th Infantry was as far from what he thought was the master race as it was possible to get. Looking around Alex realized that if that fog had not lasted as long as it did, this could be his little army that was lying on the ground as the Germans drove off. Alex had never considered himself to be a very religious man; but looking at it all, Alex knelt down on the ground, bowed his head and said his thanks to God.

The ground was frozen solid and soon so were all the German bodies. Any attempt to dig graves without heavy earth equipment was out of the question, so Alex called H.Q. and reported. He was told to leave the battlefield and return to H.Q. with all speed, and that is just what he did. When Captain Vetov arrived there he made a full report and was told the colonel wanted to see him. When he reached the colonel's command tent he had to wait, so he pulled his chair a little closer to the stove and went right to sleep. He did not mean to; it just happened, he woke up with a hand on his shoulder. It was the colonel himself lightly shaking Alex awake. He woke up with a start and jumped up with a salute and an apology for going to sleep. The colonel just smiled and said, "Come into my office," and Alex followed. Offices in tents are a lot different than those in buildings and a lot smaller. The colonel started off by saying "Captain, you have done a lot for the 4th, but the 4th needs a lot more. Captain, I'm recommending you for promotion to major and that will take time and for right now I want you to stay here in battalion. We've lost a lot of good men these last three months and have stopped the German counterattack. We now need to drive them back. They are in pockets all over, between here and Germany and most are trying to get back to Germany. We do not just want to drive them back to Germany, we want to capture as many as we can before they get back. This way we won't have to fight them all over again, and we sure do not want all that armor to get back to Germany. Vetov, this is what you've been doing since we landed on Utah Beach on June 6th. You're good at this and now we want you to plan and assist the whole battalion. Keep your jeep, driver, and radio man, get your gear together and get some sleep. Tomorrow, move yourself over here and get started on your new job."

It was now time for the Germans to be pushed back into Germany. As soon as all the American dead and wounded were taken care of, the 4th started their inward push. The skies were beginning to clear and Allied aircraft were all over, attacking any German armor on any road or elsewhere in the open. Again the German army was on the defensive and had to be dug out of one place after the other. The 4th was now back to clearing out the remaining Germans or as the soldiers of the 4th called it, "mopping up." Patton, the Air Force, the paratroopers, and the generals get most of the praise and glory. The infantry gets the work, and they have to walk to get that. It is true they got to ride in trucks a lot now compared to six months earlier, but the work was the same.

After four weeks at battalion tracking down German troops that were still behind American lines, Alex was released and returned to Fox Company of the 22nd. Here he was Captain Vitov. But as things change in war, now he was asked to clear an area of about 60 square miles. He had a little over 30 vets and well over 100 replacements. This area was mostly industrial with about 25 square miles of farmland. Alex called this farmland his box. He had to clear it first before going into the industrial area. Marking it into 25 small squares, he took three of his platoons as spear point units and the fourth as back up for any hard spots the other three ran into. The other three quarters of the battalion was assigned to a more heavily populated center south of Alex's sixty square miles. Alex's major told him he felt that this new assignment would not be difficult and when they finished they could turn and help the rest of the battalion. This farm area would help give the green troops a little experience with minor danger. Did that man have any idea how long it would take to just walk over 25 square miles even if they never even found a rabbit on it, much less with some Germans that might shoot at them. Sometimes Alex just could not understand how some people thought.

A single front line was a joke as there was no way he had a fraction of the men needed to cover it all. He decided to make three spear points going in, with the fourth platoon as a back-up for all three spear points. Three platoons could cover a little over two miles and a half if they spread out like they were trying to find lost cattle on a ranch. It was no way to try to find German fugitives. Walking over 25 square miles did not leave much option of choice. This still meant a walk of 50 miles for every man. Even if there was never a shot fired at a rabbit, this was going to be a long hard two days. What if they even found a few Germans that surrendered? This would take men and time to take them back, and time and men was something they did have to spare. The fourth platoon could handle some of this but then there would be little to no back up and that was not acceptable. The only other choice was to not cover all 25 miles and that was against orders and not acceptable either. Basically, Alex turned his whole company into a series of scouts that were followed by enough firepower back up to take on small points of resistance. Alex had heard so much regarding the idea that the Germans were whipped—that they just needed to be rounded up. He wondered how any thinking man could still say that after what they'd faced the last three months. They pushed in on their first little square with no problem at all. Then they turned around and came back on the other half of the square.

By the time they got back from their first ten miles of walking, Alex was seeing something that made his heart freeze. Many of his replacements were walking like it was a stroll in a park. They could have walked right over a German patrol and not even seen them. These men had not only made the patrol of no value, but if they had run into any resistance at all they would be dead and would maybe have caused the death of several other better men. One man had even slung his rifle over his shoulder to carry it. If a German jumped up in front of him he would not have been able to shoot back. Alex chewed their asses off but he was still not sure he had gotten through to them as they started back up the next ten-mile march of the patrol. At the end of this five miles, they turned around and started back. There was a small building that looked like a storage building of some sort. Close to it stood a farmhouse with the usual few small structures around a farm. No one seemed to be around it and it was on a road that bordered their assigned area.

Alex had stopped and searched through his Ziess binoculars from three miles away. This was the first building on their patrol. It had looked deserted from that distance like a lot of farmhouses had looked in the past. An empty-looking farmhouse was more scary than a rattlesnake to Alex. Three more miles of walking brought them less than half a mile from that farmhouse. Here Alex ordered a stop, set his men into a textbook approach, and started making their way toward the farm. Several of the replacements looked just like they'd looked in maneuvers back in Basic. They were going through the motions like they were half asleep when an MG 42 plus rifle fire started from that house. A string of 8mm bullets cut the top of one replacement's helmet and head off like a saw. Three more were hit and Alex did not have time to think about them right now. Ever since he'd become the CO of the company he knew sometime soon some Germans were going to open fire and too many of these men were going to die. They had well made it into the fifteenth square when all hell opened up on them from the farmhouse. The back up platoon came straight in while men on both sides slowly moved up toward the house using any cover they could find. The plan worked perfectly except now there were now two dead and six wounded. At this rate there would be too many casualties before the ground was cleared. The company always carried at least two bazooka teams when moving in full strength. As the whole company was acting just like a super big patrol, the mortars, machine guns and other heavy unneeded supplies remained with the trucks.

When they were close enough, both bazookas opened up on the farmhouse. It was not long before it was in full flames and Germans on the back side were running out. The riflemen on both sides of the house took care of every last one of them. Alex had his radio man call back to his trucks to go ahead and move up toward their pick-up spot toward but not close to the building on the corner. Alex told them to stop on the road close to the burning farmhouse and to not approach the larger commercial building still two or three miles away. Alex picked four of his rookies who had seemed to him the most unconcerned to pick up the dead and carry them to the road. The rest of the rookies were all assigned to go with the wounded and get a good look at them, as this war was not over yet, and he wanted them to see what German bullets did to bodies. When the trucks arrived it was getting late and they still had that commercial building to clear. After making sure the wounded and dead were being taken care of, Alex ordered all the company machine guns and lots of ammunition loaded into one half-track. He told that driver to remain back out of panzerfaust range and stay alert. Then to come as soon as he was called. All other trucks and men except for the second platoon were to stay behind with the trucks. They were to only pull up behind the half-track when ordered to do so. Watching that building like a hawk, his second platoon men approached. Alex decided it was a mechanic shop or perhaps a small machine shop as he got closer, looking at all the things around the outside of the shop. About that time a shot came from that building and an American fell, within a few seconds another shot and another man went down. Again the bazooka man that Alex had close to him was told to put a bazooka round through that window and the man fired. The round hit above the window but the explosion knocked the window out. "Another round," was all Alex said as the number two man of the bazooka team loaded the bazooka again. That round went inside the building and it exploded. At the moment of the explosion two experienced vets rushed forward, one on each side of the window. One man tossed in a hand grenade and it exploded. In about ten seconds the other man tossed in another grenade. They both rushed to the door and one stood to the side and yanked the door open, the second tossed in another hand grenade, then the first man stepped to the door and emptied his M3 sub-machine gun into the building in a spray pattern from left to right then stepped back. The man with the M3 changed his magazine and stood by the door for a few moments then got down and peeked quickly from close to the ground. He looked again, a little longer this time--then pulled his head back and spoke to the other soldier, who took a quick look and then a long look around. Then he held up two fingers and made a come-on-in motion. Two more vets jumped up and ran for the window. They took turns taking quick looks into the building. The building contained one dead German sniper. His first shot had killed an American—his second wounded another.

In less than two miles covered, there were eight casualties. Alex was always known and respected as an officer, but now he went ballistic. He told his company that their orders were to clear every German soldier from off their assigned area. They were going to do it as long as there was one single man left in the company. At this rate there was not going to be any that made it home alive, except the vets that knew how to fight and still live. He guaranteed that every rookie replacement was going to be dead within 72 hours unless they learned how to be soldiers. He told them, "Those four vets just showed you how to stay alive. It is not by hiding in a hole or looking at birds. It is by killing Germans before they kill you. If you think you can just walk around out there and still be alive tonight, then you are too stupid to live anyway. If you are a target for more than one second you will die. If you cannot see that hidden German you will die. If you let a German get a shot at you, he will take it and you will die. You do any of these things and you will never leave this ground alive. Every second you are out there you must know where that next shot is going to be coming from, and if you do not, you are going to die. Search every place a German might be with your eyes and use your brain. If you are going to get yourself killed, this company is at least going to get some good from your dead body. I am going to watch every man I can and your platoon lieutenants, sergeants, and my vets are also going to watch. Any man that just strolls along is going to the point of every patrol until he learns, or he is shot, or someone that is even worse is sent to take his place.

That way, since you are going to die anyway, your body might as well save a smart soldier's life."

He was not trying to be super hard on these new men; it was for their own good. Alex cared for them very much but like basic training he was trying to turn the green recruits into soldiers even if it meant scaring them into it.

Back in camp there were reports to fill out and two more letters to write to parents. Requests for more replacements and supplies. Then Alex took a shower and got some sack time; tomorrow was going to be another full day. Now Alex called out five men to take point in a rotating order and sent them out again. This time every man was looking at everything like he had X-ray vision. The new point men were as scared as could be, but did their job well anyway. There was another firefight but every man returned with only one wounded.

On the fifth day they approached a large industrial complex and Alex knew, if there were Germans, it was going to be well-defended. He called for armor back up but was told all armor was needed elsewhere. They started in slowly and began taking fire from a large round building with a platform on the top. The Germans had a machine gun up there, but suddenly the platform just exploded. Alex turned around and saw a single Sherman approaching. Every five seconds or so that Sherman sent another shell towardd that complex of buildings. At about a half mile the big fifty caliber machine gun on top of that Sherman tank opened up, showering the whole complex with those big fifty caliber bullets. As it got closer even the smaller thirty caliber opened up. As it ground to a halt beside Alex, he looked up into a grinning sergeant's face. He said, "How's your hearing?"

Alex recognized the same sergeant that had helped him in the early days of the invasion. Bullets started pinging off the Sherman and Alex quickly ran to the rear of the tank. Alex reached the little steel box, he took the phone handset and said, "Thanks sergeant, this is the second time you've shown up to help me and my men out of a tight spot."

"Sure captain, I saw the RR tracks on your coat. Now hold your ears a second. Alex covered both ears as the tanks cannon fired another few rounds. Over the phone the sergeant said, "Cap, I am going to be busy, we'll talk when things quiet down, block those ears again."

This time Alex only held his left ear while pressing the phone tight on the right ear. The big booms followed and the phone did a great job of blocking the roar of the cannon. The Sherman did not move forward with the troops as that would put it in Panzerfaust range. However it did continue to fire at all the spots that looked like good targets. Approaching the complex of buildings, Fox Company started entering them. This was when the top hatch swung open and the sergeant climbed out and hopped to the ground. Both men shook hands.

Alex's first question was, "Where did you come from, I was told there were no tanks available."

"There were not any," the sergeant said, "but me and the boys agreed to come anyway. We heard your call, and slipped off. We are, in fact, AWOL at the moment and need to get back as soon as we can. We were going to move in closer but the last time we were with you we had the two MG 42s to support your men up close when a Panzerfaust exploded right in front of my tank and I knew I was already too close."

Alex said, "So that was what it was; I felt the explosion but could not hear it well so did not know for sure what had happened."

"Maybe we can get together sometime. somewhere for a drink," the sergeant said. "No time to talk right now; don't want to get caught AWOL again. As your men are now entering that first building, it is no longer safe for my tank to fire into it as we might hit Americans." In a moment the sergeant was back in his Sherman clattering back up the path. The men were in those buildings fighting at pistol range. They were so close to the enemy it would be hard to turn their rifles among all that machinery. Alex hurried after his men until an 8MM hit the side of his helmet. It just left a crease in the helmet. But to Alex it was like someone had hit his helmet full-on with a baseball bat. It also reminded him that he'd done just what he had told his men not to do. No straight lines--zig zag, duck and weave and look at everything in front and the near sides of you constantly. Putting his helmet back on, Alex started practicing what he'd preached to his men.

This was some sort of food processing plant and was totally full of machinery and huge storage bins. Men from both armies were busy throwing hand grenades at each other and this was destroying the machinery more than helping the soldiers. Their grenades seldom went where they needed to go as so many pipes often blocked their path. They were bouncing around everywhere and exploding all over the place. Here the men with pistols, short sub-machine guns, and carbines were more effective than the men carrying their M1s. A German would pop up, fire a quick shot and right back down again. Private Hagman was crawling down the aisle while looking under the machinery. Every time he saw a pair of German boots he would shoot his 45 and when the German fell to the floor with a bullet in his foot Hagman would shoot him again. This worked so well that he used up all three of his seven shot magazines. Sergeant Dourity tossed him his two extra magazines. When all five magazines were empty, one of the other men handed him a captured P-38 and Hagman finished the building. Before entering the next building Sergeant Dourity told the men to stop using hand grenades. One thrown in the last building had hit some machinery, bounced back, and killed the American who threw it. With luck, that was the only one killed or wounded by their own grenades. Nevertheless, this was plainly too dangerous inside a building full of machinery.

Alex sent one platoon to the left side and one to the right side as he sent the other two into the complex of buildings. Naturally, they would have reached the back of the complex long before the two platoons could move through it.

Alex feared that some troops might wound his own men while

fighting inside. Both American and German bullets were flying through those windows and the thin metal sheeting the walls were made of. After more than two hours of fighting side by side, many wounded Americans were brought out from behind the fighting. Alex had both the other platoons send in one squad of men from each platoon as reinforcements. One of Alex's sergeants that was wounded in the right shoulder came to Alex and said, "The men inside need more forty-five ammunition and pistols if any are available."

As Alex had been carrying both his prized Colt and the equally prized Luger, he had never stopped his men from carrying captured German pistols with them. The American army had little use for pistols at that time except for back up for commissioned officers. The Thompsons and M3 grease guns were 45 caliber sub-machine guns so every unit equipped with subs had 45 ammunition. Officers with 1911 45 pistols had three clips [magazines] –one in the pistol and two in belt pouches. No more were carried into battle. So when hand guns were used in action, after seven shots the clip had to be replaced in the 45s. After 21 rounds were fired, each clip had to be reloaded by hand, a slow job indeed. Alex asked the two platoon leaders to pick a squad that had several handguns in it. Both squads went in carrying an ammunition can full of 45 cartridges as well.

Alex began to worry they were going to run out of daylight before clearing all those buildings. The two platoons still on the outside slowly moved forward as the sound of battle progressed inside the compound. The two lieutenants inside were rotating their men forward from one room to the next. So not one squad faced the enemy in such close quarters for more than one room. Inside the fence that surrounded the entire complex, there was one small building about the size of a small farmhouse that turned out to be a German ammunition dump. Not a single German fought to defend it. Alex was sure that everyone knew that with walls made from corrugated steel, any bullet going into that ammunition dump could easily make the whole thing go up like a monster fireworks display.

After it was captured and broken into, every man that had used his captured Luger, P 38, or PPK pistol wanted to get plenty of German pistol ammunition from that ammo dump. After they cleared the last building they headed back to that building to get stocked up. Alex found something he thought was much more valuable, a stockpile of Panzerfaust 100s. Even the latest American bazookas could not be compared to the new German ones. Alex now had crate after crate of these, along with at least a thousand pounds of German high explosives. This was the type that the Germans were using to blow up bridges and set booby traps to kill Americans. He well knew the army's warning to not use captured enemy weapons. As the unique sound of many enemy weapons told men who they were facing. Bazookas had been Alex's small artillery when he could not get the big stuff. Now in his hands were truly handheld artillery and the temptation was more than he could stand. He ordered in an Army 6x6 truck and loaded it up with Panzerfausts. A second 6x6 was filled full of Panzerfaust rockets and 9mm ammo. As the American army had come so far in six months, his company was often short of supplies. Alex knew in emergency situations it was all right to use enemy supplies. So while he was at it, Alex ordered in three more army trucks "to be used as needed in emergency situations." He got the trucks.

All this went to a storehouse that his men had just liberated. His men loaded these trucks up with canned ham, sausage, etc.

Since no one really knew if the local water might not be good, that offered an excuse to load up about 150 cases of German beer. They had orders to not leave any supplies behind that might help or benefit the German army. Of course, that meant to destroy enemy supplies, but Alex took it literally: "Do not leave any enemy supplies behind." Alex ordered another truck to be filled with 300 more cases of German beer. Even this large amount was only about half of what the storehouse contained. Just the same, Alex was not a hard drinking man and very rarely even drank enough wine to feel "the buzz."

There was a section of this warehouse that had a section locked off in a fenced in area. A huge sign in German read 'Officers Only on the locked gate. Alex could only read a little German but that sign was easy. One of his lieutenants was very knowledgeable concerning wine and could speak and read German. Alex turned this job over to him as to what would be of benefit to Fox Company. He warned them of the fact that any man drunk on duty when in contact with the enemy would becourt martialed. There was still one unloaded truck so Alex went back to the ammo dump and loaded up more high explosive equipment and took a dozen MG 42s with ammunition as well.

When all four of the new trucks were filled up, Alex sent for six more of the ones already assigned to him. Alex told the lieutenants, "We're going to burn all that food in the morning. Since Fox Company has fought so hard for two months and eaten cold K rations in freezing temperatures, they may file in and get whatever they want to eat tonight."

He was no fool. He knew exactly what was going to happen. The men filled their pockets and both arms and the sergeant at the door gave every man a bottle of German beer as he left. The men were not allowed to have anything stronger than that one bottle of beer. Most of the entire company slept that night rolled up in their half tent rather than setting it up. That night the men were doubled up on sentry duty and changed men every two hours. This was just in case full stomachs made them sleepy.

Alex got in his jeep and drove back to the little Belgian town they had come through earlier, spoke to a few people and returned to camp. Shortly after daylight more than two hundred Belgian men and women showed up with wheelbarrows and farm wagons of every kind. They probably took every tool, blanket, and morsel of food in sight.

Alex called all his men off the storehouses except the ammo dump. Alex left one squad behind with the instructions to destroy any foodstuffs or items left for the Germans to use. There was very little remaining. That squad was left enough of the captured

German high explosives to do the job three times over. Then they were to get in their truck and catch up with the outfit.

The very next day in a heavy section of forested land, they ran into more German soldiers. Alex said, "This is a great time to test out those Panzerfausts." He ordered his lieutenants to stay put and engage only in long distance sniper work. There was a small road leading back to where the company trucks and supplies were. He went by himself, except for one orderly. They had not walked a mile when the orderly was shot and Alex hit the ground. Not another sound was heard. He crawled over to his man, but it was no use. A sniper bullet had passed through the helmet just over his right ear and come out his left ear. As Alex looked at the wound he realized that bullet must have come from somewhere up high and not far away. Alex tried the old trick of taking his helmet off and putting it on his bayonet. Nothing happened so Alex know the German was good at his job, up in a tree, just waiting to get the cross-hairs of his scope on him. With a sniper shooting from that high up just lying on the ground would not protect him. Alex lunged for a large tree between himself and the sniper, a second shot missed his fast move. German sniper rifles were bolt action, so when they were fired, the bolt had to reload the chamber. A good sniper could do this in a single second, but he was in a tree and had to hunt for his target again so just maybe he had two seconds. It was dead winter and most trees had long ago lost all their leaves except the fir and pine evergreen. Only one fir fit the description that all the facts called for. As Alex jumped for the large tree he wanted to stand behind, he raised his M1 and fired into the center of the sniper's tree. His hope was that this would distract the sniper long enough for him to get a safe position behind that larger tree.

Alex had been carrying a rear view mirror he broke off a destroyed car several months ago. He had used it many times in order to see around corners rather than expose himself. When he looked he could see a dead German hanging over a branch where the German had tied himself to the tree.

When Alex reached his Jeep, a sergeant asked him, "Skipper, where did you get another German sniper rifle?"

"Picked it up on the way back," was all Alex said. "Sergeant, take half your your squad and go get Jenkins, a sniper put a bullet through his head. But be careful; there are still Germans between us and our front. I will get some supplies and the other half of your squad is going to help me, so get them up front."

Turning to the seven men that were left, Alex told them to come with him. When Alex's driver, Corporal Walls, saw Alex, he walked over to him. "Get my two machine gun crews to tie both thirties on the hood," said Alex. "Then empty the trailer and hook it up. You men go help the corporal, and double time it."

"You three replacements, get your gear, double time it back here, and stow it in the back of that second 6x6 over there. To the truck driver Alex called out, "Pull off the front of the tarp and grab some of those Panzerfausts on your truck. I want enough to fill my jeep's trailer, then add another two layers on top. Round it off with another two or three and tie it down tight."

By this time in the war, Alexander seldom got to know his re-placements by name as he had now lost about four hundred men between the Hurtgen Forest and the Battle of the Bulge, there just was not time. However, their names were on their uniforms and when things were slow Captain Vetov would read them and call them by name. Times like this it was a look and "hey, you," They were almost strangers to him. Alex still cared for all his men but this was just a fast-moving war. "You help get that tarp back," he said, "and hand those boxes down while you two stack them on the ground."

Walls had grabbed the company master radioman and returned with the men and the trailer ready to load. The Panzerfausts fit best sideways in the trailer so the men loaded things fast and tight. Captain Vetov beckoned the radio man, "Get me battalion."

He made sure the Panzerfaust extra rocket ammunition boxes had filled the back of the jeep. The radioman said, "Battalion's on, captain," and Alex stepped to the radio. "This is Captain Vetov. May I speak to the major? A brief pause, then Alex spoke into the radio phone. "Give him this message. Situation yellow in section J7, heavy resistance, little advancement, expecting much improvement shortly."

Looking at the trailer Alex figured they had loaded fifty or so of the German rockets. The men were looking on so Alex spoke up. "You know what's on that trailer. You also know that Jenkins was killed coming through those woods. If one bullet hits that trailer the four of us in that jeep will be collected in small, bloody pieces. Follow us quickly but carefully. These woods are definitely not cleared."

Walls started at mid-speed until the road started getting rough. Then he slowed as he thought of how many high explosives were in that trailer. Alex said, "Corporal, the Germans are very good at packing these things and some bouncing is not going to set them off. However if a single bullet hits home on one of them, we are all gone."

Alex was a little too convincing and now he had to keep telling Walls to slow down. They made it fine and in a short time about fifteen Panzerfausts were carried forward. Every man who took one was given instructions on how to use it. During this time period both 30s were set up for a good field of fire. Alex decided it was too late to use his surprise today. Even if they made a great gain, they would not have time to take advantage of it. That evening Captain Vetov made the rounds of his men discussing their daylight targets.

Just after dawn, Captain Vetov carefully sighted his M1 and dropped a German soldier. During the night many American troops had worked their way within fifty yards or so of the German lines. That morning when the Americans opened up with their captured Panzerfausts the Germans found themselves on the receiving end of an unexpected artillery attack. However they quickly pulled back into their line as soon as the artillery stopped. Of course, it was not American artillery but their own weapon being used against them. The results were the same. The Germans fought but were outnumbered. By now all the Panzerfausts had been reloaded. They had plenty of extra rockets and started the artillery bombardment all over. The Germans retreated again until they got out of rocket range but soon came back after the rockets stopped. With every move their numbers were dwindling. This little play was repeated over several times until the Germans did not try to return to their reinforced positions. There were not enough soldiers left to hold them anyway so they retreated and stayed back. In doing this they left their fox holes and prepared positions. Two American machine guns and over one hundred M1 rifles both hurried them and reduced their number. The whole battalion was on their heels, and for the Fourth Infantry Division, this was the last big organized fight that they experienced until they faced the German army at the crossing of the Rhine River This did not mean it was their last skirmish by any means. Every time they had to cross a river or even any body of water over six feet deep, the Germans made it a killing field and Germany was full of these rivers, streams and creeks.

10

PLUMB RIVER

C alled into the colonel's office again, Alex was handed a pair of gold oak leaves and a congratulations, "Major Vetov, your promotion has finally come through. Maybe now you will not always act like a sergeant and be out front of your men. I hope you stay behind your men, but I doubt it. Now that you are a major, you would typically be transferred to a new battalion. But things are different now, and you will stay right where you are. The other major has been transferred out. You are in sole charge of the battalion as of now. If you want to keep or change any or all your staff, that is your call." The colonel continued with his perspective on the German front. "They've been telling us for six months the war is nearly over and we've had the hardest and bloodiest fights during that same six months. We have reached the Plumb River in spots and I want everything on this side cleared before we cross it. This war will never be over until that son-of-a-bitch Hitler is dead. The Germans have blown most of the bridges and have formed strong pockets around the ones they have not blown. This is to get their equipment and men out of our side and use them against us on the other side. You and your battalion are to stop the Germans from getting across the river in sections B seven, eight and nine and if you get the chance to save and capture one of the two bridges that are still left, please do so. We know they are already set with explosives and will be blown if and when the German high command sees they're going to be taken. The ice is already breaking up and the river is high from melting snow. It's going to be hard to cross without a bridge, but it looks like that's going to be what we have to do. By the time you get those three sections cleared out, maybe the ice will be gone and the high water will have droped. Good luck, major, and keep us informed on all pending operations."

Major Vetov went immediately to battalion H.Q. to get things started. He had already been running it anyway, but now he could make some changes he had wanted to make for a long time. When he entered the command tent, everyone snapped to attention and saluted. Most were smiling. He went directly into the commanding officer's office and was pleased to see it had been cleared out and made ready for him. After getting all his gear from his old office brought to his new office, he looked at photos of the two bridges. Gazing at the aerial photos, he wondered if there might be a way to capture one of them. Well, these could wait. His first order was to cut off the Germans trying to get to the other side of the Plumb River. Each of these sections had its own problems, most of the land was normally rich farmland before the war, except right along the river itself. That was used for a lot of river transportation. Allied air power had destroyed much of this and the frozen river was just now clearing itself of the hard winter ice. The roads were just beginning to melt into mud. Alex knew that Germans would try to convey much of the heavy German equipment so they could make a break for the German side of the river during the night when the mud refroze and there were no aircraft overhead. The coldest time of the night would be the last few hours before dawn so that is when the men needed to be at their best. Enemy troops could begin moving as soon as it was dark to avoid aircraft. Passing through the conquered countries, people provided much of the information about the German army. Now they were in Germany, so his men were going to have to go out and get all their own information.

There were still strong pockets of German resistance on this side of the river, especially around the two bridges. There was a large pocket of resistance also around a large set of docks and up-river in section 9. Directly across the river on the German held side of the river there appeared on the aerial maps a large number of buildings along the railroad that was on the German side. This must have been a place where the farms brought their crops for shipment by river and rail. Studying his aerial maps Alex noted how most of the roads in the area went toward or joined roads that led to this area on both sides of the river. While there were small areas of woods along the river valley, there was no place that a large number of tanks, trucks and large equipment could be hidden during daylight hours. One tank might be hidden in one barn but there was no place anywhere in his sections that could hold large concentrations of German equipment. Infantry yes, tanks and trucks no--so what was the German plan? Back to the Aerial maps again, checking out sections C 7, 8, 9—still nothing. D was the same, no place to hide large heavy equipment. Over in D11, however, there appeared to be a large mining complex. The aerial pictures did not give enough detail to be sure what Alex was looking at. Looking at the roads was a different story. They were larger and looked well-used. One came across section D11 into D10 curved into C10 and over into C9. Here it crossed another road that headed right into B9 and the bombed out docks. The river road running alongside the Plumb River ran straight to the larger of the two bridges.

Getting a magnifying glass, Alex checked out that larger bridge on the map and saw that it contained a roadway and a rail line on the far side. Alex started putting two and two together and he thought he knew what the Germans were up to and it was going to be right through his sections. Starting tomorrow, he was going to have to show he was running patrols to round up small groups of German soldiers. These were Germans that had been left behind the American front lines. The Americans were flushing out these pockets all over this part of Europe. Even more important he was going to use these patrols to scout out information. Like any good chess player, if he could find what the Germans were planning, he could cut them off and win. This must be done without either the Germans nor the Americans knowing what was going on. A new major, especially, had to fulfill orders to the letter; he was just going a little further. Just the same, at this point it was only a guess and Alex needed a lot more information to put details and a plan into play.

Mopping up was what the 4th had been doing even before their boots dried out from the salt water of Utah Beach. Alexander Vetov was as good at this as any man in the 4th.

On this night, it was already the wee hours of the morning before Major Vetov fell asleep, but he had to rise early to present himself as their new C.O.

After the formalities were over, Alex called all his battalion captains together to lay out their first orders. From the start he laid out how the clean-up program was going to continue. This included how to do it with the smallest loss of American lives as possible. It must include knowing all about everything and every place they went, for their own safety. All details were to be reported to H.Q., regardless of how insignificant they may seem so H.Q. could best function. Leaving this meeting, Alex overheard one of his captains say to a newer captain. "I've known Vetov a long time and he was a great captain. It looks like now that they've made him a major he's turning into a paper pusher."

Alex just smiled, as this is just what he wanted them to think until he knew if he was right or not.

As quickly as he dared, Alex assigned some of his best and experienced squads to check out the roads and areas down which Alex thought the German armor might be coming. They were given specific instructions to not get into a firefight unless completely necessary. One squad was sent across country, mostly at night, to try to get close to the site of the mine or whatever it was. Another was sent to the bombed out docks also with instructions to stay undercover. Word came back that the roads were old and built up higher than the ground around so they were dry and solid. There were definitely tanks and artillery under camouflage at the mine site. The bombed out docks were alive with German troops.

Checking his weather reports, Alex saw that two nights away was the new moon and the forecast was that the skies would be cloudy for a day or two. Alex wrote a report simply stating he had good information that a heavy German force was going to be making a dash for the bridge at B9 with enough strength to achieve a break-through. More information would be called in by radio if this proved to be a fact. The message was sent in person, as he was not sure it was correct, and did not want to use the radio, code or not. This would give Alex an excuse to use his radio as he laid plans for the coming action. Calling in all his captains to H.Q. he gave them all the information that each captain would need and instructed them to only use theirs in ways that would typically be used for mop up operations. Each captain was sent out to do his part. Kilo Company would pull their men in to cover both sections

B7 and 8. Next Alex turned to his artillery. They were going cross country to intercept the German heavies where Section B 9 and C 9 come together. He was going to take every piece of artillery that battalion had and even three quarters of his mortar and bazooka teams. He was leaving behind his eight Shermans to use as backup, ready for a fast call to any point where they may be needed.

Even though it was only 1400, Alex wanted to move out as soon as possible. Calling over an MP sergeant, Alex handed him the sealed letter to the brigadier general at regiment. He said, "As soon as the last truck leaves the compound drive very slowly to regiment. When you get there, tell the staff that you have orders from Major Vetov to give the sealed letter only to the general himself."

Alex waved the first half-track to start and he waited until about ten trucks had passed when he could stand it no longer. Corporal Walls, let's get in that line." Turning to his radio man he said, "The second you hear a call coming from regiment, hit the scramble button and hold it down until we are in action. Or until I see I've been wrong and we start back."

The sun was going down as they reached the other road going down to the docks. This was all farmland and there was heavy undergrowth covering the road on both sides. They were not tall fences and no doubt in good times the German farmers had kept the weeds and other growth out of their fences. However, after years of war, both sides of the road contained thick undergrowth. In places there was only three feet of cover and nothing that would stop a bullet. Some places, small trees rose six to ten feet tall. Surely this would not work like the hedgerow country, but would hide their 105s . There were a few farmhouses and buildings back away from the road.

Alex only had three high velocity 90 mm tank destroyers and noted two barns less than a mile down the road, one on each side of the road. He sent two of his 90s to hide in the barns and the third to go on farther down the road to stop anything that got through. Without his saying a word, his 105s had divided to both sides of the road and found themselves the best place they could find to hide. Bazooka teams only needed a little brush to hide themselves and they had done the same thing. Three company was spreading themselves out as in the distance came the clank of armor and the sound of many motors.

Alex turned to his radio man and said, "Headphones only, let's have it." Alex held one side of a head phone to his ear in time to hear his commanding general using language Alex had never heard him use before.

Alex said, "Major Vetov here, sir."

A little calmer the general asked, "Vetov, where the hell are you?"

Alex answered, "Right where I said I would be, sir, and I am looking at a column of German tanks coming right at me."

Without question, the first tank saw something and sent a big 88 shell down the road into the fence line. When it did every 105 started shooting at the lead Tiger tank or the tanks and trucks following. The two tank destroyers and a few 105s hit that Tiger several times. As strong as a Tiger tank is, so many anti-tank shells hitting it at the same time left nothing but a burning hunk of metal in the road. The American artillery was massacring the front of the German column. Back a ways, the German armor was coming through the fence and into the fields on both sides. It was now growing too dark to see much but the 105s were still taking out German trucks and equipment. The fires set shone a strange light over the battlefield.

Americans were using this light to fight the Germans, but the Germans were using the muzzle flash of American guns to fight back. American troops were now shooting up flares to help light up the advancing Germans and there were many more than Alex had expected. As American machine guns have a steady flash of muzzle fire, this attracted a lot of return fire from the German side. One by one American machine guns were destroyed, but the American mortars were taking out Germans with every shot, but there were so many of them and they just kept coming by, swinging further out into the fields where there were no American troops. The ones that got around just kept going and the American fire followed them until they were out of range. The rest of the night was spent mopping up, taking care of the wounded and collecting the American dead. Alex called the general back and said, "Sorry sir, we whipped them but we did not stop them all. We have heavy casualties and need much more medical help than we have, sir."

The general answered, "Men are coming to your aid and have been since your first shots. When you get your men taken care of, get yourself back here."

At this point Alex did not know if the general was pleased with the win or very unhappy with the commanding major.

By daylight there was at least another couple hundred men on the field besides the ones Alex had brought with him. First, ambulances and trucks were loaded with wounded both American and German--then trucks started gathering up the dead. Alex again called regiment and asked for permission to go after the Germans that had fled. No one other than the general would give him an answer, and the general had been up almost all night and was asleep.

When the general did call back all he said was, "Vetov, get yourself back here now."

Calling his driver, Alex said, "Wall's, get me to regiment H.Q." and off they went. It took over an hour to get there and Alex tried and tried to think up a good explanation. There was none that the general was going to like and Alex knew it. Once in the brigadier general's outer office, Alex realized what he looked like after spending a good part of the night on the damp ground dodging German bullets. He looked like he'd spent the last few days wrestling hogs in a hog pen. When he was finally ushered into the general's office the general and several staff were all there and looked like they were getting ready to meet General Eisenhower himself. Of course, the general always looked like that, even on Utah Beach he'd looked like that--except for the fact that then he was wearing a helmet and was now sitting in his plush chair.

The general continued looking over papers for several minutes. When he did look up, Alex gave him a salute and held it. The general gave him a half salute and said, "Major Vetov, what the hell have you done? Man, you have come up through the ranks. Haven't you yet learned what the chain of command means? I pulled for your last three promotions as you were a good front line officer, and had good instincts about front line fighting. You looked out for your men and had good battle records, except for one thing. You always did things your own way and now you have done your thing without even informing your superior officer. Now we have had more casualties in one night than any other single battalion has had since we crossed into Germany."

At that moment all Alex could think about was how far back he was going to get kicked. Were they going to take his commissioned officer status away, or even worse a court martial and who knows what else?

At that moment Alex decided it was best for him to just answer questions and not try to defend anything he had done. Sitting back in his chair the General asked, "How in heavens did you know when and where the Germans were coming from?"

Alex said, "Sir, I figured it out, sir."

The general said, "Where did you get your information from?"

Alex answered, "Sir, I figured it out myself, sir."

"If you figured it out all by yourself, major, why did you not know you were facing over one thousand German troops and thirty-one armored vehicles."

At this Alex looked surprised and said, "Sir, no sir. I missed that, sir."

After a long look the general said, "Well, you at least admit you do not know everything, major. You look like you fell into a mud puddle. Major, go and get yourself cleaned up and get some sleep and be back here at 0700 in the morning looking like a major. We are going to Division H.Q. And get this whole story. Dismissed, major."

And it was over at least until the next day. A great weariness descended upon him. He had had little sleep for the last three days and none at all in the last fifty hours. A hot shower, food, sleep, and a clean uniform helped.

Getting dressed the next morning, Alex tried to make up his mind if he should just wear his battle ribbons or also his medals. He had picked up quite a few by now: three full rows of combat ribbons, four medals from the French government as well as the ones from the U.S. Army. Now he looked the part of a 4th Division Major, even if he was a very young one. At H.Q. there were four staff cars waiting, Major Vetov was placed in the last one and off across Germany the column moved.

It took over three hours to reach division H.Q. That was located on a large estate like some of the ones Alex had seen in England.

In a large dining hall there were about 20 men gathered and Alex wondered if this was a court martial. No, that could not be. The Army had a very exact way of conducting a court martial and, for certain, the army never does anything that is not by the book. That fact stung a little now as Alex realized that was exactly why he was here now. All the ranking officers were seated around the table and this was something Alex had never heard of in military matters.

Two star Major General Harwell, while remaining seated, said, "Gentlemen, this is an enquiry as to the events taking place in Section B 9 three days ago. The primary goal of this meeting is to find out how this engagement took place without the knowledge of division."

It was a long day as Alex explained how his orders were to hold his assigned ground, mop up that assigned area, and look for any way of capturing one of the two bridges over the Plumb River. Lastly, he'd been commanded to stop German troops from getting over the river to carry on the fight. Alex explained how he had studied his position to best fulfill his orders. His men had scouted around to try to locate any large collections of German troops. If they had armor, he could only figure one place they might be hiding that had roads sufficient to get them to the river in a hurry. As this was only a hunch, he did a resonance in force to check out his idea. Then when everything came together he was sure the Germans would be on the move within hours so he moved to block them and see if he was correct. He had sent word back by personal delivery to division as he'd had an experience in which the German army had nearly destroyed his entire company by listening to their radio signal. He also explained how he saw no real difference—that is, he'd done almost the same thing tracking down and destroying Peiper's tanks, for which he had been given the Silver Star and a commendation. It had never been his intention to not follow orders but only to fulfill them to the best of his ability. Many questions were fired at him for hours, but he told things just as they were. He left a few things out very much on purpose.

When it was all over, General Harwell said personally to Alexander that he needed to be careful about keeping division informed on all plans and movements. Then with a half smile and half smirk he said, "Young man, are you planning on going into politics after the war?"

With a look of surprise, Alex said, "No sir, I had never even thought about it, sir."

The general said, "You ought to think about it, son. You would make a very successful one."

When they got back to battalion, Alex was treated with a cool attitude by most of the officers of equal rank or above. His captains greeted him cordially enough, considering every one that had been in battle with him that week had lost many friends. That put a strong damper on things. Army publicity boys put out the story that division had faced and fought what was probably the last big fight on this side of the Plumb River, with the loss of much of Germany's remaining armor on this side. Alex's battalion had won a great victory but at very great cost as well in both men and equipment. He was still in charge of the same three sections and still had the same orders. Just a lot less to do it with until new men and equipment arrived.

The bombed out docks had never left his mind, and now he wondered how many of those Germans that had gotten around him had made it there. If they had, that meant a large number would be trapped with nowhere to go.

This was just too good to pass up and this was his section. It was also his orders to "mop up" Germans trapped on this side of the river. He notified the colonel that he was going upriver to check things out while he waited on reinforcements. Taking two platoons from Kilo Company that had not been in the earlier battle, they took a back road around the main river road and approached the docks, remaining hidden. They watched a long time and it did not make sense that there were fewer Germans there than before. There was a change, however. The whole area had been moved around. This made no sense at all; something was going on. After dark, Alex and three men slipped down to the far side of the docks close to the river. After it got dark a few dim lights started to appear among the bomb damage in the dockyard. Then a motor cranked and one of the upside down barges began to move away from the water's edge. The moonlight shining on the river reflected its light on the river and Alex could see two steel cables come up out of the water and become somewhat tight across the river. Here, the Plumb River was only about fifty yards wide and the banks were fairly steep. It was late February and the river was running bank deep with all the melting ice and snow from upriver.

A small German scout car pulled a mid-size barge up close to the riverbank and a small German artillery piece was loaded into it, then another. A larger motor than the one before cranked and the barge began to swing toward the river. On the other side of the river a light flashed three quick flashes and the barge was pulled into the river. The four Americans watched as the barge made a round trip and while it was going and coming they could see several welders working among the damaged barges–that were being repaired. This could be easily seen as welding torches create a lot of light. This light also showed the steel tracks of several heavy tanks and the wheels of trucks. The upside down barges were being used to cover the German vehicles. The Germans were rapidly repairing this damaged barge yard. Even more surprising was the fact that when the barge returned, it was loaded with men and equipment. It was not long until the barge was reloaded with two more small artillery pieces and started back across again. Several barges, most upside down, were scattered along the riverbank like a spilled box of matches. Just like bombing would have thrown them around. A crane came to life and an upside down barge was uprighted close to where Alex and his men had chosen to hide. The men could smell the welding work had already been done on these barges and they were ready for use. Some of this was making sense and some pieces just did not fit together.

Higher upon the bank a guard dog started barking like it was going crazy and the Americans could hear the guards talking. One of Alex's men knew German better than Alex did and announced that they were coming down to inspect the barges and follow the dog. Alex had never gotten 100% of his hearing back anyway. There was no choice but to move as close to the water as they could and go into that super cold water to get around the end of one barge. The dog could not follow their scent in the water. There between the one barge was a second barge that was setting partly over the other one to make it look destroyed. Underneath the barge on top was a boat like the navy uses. It was about 25 feet long with a motor mounted in the middle of the boat. It had a lot of working tools and welding equipment that were being used in working on these barges. These tools were covered front and rear by large tarps and the boat was tied to the inside of the upside down barge. Very softly, Alex instructed them to get in. The two ropes were cut and Alex and his men pushed the boat out into the river and quickly slid under the tarps. The current was strong and no one seemed to notice the boat drifting away. But Alex waited a long time before taking a peek. The current had taken them to the German side of the river. As the current took them to that side it had already shoved much trash and debris to that side as well. Not far away was the biggest bridge of the two in Alex's sectors. He briefly thought of trying to start the motor but instantly realized that was a stupid idea as that bridge was well-guarded. They stayed under the tarps and tried not to shake too much as they were all wet and very cold. After a while the boat bumped into something, moved a little and then stopped. Before looking, the men listened for a long time, finally Alex took a quick look—then a few minutes later a longer look. The bridge was built with steel beams coming up from a large concrete base a short way out into the river.

Their boat had stuck between the concrete base and the river bank that was also filled with trash and debris. The boat was right up against the concrete base and Alex thought he might be able to get on the base and pull the boat outso they could float around, continue downstream and maybe find a place where they could get to the American side. Try as he may, that boat loaded down with tools was as tight as if it was welded into place. The current coming downriver was stronger here and it held the boat like steel. Alex got back into the boat and told the other three men what the problem was. They continued talking very softly, even though the running water around the concrete piling was making quite a bit of noise. One man said, "Maybe I can get some of this trash out of the way and we can float through."

Another said, "If I can slip some of these heavy tools overboard without making any noise it will make this thing lighter." Moving the big welding machine was out of the question but there must have been a half ton of other things in the boat. Alex agreed to both ideas and he climbed out onto the concrete to try to get a better look in the semi-dark. On the downriver side of the concrete where the steel started there was a ladder going up to the bridge. Since it was on the inside of the bridge and no one could see him, he could barely see a steel walkway up above him. Climbing up to it he found a service walkway leading across the river. It had several large pipes on the inside tied to the bridge and a little work platform where the pipes could be reached. There was a fairly large bundle of wires under his feet. In spite of the darkness Alex could see a large bundle of packages hanging under the bridge. Some of the wires went down to the bundles and Alex knew just what he was looking at. He got down on his knees and started cutting wires. Then he hurried to the second bundle and started cutting them. At the third bundle his knife was getting dull and both hands hurt as he had been using both. There was now just enough daylight to see the shapes of things around him. Alex had thought that maybe the walkway went all the way across the river and they could escape that way but it did not. He had no idea it had taken him so long as he hurried back to the boat. Getting back to where he'd first cut the wires, Alex stopped about ten feet past the cut, pulled the pin on a hand grenade, and carefully stuck it under the wires so the firing lever would fly off if the wires were moved. He quickly climbed down the ladder and into the boat. It had been worked free and the men had the boat tied to the downriver side waiting for him to return. They got in and re-covered themselves with the tarps and Alex saw they had put every tool in the boat over the side except the welder.

Drifting down the river, Alex wished he had stopped long enough to cut off a few packs of German explosives from one of the large bundles and put it with his hand grenade to have blown a section of the service walk off the bridge to make it much harder to repair the damage he'd done. Knowing how important it was to get the word to H.Q., Alex waited fifteen minutes then threw the back tarp overboard and started the motor. As soon as the motor kicked in he rushed to the tiller in the back of the boat and headed to the American side of the river. Sure enough there were G,I.s pointing M1s at them as they climbed out of the boat. His first sentence was, "Thanks guys, you never looked so good. I need a radio to get regiment right now. Grab that boat; we may need it." Reaching his colonel, Alex quickly explained the situation and told him that he had disabled the explosives on the bridge and if the bridge was attacked in force before the damage could be repaired they had their bridgehead over the Plumb River in their hands.

The colonel said, "Vetov, have you never learned anything yet? Only division or corps headquarters can make such decisions. I hear that H.Q. is more interested in getting all those bridges blown up to keep the Germans on this side from getting away. Go back to your men and get them ready to join the line as we push forward tomorrow."

Alex hung up and told the radio man to get General Harwell at division and as quickly as possible. When division answered, the radio man asked for an emergency call from Major Vetov. It was denied. Alex shouted into the radio, "The B eight bridge is open right now. This will not last more than for a few hours, you son of a bitch. Unless you let me talk to General Harrwell right now, hundreds of G.I.s are going to die because of you."

The general came on and the first thing Alex said was, "The B eight bridge is open right now, general. This is Major Vetov and you can put me in front of a firing squad if you want to, sir. I cut all the demolition wires myself before daylight, sir, and it will not take the Germans long to work it out and repair those lines. If that bridge is attacked now the 4th will be across the Plumb River before tonight, sir. I called my Colonel and he did not believe me, sir, you can do anything you want to with me but this will save more of my men's lives, I lost too many already." Again Alex hung up, called his regiment and said, "The bridge is open; take the Shermans and everything you've got and hit that bridge fast. I will be there as soon as I possibly can.

Major Vetov commandeered an army truck and headed for B 8. Those oak leaves still had some clout in this Army. When he did arrive, one of his captains saluted him and said, "Sir, you are no paper pusher, sir."

When Alexander arrived at the bridge it had already been taken by his men. A captain said, "It was the proudest moment in my life when I watched one of our Shermans go over that bridge, sir. There is still hard fighting on the other bank, but we have a good foothold over there and the Third Army is bringing up full reinforcements and we already have full air support. By this time tomorrow we should have control of everything for ten miles in all directions. Alex saluted the captain again and said, "Is my driver here? I need to get out of these wet clothes."

After a hot shower Major Alexander Vetov did not even get something to eat, he returned to his tent and fell asleep.

The next morning there were two MPs waiting outside his tent. They were polite but insistent. He was to return to division with them. Explaining he had not eaten anything in over thirty hours they took him to the mess tent. There Alex felt like the condemned man eating his last meal, but he didn't really care. After he ate he got into the MP jeep and headed for division. As rough as that jeep ride was, Alex did not care and he went back to sleep anyway.

Facing General Harrwell again, all Alex knew to do was salute. Again the general returned the salute just as he did the last time. The general was sitting while Alex stood at full attention. After a long wait the general said, "At ease," then after another long two minutes he said, "Have a seat. Major, I have no idea what to do with you. I should have you shot just like you recommended I do, but that would be a bad thing to do to one of the bravest men I have ever commanded. As well as being the hard-headedest, most uncooperative, disrespectful men ever to wear the uniform. You should have the Medal of Honor right before you are drummed out of the service. You cannot be rewarded, as you have not observed military protocol. You cannot be punished as you have showed initiative and done this division great service from the day your boots hit the ground on Utah Beach. Hell, I have no idea what to do with you. Your men will die for you and you have the greatest respect of any major in the 4th among the non-coms and enlisted men. Most commissioned officers hate your guts. Yet in spite of your rank you are looked at as if you were still a sergeant, and I might add you still act like one. You were one of my most promising officers and yet," a long pause, "I do not know what to do with you. After the last episode you pulled, do not imagine I didn't see how you played the jailhouse lawyer at your board of inquiry. I should transfer you out, but I would not do that to any other commander in any branch of the service. Until I get this figured out you are going to come here and work in division intelligence as a major. Do not ever try to play sergeant on me again. Is that understood? Your days of pulling a trigger are over. You figured out the German escape plans by looking at maps and reports. That is now what you are going to do, for the 4th and not for Vetov. You have two weeks to get your battalion squared away and ready for a new commander. You know that it should have only been given to a lieutenant colonel in the first place, you were just so damn good you got the job."

Returning to his tent, Alex started getting his things together. Corporal Walls was the first to ask permission to enter. Then he just blurted out, "Every man in the battalion wants to know what happened and what was going on."

Without going into details, Alex explained he was being transferred to division intelligence in two weeks. Did this mean a step up or a drop? Walls wanted to know. Alex said he would just have to wait and see, as he was not sure himself. He only knew he would no longer have his battalion.

"Do I go too?" Walls asked.

Alex grinned. "Hell, yes you do. You will have to go as my adjacent or assistant but we will work that out. I've got two weeks to get everything together for the new commanding officer to take over. I want everything in tip top shape when he gets here. Spread the word to bring all my captains in. I need to talk to them. What has been done about that dockyard?" Walls disappeared and Alex headed for battalion H.Q. with his map case and his personal notes. Walls was gone and of course so was his jeep, so Alex walked the fifty plus yards up to H.Q. In his old office, Alex received all the aerial photos of the dockyard and looked them over noting that they were all the old ones from three weeks ago. He called regiment to see if they had any newer ones and was told no. With some hesitation he called the lieutenant colonel's office to request new aerial resonance photos of the docks and the building across the river. As this was the same man he had called last week and was told to stand down, he was on edge. He needed to update photos, however, and since he was still in charge of B 9 he had the right to request them. The corporal that answered informed Alexander that the colonel had been transferred and as yet no new man had been transferred in. He was further told that he would have to make his request directly to division to request a new photo run over B 9.

Alex thought about this before calling, but he knew what he had seen at the docks. This was still his section and he needed updated information, so he called division intelligence and requested the new photo flyover. Speaking to a Captain Wallace, Alex was told that his request would require him to submit forms IPR 409, 411 and 412 for immediate information request. It would take two to three weeks going through channels, and still require IPR 409 and 411. Alex suddenly realized, No wonder this war is taking forever to get things done.

The voice on the phone said, "Sir, are you the Major Vetov that is coming to join us in the basement."

Alex said, "Yes, I am being transferred in two weeks, why?"

"Major, your reputation precedes you. Better wear your winter coat as you are going to get a cold reception here in the basement."

"Basement, what do you mean?" Alex asked.

A soft laugh came over the wire. "Then you do not know we are literally in the Estate basement. The cold reception? That's because you are a field officer without background in intelligence and as a major you will outrank every man here but five and three of those are majors. This is the funnest thing that has ever come into our little group. I think it's great, and I know several of the others do also. The top five think it is terrible that an outsider with the rank of major is being forced on them by our general and recommended by our three star 4th Division General himself, They're all scared to death of you and who you have backing you up. Tell you what, major, form 412 is the reason for immediate aerial recognizance. Tell me what it is, and I will fill it out for you right here. I have enough on file here to fill out 409 and 411. I will mark it urgent and send it up to corp tonight and they'll review it tomorrow morning, first thing. You understand it will be your name on all the pages. If it is ever questioned, I never talked to you and I have no idea how it got through. The general's office approves all dispatches before they go to corp, but there are thirty or so going out this evening and his office will just stamp them all approved before sending them up. They will send them back to me for shipment and I'll wait till I get them back to use the urgent stamp so it will not require extra attention.

"Now I need the reason in great detail or it will get dropped to the bottom of the pile."

"This is going to take awhile," Alex said, and started the story of his examination of the barges. How the Germans had been repairing and welding supporting steel runners to the bottom of large grain barges so that they could transport tanks and heavy equipment across the Plumb River at night. He personally had seen them moving artillery across with an elaborate steel wire apprentice. This had always been the German plan—to get their men and equipment across and the bridge was just a distraction. As his battalion had taken the bridge, the Germans must have gone into high gear to get as much as possible across."

The captain asked a few questions and said, "There is a lot here so let me get started. Remember, we have never met or talked. Welcome aboard, major, we are going to work well together."

Thinking it over Alex said, "Well, now I know I will not be alone up there. There was nothing else Alex could do about plans for the docks until he got those new photos. There was tons of other work to do and it was again late before he returned to his tent for sleep. The next morning Alex had breakfast and got right to getting things taken care of. He was in his jeep when his radio man got a call. With a white face he handed the head set to Alex and said, "General of the Army R. O. Borton for you, major."

Walls stopped the jeep fast as Alex puts his headphones on, "Major Vetov here, sir."

"This is General Borton. Major, how close are your troops to that river crossing."

Alex said, "Most are less than a mile and some are within a half mile, sir."

"Major, get all your men out of there as fast as you can. Everyone needs to be ten miles away or at least as far as they can get. Our Air Force is bringing in enough bombs to turn that whole area into fine dust. When your men hear our planes coming they need to send up red smoke so they do not get bombed. Got that? Red smoke. There will be several air strikes so do not try to move forward until you are ordered to do so. By the way, major, that is the kind of intelligence work we need more of. I have the photos you requested on my desk and I have compared them to older photos and believe you are right."

Within a minute every American two-radio was sending out warnings of the incoming air strike. Within forty-five minutes a flight of medium Mitchell light bombers zoomed overhead and then the clear sounds of bombs fifteen miles away could be heard. Alex ground his teeth as he believed there had not been time for many of his men to get out. Before the Mitchells were even gone here came not less than twenty Thunderbolt fighter bombers. These are followed by P-52 Mustangs. With every flight Alex could imagine some of his men getting plastered. Now things quieted down and he had his radio man start calling his units.

"All report they are having no problem as all the air strikes seem to be right on the docks and across the river. Every caller was told to keep moving as the orders were to get ten miles away. Even while he was talking, a large flight of British Halker Hurricanes came in and pounded the target. As they flew off, the cloud of smoke and dust was larger even at this great distance. For nearly an hour things were quiet except an occasional explosion from the docks or across the river. Then at a distance came the sound of a single aircraft. It flew back and forth over the bombed area and flew off again. Later on, Alex learned that an all points alert had been sent out for all Allied aircraft available to come and hit this special target. This late in the war there were a lot of aircraft and many were just waiting to get another target. Alex wondered if that captain might have spiced up that report a little or maybe a lot. Late that day Alex sent a scouting mission to check things out. There was not even enough a road left around the dockyard for the half-track to drive into the dock area.

At the first of Alex's two weeks before being reassigned, replacements of men and equipment started arriving. Alex was pleased to learn that many of the large number of men reported wounded on the road the night of his cross country run to cut off the Germans, turned out to have minor wounds and most would fully recover in time. This helped a little in his preparations to leave his men. Another thing that helped was to learn that a well-experienced battlefield lieutenant colonel was going to take over. Then the heavens fell in upon him.

He knew things were not going well between him and Becky but he had told himself that once they got back together things would work out. On this day there was a little bump in his envelope from Becky and as he opened the letter a small piece of tissue paper fell into his hand. Just looking at it Alex knew what it was before he unfolded Becky's engagement ring. Getting into his jeep, Alex drove several miles outside camp before he stopped and tears came. It was an hour before he could read his Dear Alex letter, as he covered it with tears and shaking hands. Becky's old boyfriend, a soldier in the British army had gone missing in action two years earlier. He'd been reported as killed in action while in reality he'd been in a German prisoner of war camp until it had been liberated. When he had returned to England he was in very poor health. Becky had been nursing him back to health and the old flame just sprang back up. She was very sorry. She'd loved Alex but things change. She wished him the best of everything but she was going to get married just as soon as her British boyfriend was discharged from the army.

It was dark when Alex got back to his tent and he went right in and closed the tent flap. By morning he had pulled himself together on the outside but was jelly inside. He did his work like a zombie. Everyone left him alone as Walls had seen Alex open the letter. Walls was a good man but he'd always talked too much. Every man in the battalion knew Alex had got a Dear John letter.

Staying busy was Alex's best way to deal with things, so now he just moved even faster. By the time of change of command the next week, Alex was at least acting like his old self.

11

INTELLIGENCE

Moving to intelligence was an altogether new way of life for Major Alexander Vetov. First, he was moved into some newly constructed officers' barracks behind the main buildings on the Estate. Next he was assigned an office in the basement of the main estate building. Only the five ranking officers had private offices. Captains and down were all in one large room with many desks. Two more sections contained the communications office, then the photo and mapping division. The main floor was all army executive offices, a large conference room and the rest of the once rich estate owners' smaller rooms full of desks. The two upper floors Alex never got to, so it was anyone's guess. The bottom floor was always a bee hive of activity, while the basement was a closed off little world unto itself. Several women worked there and some of the men did not even wear uniforms. Often the more casual worked without ties and with sleeves rolled up. The air circulation was nearly non-existent and most were smoking. Many doors had a "no admittance without proper clearance" sign on them and Alex learned he would only be given clearance to some of these rooms with passes that he guessed he would have to earn. A guard stood before the two rooms that said photo and maps and the other door was communications. His major's rank got him into these two rooms and here he found a Captain Wallace who smiled at him and said, "Glad to meet you, sir," and winked at him. This captain

---

was in charge of the commutations room of intelligence and Alex knew they were going to get along just fine. Four offices were labeled major and three had last names under major. On Alex's door major was all it said, and for the first few weeks that was just how Alex felt, the man with no name.

The six head intelligence officers started every day with a meeting to discuss the day's plans, but most of the time they talked like he was not even there. For his first full day Alex spent most of it in photo and maps. He started the second there also. He asked where the large battlefield maps were and he was told they were all in the main conference room on the main floor. Well, it was all or nothing, and he headed upstairs wearing his Intelligence sign around his neck and making sure his oak leaves were shining. The guard at that door saw the Intelligence sign around a major's neck and he opened the door for Alex. Then he closed it behind Alex as he went into the conference room. Alex was surprised that only the highest ranking officers were being saluted. It does make sense, as men were going everywhere all the time. One large map showed the top left quarter of Germany with arrows and a blue background indicating wherever 4th Battalion of was. The third battalion was in red and varied colors for the rest of the American forces. The British forces were in brown with their names and numbers written in. The far side showed all the Russian army in black with several curving black lines with dates printed beside them. This showed where the Russians were on what dates, but gave no other information like the American and British movements did. There were small pins with numbers on them all over the place on the map and there was a large loose leaf book on a stand that was on wheels. Alex looked at his B sections, glanced at the several numbers there and located them in the book. It contained a lot of information and showed file numbers. Alex had his map case and in it he had a notebook that he took out and was comparing things when the general and several high ranking officers walked in.

Alex came to attention and saluted. All the men returned the salute but not with much enthusiasm. The general looked at Alex and addressed the others, "Gentlemen, for those of you that do not know our latest addition to intelligence, this is Major Alex Vetov."

Alex had met most of the men and was introduced to all, then the general took Alex aside and asked what he was doing in the conference room. Alex said, "I'm trying to learn everything I can about anything that will help me work in intelligence."

The general said, "Son, no one is allowed to write down anything shown on these maps and leave this room with it. Even intelligence is not supposed to be in here without an appointment. Intelligence has most of this information in Maps and Photos downstairs." Turning back to the others, he said, "Major Vetov has a very interesting service record, but major, we need the room."

Alex apologized and excused himself. In his rush to get out of the room he nearly ran over his new colonel coming in. The colonel had a shocked expression on his face as he saw it was Alex and right behind him came the general. Alex saluted his CO and departed down the stairs for Maps and Photos. The next morning in the intelligence officers' meeting the colonel said to the group, "I met Major Vetov yesterday morning coming out of a meeting with the general and division staff before I went in. Every man there stared at Vetov as the colonel then started the meeting, but from that day forward Alex was no longer on the sidelines. Nothing more was said about it, but things changed in the officer meetings.

Considering the line of proposed advancement from his old position at the Plumb River Bridge deeper into Germany, Alex was given the job of getting as much information as possible about German forces directly in front of his old regiment. He dove in like a harbor seal, studying the maps and aerial photos until his eyes hurt. Most of the staff worked long hours but Alex worked longer than anyone. He also reached out to other agencies all the time. The Officer of Strategic Services (OSS) often had bits of information that really helped on matters that military intelligence did not have. He made phone friends with British military intelligence and those guys were really great regarding all kinds of information. He found out what information he was allowed to share, and who tightened his ability to get more information. If he could have, Alex would have had half of all the Army Air Force photo reconnaissance flying just for the 4th. He succeeded in getting the newest and latest photo enlargement equipment into division H.Q. As Patton's 3rd army was running in front of the 4th he was getting all the information he could on where the 3rd was and what resistance they had met and seen. In turn he was sharing all he knew and what he thought the third was facing. Many times he was right in his estimates and now Patton's intelligence people were doing a lot more sharing. Every day Alex was notified what Patton's tanks had seen and what they thought they had run past. Being careful not to go around his lieutenant colonel or full colonel, he passed this information on to them and they passed it on to the general staff in daily planning sessions.

Often questions would arise to which the colonels did not have the answer, so they started bringing Major Vetov with them to staff meetings. Alex's findings and thoughts about what could work in the advance of the 4th sparked a renewed striving among many of the intelligence staff to present their ideas as well as just gathering facts. Then they'd reason together to come up with the best ideas. These ideas would be exchanged with other intelligence units before being presented in the respective division staff meetings. Intelligence in the entire 3rd and 4th army improved as they marched across Germany. This was not to say there wasn't still a lot of hard fighting for the troops. All the rivers were the worst as every one was used by the German army to slow the Americans. When they approached the Kyll River on the fourth of March all the bridges had been blown and there was enough forest on both banks to provide cover for both armies from which to fight. After learning from OSS that boats were being brought in to cross the Rhine River, Alex called British Intelligence to find out where those Bailey bridges were that they'd used in Holland. Then he suggested to his colonel to call and ask the British for the loan of the Bailey bridges. As they were just sitting in south Holland, Alex had a good chance of getting them. The call was made and the British said yes, so Alex started the basement staff into studying the aerial photos of the banks of the old bridges on the Kyll River. Now that it was March, the water on the river had dropped and the current was not bad. The river itself was a very twisting , turning river. This made the current run the strongest against the bank that made the water turn. It made every other turn easy on the American side and then in a mile or two it would reverse itself. Boats could be put into the easy flow on the American side, float down a short distance, and then come out on an easy flow bank on the German side. The exact spots, however, needed to be seen from the ground.

Doing this himself just made his feet burn for the chance, but he knew better and called upon the new CO of his old battalion and asked if some of his old scouting squads could do this for Intelligence if the scouting was approved by division. Alex asked, "Who is going to ask division?" and no one volunteered. So Alex said he was going to ask himself and took it to division staff. When it was accepted, everything was put into action. Next morning of the sixth the 4th division arrived and started shelling the German side and the Air Force came in to help. Walking the artillery fire back just a little away from the German side of the river gave Alex's old scout crews time to examine and photograph places that looked good for launching boats into the river. The scouts also examined five bridge crossings that had been blown up but still had concrete embankments on both sides. As soon as Intelligence had the information and pictures, it was all developed and studied. Before daylight the boats began to arrive. After a heavy artillery pounding of German positions, boats were launched and over 600 Americans stormed ashore on the other side to hold that bank By mid-afternoon they held over five miles of riverfront on the German side of the river. Both the Bailey bridges came in on big British trucks, along with three British troop trucks The British had brought their own men to assemble their bridges. By 0430 the next morning the first Bailey was across and the first of Patton's 3rd army Shermans were across. In less than an hour the other Bailey was across about five miles downriver and the 4th army armor was heading across. The two American armies had hit the Kyll River and in less than fifty hours on March sixth and seventh they accomplished the entire operation. It had been planned to take at the least four or five days and every one was very pleased with this.

Listening to the radio reports in the communications room, Alex was trying to get the latest reports on moving toward the Rhine River. A report broke in declaring that a spear head group of the 9th Armored Division of the 1st American Army had rushed forward to the Rhine at Remagen, Germany and lo and behold the bridge across the river was still standing. Everyone knew the Germans were trying to get as many of their troops with as much equipment as possible to the east side. It had been reported that all the bridges across the Rhine were destroyed. The bridge into Remagen was still standing intact, with German troops and equipment going over to the east side. The ninth Armored rushed down with their tanks to cut off the escaping enemy. This was easy as the retreating German troops did not have any heavy armor with them that could stand up against the American Sherman tanks. The Shermans rushed the bridgehead on the west side and drove the defenders across to the east side. Every German that was on or near the bridge hurried on across. Then the ones too far away to get over just scattered. There were German defenses on the west bank but they were not ex-pecting to see an American army coming for them. They were not equipped to hold off American tanks and were soon neutralized. Everyone knew that the Germans would blow up the bridge as soon as the Americans had control of the west side. One Sherman tank pulled up onto the bridge and started across, firing his cannon and machine guns into the defenses on the other side. He did not slow down as he advanced and every man stood looking, expecting the bridge to go up in a ball of fire. When the Sherman started getting close to the German side, the Germans did set off one section of the bridge and lots of debris and smoke flew in every direction. All the bridge had been wired with explosives, tons of explosives, but only one section exploded. When the smoke cleared, the bridge was still standing and that Sherman just kept on going.

More Shermans pulled onto the bridge and took off after the first. Most men still thought more explosions would follow the first, but there were no more. Men and all kinds of equipment went over that damaged bridge. A voice screamed over the radio, "It is still standing, we are going across; it is still standing and we are going."

Everyone in the basement was just standing and listening to that broadcast, when Alex said, "That was the bravest tank crew on this earth to try to get over that bridge. Hell no, those were the bravest men to ever put on an American uniform." With that Alex ran out of the room. He took the stairs three at a time up to the first floor and ran for the conference room. Rushing through the door-way he shouted to all. "We are in, the first Army has crossed the Rhine, and we are over the Rhine and have a bridgehead. General, we are in Germany two weeks ahead of plans."

Everyone was looking at Alex like he has gone stark raving mad when others came in and declared it was true. The general looked at Alex and said, "Get me details, get me details." Alex was out of the room as fast as he'd come in and went down those stairs a little more carefully than he had come up. Joining the men and women around the radio, a breathless Alex said, "What's new?"

"All we hear is fighting," someone said.

Alex grabbed a pen and started writing, he spun around and bumped into the general himself. "Sorry sir, got to get this off," and pushed the note into one of the radio operators' hands.

"Send to all units, starting with the Air Force. Those men need help right now, the whole German nation is going to counter attack them with everything Germany has. Taking that bridge will all be for nothing unless we can get there first, with the most, and the Air Force can get there the fastest."

Quickly turning to another man he said, "Whatever the Germans still have in air power they are going to use to bring that bridge down. Our men need fighter cover and anti-aircraft fire power."

To another he said, "Find out what heavy artillery the Germans have close to Remagen, what it is and how much they have. Those boys are going to need anti-aircraft guns to protect that bridge as fast as it can be moved. Get me 9th Army intelligence and ask what we can do to help." To another Alex said, "Send someone out and get every person in our intelligence unit as we are going to need them all."

Turning to the general, Alex said, "Sorry, sir, every second counts and turned back to his note pad, writing as fast as he could. When he did look up the general was gone and Alex knew he had not followed protocol. To hell with protocol! Right now the army had to be ready to outthink and out-move the Germans. Three things: first, protect that bridge, without it our boys will be cut off and whipped. Second, getting the information these men need today meant the sooner the end of this war. Third is to find out if that bridge was going to stay up. After all, a section of it was blown up.

"We need information and we need it all right now so we can get it to the right men." Alex was working on how the Germans might be trying to destroy that bridge when the first Army intelligence called back. When he took the phone all he said was, "Major Vetov with the 4th Intelligence. How can we help?"

After a few minutes of talk Alex again said, I cannot imagine how busy you guys are, so any of the footwork we can do to help, we will do it."

The next call Alex received was from OSS, the office of strategic services. These were the people who controlled spying behind the lines, undercover operations, and other top secret army information of all types. The gears of Intelligence were meshing together and working very well to get the job done.

Fourth Division was given the job of getting every piece of anti-aircraft guns together around the bridge as quickly as possible. Even finding who had what and where it was, was hard to do. Another night of little sleep, but things were coming together as anti-aircraft units were on the way. Even though Alex and his unit were not part of the 1st Army, they were treated as brothers. Now word was coming in regarding who was doing what, even the Germans. Surprisingly, even though the Germans were fighting hard to push the Americans back, on the eighth of March the Americans did not face more than they could handle. American engineers were trying their best to shore up the damaged bridge while starting to build a new platoon bridge across the river. The one thing that was expected did happen. The German Air Force that was supposed to no longer have aircraft came in with both fighters and light bombers. The Germans had never gotten involved with heavy bombers except for a few as an experiment. For the Germans, the light bombers were much more useful. Of course, the presence of German aircraft greatly increased the danger to both the old bridge and the new one under construction. The only good side of this, if there was a good side, is the fact that all their planes were only interested in the bridge and mostly left the American troops alone. Before it was over the Germans had sent in well over 300 fighters and bombers. This was well over the number Allied intelligence thought they could get together.

With every hour more American anti-aircraft guns were showing up. The large group of German planes on the second day hurried up the arrival of more American guns. The ninth was a different story. Germany brought in large numbers of troops, armor, artillery, mortars and fought hard to push the Americans back into the Rhine. The American Air Force showed up in large numbers to give cover for American troops and to defend the bridges. The American heavy bombers plastered every road, bridge, and railroad, and at night the British took over without a letup in air power. It was a good thing they did, as the German Air Force showed up again in force. The top brass could not believe that the Germans had that much left, especially the air power. That night the old bridge was closed for six hours as engineers tried to make major improvements in its strength and repair the one close-by hit by a German bomb. Night had been when most men working on or crossing the old bridge felt reasonably safe. That night there was a German night raid against the bridge. Plans were changed that night as it was decided that the lights and especially the welding torches made too good a target. The night work would not be stopped until at the first siren announcing the arrival of German aircraft. This would call for a blackout and men to take cover wherever possible. When the all clear was sounded the men were right back to work.

That night the Germans tried something different. While the German bombers were dropping bombs from a higher altitude than normal, one of the 37 MM American anti-aircraft crewmen noticed a lot of floating objects in the river. He lowered his barrels on his thirty seven and shot one, there was a tremendous explosion. He sprayed the river with his thirty seven and many of the objects exploded with tremendous force. The Germans had brought many navy anti-ship mines and released them upriver, timing the current for the mines to reach the bridge at the time of the bombing attack. These nines are powerful enough to sink warships and could have done great damage to the bridges. One of the mines got stuck in the rubber float pontoons of the new bridge, but the rubber floats were soft and did not make the mine explode. One mine hit something in the river and exploded and several were exploded by 37 MM shells. Several others floated under the bridge without hitting anything. These were both contact mines and magnetic mines so they had to be released away from each other so as not to cause each other to explode. With daylight came huge explosions close to the bridge but none hit it. The next day some of the huge searchlights that had been brought in to search the night sky for enemy aircraft were now deployed as far upriver as the Americans had control. Then all along the river they searched the night river to see if any more of the ship mines might be in the river again. Also early the next morning four high-speed boats started for the bridges timed so the sun would be in enemy eyes. All four were shot and exploded by cannon fire from the west bank, sun or not. Not long after that, a new high pitched whine was heard as three of German's latest top secret 234B-2 turbojet bombers came flying down the river at speeds no American fighter could catch. This same speed made it very hard for American gunners to swing their guns fast enough to shoot at them. One was shot down in spite of its super speed. The other two dropped their bombs and missed. It was thought that the planes were so new that their pilots had not learned how differently their bombs were going to fall at over five hundred miles per hour.

March 9th was going to be a long day as Germany opened fire from a huge long-range cannon that was so large it could only be moved by special railway cars. It was known that these railroad guns had a range of twenty miles and fired a huge shell. At the same time the Germans opened up with several 600 MM mortars. This is almost as large a shell as a 24-inch navy cannon fired from a huge mortar tube. These guns could have brought down the bridge if they hit it. They had no spotters to correct their fire so the shells hit all over the place doing a lot of damage, even killing a number of German civilians as well as American troops. Not one shell hit either bridge. However the shock waves did damage the new floating bridge.

This was repaired on March 10th and also on this day the 4th division was called to a halt and a full camp was set up. The entire division was given a rest. Hot showers, hot food and resupplies to get ready for one of the largest river crossings in Europe. The Rhine River in Germany is one of the really big rivers in Europe. While most of the 4th was getting rest and preparing for the rush to the Rhine River the Intelligence division was hard at work. For this big push every planning, intelligence, resource, Air Force and supply part of the American army came into play. The navy and coast guard was brought in to supply the assault craft that had been used on D-Day. Just getting them from the English channel across Europe to the Rhine River was a major undertaking.

That night there was another try to down the big bridge at Remagen. The German navy sent seven underwater demolition swimmers. These were wearing top secret Italian-developed underwater breathing gear. These were non-bubbling underwater breathing apparatus far advanced from anything the Americans had. What the Americans developed was also top secret but still left a line of bubbles in the water. Another top secret item that did work was a motion and magnetic underwater detection equipment that turned on underwater defense lights. All seven swimmers were shot and killed before reaching the bridge. While the taking of the Rhine Bridge at Remagen was a very important part, one bridge head was not enough to win this war. The Allies needed bridgeheads all up and down the Rhine River. The 4th Division was assigned to be a follow up division and not be the front of the spear this time. Maybe the Army had decided to let some other troops do it for a change. Regardless, 4th division Intelligence did not get a shot at working plans to cross the Rhine, but neither did it ever get to rest. On the 14th of March Alex got the word that Hitler had made another try at downing the bridge at Remagen. This time the V-2 rockets had been aimed at the bridge

and did not even get as close as the railroad gun had done. The closest one landed a quarter mile away and, like the cannon and huge mortar fire, only killed people that were in the vicinity. The scuttlebutt had it that the Americans were going to let Montgomery and the British cross the Rhine first upriver. On the seventh of March that wonderful old bridge came crashing down into the Rhine River all on its own. Many Americans lost their lives as the engineers were still trying to save it and it was still transporting troops to the east side of the river.

There was much debate over whether Patton disobeyed orders to stand down and wait for the British to cross or not. Whichever, on the night of March 22 with out a single artillery shell being fired or bomb dropped, General Patton loaded his 5th Division into boats and crossed the Rhine River with a bridgehead six miles deep in the east side before his boss, General Bradley, even heard about it. Alex was not the only one in the American army that did not always follow protocol. Everyone knew that Patton and Montgomery had always been at each other: in Africa, Sicily, Italy, even in England, and it sure showed now in Europe. It was said that when Patton was asked why operation Market Garden failed his answer was, "It had to, it was Montgomery's plan."

Of course, you can hear anything in the army. A lot of people did not like Patton, and it was sure he said ill-advised things and his obscenities were known far and wide. The 4th had been cleaning up Patton's messes all over France. Still there was something Alex liked about old Blood and Guts Patton. He got things done. The next day, the 23rd, the rest of the third army crossed the Rhine near the town of Worms and was to be followed by the 4th Division a few days later. That day the British and Canadians also crossed and the next day another 16,000 troops crossed. Maybe it was because all these bridgeheads into Germany had pulled some Germans away. Whatever, on the 25th the American army was able to make a break-out from Remegan and started spreading over Germany.

As more bridges were being built over the Rhine and other rivers to bring more troops into Germany, this brought on another major counterattack on the 27th. Two days later the 4th crossed the Rhine and started mopping up all the troops that had been left behind just like they'd done since D-Day. This work is not as famous as the 3rd army or the 101 Screaming Eagles running around former Nazi Europe. However, when reading the number of casualties the 4th suffered and the long list of combat ribbons the 4th soldiers have, one realizes they should have at least been close to the top of the list. Then again there were many Service units that served in WWII that should be mentioned. At least by now most every one was sure the end was in sight. Now Intelligence became more involved in new areas of information-gathering. There were millions of displaced persons all over Europe, most of which had been slave laborers. While many were in prison camps and sent off to work, others were a little better off–in higher grade work camps. Among this mass of people there were those who knew just about everything as to what the Germans did or tried to do during the Nazi reign. Alex was told by his colonel that this new area needed attention that he was well equipped to handle. Where they were located in northern Germany was close to where many Dutch, Polish, Russians and Belgians were being freed from former work and prison camps. These ex-prisoners were now kept in internment camps until the Allies could start getting them back to their homes. Millions of people could not just be released into a war-ravaged landscape to try to get home on their own. They would starve to death trying. Major Vetov could speak English, Dutch, and Russian like a native and he also knew enough German, French and several other European languages. He was the perfect man to head up a new division of intelligence to extract information from this multitude.

Wondering if this might just be a way of getting him out of their unit, Alex well knew that many thought he was too close to the general and had far too many connections with other areas of Intelligence. Most Intelligence units were in competition with each other. Vetov came along and stuck his nose into places he did not need to. While this made him friends in many places, it also made him very disliked in others. Then the unexpected happened--five American agents came to see him. Two were from the Office of Information or COI. This group was a collection of those from military Intelligence, the FBI, and the American State Department. The other three were from the Office of Strategic Services, this group had been the group that worked in the dark during the war—beginning in 1942. They had been given the open door to do about anything they thought would help win the war. They are best known as the America spy network, but they were involved in much more. They told Major Vetov that they needed a military Intelligence man to come fill a very important position and they thought he was their man. Alex was told that what he heard next was top secret and nothing could ever be revealed to anyone at any time, regardless.

If he took the job, it would have to be all or nothing. Alexander agreed and they began relating the story of what had happened and what was needed.

For several years all parts of Intelligence had been learning about Hitler's use of the Gestapo, the SS, and German army to round up and incorporate prisoners inside Germany and all conquered countries. This had demanded the building of large concentration prisons holding hundreds of thousands of prisoners. This became the slave force to build up the German empire. While most were just assigned to common work, there were also untold thousands of scientists, top engineers, doctors, mathematicians and many others that could be forced into working for the Nazis. These were separated according to their abilities to help run their German production especially in their conquered countries. As each country was conquered, the best of the best minds were grabbed up and put in special places or prisons. Whatever force was needed was applied, most often their families were threatened. "Work with the Nazis or terrible things will happen to every one you love, care about, or even know."

If this was not enough they were subjected to torture techniques that the Gestapo had perfected. Wherever they were needed to do the most for the Nazi empire, they were sent. One of the top places was an area in the north of Germany. This area had to be protected from the Allied air forces and the best way to do this was to keep it from getting bombed. The best way to do this was to make it look like three large concentration camps. In fact it was two large work camps and one large research facility made just like all the many concentration camps scattered over Europe. After all, Allies would not bomb their own people.

It was mainly the British who learned most about the three camps in northern Germany and knew they were work camps for some of Germany's top secret projects. As Allied troops started getting close to the German border British Intelligence decided it was very important to raid these camps and find out what was going on and to save many prisoners. This was going to require a very large operation as they wanted to take and hold this location. If paratroopers attacked it too quickly they could never hold it, as the Germans would use all their power to take it back. So they had to wait until they were close enough that British ground forces could break through and rush to their aid. If they waited too long the Germans would destroy everything and everyone there. Then they'd pull out as they had done so many times already as they were forced back into Germany. Even Montgomery's great plan to rush into Germany with paratroopers by using the largest combination of all Allied paratroops available had failed as the German army was still too strong. Careful planning was required and was carried out with British and Canada paratroopers en masse to liberate these camps. When they went in they did so with everything they had and sent in another spear head to get ground troops there as soon as possible.

The arrival of a sky full of paratroopers and gliders landing so close to these three camps worked better than even the planners had hoped. Most active German troops had been moved from the camps to fight the Allies, as they were coming so fast. The camps were guarded by old men and young boys that were not strong enough to fight all those British and Canadians and they just ran away. A few tried to burn files and such but there just was not enough time as the British were all over them. As the British burst into the three camps they found out that only two were work camps. Even though the third looked just the other two, it was really a full research, development and study facility. Even another was only partly a slave work center as nearly half was reserved for willing German and collaborating scientists. These had very nice apartments and recreation centers all constructed to look like prison barracks from the air. The other half was in stages—some reasonably nice places down to nothing much more than prison cells. The third was truly a typical German work camp and all three had rail-lines leading into and out of them. Following the rail-lines a double line of train rails ran right into a building built into the side of a hill. When troops entered they found it was really leading right into the mouth of a huge man-made cave. This was a full factory that appeared to have been in operation until the paratroops started appearing. The British clamped down on everything and even though they were supposed to share all intelligence with the other allies they did not.

Nonetheless the Americans had seen the large military operation and asked the British about it and all they said was it was an operation to liberate another group of concentration camps and nothing more. Bits and pieces of information started leaking out and the American army demanded under the agreed plan to share military information to be made a part. This led to foot-dragging on the part of the British until a lot of pressure was applied. Then the British agreed to allow a delegation of the American army Intelligence corps to come in. One of the largest and richest families in Germany had a summer estate known all around as the Krump estate that bordered the grounds of the prisons. The British said that this estate had been used by the Nazis as the headquarters for their operations there. The the Americans could move in there to complete their part of the shared information. With its huge ballroom and dining rooms, an OSS agent added that he thought that the estate had only been used as fancy living quarters for leading Nazis. That was just what the Nazis had used it for and not as the office for the camps. He also believed that the British thought that this would be a buy off that would give the British more time to get the info they wanted before the noisy Americans got into their newly conquered finds.

He continued, "Major, we have studied your records and believe you can play the game and get in and learn what we need to know. There is one more thing, you need a level playing field, and as a major you do not have it. The British operation is being run by a British Colonel so you need to go in as an American Colonel of Intelligence.

Things moved quickly now. Alex was flown to England and was taught much by the OSS in the two days he was there. It was there he was quietly promoted to a full colonel, introduced to several OSS agents and others, all now wearing American Army officer uniforms that would aid as props for his new mission. He sat in the back seat of a four door Ford sedan painted army green with a white star on the door to show it was American army. He was followed by six army trucks as he passed the British sentries into the compounds of the Krump estate. It looked like something in a European travel brochure from the 1930s. As he stepped from the Ford, more British sentries snapped to a salute and Alex climbed a tall stairway to the massive front porch. More sentries with salutes and there he was greeted by a British Colonel who greeted him as an equal and showed him into his new headquarters. The huge Krump library was to be his office and he was shown around part of the estate main building, ending in his bedroom. Alexander's first thought was, 'If all that gaudy furniture was moved out he and his men could have a basketball game in there.'

It is not long, however, until Alexander found a great deal of information in both the library and bedroom. Then he became too involved to care if the rank climbers liked him or not. He was close to one of the larger work camps just inside Germany that housed nearly two thousand slave workers who had worked on some of Hitler's secret projects. He had moved into an estate house that the Nazis had used as the office and home of camp director of the workers' camp. Or as an entertainment center for Nazis. The OSS agent thought it didn't make any difference. It was time to get on with his real job of discovering what the British had already learned. This was not far from the large man-made cave where the Germans had built the new German jet engines and rocket motors for their last ditch super-weapons to win the war. This took a lot of skilled workers as well all the advanced and scientific minds of the countries that Germany had conquered mixed with a liberal sprinkling of German scientists as well. Alex was given a staff of 26 which radically increased--doubled and doubled again several times over. Practically everyone on his new staff were very fluent in German as that was what they were working with. For the same reason it was the German language by which they talked things over and in general was by far the most used language his staff used. Alex had learned more and more German as he came through France. Reading and speaking German every day for hours, he became as fluent in German as English, Dutch or Russian.

It now seemed that the American and British governments were getting a little better at working together as both were very interested in what the Germans were up to. In fact, the British were much more involved than the American army. Major Vetov jumped right over being a lieutenant colonel and made a full colonel. However, he was not sure he could always act the part. The documentation alone in that work camp was buried in thousands of pages of information on the projects. The amazing thing was it had all been left behind and Alex well knew that German troops everywhere had destroyed most all documents while retreating. It could be that when the British had launched a large paratroop operation to capture and save the prisoners in the three camps in the area, the German officers and men had been more interested in getting away than burning everything. Basically it seemed as if there was nothing removed from the estate and Alex agreed with the OSS agent.

Since things were getting done in the camps and Alex's people were doing most of the work, he was returning to the estate every evening. This gave him the opportunity of exploring the huge main building. Most of his officers had moved into the 26 bedrooms and the rest into the barracks out back. The basement was the same size as the house with a huge wine cellar that had probably been full at one time. Now there were a few bottles here and there. At the back of the wine room there was a huge steel gate that had been cut open, leading down a long underground hall maybe fifteen feet underground. Here there was a huge thick door that had also been cut open leading to a large underground bomb shelter. The house was a hundred years old or more but the tunnel and bomb shelter looked only a few years old. The shelter was equipped with beds, bathrooms, and one could tell had been well supplied, but now had only scattered things lying around. There were several separate bedrooms extending out from the main room. Another room was larger and looked as though it had been an office with numerous electric lines leading in through the back wall away from the main room. Most looked like they were phone lines that had all been cut. Alex thought it strange that these lines were not coming from the bomb shelter or the direction of the house. He put this out of his mind and went back to his huge bedroom. Six people could have slept in that bed and Alex wondered how many women entertained German officers in that bed. Thinking about the bed, he was not as comfortable that night as before. Trying to change his mental images, he thought again about those wires and why they were coming from the back wall.

The next day it was back into the camp and into the housing quarters where Wernher von Braun lived when he was there. Braun was an artist as well as a designer of rockets and his walls were covered with pictures of his drawings of rockets. Several showed his rockets out in space looking back at the earth thousands of miles below. It clearly showed that von Braun dreamed of rockets that could go into outer space. Alex thought, 'How can any man be so smart as to make a rocket that could fly to London and still be so dumb as to think a rocket could ever be made that would fly into space? That was comic book stuff, not for real life.' However, von Braun was working on a rocket to try to reach America, so who knew? He was not in von Braun's apartment to daydream; he was there to find papers on von Braun's research about rockets as weapons. In his files there were hundreds of sketches of rockets and rocket motors. Alex needed some of his people that understood these things to go over them and separate good ideas from pipe dreams. Other offices offered other ideas and again Alex made notes as to who needed to come into which office and determine what was worth sending to the US for more study.

The British had basically finished their work here, going through this second compound as if, after all, it was nothing more than a protected part of the three compounds. The cave factory and the village that the Gestapo had taken over were far more interesting. From the air and photos, this compound looked just like the other two, but on the ground it was very different. On the walls the machine guns were pointed out and so were most of the searchlights. There was a barbed wire fence eight foot tall on the outside of the wall with well-worn paths where sentries patrolled to protect the people inside rather than to keep them in. The nearly half that was where the non-Nazi leading scientists were kept was reversed and prisoners were guarded. So to keep things closer, Alex made an office in the recreation area for his growing staff and housed his people in the old scientist quarters as this placed them close to the work, and gave them a good place to live and work without having to build any new places. This turned out to be a big help in getting more done.

Regardless of the reason, here it was, and getting it all together was a job of unbelievable proportions. One of Alex's biggest problems besides the size of the project, was that both British and American people started showing up in huge trucks wanting to haul off the jet engines and rocket motors. Now OSS showed up and somehow they had the power to say no to anyone. Alex already knew several of these guys as he had talked to them many times by phone and radio. This is also when Alex was told that the British had already hauled off several trainloads of files, rocket and jet motors and tons of equipment before the Americans had even been allowed in. Alex now knew he was starting at a terrible disadvantage. Still Alex had tons to work with and there was no need to cry over spilt milk. This really helped and Alex made half the second floor and most of the main compound available for them. For the first time since leaving the U.S.A. Alex had never seen so many women coming through those front doors to work on all the paperwork. It was not just secretaries by any means. It was analysts, interpreters, scientists, and specialists of all kinds. They were definitely not all Americans--many were British, a surprising number were Dutch, and there was a sprinkling of others. The war had revolutionized life so very much in America and all the war-torn countries.

As millions of men were pulled out of America to fight the war, millions of women stepped into their shoes, not only to keep things running, but to increase production in every facet of life. Many thousands joined the military to help fight the war. Men in the 30s and 40s's would never even dream of allowing their women into combat except as nurses. Of course, at home these same women were building B-17s and then flying them to locations where they could be shipped or flown overseas. During these years it was women that stepped into science, research, technology, and development of all sorts because so many men were gone. Women had always worked in these fields but now they nearly took it over.

Much more was happening among these women. They were designing better airplanes, improving medical equipment, and many were studying and breaking enemy codes, interpreting aerial photos, learning foreign languages and understanding how the enemies were doing what they were doing. Before D-Day thousands of the so called behind-the-front-lines women poured into England to support the American military. Some wore American army uniforms and earned rank just like men. Many were civilian employees still paid by the department of defense. As more and more of Europe was taken back from Nazi rule more and more of these women—especially the ones in medicine and intelligence—came to Europe. Here they joined with the multitudes of European women that were like-minded and trained. Now this was a whole force to do the kind of work that Colonel Vetov needed. Regardless of where they were from, they all had been carefully screened before they were allowed on the project. While they were wonderful workers they constituted a small number compared to over a million young American men, most of whom had not seen an American woman for years. This did create a significant problem. The good thing was that Alex had a woman lieutenant colonel, five women majors, and a large assortment of both commissioned and non-commissioned officers to oversee things. They did a great job in intelligence work and in keeping things under control. They lived and worked in walled-in enclosures, some of which had been a prison. This did much to help keep the women safe from all those desperate American men. On one occasion Alex did tell a general that when things first started he thought he was going to have to machine gun hundreds of American soldiers to keep them at a distance. The high ranking female officers did a great job of keeping things under control. There were a lot of jokes about the women being kept in a prison.

As soon as the camps were first liberated, the British army guarded everything. Now there were American MPs along with the British everywhere. Many of Alexander's command were surprised that their commander could converse in so many languages. As the work progressed Alex realized what a treasure trove of information and workers he had at his disposal. The German habit of keeping track of everything showed just where the product that was being made was sent to. When, how much, what dates, how things were sent and everything else... A main item here was that tomes of "Missing files had back up copies stored elsewhere in typical Nazi fashion. The Americans flatly declared that none of the jet engines or rocket motors or their information could be carried off. until a joint commission of both American and British agreed as to what each could transport. This stopped nearly all trucks from carrying anything off. A new problem arose as now a Russian General and his staff showed up demanding equal access, as the three nations were partners in the war. Alex and the British Colonel met with him and got nowhere as he had letters from Stalin himself demanding access to all information and an equal division of items from the cave and work facilities.

The conversations did not go well until Colonel Vetov declared he was sure this could be worked out to give Russia an equal part. After all, they were equal partners in the war. The British Colonel nearly choked on the pipe he was smoking as Alex added, "This can be done just as soon as American and British Intelligence are allowed into the countries that Russian armies have occupied, to gather up all information in those countries as equal partners in this war. The Russians stormed out and the talks were over, the next day the Russians packed up and left.

As the Russians left, Alex spoke to the British Colonel and said he thought that this particular problem was solved. Alex said he would like to go back to his quarters for the remainder of the day as it was already getting late. He bade the colonel good night and headed back to the estate in his Ford staff car. He wanted to take another look at that room with all the wires.

Alex did not like unanswered questions. Why were all those wires coming in from outside? They were installed at the floor level on the back side of the room and they had all been cut. This did not make sense and Alex wanted answers. As it was already dark, Alex got something to eat and went down into the basement to look at things again. Everything was just as it had always been and there were no apparent answers. Where were those wires coming from? Maybe there was something outside in the sprawling gardens of the estate that would give him an answer.

It was late and most of the staff had gone to bed so Alex did the same. Early the next morning after a quick breakfast, Alex headed for the estate office that oversaw the local operations. They had the plans to the estate that dated back to before the war but nothing contained any info about the bomb shelter. Alex asked if there was anyone around that knew about the estate gardens. He was told there of an old man who still lived on the grounds who had been garden-keeper even before the war. He found him in a small cottage behind most everything on the sprawling grounds. Alex introduced himself in a very friendly way, asking the old man if he was the one that had kept the gardens of the estate in such fine shape. The old man brightened and said he had worked for the Krump family from the late 1800s except for the time he served in the Kaiser's army in WW1. He had been wounded in WW1 but Mr. Krump had rehired him in spite of his being somewhat disabled. Like a lot of old people he was very glad to have someone to talk to about his life-work of keeping the gardens. When Alex asked the old man about why a large part of the gardens had been dug up—it must have upset him. There was an expression of anger as the old man raved about how much was destroyed. He had to prepare the ground and replant the garden after the shelter had been installed. To make matters worse, he had to arrange the garden so all those big ventilator shafts were surrounded by foliage. That way it would still look good. If that was not enough, he was required to keep the leaves and branches out of the mesh surrounding the shafts so the air could flow. Alex had seen the vents both inside the shelter and outside in the garden. Alex knew they were there, but thought nothing about it since an underground shelter had to have air shafts. Again he told the old man he had done a magnificent job and wanted him, if he was able, to oversee the restoration of the gardens as they had not been properly taken care of in recent times. It was like giving the old man a new lease on life.

Upon leaving, Alex said, "Whatever you need let me know, and I will take care of it." Then as if it was an afterthought, Alex asked, "Can you show me where the bomb shelter is below the gardens?"

The old man hobbled out of the cottage and walked to a spot, pointed to the ground and said, "It ends here."

Helping the old man walk back, Alex began counting his steps as he walked, all the while making comments about what a great garden the old man had created and cared for. After a bit, the old man stopped again and said, "This is the big room. They dug up this whole area..." He waved his arm around in a circle. This was all beautiful flowers then; now it is not much. From over there it was just a long tunnel into the main house."

Turning the old man around, Alex helped him back to his cottage and thanked him again. This time Alex headed as straight for the house as he could, though the plants and shrubs made it impossible to just walk straight across. He took the heel of his shoe and drew a line across the path. He started counting his steps again until he reached the big room and made another line in the path. Reaching his office in the estate he made a few notes and headed for his office at the work camp. Once there, Alex made a call and asked for a crew of six trusted workmen that could keep a secret to be at the estate at 1900. They were to bring sledge hammers and concrete chisels, wear heavy work gloves and eye protection and bring a strong three foot chain and a big lock making sure that it had only one key. Now it was back to the business of the day.

At 7:00 p.m. the work crew arrived and Alex took them down into the basement. After passing through the big steel gate, Alex took the chain and lock that the workmen brought with them and locked it up. Then he ushered them to the back of the bomb shelter in which Alex wanted the work done. There he pointed to the back wall and said, I want a door-sized hole in that back wall. While the men got started, Alex began checking out other parts of the bomb shelter in much more detail. Within two hours one of the workers came to find him and said, "Colonel, you are going to want to see this."

The workmen had a round two-foot hole in the wall and were shining a flashlight through the hole. On the other side there was another room even bigger than the one they were in. There were many desks and bookshelves like a library.

Alex said, "Give me a door-sized hole, but do not go in or look around in that room. There might be booby traps as this is a hidden room. Regardless, I want specialists to go inside first. Then he sent two of the men out to get a wheel barrow, shovels, a big electric fan, extension cords and more flashlights. The room was already full of concrete and brick dust and Alex knew that before they got a door-sized hole they were going to need to have a fan to clear the dust. The Germans used 240 volts for all their equipment so that was what the men brought back with them. They worked until midnight when Alex sent them home. After he locked the gate behind them he went back and walked through the hole that was six feet wide and reached the ceiling. He just could not wait. He found the light switch and turned the room lights on. By now he could speak German very well but it was still hard to read in detail as he had to mentally change the written words into English or Dutch to fully grasp what was going on. A true multi-language person can think in any language he knows without having to use a base language from which to work. Russian, Dutch, English were all equal to him, while French, German and Polish still required some work.

As he got deeper into this room Alex found nine very large bank type vault steel doors in the walls. They were all locked up solid and even the rows of filing cabinets were all locked. In fact, most of the desks were as well. On one wall there was a whole row of large electric switches, all labeled in German and Alex's eyes saw several labeled Geblase with a number. Geblase is German for 'blower' in English and, flipping a couple on, Alex heard the sound of motors coming on with every switch flipped. Then Alex felt and smelled the cool German night air replacing the stale smell of the underground bunker. He looked around for hours but finally gave up and walked back to the large steel gate, unlocked it, walked through and re-locked it behind him as he headed for the stairs and to bed. His alarm wakened him at his usual 5:00 a.m. and he felt like he had just gone to sleep. He reset it for 7:00 and went back to sleep. At seven he did rise, called his office on the first floor, and told them to call his office in the work camp to tell them he will be staying at the estate that day. After another light breakfast he went into his estate office and went to work as if it was just another day. The first day he'd moved in, he had found a listing of all the books in the estate library.

During the war it had been used as the office for the commandant for the work camps. There had been a huge painting of Adolf Hitler that reached from about a foot above the floor to at least ten feet up the wall. Of course, the British had torn it down when they took over. Behind it, was a painting of the Krump family from fifty something years ago standing in front of the estate. It was not nearly as tall as Hitler's painting had been, but was just as wide, showing most of the main buildings and the beautiful grounds. It was firmly bolted to the wall across from what was now Alex's desk. The desk was in front of two huge windows that opened onto a veranda looking across the estate gardens. These windows were from the floor to a height of over nine feet tall as well and about eight feet wide. Both windows had double doors that swung open wide. This allowed a good flow of air in warm weather. The house and painting appeared to be from late 1800s and would have matched any building from Paris or Rome built at the same time. Now that Alex had found a treasure trove of information hidden below ground on the estate, it made no sense at all that the commandant would not have something about it in his office. It was true that the British had been there for days before Alex had arrived. Surely they had gone through things, but if they had found anything about the underground beyond the bomb shelter, they would never have walked off and left it. There had to be something, somewhere and the Germans were very good at hiding things--things like a huge manufacturing and research facility disguised as prisoner of war camps so they would not be bombed. Search as he would, Alex could find nothing.

When 7:00 p.m. came, so did Alex's six workmen. This time they came without anything except their work clothing. They had left all the rest behind last night and Alex had requested nothing more be brought. Alex did get three brooms and some cleaning equipment from the estate house and handed them to his workmen. Last night the blowers had been left on but every light had been turned off. As Alex inspected the wall they were tearing through last night, it became apparent that the Nazis had simply bricked off part of the room. They plastered over the brick and did a perfect job hiding their work to make it look just like it had been built that way. Their only mistake was they forgot about all those wires or had continued to use them til the very last, then cut them off. Alex wanted that entire false wall removed and started getting it torn down. There was a large coal room that was used to feed the furnaces that heated the hot water and boilers that steam-heated the entire main house. As the weather was beginning to get a bit more temperate, the Allies were advancing. The Germans had not bothered to refill the coal bunkers. When the British had taken over, all they really needed was hot water and there was plenty of coal for that. So three of the four bunkers were empty and Alex had his workmen take the broken up wall and hide it in one of the empty bunkers. Shovels, brooms and dust pans cleaned up the mess and Alex located a welding crew and had the steel gate leading into the bomb shelter repaired, with a new very strong lock installed rather than the chain on that gate. Alex moved on to have the steel door repaired also with a new lock. A colonel in command does not have to explain anything so no questions were asked. The workmen were told this was top secret and under no circumstances was a word to be said to anyone other than himself. They were forbidden to even discuss it among themselves outside of the room.

The crew Alex had was doing a great job at the work camps and the cave manufacturing and research facility. So he pulled 31 of his best and brought them back to the estate, telling them this was top secret even much more so than what they had been doing. He set them up in the bomb shelter, calling it a great place to work, and got them started in the big room with all the files. He found a couple of men that were good with locks and vaults to try to work on those vaults leading away from the file room. They finally gave up and could not understand why Alex did not just go after them with cutting torches. Finally Alex told them that he had reason to believe they might be booby trapped with enough high explosives to blow up the entire area. The last day there they were afraid to even move the vault dials anymore. Somewhere there were people who knew how to get into those vaults. Everyone on the team was told to search for anything they could find that might reveal the information. After this announcement one of the women came to Alex and said, "Sir, I am a code breaker. Some of the things I've been working on are nothing but a list of numbers that appear to have no meaning. When you said we needed numbers, I wondered if they may be what you are looking for. Within the hour the first vault door swung open and it again was a very large room. On open shelves there were stacks and stacks of money. That first shelf held enough French franc to fill a railroad car full. There were logs of where the Germans had gone into every bank they came to and emptied them. Not only banks, but businesses of all types. It seemed one of Hitler's plans was to take away France's money so they would have to submit to German rule. This was repeated country by country and it only started with money. This room held so much gold, silver, and precious jewelry, indeed anything of great value, that it would take many trucks to haul it away.

The second vault consisted of records of millions of people from all over, with Germans being the largest section. It seemed that the Nazis wanted to know details about every German citizen. It was an intelligence section on people. The second largest section was labeled in German, of course: U.S. Army. Curiosity got the best of him and he looked up 4th division, then the Vs and, sure enough, there was *Vetov, Alexander* and three pages on him. He'd heard stories of American prisoners being interrogated by Germans holding files on them. Then the Germans would read things they already knew about them to get them to open up about the war. Now he knew how they could do this, There were millions of files in this room.

The third vault really was the icing on the cake. Just inside the door was a huge architect's rendition of a museum far larger than any in the world. The Fuhrer, Adolf Hitler's world of Art. Here there was no cash as such but many pallets of gold, shelves and shelves filled with very expensive jewelry, and hundreds of pieces of art.

Rows of filing cabinets with thousands of photos and papers. While his people were still trying to get another vault opened, Alex continued to look at all the things inside this vault. This is when another agent came over and said, "I think you need to see this, sir. He was led to a section set by itself. There were many pictures of either caves or large mines that were stacked full of paintings, statues, even some furniture, along with hundreds, if not thousands, of crates–all with the Nazi emblems on them. On every file was the same label "for the Fuhrer's museum." All had listings of contents, locations and maps showing where these locations were. Grabbing a handful of these photos, maps and listings Alex headed up to his office. He knew he was holding proof of the locations of the greatest art in the world but did not know what to do about it.

On the way to his office, Alex tried to decide what to do about this. It was just too unique of a find. It was far more than wealth; this was a section of one storeroom listing art that had been gathered from all over Europe. This included what had been stolen from German Jews and other rich Germans that had stood against Hitler. Hitler was planning on building the world's greatest and by far the largest art museum in the world. Along with the art was stored vast amounts of gold and multitudes of things of very great value. And here was a list of many of the places more was stored. What to do? This was far too great to pass along channels, and his problem all along was his leaping over the chain of command. Alex asked for a few days off for personal reasons and, as he had all things running well, he was granted the leave.

Locating General Omar Bradley, he got permission for an emergency meeting with the second most powerful man in Europe. He caught a military flight to Paris, France where the general was at that time. Colonel Alexander Vetov took a brief case of papers and photos with him. When he finally faced the general, Alex explained what and when. He apologized that he just did not know what to do with information of untold billions of dollars worth of treasure and had decided to turn it over to the leading general in Europe to make the decision. General Bradley said to leave the papers and just go on back. He would take it to Eisenhower and decisions could be made from the top down. Then General Bradley asked Alex what was going on "over there" and this took a few hours to explain. Final the general said, "Just go back and say nothing until you receive information from Eisenhower."

Alex went back to work, first locking that room and posting a full time MP at the door. Then he went to the girl that had made the original discovery and told her nothing could be said until word came from General Bradley himself.

There was so much going on that Alex set the art aside in his mind. The latest in the control of the V-2 rockets included plans for a rocket 68 feet tall that the Germans thought could hit New York City or even Washington D.C. itself. This would make the Americans think twice about continuing this war. Like all good intelligence, bits and pieces come together to paint the real picture. Alex thought that may be a place to start, but it had to be proven before it was fact. And facts were pouring out of that estate in northern Germany through the end of the war. While military matters slowed as the war ended, the need for intelligence did not stop. To fully understand this it was needful to go back to what happened after the Rhine River was crossed. To do this they needed to go back to the 4th Division and Captain Wallace in Intelligence. Then to Sergeant Dourity, who was now Lieutenant Dourity and even more to Private Hagman, now Sergeant Hagman, to look at the end of the war.

12

GETTING IT FINISHED

The rest at the 4th Division rest camp was over but the war was most certainly not over for the 4th Division intelligence department. It was up to them to find the enemy so the 4th could flush them out. Some Germans were fighting for Hitler or death, while others were sick and tired of the war. These last just wanted to go home and hoped they still had a home to go back to. A fight to the death made the war last longer and destroy much more than it could have. Again Patton was full speed ahead and let the rest of the armies finish things up. When the 4th Division had crossed the Rhine, it was what the 4th had always been, the boots on the ground to do the job of digging out what had been bypassed. Many of Alexander's soldiers that had fought under him had become outstanding leaders in getting this war finished. Some had advanced in rank, while others never increased their rank or very little. Nonetheless, they were fine men, and many others would have been fine soldiers if they had lived or not been badly wounded and returned to the States. Three of these men who played very important roles in the closing months of the war had a little of Alexander's nature themselves. This can illustrate what part the 4th Division had in closing down the Nazis in the last days of the war.

Captain Wallace worked 4th Division Intelligence Communication and was very good at keeping the troops on the ground informed with the information that kept them alive and let them know what to expect. Like Alex, he did not always play by the rule book to get the job done. He was never advanced beyond captain for this very reason. The bravery and common sense of Private Hagman, along with a natural mother hen nature over his men, had turned him into a very fine sergeant. He was known and respected throughout his whole company. Sergeant Dourity had also received a battlefield commission and was promoted to second lieutenant and then to first lieutenant. His men would say Lieutenant Dourity could smell a German soldier at half a mile, an MG 42 at a mile, and a Nazi SS at two miles. It was experience that had taught him to read all the signs and the land around him, but what mattered was, he was a great officer. Of course there were many more just like these three. They will give us a good idea of the last months of the war. A man building a house does not get the attention that the man fighting a housefire does. So the 4th seldom, if ever, got the attention that made it into the newspapers in the States.

When Lieutenant Dourity took his men ashore on the east bank of the Rhine, within two hours they were in a firefight with German troops that were not supposed to have been there. The Rhine River was Germany's main waterway; it had handled a large part of Germany's commerce for hundreds of years. Therefore there were buildings of all types, not only along the riverbanks but for miles inland as well. As always, the attacking Allies pushed forward like fingers of a hand that left spaces between each finger. Guess who got the job of taking care of these spaces--the 4th and other divisions like them. A big part of the problem was that, as the British and Americans pushed inland, to get out fo the way, many German troops in this tidal wave simply moved to the side and let their enemy pass. Thankfully, some of these Germans were tired of the war and tired of fighting. To counteract this and make all Germans fight to the end the Nazis would hang hundreds of civilians and some German soldiers from lamp posts. They also used trees, signposts and even houses, all with signs on their bodies declaring them traitors to the Fuhrer.

Every inch of ground and buildings had to be cleared. The fact that most were empty made some men become careless and it got them killed or wounded. While large industrial complexes looked the worst and often were notorious at hiding the enemy, even a small house or shop could still contain a deadly occupant.

Sergeant Hagman led his men into a complex that reminded him very much of the one where he'd laid on the floor and shot German feet with his pistol. Then he killed them when they fell to the floor. That was months before, when Alex was leading his platoon. Now he was leading his squad to do the same job and there were not enough men to do the job this time. When you are in the army you use what you have and somehow get the job done. He and his men started into a building and in seconds Hagman glimpsed movement and the fight started. Again Hagman pulled his pistol in such close quarters and started clearing the building. The only advantages he and his men had this time was the fact that all but one of the enemy were trying to use rifles in very close quarters. Second, only a dozen or so of them fought until the rest gave up. One of Hagman's squad was killed and two wounded. At this rate he would not have any men left after a week. Luckily, by the third day he only had one more man with a slight wound and none killed.

Every day replacements were coming into division that were being assigned to companies as needed. Many of these replacements had not even started to shave yet, and the vets thought of them as children. Some of these did not live long enough to find out how to stay alive in combat. In the early days of combat, it was fighting nearly every day and most hours of that day. Then 17 and 18-year-olds learned fast or did not learn at all. Now with the fighting being an on and off thing, the new replacement often grew careless, to their regret. A big part of the problem now was the huge amount of ground to cover and how quickly it had to be done.

This turned into movement every moment of daylight and far too fast. Exhaustion and not enough time for the soldiers to learn to properly open a door, caused far too many men to get shot. Still war was war and it had to be done whether there was time to do it or not. Another thing changed a lot also. Now seeing a large group of armed German soldiers did not necessarily mean a fight. It no longer meant even white flags. Sometimes the Germans just kept walking. Most were headed west into American lines as they did not want anything to do with the approaching Russian army in the east. To them it was not a matter of surrender as it was just a fact: they had lost the war and were not going to fight any more.

Still there were pockets of determined Germans that fought very hard. Some fought until they ran out of ammunition and then just walked off. In the past when a German surrendered, he held up a white cloth and the man came out with his hands raised. Sometimes that still happened, but a new thing was happening more and more. A German soldier would simply stand up, lay down his rifle, turn his back and walk off in whatever direction he wished. It was like him saying, "Shoot me if you wish, it is all over. I am out of it."

Most Americans just let them go and continued on as though nothing had happened. Regardless, replacements were still required in the 4th Division far too often. As the country opened up into more open farmland, army trucks carried the 4th Division to catch up with Patton's third army. Pulling into one small village the entire population was standing in the town square. Every person young and old was so scared many were trembling. Women looked like they were going to faint and some children were crying but most of the children were too scared to cry. It was like they knew if they cried the Americans were going to eat them. They were all huddled in a mass and the captain was afraid there might be some die hard Nazis hiding in the middle of the group to kill Americans. It had happened before. So American guns were pointed at the crowd of German civilians. As soon as the Americans were sure there were no Nazis, the troops started passing out Hershey candy bars to the children and k-rations to the women and the old. It was like a curtain had fallen, children were hungily eating the candy bars, troops were being embraced and the tears were now tears of joy rather than fear. As the troops climbed back into their trucks the captain came to each truck and asked if the men had kept any food for themselves. One young private said, "Captain Sir, after today I don't care if I eat tonight or not."

Still, less than ten miles down the road, they were in another strong firefight. This was Germany in 1945, in a dying country that did not know what to do. This fight turned out to be a big one that lasted until after dark. The Americans held their ground but only fired at known moving targets as the night grew darker. Morning showed the Germans had left during the night, leaving behind their dead and wounded with one German medic trying to take care of several badly wounded German soldiers.

An American medic joined him and all the wounded were taken care of regardless of uniform. That day was the strangest day in Sergeant Hagman's life. His platoon had been ordered to check out a small farming village off on a side road. They were being led by their lieutenant in his jeep, followed by the five army trucks holding the entire platoon. This was beautiful country, having never been bombed or touched by war as could be seen. Then over a rise in the road came marching German troops headed toward the Americans. It was wonderful weather so the canvas tops of the trucks had been removed so all soldiers were out in the open air. More and more Germans were coming over the rise in the road and they were all still marching like they never saw the Americans. The captain didn't know what to do as his men were heavily outnumbered and there was no place to go. If they tried to back up and turn around to get out of there those hundred or more Germans could riddle them with fire before they got ten yards. All the captain said as he walked up and down the trucks was "hold your fire; there are just too many of them."

The Germans just kept coming in perfect marching order, but not in the German goose strep. All the Germans were well armed and several had MG 42s over their shoulders They stared stonily at the Americans and the Americans stared back. As they started past, a German officer with another German soldier approached the American Lieutenant. They saluted each other and started a conversation. After a while the German officer saluted our lieutenant again, then returned into his men's ranks. There was well over two hundred men in that column of German soldiers. Many were walking wounded and our lieutenant offered our medics to help. The German officer halted his column, thanked the American captain and told him his own medical staff had done all they could but some American medication would be greatly appreciated as they had run out long ago.

By this time the American troops had unloaded from their trucks and offered first water to the Germans, then cigarettes, food, etc. Last, the captain offered to turn over two of the American trucks to carry the worst of their wounded men and the German officer accepted with great thanks. The American captain ordered that two five gallon cans of water and several cases of K-rations be placed in the trucks with the wounded Germans. Finally the German army walked past and on down the road while the lieutenant went to his jeep radio. The captain, looking at his men said, "For the first time I not only believe this war is nearly over, I believe that things are going to be all right."

Everyone just stood there as the lieutenant talked for some time on his radio before coming back and stopping at each truck to explain that the men were going to have to take turns at riding and walking as there were now not enough trucks to carry all the men. There was not a man that complained; all appeared very happy. The German colonel had marched his men from fighting the Russian army to find the American army to turn themselves over to the Americans rather than to the Russians. The German colonel had wanted to turn his men over to an American officer of at least equal rank or more. Watching what was left of a German regiment march by still armed while less than fifty Americans sat in their trucks was something none of these men would ever forget.

Going on in to check out the little village was a very anti-climactic thing to do. They did their job, got back in their trucks, returned to the main road and started back to join their regiment. After the lieutenant's call, the regiment had stopped and sent all their free trucks back down the road to pick up and bring all the Germans back to camp. The American general himself was there to accept the surrender of the remnant of a German regiment and to not only accept their surrender but to welcome them as a part of the end of the war. All the German soldiers stood fully armed and in perfect formation until their colonel officially surrendered. Then all the Germans started filing up to the front behind their colonel, laying down their rifles, hand grenades, ammunition belts, bayonets, knives and even packs. Then they returned to their ranks and stood at attention until their colonel called "at ease" and all went into the perfect at ease formation. After speaking to his men a few moments, he told them to take the "at rest" and be seated on the ground, which they did. Some of the Germans began to pull out small potatoes or other scraps of food to eat and the American general ordered the Americans to provide food and water for the German troops. The Germans were to remain at the surrender grounds that night and each German soldier was allowed to retrieve his pack, prove to an American guard that there was nothing dangerous inside and take it with him. Also personal clothing, shelter and some were allowed to get shovels and other items in order to have a safe and sanitary camp. Of course, this was done as all items were inspected for weapons. There they remained under a light guard party until the next morning when they awoke to the aroma of hot coffee, a cooked breakfast and trucks to ride in. Only then were they loaded into the trucks and sent to a processing center with a handwritten letter from the general on just how these German soldiers had surrendered to him.

The next day, approaching a farm house and barn, the squad received fire from both buildings. There was little cover to advance behind toward either building and Sergeant Hagman did not want to get any men killed or wounded so he stopped his men and called for back-up armor. Then for thirty minutes both sides just exchanged long range rifle fire as Hagman waited on the armor he had called for. Then an American half-track came clacking up the road. It passed the American troops and approached the farmhouse with its fifty caliber machine gun spraying the house as it advanced. It just kept getting closer to the house when a Panzerfaust hit it right in the front grill. The front section of the half-track exploded in a ball of fire. The back gate of the half track opened and a half dozen men made a run for it back up the road toward Hagman and his squad. An MG 42 opened up on them from the barn and half of them fell. Some of the Americans had kept the burning half-track between them and the barn and they made it back to Hagman's position. The 42 just kept on spraying the Americans on the ground that they'd already shot down. Two of Hagman's men rushed forward to try to help their fallen fellow Americans and they were also cut down. Back on the radio Sergeant Hagman called again and explained what had just happened. Again the Americans just waited, but not for long as two American P-52s came in low and fired rockets into both house and barn. These rockets were designed to explode German Tiger Tanks and there was little left of either building. Even though both buildings had been exploded, the squad approached with caution.

The sergeant looked for survivors in the barn's wreckage and there were none. He did find the used launch tube of an old model Panzerfaust like those used back at the beginning of the war. That explained why it did not have enough power to blow the American half-track all to pieces. How strange this war had become. One day they were passing out candy to German kids and accepting hundreds of German soldiers that had surrendered and come to them. The next they were faced with a death squad that had to know they were going to die yet still killed more American soldiers before they died themselves. Regardless, it was for sure this war was still not over as long as some Germans had a gun and ammunition. As military ambulances came to pick up the wounded and a truck picked up the dead, the sergeant loaded what was left of his men in one truck along with the two remaining uninjured men from the half-track. Their second truck returned empty. Every day the company sent out patrols, but after what had happened to Sergeant Hagman's squad, they stayed in camp that day.

Were they given easy patrols because of what they had just been through? Or did it just happen that the next two patrols were easy and not a shot was fired. That was far from how things went just six months ago. Word came that the American army had met up with the Russian army. This seemed to make everyone think that they could see the end of this war and live to tell about it. Three days later the 4th Division was called to a halt and informed they were going no farther east. High command had decided that the German country to the east had been given to the Russians to finish things up over there. Some American troops were to be stationed along certain lines while the rest were to go back and finish mopping up all German resistance in west Germany. Hagman's Battalion was assigned the task of holding the line here along the new border between the Americans and Russians. It turned out this was no cake walk assignment.

First there were thousands of German civilians along with German soldiers trying to get to the Americans before being cut off by the Russians. To begin with, it was a matter of dealing with all these people—providing them food, medical help and shelter. Then they had to send them deeper back into Germany for others to take over that job. Even separating real civilians from German soldiers was very hard sometimes as many soldiers had shed their uniforms for civilian clothing. Very few American soldiers understood more than a few words in German or none at all. Finding some Germans that spoke English was a little easier and every one that did was grabbed like they were gold to help the Americans. As huge as this job was, it paled in comparison to what happened as the Russian army approached the American lines. The Russians demanded that the Americans return all the fleeing Germans into Russian custody. On more than one occasion, Russian soldiers firing at fleeing Germans had bullets fly across the American lines. On numerous occasions the Russians opened fire on fleeing German civilians and, yes, some German soldiers were mixed in. This was not only rifle and machine gun fire but the Russians used mortars to within a few yards of the American lines. A few American soldiers were caught in this fire and American soldiers died from Russian bullets and mortars. Americans were strictly forbidden to fire back, but some Americans felt the same as when they'd watched the Germans shoot down French civilians, men, women, and children as hostages in France. There were a few Russians shot by angry Americans, neither side wanted this to get reported as this was allies shooting allies. Some stories did leak to the press and many stories were brought home to America in men's minds.

Parts of the 4th was scattered across occupied Germany to try to bring some order back to a war-torn country. This was no longer a place, under most conditions, for airplanes or even tanks. Light armor was used in small mop up operations, most was back to the boots on the ground, and the 4th had plenty of experience at that. When the 4th was sent into Bavaria to finish the war there, it was almost like the war was already over, except for the fact that this was where many high ranking Germans had built their mansions to live in after they became the rulers of the world, along with Japan and Italy. There were only a few hard fights in Bavaria compared to what they had faced in the past ten months. In fact a bigger problem was keeping all those American soldiers from chasing all those beautiful Bavarian skirts. This along with rich houses full of food, drink, and great riches was hard to control. As Bavaria was nearly all untouched by war, it was a rich beautiful countryside that roiled into the high mountains to the south and east. Add to this, there were days on end when not a shot was fired. American troops let their guard down. As April turned into May, word came that surrender talks were underway and on the 9th they were confirmed.

Captain Wallace was still in the Intelligence basement job of leading the Communications part of Intelligence. His job increased with every week as some of the other Intelligence officers and their personnel work actually slowed down a little. The center was flooded with a non-stop flow of radio and other communications. Everyone was not expecting intelligence to have all the answers as to who needed to be when, where, or whatever, but they acted like it. Then Wallace had to be very careful about what was said and to whom. Before the 4th had reached the east bank of the Rhine River every radio in the division seemed to be on the air. When the division had come ashore on D-Day the whole division only had a handful of two-way radios. Now it seemed like every sergeant had one. They did not, of course, but to Captain Wallace it seemed that way. It was his job to oversee all this, to separate it into needed information, to get men and equipment to where they needed to be. Above all, to get them there at the right time with the right equipment. Going beyond this, having learned Alex's way of doing things, Wallace tried to foresee what all the next moves of the Russians, Americans and Germans were going to be. This way, communications would be able to handle things as needed.

Alexander Vetov had been a master chess player at this and had taught Wallace and his communications people much about how to do it. Shortly after crossing the Rhine, a platoon got ambushed and called for a Sherman to come help them out. Wallace called the air resonance maps department and had them bring him a map of the latest aerial photos of the place where the platoon was fighting for its life. Calling the Sherman directly, Wallace told the sergeant that the road directly into the area appeared totally blocked and to detour over to another road, then cut back so he could get there. The Sherman arrived in time and the sergeant that was in charge of the

Sherman said that, without Wallace, he would have never found his own way around in the manner intelligence had first instructed.

Combining the routes that Patton's third army had taken with the resistance he had met told another story as well. Since Patton only fought one way and that was to advance as quickly as possible. He told his tankers, go through them, over them, even under them—just do not stop. The Germans had learned in a hurry to fight and then get out of the way to live to fight another day. Putting this all together with front line information coming in non stop, it painted a very clear picture of where the German troops between Patton's third army and the advancing 4th actually were. Not just Wallace and communications but the entire crew of the 4th intelligence never shone so bright as they did the final two months of the war. No one is right all the time but this little group started scoring from 65% to 80% correct on their calls. This allowed the 4th to have just what was needed at the right place and at the right time. Like Vetov had done before him, Captain Wallace often did not wait for orders to run up and back down the chain of command. This made a lot of ranking officers very upset with him, but it was hard to say too much with a man that was up to 80% correct in his calls. It did, however, lock Captain Wallase into the rank of captain until the war was over and he was sent home and discharged from the army.

On top of the super load of work already on communications, another job was dropped in their lap and that was reporting on the vast movements of civilians in their war zones. Before the 4th had crossed the Rhine, refugees were always just trying to get away from where the battles were being fought. Now that they were deep into Germany and Patton had moved so fast, along with other American and British armies, these hordes could smell the end of the war. But the millions of displaced persons did not know where to go. To hear the sound of battle was enough to head them away from it. They'd race in another direction until they ran into another battlefield and changed directions again. All these people were just trying to get away and were fleeing in all directions. All these groups contained German soldiers. Some just wanted out of the war, but all too many were still ready to fight. This latter group mainly hid among the refugees to protect them from the ever-present Allied air power. It was the patrolling Air Force that sent in most all the information about these refugee groups. The Air Force reported where they were, often the direction they were going, how large a group it was, etc. Same old story: it still had to be the boots on the ground to do something with the information.

If there was any part of the 4th intelligence department as busy as communications, it was the men and women working the air resonance photos. The Germans were very good at hiding their troops and armor from aircraft but these men and women knew just what to look for. They spent untold hours examining photos with magnifying glasses, then comparing them to older photos. Any changes often indicated there were Germans at a certain place or there would have been no changes. This went to communications for a closer inspection from aircraft or on-the-ground observations. More than half of the armor, trucks and other vehicles found this way were just sitting without any fuel.

One day Wallace was called to answer a question from a sergeant in the 22nd. "What do I do with a twelve or thirteen-year-old female hell cat that will not give up? We have her tied down with cargo straps but I don't feel right about putting her on the truck with captured German soldiers."

Wallace answered, "That is your C.O.'s problem not mine, sergeant."

The sergeant came right back, "That is the rest of my problem, sir. Both my captain and lieutenant are dead, there are only two other sergeants still alive in my platoon and I outrank them. I am now in charge of my platoon and only have 22 uninjured men left while trying to hold 38 prisoners. We only have one truck still running and I have not been able to get through to my company or battalion. The battery on this walkie talkie is just about dead so I tried the Intelligence special frequencies. That was it--the walkie talkie had given up."

Wallace had received no information at all about the platoon except it that was the 22nd and the sergeant's name and even the name was very weak on the almost dead battery. Wallace was not sure he had it right. He called the 22nd and wanted to know if they had a Sergeant Kirkpatrick, as Intelligence had received an emergency call from a cut off platoon in a desperate situation. This got instant attention and Wallace left it with them, never mentioning the crazy teenage girl again. Two weeks later, Captain Wallace was told there was a Sergeant Kirkpatrick that wanted to meet him. Intelligence was off limits to the sergeant so Wallace had to go upstairs to meet Kirkpatrick. The sergeant made an attempt to salute Wallace with his left hand, as his right was in a sling. Staff Sergeant Kirkpatrick told Wallace quite a story of what had happened that day when his platoon got ambushed and nearly wiped out. The platoon had gone in with a half-track, the captain's jeep and three trucks. There had been two quick explosions as the half-track and jeep were hit by Panzerfaust. The troops had piled out of the three trucks into rifle and machine gun fire from both sides of the road. As they started fighting back, two more Panzerfaust took out two more trucks that had already discharged their troops. The American platoon was a well-experienced hard-fighting outfit, and after a long hard fight many of the Germans started giving up.

One child soldier and a small one at that continued to stand up and try to fire an empty rifle at the Americans. The little guy would pull the trigger and throw the bolt to reload and pull the trigger again. The rifle was empty so it only clicked regardless of how often the bolt was worked. The uniform this child was wearing was much too large and even the helmet was just sliding around on his head. Pulling the helmet off allowed a lot of long blond hair to fall over her shoulders. The Americans were stunned to see a young female in a very large German uniform pull a Hitler youth knife from her belt and charge them. As learned in basis training, a GI turned the girl's hand carrying the knife with the barrel of his M1 then swung the butt of his rifle against the side of her head. She went down so hard the soldier thought he might have killed her. Most of the GI's were trying to guard too many prisoners, while three were just looking at the girl. The one that hit her got down on his knees to check if she still had a pulse or not, when she regained consciousness. She came to without any weapons but like a cat in the middle of a cat fight. She scratched, hit, and bit with the fury of a west Texas wildcat. Finally while two men held her, another got some cargo straps from the only remaining truck and tied her down. It was good none of these men understood German as from the moment she woke up there was not one second she was not telling them exactly what she thought of them.

As the 4th progressed across Germany, most of the division moved with it, while the Intelligence stayed in the basement for a while as it just did not have time to pack up and move. As the distance grew greater and greater, it became necessary to move to keep things working as they must. Actually Wallace liked it when his bosses moved off; this allowed him more freedom to do things his way. This is also the time when more and more information started coming in about trouble between the Russian and American army. He let an American news correspondent in on a tip regarding trouble between American and Russian soldiers. Wallace knew better than to let any information from intelligence reach the press. Nevertheless the reporter had told Wallace that he'd heard rumors about the trouble, and Wallace had not denied it. He only said, "You know the army, you can hear anything you want to hear."

The newsman had written that he had inside sources about these troubles. Wallace was arrested at his desk the next day. He talked his way out of it, but was told to never again have a drink or talk to a newsman. Just because they had been seen together it nearly got him court martialed. The rules of military justice in WWII were more "you have to prove yourself innocent" rather than the other way around.

As the Americans drew close to the Russians all along their front lines, a lot of tension sprang up in spite of the first meetings of the American and Russian armies. American pilots started reporting they were being fired upon by Russian troops. Next the Allies were officially notified to not fly over assigned or captured territory "as the Russian military might fire at any unfamiliar aircraft. This would be an accident on the Russian's part, but could be avoided completely if all non-Russian aircraft would stay well away from all Russian territory." So the Allies marked off vast strips of still unconquered ground as no-fly zones and then just stopped forward American movement, leaving miles of no man's land between the Allies and the Russians. The Russians on the other hand not only took all their allotted ground but often moved into these no man's lands as well The Germans that did make it into the American lines told the same stories against the Russians. The Allies had heard for years about what the Germans had done in Russia and now they heard what the Russians were doing to the German people that were the conquered ones. The Russians made it well-known that every inch of ground they had taken in battle was theirs by right of conquest.

Patton had never liked the Russians and had always let everyone know it. Now his commentary about the Russians began to flow in spite of being told by all his superiors to keep his mouth shut. That did not work well at all and most of the people who really knew Patton said that Patton recognized he had higher ranking officers over him, but never acknowledged they were superior to him. It had always seemed as if Patton considered the 4th a part of his command as it was much of the time the clean-up crew following his tanks. Of course, Patton had always considered his troops, out in front most all the time, to be the most important part of defeating Germany. So in reality he felt that all American troops formed part of his clean up brigade. He never thought that way about the British. Patton considered the British as the ones to beat in the game of war against the Germans. When it came to Montgomery it was not very certain that Patton even considered him as an ally. Montgomery was definitely the one to beat in every action and decision. When Montgomery decided to launch Market Garden and needed most all of the Allies' supplies to accomplish it, It took away Patton's fuel and that stopped Patton's tanks cold. Rather than slow down, Patton pushed as far as his tanks would go until they started to totally run out of gas. This put many American men in danger just sitting in empty tanks, trucks and everything that required gas. Germany had already run nearly out of gas so there was very little German gas that Americans could get. This made Patton furious, as this was all Montgomery's fault. Patton had never liked him and his words about Montgomery are a little too rough to print.

A part of army intelligence started gathering more and more information on the Russian army and, of course, Patton pushed this with everything possible and still get away with it. He was not the only ranking American officer that saw this need however. As April came to a close so did the fighting, and the 4th became a huge humanitarian effort to take care of millions of people. As the war slowed there were as many people in Germany that were not German as there were German. This did not include the Allies' armies—just the millions of slave laborers that had been brought in from conquered countries. So much of Germany had been destroyed it could not even begin to feed its own, much less these millions of displaced persons. The fact that it was spring helped a great deal but forty million meals a day was just beyond comprehension. Large parts of Germany had no utilities. In fact many cities were not much more than piles of debris. The medical needs were also staggering in every way possible.

Every child in Germany learned one word of English very quickly and every time an American came their way they used it--that word was Hershey.

Sergeant Dourity was another outstanding U.S. soldier. In his first days in France he came ashore as Private Dourity, and ended up the war as Captain Dourity. Like Alexander Vetov, he received a battlefield commission, then climbed the ranks until by war's end, he was a veteran captain He was best remembered for his actions as Sergeant Dourity. When he first came across the Rhine he was already Lieutenant Dourity, leading his own platoon and well respected as an outstanding leader. For one thing he was never hidden in the back in any battle fought. He forcefully but carefully went into battle. Many men thought it was impossible to be both a point man and a commissioned officer at the same time. Dourity was a master at doing just that as he was one of those that could read a battlefield like a book. Second, he knew his men, their strengths and weaknesses and he used them accordingly. If he could keep his replacements alive long enough, he was able to turn them into real soldiers. Last and of the most importance, his men knew he loved them and was always looking out for them while still being a force against the enemy.

When hitting those industrial buildings along the east bank of the Rhine, his experience had taught him just what to do. For one thing he had about as many carbines as he had M1s in his platoon. Like most men, he loved his M1s and their power, but recognized that carbines were much easier to use in tight places. He had also picked up a lot of M3s and a few Thompsons. Another thing he had collected was a lot of Browning automatic rifles as this was the closest thing the American army had to the German MG 42. His men carried more hand grenades than any other platoon, along with more bazooka ammunition.

Grenades were to be used before going into any room or building, then were to stay on their belts once inside. The little carbine bullets and 45s did not ricochet around inside as badly as the big 30-06 did. While the BARs only held twenty rounds, they could still lay down a cover fire on any location. Dourity thought a bazooka round through a window or a hand grenade through a door was far better than sending a man in first. It was still the big rooms of storage or manufacturing that presented the big problems. These still had to be taken the old fashioned way, man against man. So Dourity had taught his men how to read an industrial complex and had these men teach the new men as they came into the platoon. In Dourity's platoon, the training never stopped but it was different from camp training. Most of it was now the experienced men talking to the new men and telling them how to survive and work together. Then they explained how to look at everything and read what they saw. A front line combat solider never fully relaxed, he expected the unexpected, and calculated everything. While on the line there was no such thing as safety and every time a shot rang out there was a lesson to be learned.

The transition from being a civilian to a soldier did not happen during basic or even advanced training. It happened during the first months of combat, it happened when one of one's best buddies was killed. In fact, it took months to become a front line combat soldier and the learning never stopped. A peaceful road could turn into an ambush as it did one day in mid-April. The day could not have been more beautiful and the German countryside was full of life and spring. There was not a sign of the war around them when a Panzerfaust just exploded into the second squad, killing five and wounding the other four. At the moment of the explosion an MG 42 opened up, spraying the entire platoon along with rifle fire and at least one Schmeisser. The point patrol disappeared as they were shot or they just hit the ground. Whether the captain's jeep was targeted on purpose or not, it and its radio was shot up. As usual, Dourity was with his men and not in the jeep. As men piled out of their three trucks, gunfire reduced their ranks but this experienced platoon fought back. Finding cover wherever they could, they returned fire with everything they had. It was effective fire and the German ambush began to die off until it ceased altogether. The damage done to Dourity's platoon was massive. Over 20% of his men were killed or wounded. Eight were dead and fourteen wounded. The jeep radio was dead and the short range walkie talk-ies did not have the range to reach anyone.

All three trucks had been hit many times by all the gunfire. Only one would even start and water was pouring from its radia-tor. Dourity knew that truck would not run far but hoped to get far enough to be able to reach the rest of his company that was spread over the area. He posted guards and sent out some short distance patrols to make sure the Germans did not return. Every other man still on his feet became the best at being a medic as they could. They filled the radiator with water from their canteens and started off.

The truck was soon out of water and a truck with no water does not run far; it did reach some high ground and finally the little walkie talkie reached help. It was still nearly half an hour before the first army ambulances arrived with a part of Oscar Company. Shortly, six more trucks and ambulances came as well. After his dead and wounded were removed from the field and carried back to Regiment Medical and graves detail, then Dourity talked to his men that had been out as guards and on point patrols. "I want to know where those SOBs went to; any signs of where they went, I want to know.

There were lots of signs of where the retreating Germans had gone--a little too many Dourity thought, but he took with him two fresh platoons and a few of the men that got ambushed and were still unhurt. The platoon that had taken such great losses he told to return to camp.

After they got started following the Germans, Captain Dourity began to notice a number of men that had just been in the fight had hidden themselves among the two new platoons. The new platoons were giving them water and ammunition and walking around them to hide them. Dourity smiled and said to himself, 'There are times to enforce orders, and times just to stay quiet. Man, how proud of these men can any officer ever be.'

The Germans were on foot and there were blood trails. They found two dead Germans on their walk and several wounded that had been left behind. Captain Dourity had tried to bring a Sherman with him but the ground was just too rough and a Sherman could not get through. Even a jeep could not find a way through, so it was just the boots on the ground that made it. As the Germans did not have any transportation, they had chosen the very roughest ground to retreat into. Taking this all into consideration Captain Dourity came to the conclusion that the Germans he was facing knew they'd lost the war but were determined to fight to the death. This was going to be a hard fight and these Germans had picked a place to die in, knowing the Americans could not bring in any armor as it was just too rough. This fight was going to be man to man and the Germans were not going to give an inch. Dourity was determined to not get ambushed again as had occurred before.

This time Captain Dourity brought with him a SR 35-pound back-pack radio that had a pretty good range and both platoons had their walkie talkies. After they'd been walking for a little over three hours, he called a rest for fifteen minutes and spoke to his two lieutenants. He told them he wanted to send them out shaped like a winged bird with the tip of each wing leading out first. One squad at the very tip like the tip of a wing followed by two squads making up the main part of the wing. In the center would be a squad like a bird's head probing ahead. Behind the head would be the body made up of the remaining soldiers and all the extra personnel, he and the SR radio, medics and two mortar units. The other three squads would form the other wing. The wing tips would move first, followed by the rest of the wing rising. Then the head would probe forward and, as the base of the wings reached the bird's body, they would all move forward followed by the mortar and medics. One lieutenant would be in the middle of each wing and remain in contact with the SR. As soon as any part came in contact they were to take a defensive position and call the SR. The Americans started moving forward with great caution.

Within twenty minutes there was gunfire from the left wing and Dourity told that lieutenant to hold his ground but do not attempt to move forward except to bring the whole wing into contact with the enemy. Now Dourity ordered the right wing to swing around in a quarter circle movement until it came into contact. From the first shot from the right wing, the head moved forward again. When the entire force was fully in contact, Dourity ordered his mortars to open fire on the center of the enemy force—then slowly widen the circle of fire Every American stayed where they were until every last mortar shell had been fired. Then the troops moved forward. The mortars had done their job but there was still a lot of fight in the Germans. The ground was rough along with a heavily forested land. It was beginning to get dark by the time the fight was over. The Americans had 18 prisoners—every one wounded in varying degrees and they counted 26 dead Germans. In the darkness of the forest it was sure the Americans had missed some. But Captain Dourity wanted his men out of there before it was too dark to see, so they started back. When they found some reasonable ground to protect themselves, they stopped to spend the night. Only two more men had been killed but there were another eleven wounded, though all those were expected to recover.

Within a week the whole 4th Division had been ordered to move down into Bavaria. As far as the countryside was concerned it was like leaving the war behind. Once set up in their new camp, all commissioned officers were called into battalion meetings. They were told that German troops still remaining in Bavaria were some of the most diehard troops in the German army. This beautiful country had been the playground of high ranking German officers and Party officials. So it was very important to not let up in any way or any time. This area bespoke prosperity and showed little sign of the war at all. The people were a different matter; if looks could kill every American would be dead. Captain Dourity thought that all that richness would be protected by the diehard Nazis, but he was wrong. None of it was. The German troops had moved back into the mountains so the 4th blocked those roads and proceeded to check out everything else. It was hard to keep men on their toes when they went days without firing a gun, and the abundance of drink and fine German food did not help at all. As April came to a close, orders came: "Do not move into the mountains. Just guard the roads." In camp the scuttlebutt was that Hitler was dead and the Russians were tearing down Berlin brick by brick.

On May 9th the Germans officially surrendered. The world went crazy with delight as it should have. Men like Captain Dourity, who had fought men that preferred to die fighting than to surrender was not too sure that the fighting was over--official surrender or not. American planes flew back into the Bavarian mountains and dropped leaflets and a few troops started coming down and giving up, all with tales of their being ridiculed, cursed and worse by the Germans that swore to never give up regardless. Many of these were saying it was an American lie and the Fuhrer and the Nazi party could never surrender. The question on everyone's lips was 'When do I get to go home? The war is over and I am still alive. When will this be over for me?' Anyone with eyes saw there was much still to be done so most GIs just worked to get it over with. Then the scuttlebutt started that the 4th was going to be shipped to the Pacific to fight the Japs. That changed things a lot and many men were not quite as much in a hurry to go back to war on the other side of the earth as they were to just being home again. Roadblock duty was not fun at all—especially as they heard stories of 101 men and other units trying to drink up every bottle in huge wine vaults in all those mansions. Of course, those stories had to be exaggerated, didn't they?

Most of the 4th was scattered around Bavaria to try to help the people and maintain order. This was a huge job indeed and it seemed that no one had done much planning to get it done. For a little over a month the 4th worked at their new job and finally they were told they were going back to the United States and retrain and refit before being sent to the Pacific. Getting an entire division back to the United States was a huge job within itself. The call from America, both the general public and political, was get the troops home from Europe and let's get this Pacific war over with as soon as possible. In fact, with every passing day the word grew louder, 'We won; now get out of Europe and let it take care of itself.' Unfortunately this included intelligence and army intelligence. It was disbanded so fast it was like they were using a bulldozer to clear an abandoned building. Some Army intelligence people had to stay as long as there were American troops in Europe but whereas there had been thousands, now there were hundreds. Where there had been many hundreds of different offices directing Army intelligence, there were now twelve and soon it was cut to four. In the early days of 1945, Alex had over six hundred men and women working under him alone. Now there were less than three hundred in all Europe including all the different intelligence agencies. Alex would call another office and find the phones had been disconnected.

Then an army truck would pull up to his office and a private would come in and ask, "Where do you want these files? I have a 6X6 full of them."

"Where did they come from, private?" someone in the office would ask.

"I have no idea," the private answered. "I was told to drive this truck to your location is all I know."

It was not long until there was not enough space in the hallways to even walk, as files were coming from everywhere. As most agencies were closed and no one knew what to do with the files, they just sent an agency that had not been closed. When that one was closed the files would all be sent to another location. Alex had lost so much of his staff that there was not even enough help to look into those boxes and find out what was in them. Ranking officers over Alex were being discharged right and left and no one knew what was going on. Finally in desperation Alex called London to the joint chiefs of intelligence and asked to speak to different people and the only person he was finally able to talk to was an unknown colonel. Alex explained his situation and the colonel said, "Go through it, pick out what is important and burn the rest. The war is over so I don't see how any of it is still important," and he hung up.

It would take lifetimes to go through all those files as every office that had been closed down in Europe sent their files to the few that remained open and Alex's was one of the few. Finally he got permission to move them to an empty army warehouse as there was now lots of them empty and they were good for storage. Here and there he picked up experienced intelligence personnel from closing offices to rebuild at least part of his own office. Once he got his new staff up and going and had attempted to reorganize, he had back business to take care of and then a little at a time he had some of those files brought back. One day a general walked in and said, "What the hell is going on here?"

Alex tried to explain until the general said, "If Washington has its way, this time next month the army will not have enough soldiers left in its army to have an honor guard for the president, damn those politicians. Soldier, keep your mouth shut and hide as much as you can and just maybe they will forget you are here. He turned and left.

There was still so much to do, he had to depend on a few of his new people to try to make heads or tails of those files. Some were packed up and sent to Washington, some were burned, while most were returned to storage for review by others or even his office at a later date. There were so many things that thousands had been doing that now a couple of hundred men and women were having to take care of only the most pressing. The army, politicians, and hundreds of other groups were trying to disassemble the military and leave only a few for national defense. It seemed utterly impossible to keep millions alive in the rubble of Europe with all its other problems. This made it actually amazing how often intelligence was called for answers.

13

THE HIDDEN WAR

Many men in the military, and especially the intelligence community saw a very real new threat to peace in Europe and it was their old ally, Russia. The peace accord had divided Europe into post-war zones where most all of Western Europe was returned to prewar governments as fast as they were liberated. Every inch of ground that Russia had conquered remained under Russian control. Yes, when Russia got men and a communist party firmly established and in control, they announced that a country was independent. It was as independent as a puppet on its strings and not allowed to have a brain of its own. As its production got kick-started again they had to pay Russia back for "liberating" it and paid a maintenance fee for protecting it against the West. All wars from the beginning of time had used spies and intelligence to help defeat their enemies. Much of America had slipped back into its old self before WWII, saying, "We are protected by oceans on both sides. Just win WWII and pull out of everything outside our own borders. Do not dare to even suggest that our friends and allies, the Russians, could do anything wrong. That's an insult to all humanity."

Even before getting into the war the necessity of getting information had become very apparent. For this to work, different agencies had to work together and F. D. Roosevelt ordered the formation of the Coordinator of information [CI] which included all military, the Federal Bureau of Investigation and the U.S. State department to work together. This helped but it was like telling all football teams to work together. They do as long as each team can still win each game and top the others. The Office of Strategic Services was connected to these but by a long thin thread. This was a spy network, deeply involved in clandestine operations that had to remain top secret if only to protect its own agents. Somewhere along the road of war, Roosevelt was asked to create a better fully-functioning Centralized Intelligence Division to better get and keep things working together. How, when and where this was started, developed and employed, few if any were permitted to know. The command in this was supposedly this group known as CI. Maybe this was done on purpose to hush the later more secret things so the world would not know there were two different agencies. We do know that on September the 18th a large report landed on the president's desk marked: Top Secret CI for the President of the United States, HIS EYES ONLY. From that day forward the fact that the United States had such an organization was known to the White House Cabinet. In time it was slowly revealed to the remainder of the military that had not been already informed. Some in government and the press had a fit that the United States had an organization that not even the U.S. Congress of the United States could look into without special permission. This was called UN-American, for anything to be withheld back from the people. That of course was foolish because throughout history many things have been barred from the public by governments or leaders.

Still the idea of ending all secrets was a pipe dream that America wanted to believe. Therefore the American military was cut to the bone and even most of the bones were thrown away. Twelve days later the military was ordered by Truman to dismantle the OSS as good neighbors do not spy on each other. There is no telling how much pressure was put on Truman to get him to do this. The military had to obey the orders of their commander in chief, so the OSS was dismantled but the military kept just a few by changing the name to the Strategic Services Unit. They kept their orders and disbanded the OSS while creating a new SSU without informing all of Congress. They did notify the few Congressmen that had enough brains to understand that a nation can no longer have a working army without Intelligence. It's like maintaining an army without feeding it or paying it--things just do not work that way. The military approached Truman and others trying to get them to approve a new or improved CI. Somewhere down the line after September 1949 an A was added to CI and it officially became known as the CIA or Central Intelligence Agency. The years between the end of the war and 1950 were hard years for Intelligence as it had to rebuild itself from the ground up and Congress thought it was a waste of money anyway. After all it was happy times again and times of great prosperity and America would never face war again. Besides was that not what we just fought WWI and WWII for, to make sure there would now be per-petual world peace?

One of a few that never left intelligence, even though he was moved around in it with the changing of the wind, was a colonel named Alexander Vetov. When General Patton was named the Governor of Bavaria, he fought to keep as much of the Military Intelligence and OSS as he could, so he could keep an eye on those no good SOB Russians. Many times when he was ordered to cut intelligence personnel they were reassigned to Patton's displaced person divisions or some other title while staying on the job. When Patton learned that the 4th was going to be returned to the Sates and then sent to the Pacific he personally requested that Colonel Vetov be transferred to his office of the governor of Bavaria. Shortly thereafter Colonel Vetov requested a few personnel including a Captain Wallace to work with him. Patton wanted to know as much about those Russians as he'd wanted to know about the Germans before the end of the war. The fact that Patton could not keep his mouth shut ended his leadership in the army. He was far too famous to turn out to pasture and far too much trouble to be sent to the Pacific to fight.

Even before the end of the war Intelligence was already on the chopping block and being cut right and left. Even the thought of keeping anything from the British or Russians now was just unheard of officially. Most all the intelligence personnel was very selective as to what they shared and to whom. After all, the British had not shared with Alex until forced to and only after they had time to get everything they wanted. The Russians shared nothing so why share anything with them? Business suits now began to hang in Alex's closet, along with his uniforms; and he was out and about in them often now. He was seldom ever seen in his Army staff car, and drove himself around in a French car most of the time. One of the people that Alex had requested to come with him to every posting after leaving the Krump mansion was a fine intelligence officer named Margret Hollis. Most of the time that Alex was in the French car, Margret was with him. Many of these trips were for fact-gathering, and Margret could speak German as well or better than Alexander could. The icing on the cake was that she could speak Russian nearly as fluently as Alexander could. They could go anywhere and blend right in. It was amazing how much they could pick up as a couple from people they met. When they did use English, even though Margret was from Kansas City, she spoke with such a strong command of the British vocabulary and accent that she always passed as British. Spending three years in England doing intelligence, she had perfected it. Her Bavarian German was that of the elite Germans. She kept a small but very good wire recorder in her purse when they were out together.

They made a perfect team of spies and as Patton could not keep his thoughts about the Russians to himself he was relieved [the nice word for fired] as governor of Bavaria. Colonel Vetov was moved to the American section of Berlin to continue his work. His people followed him one or two at a time until they had the whole team. The very latest in equipment was brought in and the CIU had the best spy shop in Europe. Now they primarily used the Russian language when they were out on the town. He and Margret posed as a well-known, very rich British business couple helping to rebuild Berlin's business for world trade. The CIU had provided Margret with a full set of papers and a background of being born in the Ukraine as Katiya Vastlier, moving to England in 1926. Her papers were based on a real person who had moved to England on that date and disappeared in a German air raid in 1939. Her body was never identified so the real Katiya became the perfect cover as the second Katiya. She slowly started using Katiya instead of Margret, telling her friends and acquaintances that during the war and living in England the name Margret had worked better for her so she wouldn't sound foreign. Now that the war was over she'd gone back to her real name of Katiya.

She had a British passport and greeted all Russians as having been great allies in defeating the Nazis. They had box tickets in the Russian section for both the opera and ballot. Their going back and forth into the Russian zone was so common that the Russian border guards knew them by name. They rented a large villa in the British zone and opened their import export business in the building that shared the CIU offices. Using a large building also gave the CIU a cover. They were now provided with a large Lincoln with a chauffeur. Alexander used his US passport and talked about his life as a major in the American army. Of course, the fact that he was in intelligence never came up. He also greeted all the Russians as fellow country-men and great allies in winning the war.

Russian officers also thought of Alexander as a Russian-born ex-ally American officer during the great war against the Nazis. In all this they liked and accepted him as an ally and brother Russian. The war had just ended and it was time to celebrate. The tension trickling down from higher ranks had not reached the lower ranks of their Russian army in force as yet. The Russians wanted to talk and they talked about everything. When Alex asked them about their homes in Russia and their families, they conversed into the night, covering their whole lives from birth to the unit they now inhabited while stationed in Berlin. They told about all their units and what they did in their units. The food at home in Russia compared to the food they now were eating as Russian occupation soldiers. This, of course, led to what they were now doing and all the stupid orders they felt they were now receiving. It would take Alex the other half of the night to type up all the information he had received in only one evening of being out on the town with Russian troops. Alex had well learned that all information was good and one never knew when it could be put together with other information into crucial information revealing a much bigger picture.

After the first few months in Berlin, between Alex and all his other CI agents, they knew every position and unit name and the number of Russian troops in Berlin. They also learned about the improvements that were being made on their T-34 tanks and other equipment. In fact, they had gathered much information about Russian troops and equipment outside Berlin as well. They put this together with bits and pieces picked up from American, British and French forces stationed in Berlin. Through shared intelligence from these allies and the photos taken of moving cars trucks and aircraft, Alex's staff could inform the American army exactly what the Russians had and where it was. However as time passed, things tightened up and tensions grew, especially as the border guards started becoming more strict. Even the attitude between the American troops and the Russian troops slowly but surely began to change. Since the beginning of time, among soldiers there was always fighting between men over the women. When this was with a Russian soldier fighting an American soldier over the same woman, the Russian's buddies became involved. On one occasion someone drew a knife. Of course, every one claimed that it was the other side. By the time the story spread on both sides, hot tempers flared and for a while traveling between the east/west zones were closed to enlisted men on both sides. For Alex, it was still pretty much open as he was known as a businessman that had been an American officer. After all, he was Russian-born, spoke their language, and liked all things Russian. When he wanted to cross at any checkpoint, if there was a delay he had a long list of Russian officers to call upon. Besides this, many of these border guards knew Alex well and also knew he was friends with ranking Russian officers. In addition, what Russian was going to pay much attention to anyone with the name of Alexander Vetov? When the crackdown started getting tight, Alexander became more careful when he was in the Russian zone.

Alex still met with his Russian friends and even East German businessmen about how his business could be helpful to both sides. The war was over and shouldn't allies help each other get back to a better life. If a little money passed back and forth, that was just a bonus. Then add to this fact that Alexander and Katiya were very involved in the German and Russian arts. It dropped them right in the middle of those that had power in East Germany. Every opening or closing of a new opera or ballet involved a party with the most important people and Alexander and Katiya were always invited as important business personalities. They were always black tie affairs and Katiya had to be careful in her Paris gowns to look perfect, yet still not outshine the women from the East. To make these women anything but best friends would hurt their cause. While Alex gained much information, it was Katiya's conversations with the wives and girlfriends that brought back boatloads of information. If she did not have perfect recall, it was very close to it. Alex always thought she had a photographic memory. Many times Alex said that Katiya knew more about what was happening, not only in Berlin, but in all East Germany than all the Russian high command did.

One Russian Colonel in particular cozied up to Alex and Katiya--a colonel Mikhail Sokuiov. He showed them around the best sights in East Berlin, and the best restaurants and showplaces the Russians had prepared for foreign visitors. This was to show off the

great progress the East Germans were making under the direction of Russian Communism. Colonel Sokuiov wanted to know all about Alexander's new company and the work he was doing in east Berlin and other parts of Germany as well. Alex and Katiya both knew this had to be more than just a friendship so he had CIU check Sokuiov out. Sure enough he was Cheka, a division of the KGB that only had to answer to Stalin himself. That meant that the Russians knew who Alex really was. Well, this was alright; it just changed the game. It could be used to CIA's advantage, but it had to be carefully played. Most times when Alex and Katiya were in East Berlin for the opera or ballet, it "just happened" that they ran into Colonel Sokuiov with a beautiful woman on his arm. Sometimes the same woman, sometimes with someone else. Most times he would insist they have dinner together at only the very best places or at least drinks.

Things were going great until one day at the Russian ballet Sokuiov told Alex he wanted Alex to meet a real Russian hero and Alex turned around and looked into the face of Dimitry Zoliff. Alex was a very good spy by now and he reached out his hand to shake the hand of the famous general. Dimitry responded in kind as though neither had ever met. After a few words passed all around the general went on his way and Alex and Katiya returned to the ballet. If this was not the longest ballet Alex had ever sat through, it sure seemed like it. How much did the KGB know; did they know Dimitry had worked with American Intelligence? Even if they did, it was to defeat the Nazis and we were allies. What did this mean?

He sent a secret carrier back to Paris with all his questions and waited. Alex's trade and reconstruction company had offices in Frankfort and other cities and in a few days he was asked to fly to Frankfort, then by military transport on to Paris. A whole week was devoted to discussion as to what moves to make, and if this or that happened what to do, and hundreds of other moves. Several things came up as necessary: first, things must not seem to change in Berlin except to act a little more like a rich American businessman. Katiya would make more "shopping" trips to Paris and actually spend a lot of time shopping in the very best shops. Alex would be seen even more in his business of import and export. Then they'd wait to see what would happen next.

Making another trip into East Berlin by himself, Alex "accidentally" ran into Sokuiov at lunch and they talked like best of friends. Sokuiov asked where Katiya was and Alex truthfully told him she was in Paris on a shopping trip. Then Sokuiov quietly asked Alex if he and Katiya were married. They were living together and acted married, but she did not share Alex's last name. Alex said, "Yes, we are together and I love Katiya but we have never married and never plan to do so."

Sokuiov smiled and said, "We Russians understand such things better than Americans do." Before Sokuiov departed, he leaned over to Alex and said, "Since you are here alone tonight, why do you not come with me to an officers' club."

Alex sat quietly for a long pause as though he was giving it long hard thought and then slowly said, "Well, maybe for a little while."

From the moment they walked through the door of the officers' club they were served drinks by topless women that were almost totally naked. There was no question Sokuiov was trying to get Alexander drunk and off into a side room with some of these women. True to his word, Alexander went back to his place early. The next day while at work Alex got a call from Sokuiov and they talked. Alex thanked him for the evening but without enthusiasm. Alex wanted Sokuiov to think he was a moral man that was true to his woman. That should give the KGB a lot to think about.

The intention of Katiya's trips were to Paris was to deliver the top of the top important information back and forth, as no KGB agent would dare touch her. Besides that, every flight had several CIU agents aboard. In fact, there was protection throughout all her trips. When the enemy knows who is an agent and the agent knows he or she is known and people on other sides know, it really makes for a weird situation.

While the CIA had been unofficially started in December of 1945 it was not officially sanctioned by the United States Congress until September of 1949, calling it Central Intelligence. Now the agency was no longer the bastard child but was a full-fledged part of the American government. It was still several years before the word 'agency' was officially added to central intelligence. Between 1945 and 1949 things in the world had changed a lot. With every change, intelligence became more important and CIU gradually blended into CIA. If Berlin was not the most important CIA office in Europe it was most certainly close to the top. For several years everyone on both sides thought that if there was a flashpoint that could start a third World War it was going to be Berlin.

When Germany was cut up like a pie, Russia got a big chunk and America, France and Britain got small pieces. Berlin was deep in the Russian zone and it was also cut up into the same version of the pie. The Allies had four main ways into Berlin, the Autobahn highway, rail, the canals and restricted air routes. Everyone knew that Berlin was full of spies from all countries that had been involved in the war and probably most of the countries that were not.

By 1946 trust between the Russians and their former allies had evaporated. Somehow in the middle of this were Alexander and Katiya. Russia (or East Germany if you prefer) was hoping to use Alexander and Katiya in one way or the other to their advantage. Yet these two were the perfect spies at getting information. While the communists were actually watching, they got it anyway. Think about it this way: Alex and Katiya were putting together pieces of a puzzle. All the while the other side was trying to mix in fake puzzle parts from another puzzle with pieces that looked just like the real pieces. Yet these two, with the help of their staff workers, came up with the right picture most of the time. This was such a hard thing to do; no one on earth could always get all the parts right. As East Berliners rushed to the West, the communists cracked down harder until strong fences went up and guards started shooting down those that tried to get away. As days passed Alexander no longer had such easy access on his travels back and forth from West to East and back again. One day when Alex tried to get into East Berlin he was stopped and his pass was confiscated. At that time he was told the he was now on the prohibited list and could only go in with special permission. To get that permission he had to present a written application not less than five days in advance, with a specific reason to enter. Alex knew that the communists had grown tired of playing cat and mouse with him and had cut him off.

Well, this changed things a great deal and now he returned to directing intelligence gathering as a boss and had to lay aside his role as a field spy himself. Everyone knew he was a spy so, therefore, he was no longer an effective spy. As a director of other spies, however, he was right at home, and as director of a huge import and export corporation, he had cut out such a large place that he had to remain there also. After all, the whole thing was a CIA project. As things tightened up and tensions ran high in Berlin, the CIA decided it would be wise to pull Alex and Kit from Berlin and move them and most of their staff to Frankfurt. This time they took over a country estate with plenty of room for buildings for CIA and even an airfield for small and medium aircraft. Part of the pressure of living in Berlin was removed and this made working operations even easier. Army DC-47s came and went on a regular basis and this allowed Alex and Kit to move around with a new ease. They were together most all the time now, even more than before. Those that were close to them had a running joke as to which one was the boss. Kitiya got most of the votes, but Alex said that he did not mind. Officially, he still out ranked her.

Getting information from behind those closed doors of communism was even harder than getting it from the Germans ten years before. When the communists even suspected someone behind their lines was giving information to the West, that person just disappeared. Many people who were just at the wrong place at the wrong time fell into the same situation. There was rarely a trial and the few times there were it was for show and had nothing to do with fact or guilt or innocence. It was put on to show who was in charge and remind people where they belonged. There was some backlash here, however, and some that had lost a loved one turned for help to the CIA. At this time the most important information came from the Russian and East German soldiers themselves. They never knew they were giving away important information as they got drunk or just talked. When they were with women, what they said often filtered back to CIA agents. They were not in a shooting war so their extra curricular activities had them talking a lot about everything–their companies, units, equipment and all the latest talk about what they'd just done or what they were going to do. The German women that had suffered so much in the closing days of the war, and were still suffering at the hands of Russian soldiers, were pleased to get any information back to the Allies. Again separating the millions of small pieces into fact or fiction proved very hard to do. One possible tip-off occurred when the same thing came up over and over. Then it was separated into a pile for further examination. In spite of the vastness of it all, it was amazing how info came in: the size of occupation troops--units, names and numbers. Even officers' names and ranks along with equipment, locations, duty assignments, even to the food they ate.

Combined, this gave a fairly accurate picture of what the Allies were facing. For every GI in Germany there were twenty Russians or conquered men from other countries wearing communist uniforms. When the war in Europe and Japan ended, American factories could not wait to build airliners and not bombers, farm equipment not tanks. Shipyards switched to whatever rather than aircraft carriers. The world was full of used WWII equipment that basically Americans left wherever it was, as they no longer wanted or needed it. Meanwhile, the Russians were in the process of upgrading everything to fight with, and keeping the old just in case. The British had given them the jet engine, along with information procured from captured German jets and drawings. They refined and worked until they came up with the MIG 15. The world famous Russian T-34 tank saw sturdy improvements. Having seen how the Germans used their submarines in WWII, the Russians jumped into submarine improvement and manufacture. Communist troops in many countries now had conquered more land than the Germans ever had.

America said it is over, let us be happy and get back to living. But what Russia and communism was doing scared the hell out of some of America's military and political community and they got back into the development of improved weaponry and even called back into operation many of its fighting forces. Even the 4th was reestablished and sent back to Germany to stand against feared Russian warfare with exactly the weapons with which they had finished WWII.

One area of warfare that was quickly re-organized and better equipped was intelligence. Everyone looked to the CI/CIA for help and information. As in WWII and the OSS, knowing all about the enemy was very important. The CIA recognized that slowing down the enemy was very important and the best place to start was with the millions that were under the iron hand of communism. In reality, just like the Germans had been with the Nazis, these millions were still conquered people, not liberated as they'd wanted to be. So sow the seeds of hope for freedom and see what grows up. In many places it did spring up and was crushed by Russian tanks and cannon. The West did nothing to help and in reality it could do nothing without another World War now equipped with atomic power and troops that outnumbered the small countries of Germany, Japan, and Italy's largest armies at the height of their world conquest by ten to one. When it came to NATO forces, it was more like thirty to one. The American hope now was to hold all these millions where they were by becoming so strong we could assure them of mutual destruction and maybe the end of mankind. Even to do this America had to catch up, by pass, know more and at least be as powerful as any other nation. The place to start was intelligence—worldwide intelligence.

Russia already had developed a super intelligence network. While Russia was not the only Communist country, it was where Lenin and others sparked it into a worldwide brush fire. It was Russia that had spread it and nourished it, and it was Russia that had to be held in check by bluff, power or anything necessary.

In 1947 it was looking like an impossible job to control the roar of the big bear. The U.S. looked like a fencer using his thin little sword seeking to turn away every thrust the enemy made, all the while looking for an opening to wound the enemy. In this case, however, the powers that be were only interested in staying in the defense mode. The non-stop questions were arriving by the truck load. What is the enemy doing? Why is the enemy doing whatever he is doing? How can we block his thrust and what will it take to do so? On and on the questions flew and the CIA and other intelligence agencies were doing their best to come up with the right answers. Any one wrong answer could allow the enemy's sword to draw blood. Russia felt like having the allies in Berlin was as bad as it would have been to have Hitler's army in Moscow ten years earlier. East Germany was communist, as they had conquered it, while the Allies had just stood back and let Russian blood take Berlin and a large part of Germany. Then the Allies had demanded parts of Berlin. Yes, Russia had relented a little then, but now she wanted it all back. It was hers by right of conquest and she had the power to cut it off and starve the Allies out. If a million Germans starved to death that was not Stalin's fault; all the Allies had to do was get up and get out. Besides if the Allies did get out of Berlin and faced the might of Russia, maybe they would keep on moving back and get out of all Germany.

Then Stalin demanded traffic be stopped and inspected by Russian troops to see if anything was coming into Berlin he did not want to come in. You cannot stop airplanes in the middle of the air, so Russian aircraft would buzz all non-Russian aircraft so close as to keep them from flying into Stalin's air space. Then a Russian Yak fighter got too close to a British airliner and both planes crashed with no survivors. The British protested and the Russian answer was if the British had not been in Russian air space it would not have happened. This did cause a worldwide outcry against the downing of a British airliner in an area that had been approved by the Russians for years, causing the death of many non-military citizens. Stalemated was not Stalin's way and he did not like to be criticized, so he cut the city of Berlin off from the rest of the world. There was no way for him to stop airplanes without shooting them down and even Stalin knew better than that. It would have started WWIII and the whole world would be against him. There seemed no way on earth airplanes could bring enough food and supplies to feed and take care of over a million people, anyway, so let them try. That initiated the Berlin airlift with transport aircraft from eleven nations flying in food, fuel, and the necessities of life for fifteen months while the world watched and cheered. Even Stalin finally gave in to world opinion but it took fifteen months to do it. Who knows what went on in communism during those fifteen months but there must have been great pressure pointing to the fact that this was hurting the communist cause.

One day Alex received a large batch of East German newspapers but strangely, it was the second batch that had arrived that day. Using a powerful magnifying projector Alex studied both sets of newspapers and, sure enough, hundreds of the printed dots contained a super small micro dot film. Micro dots were not new and both sides used them. The micro dot was a piece of film so small it fit inside the dot of a period or letter of the alphabet. This dot could be magnified with the right equipment into a full typed page. The CIA had the equipment to do this and a few dots were very carefully removed from the printing. Alexander studied them but did not know what he was looking at. One of his analysts studied them for a while, then came into Alex's office looking like he'd seen a ghost. He explained to Alex that some of these dots were studies of American plans as studied by Russian scientists. Most however were copies of many government pages in the original English right from American scientists about the development of the atomic bomb.

This shocked Alex so much he stopped all work on removing the dots. Within four hours he was on a fast plane to London where it was re-fuelled and took off for Washington D.C. Alex had taken both sets of everything they'd received plus all the work that had been done in Germany on these papers. Upon landing he was taken to CIA headquarters where the entire board of American-based directors of the CIA was waiting for him. All the papers and work that had already been done were taken away for analysis and Alex was questioned in detail. Their main question was 'where did all this come from?'

The simple truth was Alex did not know. He said his staff was trying their best to find out. However they were doing so very carefully to make sure no one had any idea what was going on. If the information was real it meant that there was a hidden source deep in the Russian government leaking top secret information to the American government. This could be the most important information source that had ever been available to America. This also meant that there was a spy network in America that was stealing the most important secrets from America right under American noses. A part of the commission immediately moved information to the FBI to start the greatest anti-spy program in the United States. This was not a plan to build up better security. This was a plan to learn how our security had broken down in the first place and to find those that had done it. There was no question that the most important research and development had been compromised; that was a fact.

While the commission was waiting to find out how much damage had been done and how much the Russians had, they moved to discussing who, how and why this information had been sent to the CIA in Germany. Alex had thought that Dimitry might have been involved from the moment the micro dots were suspected to be real. However, Dimitry's name was never brought up before the commission. If there was the slightest hint that Dimitry was involved against the government of Russia, the Russians would kill him and everyone he had ever talked to, and all their deaths would be slow and painful.

Several things were decided. They had to support and encourage a large anti-war faction that did not want Russia to get involved in another war. These people were pro-Russian but anti-war and might or might not be communist. Allies just wanted those Russians that wanted war to be held back from getting an edge on rest of the world. So these peacemakers had to be protected in every way possible and Alex sent a top secret notice that all activities to trace or locate them be instantly stopped. In fact, the German office of the CIA was told that "they had never received anything at all." This group of peacekeepers had to be large and in very powerful places in the government, military, and Russian intelligence. They probably would never work with the Allies, as these were not traitors. They were true Russian patriots trying to protect Russia from those in power who wanted to conquer the world. This made them the best allies in the world to avoid war.

These meetings went on for three days and every day more and more information from the micro dots kept coming in. Every piece of information was proven to be correct. On the last day twelve persons from the Atomic Energy Commission were brought in and asked questions about their security. They were all totally satisfied that nothing had ever been able to get past their security. Then over a hundred sheets of their papers were passed out among them and they were asked if they had ever seen them before. All twelve were stupefied, declaring there was no way anyone could have procured those papers. They demanded to know how the CIA had been able to acquire them. When they were told that they'd been stolen from America and sent to Russia, one of the commissioners passed out and was thought to have had a heart attack. He was sent to a hospital with two jeeps full of MPs to stay with him at all times regardless. On the fifth day different parts of the CIA spent time with Alex discussing the situation. On the sixth day he was returned to his plane with close to a thousand pages of information and requests for CIA actions in Europe. On the seventh day he was back in Frankfort with his Margret/Kitiya.

At this point he had been instructed to very carefully look to see if there was any possibility that information in the past might have been slipped to him by the same people from whom this information had come. He needed to do so with much care. If they never found out it would be much better than compromising the source even in the smallest way. Every person that had anything at all to do dealing with this discovery was placed under the strictest of security and questioned in great depth whether anything had been said, even as small as a comment about receiving two sets of newspapers.

Thinking things over, Alex and Katiya began to come up with a very long list regarding how easy some of their information had come in. Maybe just maybe Alexander Vetov had not always been as good a spy as he thought he was. For several years his assignments had been at the top of intelligence in gathering information; maybe he'd had a little help. Now this thought really rocked his boat of pride. Still, Alex knew he was good at doing what he did, so he went back to work to help protect America and the free world. While doing this, his business of free trade and reconstruction was actually doing a great deal of good for Germany. German plants were back in production, making products for the world as well as Germany. Alex was particularly proud of the Porch factories and the many products they were producing. One that had been started by Hitler was a small inexpensive family automobile that was very cheap to operate and still performed well. The English word was family wagon, the German word and name was Volkswagen. German farms were cleared from war damage and were back in production, not only feeding the German people but exporting food to much of Europe. German toys, musical instruments and a vast number of goods were now flowing into America and the world.

As West Germany prospered, the people of East Germany were

trying harder and harder to escape to the West. The East German people were cold, shivering in rags that had been new in the early 40s. Even now after all these years it was the best they had. They were living in the remains of their homes and bombed out buildings, while trying to stay alive by digging out burnable wreckage from this same rubble. A few East Germans that were helping the Russians had moved into nice apartments and even homes. If the rest were even paid enough to keep from starving, they were few in number. The poor in East Germany knew the lives of their counterparts in the West were getting better every year as those living in East Germany were just trying to survive. More and more risked their lives to get over the border to the good life in the West, and many lost their lives trying. Others were put into slave labor camps to work for nothing.

14

THE COLD WAR – THAT WAS NOT SO COLD

A t this point it seemed the communists became more interested in starting communist brush fires in countries all over the world. Communist Chinese had conquered China. Korea had been split into a communist north and a south with the United Nations being its overseer and adviser. This job was basically left in the hands of the United States. While communist fires of rebellion were burning all over the world, of course much of Europe had been "liberated" by Russia and was little more than a part of the now-Russian empire. Being an undercover CIA agent anywhere was a very dangerous assignment even in the friendly countries. Some agents were killed or caught and then kept for torture or to be exchanged to the other side for American-held spies captured by America. The last half of the 1940s were rough years for worldwide agents. In 1948 the communist People's Republic of China was recognized as the official government of China. The United States started pulling its troops out of Korea in order for that nation to make it on its own. By 1950 the United States had cut off all aid and involvement in Korea. As North Korea was a puppet state of Russia, Kim Ila-Sung asked Stalin if North Korea could retake all of Korea and make it all communist. Stalin thought that since the United States had pulled out and was no longer interested in South Korea, he could go ahead if he wished. Now a new tidal wave of war started in one small spot. Things changed now but maybe became better and easier to understand, as this was

---

open war. While the American goal had been to keep war cold rather than a hot shooting one, the word everywhere was "arms race" to see who could have the most or at least the best. China alone boasted she had the largest manpowered army on earth. China said she had more men under arms than all the non-communist countries combined. Russia was pushing very hard to develop the latest and best weapons and boasted to the world about doing it. All the while, Russia was doing the same thing in spies and intelligence, but keeping this very quiet. Then the new communist plan of limited hot war showed up in Korea.

On June the 25th North Korean troops with Russian made T-34 tanks crossed the 38th parallel and started south. Since South Korea had no outside help or supplies, this was thought to be an easy conquest for the communists. While North Korea had all the unwanted leftover WWII supplies from Russia that she wanted, Russia was in the process of rushing forward to equip its new military with new improved equipment. The bolt action 91s were replaced with SKSs and even some with AK-47s. The old rifles, machine guns, T-34 tanks, Yak fighter planes and all the rest of their old WWII military equipment went to China, Korea and other countries. Some they sold off but most went freely to the countries that were fully communist or wanted to be. The North Korean army swatted aside the south's small, poorly equipped army as nothing more than pesky flies. Two days later the UN Security Council protested the action of North Korea and sent a note of protest to North Korea. That same day Syngman Rhe, the president of South Korea, ordered all communists in South Korea to be executed in the Bedo Massacre better known as "The Summer of Tears." No one doubts that over 100,000 South Koreans were killed and no one has any idea how many more would have died if the north had not advanced so quickly. This advance mobilized every soldier the south could rush to the front, not leaving many to keep killing their own people. This action turned many South Korean people against Syngman Rhe and the south's government.

In three days the north had captured the south's capital of Seoul. The north did not even slow down in their rush into the south. On the fourth day of the war, June the 29 the North Korean army is driving south as fast as men can march. That same day General Douglas MacArthur arrived in Suwan, South Korea with a small handful of American occupation troops from Japan, all with left-over WWII guns and equipment. The only real power MacArthur had, when he was allowed to use it, was the Air Force and later the U.S. Navy with its air power and fire power. Now the situation was a little better, as even WWII prop-driven aircraft were deadly against the north's movement south. It did not stop the communist army, but did a lot of damage to their advancing army. This was amazing considering there were very few American WWII aircraft available and only a very small number of these were allowed to MacArthur. After all, one "would not send a fire truck to swat a mosquito."

A U.S. military presence that close to Russia in the cold war was unthinkable, but a few soldiers with WWII M1s could not be thought of as a threat to Russia. Practically all the aircraft were old leftover propeller driven aircraft with just a few reasonably new ones included. Even the newest ones were still WWII propeller planes. In fact most of the planes that showed up in the first month of the Korean war were aircraft that had been left behind in Japan or the Islands, discarded as American forces got the new and better aircraft that was being produced.

Even these would have worked well if there had been enough of them. It was all just as obsolete on both sides at the beginning of the Korean War. The Yak fighters that the North Korean army had were nearly as old as the American aircraft were. If MacArthur had a thousand of the American fighters that were being cut up in Arizona and sold for scrap, the beginning of the Korean War would have been a different story. There were thousands of American pilots flying them just five years before who could have piloted those aircraft without a long training period. To fill military contracts, companies were still building aircraft as WWII came to a close. Untold numbers of these were flown direct from their factories to locations where they were cut up and scrapped. To America, they no longer had any value. Transport planes were sold off, as they still had value. A few fighters were sold or given away to small, very friendly countries. At the start of the Korean War there were still thousands of these new or like-new aircraft just waiting for the wrecking companies to demolish them. If MacArthur had a thousand of these in the first month of the Korean War, history would have resulted in a different story. After all it was leftover Russian equipment that Russia no longer had any need for that we were facing.

As soon as WWII was over, America said, "We do not need this old stuff and we sure do not want to spend money on any new military equipment." Meanwhile, some small voices in the U.S army and Navy claimed they had to be equipped and they hung onto all they could. Aircraft, ships, tanks, trucks and a lot of old WWII equipment was mothballed for use at a later date. This equipment was not being improved, just stored away. If a new war was to occur they figured it would all be super jets, atomic bombs, etc. The one thing that could never happen again was a WWII type ground conflict. Never again would soldiers fight on the ground. If war ever came again it would all be super weapons and just maybe the end of the world. As the communist threat developed, America started in research and development of new weapons and they progressed fast. Whereas in WWII plants were making thousands, now they were lucky to get a contract for a dozen of the new things for "testing" purposes. Almost all government money went into aircraft development or top secret super weapons, biological or germ warfare, and thousands of others went on behind closed doors. The few occupation troops that were still in Japan were mostly green recruits that had never had a day in combat in their lives and never thought for one minute that they ever would.

Without a pause MacArthur sent his handful of soldiers north to try to slow down the advancing enemy. In four days from first landing in South Korea the Americans were facing the vast communist army and on the fourth of July they fought the Battle of Osan. No one has been able to come up with how badly they were outnumbered or to consider they were facing Russian T-34 tanks with out-dated WWII bazookas. They had to retreat with over a 150 soldiers killed and wounded. However, the North Korean army knew they had been in a real fight. They also knew they were now going to have to fight the Americans and not just chase them away.

It only took one month for the communists to conquer all of South Korea except one small pea-sized pocket known as the Pusan Perimeter. In this month many in the United Nations sent small numbers of troops to help fight this "Police Action." Still it showed that the United Nations was trying to uphold their hope for a world in peace. Right then, MacArthur would have likely accepted help from Custer's 7th Cavalry with their single shot rifles if they had been available. The West was also very careful to pretend this was not a hot war between East and West. Just a little misunderstanding to be policed by the West. By now the Yankee sleeping giant was coming back to life and began sending men and equipment into the fight. But the American money and new equipment was apparently going to Europe to face the "real threat," just like the start of WWII.

Other than a few modern airplanes, everything was still leftover WWII equipment as this was all America politicians decided to send. Even though thousands of better American aircraft were being sold off for their scrap metal value. Later in the "peace action," a very few American jet fighters flew to Korea from Japan to help. After flying to Korea from Japan and saving enough fuel to return, they only had the range to work in the very southern part of Korea and even then counted their time in minutes not hours over any target.

When MacArthur started getting large bombers, the storyline changed a bit but even then, most all the newer B-29s were held back to protect from worldwide war. Again, because Korea was a police action, it only got the scraps. Besides, we were only fighting against the North Korean army and they only had old used Russian equipment to fight with. Fighting a war from a pocket of defense could turn into years of fighting and for MacArthur that was not acceptable. He wanted to win and quickly; this had to be done by doing the unthinkable. So he did just that, against the Army and Navy's advice that his plan could not be carried out. He pulled together a naval task force right from the pages of the Navy's fight against Japan. He planned to land it in the most impossible place in all of Korea—a harbor right across from Seoul where he could rush in and cut the enemy's supply line. Then he could cut the enemy off and force them out of South Korea for a quick victory. Nature itself posed the biggest problem of all. The tides at Inchon were an average of 29 feet, one of the world's highest. At low tide there were miles of mud that no American vehicle could get through or over. The landing force would have to go in, discharge enough men and equipment to fight, and gain enough ground to hold until the next high tide. They had to hold or be wiped out and the whole invasion would be lost.

Alex was on the other side of the world but this took a vast amount of intelligence and information-gathering to accomplish. From the moment MacArthur thought of Inchon he called upon every part of intelligence to get him the necessary information. The Navy intelligence came in first with the flat statement it could never be done; it was totally impossible. MacArthur said "Nothing is impossible, we just have to find out how to get around all these problems."

Now the CIA stepped in with mountains of information on the Inchon Harbor. The maps the Navy had were not adequate at all so the CIA went to the Japanese. After all, Japan had owned Korea during the second world war and the Japanese navy were very good at gathering exhaustive information about harbors. The Japanese even knew all the harbor features in every country they conquered or even wanted to conquer. The Japanese maps showed exactly where all three main channels leading into Inchon Harbor were.

They had the exact depth and width at high and low tides. They showed the mud flats with descriptions of the mud and how deep it was—even the average water temperature year round. A great help was the fact that the CIA had started collecting information on all of Korea before the north came across the 38th. The Korean army had taken Inchon the same day they'd taken Seoul. From the first day the North Koreans had taken Inchon, they started using the harbor to bring supplies from the north. They used South Korean slave labor to do much of the on-the-ground work. This slave labor saw everything that was going on in that harbor. They unloaded old Russian underwater anti-ship mines from Russian freighters as well as guns and ammunition for the North Korean troops. The slave laborers paid a lot of attention to those underwater mines and even made sketches from memory including model numbers and production dates. These slaves were not only there when these mines were taken out into the harbor and put into the water but, again, it was the slaves that did most of the work. Their memory was amazing as they got back to shore and recorded where these mines went. To Alex and men like him, this was like working WWII all over again as the real information was coming from those that hated the enemy. This kind of information could be trusted.

Then when the American Navy intelligence division got this information they quickly put together a plan to defeat these mines. Of course, where they were was the most important but the second item was just about as important. These mines were all of the old design that were made for mining a normal harbor that did not have very high and low tides. They were most certainly not designed for a harbor that had a thirty-foot difference between a high and low tide. Most mines of the early war years were what men on mine sweepers called "mine in a box.'" These mines came in a box-like base that protected them while in shipment from being accidentally set off. This box protected them while being placed into the water, still in their boxes The boxes were heavily weighted not only to sink them but hold them stable in swift currents. On the bottom of each box was another weight fastened to the box with a long steel cable that was adjustable for length. When this mine was put into the water this bottom weight was released and fell the preset distance from the box. When this weight hit the bottom and the cable became slack it triggered a device that locked the long cable holding the mine and box together. These were floating mines like a fishing cork on a fish line. When the cable was locked between the mine and the box was locked, the heavy box pulled the mine underwater to the preset depth the first weight had locked it in. In most all harbors this worked very well, but Inchon's extremely deep tide was not like most harbors. At low tide the tops of the mines were seen on the surface and at high tide they were so far below the surface only the very largest ships were deep enough to set one off, if even then.

Also the communists were using this harbor so they left a path down the three channels leading into the harbor so as to not blow up their own ships. The Japanese maps showed exactly where these channels were with every curve. Not one American or Allied ships was sunk by these mines during the landings. Intelligence had saved the day. As the task force approached Inchon the Air Force and Navy air power pounded Inchon and all surrounding targets, especially all roads leading into the city. Air power kept reinforcements from reaching the city, not only for the landing, but even more important for the long hours before the second wave of American ships could come in with the second high tide. Once the tide started out, the water in the harbor receded faster and faster, requiring ships to unload as quickly as possible. When it dropped six feet, all large shipping was ordered out, regardless of what was still on board. When the big ships got out, the mine sweepers went back in like they had done before to clear the edges of the three channels of mines. They stayed at their jobs until some floating mines began to show at the surface of the water. Here, gunfire exploded these mines to clear even more of the water that was becoming more shallow with every hour.

As troops first started landing, there was some hard fighting but it was lighter than expected. Moving away from the beaches, however, got tougher with every mile. As the troops were landing, naval gunfire, especially from the big battleships and heavy cruisers, was so heavy behind the beaches, along with the air power, it made it impossible for the enemy to move forward. Once the troops began to slog inland even a few hundred yards the U.S. Navy and Air Force had to move its fire back to avoid killing Allied troops. In spite of the tremendous fire on them, as the fire began to move deeper inland it was amazing how many communists had survived and came out to fight. Steady progress was made by the Allies but it was now slowed for two reasons: first, there was more enemy pressure. Second, it was going to be a long time before any more troops and supplies could arrive, so what they had it was necessary to hold until reinforced. The few North Korean Yak aircraft that were stationed in the central party of Korea tried to come in to help the North Korean army. But they were so badly outnumbered by the Allies they made little if any difference. The North Koreans had thought all fighting was over in that part of Korea and had moved almost all their aircraft to the south tip of Korea where all the fighting was going on. All North Korean armor had been destroyed or at least neutralized by the naval bombardment or Allied aircraft that it played no part in the first day's fight.

During the night some enemy armor and troops had been able to work its way in but even this was temporarily neutralized by the Allied aircraft as soon as it was daylight. Things began to change. Even though the second high tide had brought in tons of equipment and thousands more soldiers, the enemy was digging in and fighting to the death to stop the Americans from reaching deeper into Korea.

As the fighting reached the foothills and then the mountains of Korea, the fighting became harder and progress became slower. MacArthur was very happy with the landing but very unhappy that his troops were not cutting into the North Korean army to block their escape back north. One thing happened now that did make things much harder on the Allies to win the fight around Seoul. The highway through Seoul was the main supply route for all supplies to reach the fight in the south. This was MacArthur's whole plan—to cut this route, which he did. Now all these northern troops, tanks, artillery and equipment piled up to fight MacArthur's invasion. However as hard as this was on MacArthur's men, it did stop most of the supplies from going south. As communist supplies dried up in the south the pressure on the Pusan Perimeter eased some. As the Allies also had been reinforced, they broke out and began pushing the communists back north again. The fight going north was all a hard fight unlike how the North Koreans had flooded to the south with little to no opposition. However as supplies ran out for the communists their flight back north became faster.

At home in America, seeing progress made every day, the American people rejoiced that we were winning and MacArthur was more a hero than he had ever been. When the 38th parallel was reached, MacArthur asked President Truman if he could cross and continue to drive the communists north. Permission was given and the fight now started pushing the northern communists back into their own territory. But now the bitter winter of North Korea arrived early and the Allies were not prepared for it. When a soldier has to fight in freezing weather without proper clothing it is nearly impossible to function properly. When that temperature goes to zero it requires arctic clothing and equipment to even stay alive. All too many American troops fell because they did not have what they needed. However, they fought on until even mediocre winter gear and supplies arrived.

By early October Washington was buzzing with the question: will China get involved? as the fight moved in that direction. On October 15th MacArthur assured Truman that the Chinese would never get involved and he pushed forward toward the Chinese border. To ensure that the Chinese would not get involved in the fight, American pilots were restricted from approaching Chinese airspace and must never enter it regardless, even though supplies were coming across the river border into North Korea and communist MiG 15s were running for it when chased by American Saber jets. On one occasion, there was much pressure exerted by the defense department to stop the flow of supplies into North Korea across the border. The power of control gave the Air Force permission to bomb the south end of the bridge into North Korea, if they could do so without even a wing tip entering an inch of Chinese air space. MacArthur was declaring the war won but requested doing whatever he needed to do to block that border. Ten days later it was discovered that there were already over 100,000 Chinese troops in North Korea and they were well equipped with winter gear, T-34 tanks, trucks, artillery and everything they needed. They came down upon the Allies like the sky was falling in.

Outgunned and radically outnumbered the Allies could do nothing but retreat. As it turned out, they were not really retreating. They had just turned around and were fighting while facing the other direction. Almost all Allied army troops had been surrounded, and the communist troops were trying to annihilate them.

This was when Katiya came home from grocery shopping in town and found a letter in her grocery sack addressed to Margret. It had been a long time since she had used that name and wondered who even knew it was her real name. She opened it and read a handwritten note that read, "Dear Margret, please tell Alex that I remember the 88-acre farm in Utah and hope it will not be too long until we can meet again with a world at peace. Have a merry Christmas and a happy new year." No name, just a "your friend."

Alex knew exactly what Dimitry was saying and made plans to just disappear from the 25th of December to the 1st of the year. Getting permission to be gone for the holiday week was not hard to do, as everything was going on in the other side of the world from Europe. Alex and Margret/Katiya left for Paris for a "Christmas Holiday." Christmas morning he kissed Margret goodbye and headed for Utah Beach. When he arrived on the 26th he parked as close as possible to where the German 88s had been. What was left of them was still there and Alex could see where the White Russians had made quite a mess in taking them out and the German encampment as well. After all these years it looked like everyone just walked off and left it for time to do its worst. As dusk came, he walked back to his car and now there was another car there. An older dignified man in a business suit opened the door and told Alex to get in. Six years had aged both men as they greeted each other in an embrace.

They sat and talked a long while and then Dimitry said, "Alex, I will never betray mother Russia, but a trap has been set for the Allies in Korea and MacArthur is walking right into it. It is not what the Chinese have done, even though they are included. It is a plan to not only destroy the Allied forces in Korea. This plan is to change the balance of power on earth and place communism in the driver's seat for the foreseeable future. It will include the nuclear destruction of America if she does not buckle under to worldwide communism. Right now the war hawks in the Kremlin think that they can wipe America off the face of the earth if they have to. Here is their plan: they are going to use the Chinese and the Korean War to get things moving. They must win more of the world to their side before they can set the last part of their plan into action. As we speak, your American Air Force is using over a hundred B-52s to bomb North Korea. Your allies have been increasing their air power every month in this war. At first they only faced Yak fighter bombers. When these were used up, better planes were sent until MiG-15s started showing up but only in small numbers. These were also our oldest fighters and the Korean pilots were not the best. This made your American pilots sure of themselves.

Then the Kremlin sent better airplanes to Korea with experienced Russian pilots to teach and direct them. These Russian pilots were careful not to go over into Allied airspace because if they did get shot down, that would prove the Russians were in the war. At the same time Russian pilots and instructors were sent into China along with regiments of MiG-15s. They taught the best of the Chinese pilots how to fly the best jets. These MiG-15s were far better than what they had to start with. Still the Chinese pilots were not the best pilots. It takes years to properly train a fighter pilot in a jet fighter, not three months. These Chinese pilots have been flying MiG-15s over North Korea for several months now and never over Allied-held ground until their ground troops got into the war. Sprinkled in among the Chinese pilots were Russian pilots to teach the Chinese pilots what can only be learned in combat. The Russians never got far below the Chinese border so they could get back in a hurry if necessary. As the Chinese began to win back North Korea, the Russian pilots would be coming back south also. The known presence of top Russian pilots openly fighting the Allies could never be known because of the damage that it would do to their overall plan. The plan is for many of the inexperienced Chinese and North Koreans to get shot down so the Americans think they are winning in the air. There is coming a day when the American Air Force will face Russia's finest pilots and latest fighters a thousand at a time. America will lose its air power superiority not only in Korea but in all Asia as well. Then all Asia will see the Chinese as the only true power in Asia.

"You see their plan requires that the world see the Allies are no longer the strongest and cannot be trusted. While we are talking, there are eleven regiments of our latest MiG 15s that have been moved into China. They are being painted with Chinese markings. These MiG-15s are 15% faster and have a great altitude increase. Far more important, these are now equipped with target finding rockets that are two and a half times more powerful than any the world knows we have. The pilots flying these MiG 15s have been in training for three years and about 20% will be Russian or communist block pilots and most of them will have had many years of experience. The plan is when the Chinese push the Allies back into South Korea, then MacArthur will send his B-29s north in waves as was done against the Japanese in the closing days of the war. First, over four hundred planes with Chinese markings are going to be flown by the best Chinese and Russian pilots and they are going to shoot down every last B-29 in Korea. All American aircraft will be greatly out-numbered while all the MiG's will be pretending to be Chinese. Then they are going to go after every other Allied aircraft in Korea and, last of all, blast Allied positions. These greatly improved MiG 15s are not our latest and best aircraft. I will not go into detail on our best as I want to help this plan to fall apart, but I will not hurt Russia. I want to do what will help Russia but not destroy the world, including Russia and America. There are over six hundred of these supersonic aircraft just inside the Chinese border to make sure the job gets done. Then they will take over most of Asia as well. This is a back up plan to make sure they will win, and they will if things go according to their plan.

"They do not want Japan and will leave it alone. After all, Japan is no longer armed and will stay out of everything. Japan is now a very productive country and China wants Japan to help make Asia the true power in the world. While it is doubtful Japan will turn to communism, China is sure they can work with Japan, After all, Japan still remembers it was the Americans that destroyed them in WWII and dropped two atomic bombs on them. What China does want is the resources of Indochina. On top of this there are a million more Chinese troops ready to come down and finish the job in Korea and then move into Indochina. This will discredit America and their allies so China can take over. The war hawks in the Kremlin hope that MacArthur will resort to using nuclear power to fight back and even hope it will be used against mainland China. This would finalize the world's negative opinion of America and would allow Russia to retaliate with its vast stockpile of nuclear weapons, and I assure you, they have many more that your CI thinks they have. Dimitry said, "Alex, I love Russia and want to protect her, but this plan cannot be allowed to work."

They talked on until daylight began to show over the mountains.

Then they parted with Dimitry only asking Alex to never mention his name to anyone as Washington can no sooner keep a secret than a paper towel can hold a barrel of water. If the KGB even suspected him, this would get him, and all those close to him, killed and might lead to the destruction of all those in Russia that want world peace.

Returning to Paris, Alex only told Katiya to return home to Germany as he had to fly to the States. Once there he requested to speak to the director of the CI in private and he told all with special emphasis on never giving even a hint of such an important Russian connection. The CI director agreed to never reveal the Russian contact even to the highest authorities. The committee met and the bombshell was dropped when Alex refused to give up the Russian connection regardless. The committee ranted and raved, threatening Alex in every way possible.

Finally Alex said, "I will die for my country, but I will not trust this committee with my pocket book. Why should I allow it to destroy the world just because it does not get its way?"

That ended everything: tempers flared, unprintable words were spoken, and they all left. Then everyone was told that all that happened was classified, even top secret from family or closest colleagues. The committee was highly upset over this as well. Just like the Atomic Energy Commission had done before, most thought it so far out as to be impossible until the director made one simple statement. "If it is true and we do not act on it, this is the end of the world as we know it. In truth this could really be the total end of the world. If we do act on it, true or not, we have lost nothing."

Now every needful person from the White House, in the Department of Defense, and military went to work. The White House started planning to know every move Mac Arthur was even considering. The Air Force started sending its B-29s a few at a time on carefully planned attacks. Even then, all were sent with Saber jets to protect them. Airfields were constructed and improved in South Korea so the Sabers would not have to fly from Japan. The military was informed this was not going to be an insignificant police action where the U.S. fights then packs up and goes home. The military would be in Korea a very long time. This little unimportant peanut piece of ground was now an important player in world domination. The navy was beefed up around Korea with special attention to aircraft carriers and ships packed full of the very latest long range radar equipment. The navy's Phantom jets were no match for elite MiG-15s but were great for helping ground forces. Both landbased and aircraft radar went into 24-hour watch on China. When any MiG-15 crossed into Korean air space it was carefully watched. The latest in radar was airlifted to Japan and Korea for long range detection. A new rush was put on troops to be sent to Korea from every Allied nation that would aid, without being told anything except that the ground situation was desperate. American production was stepped up and current weapons, not just super future weapons, were on the production lines. However, America let it slip that they also had some very much improved supersonic aircraft, bombers and much more.

In 1951 Alex was informed that a couple named the Rosenbergs had been arrested. This part of the crackdown on the leak of atomic secrets was made public. Hundreds of lesser foreign agents were arrested and charged with spying or helping foreign spies. MacArthur was also fired as he refused to take orders from his commander in chief.

A large part of America thought that MacArthur was right and China should be invaded. Slowly but surely the drive south by the Chinese army was slowed to a stop. There was now a battle line running back and forth across Korea near the 38th parallel. This was a constantly moving line as the Chinese and Allies advanced and then retreated over the same ground, accomplishing nothing other than loss of lives on both sides. Finally a so-called ceasefire was called as both sides' plans did not work out. Then Russia began looking for a better place to light another fire and make another plan. The talks in Korea went on and on like a bad soap opera. All the while, there were still small firefights back and forth in Korea. Each hill was argued over and when the Chinese said they held a position and the Allies claimed they held the same hill, the Chinese jumped up and stormed out. That night the Chinese tried to take back that hill and many times succeeded, as the loss of men meant nothing to the high-ranking Chinese officers. The next day the negotiators were back saying, "We have proof that hill is ours or they'd simply say, "We have returned to continue the talks," never admitting to anything.

When Eisenhower was elected president in 1952, many in the military and groups like the CI thought that a military man in the White House would radically change things. As Eisenhower took office in January, little changed as Congress was running the country, not Eisenhower. Even when Stalin died people thought this would change things. In some ways it did but not in the way people thought. Now there was a power struggle to see who could be the top man—not only the top man, but all the top men.

In June of '53 the people in East Germany rose up against their Russian oppressors, thinking the West would help them. In reality, how could the West help other than rushing into East Germany and there was no question that would have kickstarted WWIII. Russian troops and T-34 tanks with new improved weaponry were stockpiled already in Germany to attack the West as soon as they could. They figured they could quickly just run over the rebellion. Then in July, after three years of war in Korea, armistice papers were signed and a true ceasefire was established. Neither side gave up; they just agreed to stop fighting. All this time both sides were trying to guess what the other side was doing. The whole world was one big ant heap of spies running around like they didn't know what they were doing and thinking. However, in truth, every one of them was on a specific mission. This went on day and night as both sides tried to gain an advantage over the other.

The year 1954 opened with a bang in a new part of the world. The French had owned a big part of Indochina before WWII. Then the Japanese came and took it, as Germany had temporarily defeated France. When the Japanese were defeated, this area was reclaimed by the French. After the war, most of France's thought and energy was devoted to rebuilding their nation at home. There was not much the French could do to reclaim their colony. Also there was much organized resistance against the Japanese that now turned into resistance against the French. When the French tried to come back in, they faced a powerful force known as the Viet Minh who now turned their guns on the French as soon as they tried to re-enter Vietnam in 1946 and 47. This ended in 1954 when the French forces were killed or captured in a place known as Dien Bien Phu. As far as the world was concerned, things sort of fell apart until the World Council decided to split this former French colony into four parts, with Vietnam as two countries. The north was under communist control and the south was sort of overseen by the Allies. South Vietnam formed a sort of democratic government that faced much opposition from the start. Laos and Cambodia were permitted to initiate their own governments.

This was when Alexander and Margret were brought home from Germany and moved into their new home not far from Washington D.C. They both had new offices in D.C. Margret's office was the American home office of the European division of the CI [Counter Intelligence], while Alexander's was a new division of the CIA known as the office of internal affairs. Alex had no idea he was going to be given a new division or what the job entailed. His first day at the CIA headquarters, he was called into the office of the director of CIA. They had met on several occasions before and now here he sat being told that his was to be a two front office, both very important. The director told Alex that he'd been picked from several candidates to head up this new division for several reasons. One was his foundation in the army as a soldier on the ground during the war. While most of the CIA were former servicemen and women, only a few of those that were in charge of upper levels in the CIA had experience in field operations. They had a good many ex-OSS persons that were well-experienced. In the last few years a lot of things had taken place in the ranks of the CIA that were not going to be tolerated from now on. Some politicians had used CIA resources to push their personal agendas. Agents in the field made bad choices without proper oversight.

"Let me explain myself," said the director. "When you were moved from being a major in charge of ground troops it was because you were always able to get information on the enemy to help your men win their battles. From the reports that I have read, you were able to obtain your information from local sources, scouting, the study of maps, aerial photos and such. Your success rate was very good and you were chosen to be transferred into intelligence. Here again you were highly acclaimed and, even though you did not have a background in military intelligence, you were moved up in the ranks. When the war ended and intelligence was being dismantled, none other than General Patton asked for you to be transferred to his intelligence unit."

The director continued, "When I was asked to step up to become the director, there were two things of many that I wanted to change. The CIA was following these two things from top to bottom. First, they all said, 'The enemy of my enemy is my friend.' The enemy of your enemy may help you fight your enemy but that does not make him your friend. Second, the new CIA said that money solves all our problems. It buys its information, hires mercenaries to do much of its dirty work, and thinks enough money can buy any government. I want these ideas to be changed in the CIA and I need your help to do this.

"Next, even though we have a Far East division I personally think, in view of all my studies and reports, we need a new division. We are going to see the hottest spot for America to be the old French Indochina region which may become another Korea. I have talked this over with many top military people and finally I have asked the president to appoint a special group to study this problem and make recommendations to me and the president only. This will not be recognized openly in the CIA or to the military, or even to Congress. Telling anything to Congress guarantees it will be the next day's news in every broadcast in America. I hope I'm wrong, as I do not want our boys dying on foreign soil again, nor do I want another Pearl Harbor. So this operation will remain quiet even in the CIA. You will report to me alone and I will make the decision as to who to tell and what to tell. If you take this job you will be called the rat squad of the CIA, but you will be doing a great service for your country. You cannot go into any details of this even to Margret. I know you need time to think this over and explain to Margret what you can. I will need your answer by Monday morning."

The two men talked for a while longer before Alex said, "Sir, in 1943 I pledged my life and service to defend this country and had no idea if I would see America again. There was not an expiration date on that promise and many of my friends did not see America again. Margret will understand and I would like to take this job to continue to serve my country."

When Alexander arrived Monday morning, he was directed to his new suite of offices. The only thing on his door was a new sign. "A. Vetov, Director of Internal Affairs, office of the CIA." Alex opened the door and stepped into a new life. Starting up a new division would take a lot of work and Alex started right in getting things organized. While gathering information about the Viet Minh and their fight with the French, it was a great help that he could read French. Many French books contained information about French Indochina before the war. Others described how they had to live during the war and how the population fought the Japanese. Some told the story of how these same people turned against the French when the French tried to return. While Alex was studying up on the Indochina people and their struggle, he had his new staff start gathering up information regarding how the CIA had been getting involved in the politics of many other countries. He received permission to gather up members for his new division from all the way back during the war through his intelligence work in Germany. It was sort of like trying to drive four cars at the same time but Alexander got it done. Just having the title of internal affairs opened most all departments and files to him. However the reaction of the people in those departments was hostile to say the least. Many reacted to this as if Alex and IA was pulling their teeth with a pair of pliers and without anesthetics.

Alexander was actually shocked at how much the CIA had been getting involved in the political operations of so many nations. All this and without any real guidelines, most was left to the agents on the ground wherever things were happening. So much was done without consideration of long range consequences. When the Shah of Iran's government was overturned and he fled for his life, the CIA had come in and spent money like water to bribe, pay off, or recruit men for the return of the Shah. A super propaganda campaign was started and in 1953 the Shah was returned to power. This convinced many in the CIA and Washington that the CIA could spend their way into controlling many governments. They seemed to ignore that fact that a CIA-backed coup in Syria in 1949 had also been overturned in 1953 by their military, with the help of the communists. The CIA had worked to reverse this takeover and there was much fighting and trouble in Syria. Then Syria turned to Egypt for help and this expanded into the United Arab Republic. What happened in Syria poisoned much of the Muslim world against the United States.

Even so, in 1954 the CIA was told to pull out the stops and get the Guatemalan government kicked out and a government more friendly to the United States placed into power. To start, they had to replace President Arbenz with a man more friendly to the U.S. In spite of their best plans, the people of Guatemala and their military did not accept the CIAs picked man and turned the government over to military leadership. The political football was kicked around a lot for a long time until the CIA finally bought their man into power.

To Alexander Vetov, this was no way to run a supposed intelligence organization. It was supposed to gather information to protect the free world and not play at being king-makers. The year 1955 marked the end of the occupation of Germany by the Allies and the unofficial beginning of the Vietnam War. Alex's staff went into high gear to gather as much information on these so-called Independence fighters as they could. One thing was very sure—these Vietnam fighters did not want any outsiders in their country that were not at least Asian. This was when President Eisenhower told the CIA he wanted the best and latest information on all aspects of the conflict in Vietnam. I.A. was told to get with the Far East Division and compile a complete update for Eisenhower.

Working day and night, Alex's staff had a good report in only eight weeks. Alexander and six staff members presented it to the president and his close advisers as soon as it was finished. The reason Alex took six of his top members with him to see the president was so that any who had questions for Alexander and his staff could get better answers. This was done without any military personnel at the meeting as Eisenhower wanted to get points of view and information about the trouble in Vietnam without military input. He had plenty of that from the start of Vietnam's trouble. He wanted good information from different outlooks to get a better all-round view of the situation. After a five-hour meeting with hundreds of questions, the meeting was dismissed and Alexander was asked to come into the Oval Office for a chat. Once there, the president said, "Vetov, I became aware of you when you were a major in the 4[th.] You got things done. Though you sometimes skirted close to the edges of protocol, you were a good soldier. When you were moved into intelligence you played an important part in helping us win the war. When I learned you'd been transferred to Patton's staff, I thought Patton's anti-Russian feelings might rub off on you. Instead you became a very important person in the gathering of facts and fiction and was very good at dividing the two. Your analysis of situations has become known and appreciated.

"Now this is what I want you and your department to do for me. Your department has compiled a very good report and every question my people asked your people, they had a clear and excellent answer. I have great confidence in both you, and them. I need you and your people to continue to compile information and offer alternate choices to what the military is supplying me. Do not get me wrong. I've been a military man all my life, but I learned in my early military career to get a good look at all sides of a matter before jumping in with both feet. I need you and yours to study every move we are going to make in Vietnam from this day forward and what the results are going to be. Your advice will probably seldom be followed, as the military will be running the show over there. Vetov, get out your crystal ball and tell me what is going to happen as a result of every move we make in Vietnam. Understand what you are doing is to give an analyst a second opinion. Whatever you need, let my staff know and we will do our part. The two men shook hands and Alexander said, "Thank you, Mr. President, I and my people will do our best.".

A few weeks later I.A. sent a long revised report to the president. It mostly was about the need to step up the gathering of information without depending so much on buying it. Alex explained that he did not have confidence in bought information and the maps of Vietnam were very inadequate. He recommended that the military advisers in Vietnam be advised to be as friendly and helpful to the people as was practical, but to be very careful at the same time as there was significant evidence that many of the troops they were training were actually V.C. that had been placed into the South Vietnamese army and even their government. From this day forward bits and pieces of information were sent over several times a month to the president's office.

The Hungarian revolt in '56 was a hard pill for Alex and Margret to swallow. Like the East German revolt, there was nothing America could do short of declaring war on Russia. The United Nation's most powerful answer was a note to the Russian government that they did not approve. Every time the communists made a move anywhere and was not stopped, it empowered them to make other moves. This same year the freedom fighters in Vietnam declared openly they were communist. The worldwide tension between east and west was sitting on a knife's edge and in 1957 the United States put its Strategic Air Command and military on 24/7 full alert and kept it there. Even the schools taught the children of America that when they heard the air raid warning go off to get under their desks and cover their heads. Thousands of Americans dug atomic bomb shelters and listened to all newscasts. The government of Cuba was so full of corruption and organized crime that many people thought it needed to be replaced. A great many people got involved, but the CIA thought there was one young man that demonstrated the ability to take over that government. A young Fidel Castro said and did all the right things as he promised to kick the American gangsters out of Cuba and give the country back to the people. A guerrilla war was started to overthrow the government of Cuba.

The years between '55 and '59 defined the world of unrest between ideologies and there were political brushfires everywhere. American interests were running around trying to guide people and nations into their way of thinking and all too often using the CIA to push those interests. Fidel Castro took over the government of Cuba and was welcomed by the American government as a hero. But like many men before him, he became a dictator and not the savior of the people. When the U.S. criticized him, he turned to the Soviet government for support and they were glad to give it. Then Fidel openly declared he was a communist and hated the United States. So the CIA said, "We backed the wrong horse in that race so let's get rid of him and get someone else."

Easier said than done. With the backing of the Soviet government, Fidel remained firmly in power.

The Viet Cong now openly vowed to take over South Vietnam and increased their guerrilla operations against that government. The rest of Indonesia made a declaration of neutrality in the war and in '57 President Eisenhower increased aid to South Vietnam and sent in the CIA to start a counterforce against the communists.

Nearly every recommendation Alex presented to the director and the president was opposed to the way things were being handled by the CIA. He comprised only one division head and while the director often agreed with him, the White House accepted the old line practice of doing things. The mercenaries that were hired to fight the communists were as ruthless as the communists and did not win the hearts and minds of the people. In fact, nothing was really done to win the people; it was just an unofficial war between a corrupt government and communism, and the Americans were on the side of the corrupt government. This was simply because they thought that anything was better than a communist takeover. America would not admit the government was corrupt as it was anti-communist and that seemed to be all that mattered. Alexander told the director that if the conquered nations of Europe had not hated and fought the Nazis, the Allies would not have won WWII. Still Alex was fighting a strong well-established mindset so he turned to try to help the Americans on the ground in Vietnam with information. This group of Americans was growing with every turn of the unofficial war. American advisers trained, directed and helped to arm South Vietnamese forces. The number of dead Americans returned to the United States at that time was never reported in our newspapers even though some deaths could not be hidden from the public.

The very place the Viet Minh had defeated the French--the highlands of Vietnam—turned out to be the place that Alex's division was able to get some of the best information of the war. In the highlands lived small groups of natives that were very indepen-dent and thought for themselves. Alex often referred to them as his American-style Indians. They were a primitive people, prefer-ring to live the way they had lived for centuries. They still used their crossbows to hunt game and even to defend themselves. The Viet Cong came in and took their young men and forced them to join their army, then took their girls and women for--well, let's call it their slaves. These highlanders hated the Viet Cong with the hatred and fury that the American Indians did the white eyes in the Old West. These highlanders were real allies, not just paid informants or mercenaries. Here the information received could be counted on and as they were close to the Ho Chi Minh trail where many of the supplies were coming down from North Vietnam, much inside information was supplied. As this trail was over the border and not in Vietnam, no Americans were supposed to cross to gather infor-mation. The CIA did not always follow these guidelines--still, the Highlanders were the best at getting information to Alex's division.

This is when Margret informed Alex that they were going to have a baby. In spite of their very busy schedules, they both took two weeks off and got married. Both of them wanted a small wed-ding but it did not work out that way. They'd been so highly in-volved in their work for so long that the list of guests grew longer and longer. While the wedding was held in Washington D.C. the tra-ditional place for honeymoons were places like Niagara Falls back then. That is where Alex and Margret spent the next week. Back in D.C., both went right back to work, but shortly after returning to work Margret asked for a leave of absence for one year to start in six months. Alex had never been so happy in his entire life--nearly as happy as Margret was. Plans for a radical change in their lives, if not in their work, started taking place.

15

VIETNAM

T he minds of the leaders of the Peoples Republic of China started making great changes with the death of Stalin and the struggle for power in Russia. When all plans for Korea fell apart and the Chinese finally signed the ceasefire agreement, they had too many problems at home to get much involved in out-side matters. Nonetheless, they started making plans of their own on how to spread communism and their own interests throughout Asia. After the Chinese began to understand how they were being used in Russia's plans to expand communism even to the point of letting China get bombed with atomic weapons, in typical Chinese fashion they remained friendly with Russia but no longer trusted Russia. When the Russian communist government started to fall apart, the Chinese government said, "It is time for us to step in and be the leaders of communism for all the world. We will now use Russia as Russia used us. Not only Russia, but every region, nation, or person that can be used by mind, thought or whatever. We must plan with care with much forethought and patience. We Chinese are a patient people and we will use this to accomplish our long range goals."

The Chinese council started looking for ways to accomplish this new thought. All humankind was warlike in their very nature. The first recordings in history were about war, and how and why they were being fought. In all history war was common and peace rare, but what had been accomplished by these wars? Kingdoms were built and the most powerful sometimes lasted for many years only to be conquered as they fell apart. War was a part of humanity but should it not be used to build more than military power. From the first spears to the atomic bomb constituted one type of war. China desired to be a nation that uses all kinds of conflict to win and conquer the wealth and minds of all people.

Why had Hitler lost WWII? While many answers were presented only one stood at the top. If Hitler had waited, on many occasions he might have won, not lost. What if Hitler had not attacked Russia when he did but waited until his armies had fully recovered from their fighting that had conquered Europe. What if Hitler had given his scientists and engineers time to develop their jet fighters and long range rockets? They wouldn't wait for the atomic bomb, though the Germans were already working on it well before the Americans even started. No, in everything Hitler did, once he grabbed the power was to do it now. Hitler was not a patient man. No one knows how history might have been written if Hitler had patience.

China would not make that mistake. Yes, there was a time to move but there was also a time to wait. Unfortunately military men were so often without patience, so the military must be balanced with minds that looked ahead at all times. Then also the impatient could remind the slow to act when action was needed. China needed to find the perfect balance to win. What really won wars? The first answer was money and lots of it. Of course, money is really a word meaning a symbol of exchange, ability, control and several other things. Second, resources of all types. Germany and Japan both were relatively small nations that still had great resources in brain power, dedicated humans and other resources, but were very short on natural resources of oil, metal, chemicals and other things. America and Russia were huge, and natural resources were plentiful. Russia had so many people, her supply of manpower was practically endless. In the beginning of the war Russia was weak, disorganized and despondent. America was large in land mass and also had a large population that was sound asleep in its prosperous way of life.

China decided she must be smarter than any nation had ever been before, it must build itself up into not only the largest world population—it must also become rich and build a web to trap any that might fall into it. Communists around the world would be helped while not putting China in danger herself. China must look for ways to drain wealth from other nations in order to make China rich. Especially Japan had millions that would lay down their lives for Japan in the 30s and 40s. Germany had enough of their population that would do the same for Hitler, and they could force the rest into submission. While China had millions of dedicated communists, they still had many that were not. In fact, most of the Chinese people really did not care one way or the other. There were also many that did not like the communist way. Life must be improved for those that were good communists and especially for those that were extra smart, gifted, or dedicated. This must be done slowly for many reasons as China was still a poor country. It also must be done so China would not remain a poor country. It could use its millions of people to make it the richest nation on earth. That would also make it the most powerful nation on earth.

The military must make plans to control the country when desired. To protect the country when needed, to assist other nations in overthrowing any government that was not communist. This must be done without placing China in a bad light. One thing that would help was the fact that China had vast stockpiles of Soviet weapons that could be sent elsewhere without shining a negative light on China. Indochina was a great place to start as it shared a border and North Vietnam was already communist. This did not change the fact that there had been border trouble with China and North Vietnam for years. There had even been a small border war between North Vietnam and China and there were still hard feeling on both sides. It was still a touchy issue but the bigger picture of making the world a communist world was more important, so supplies and men flowed over the border anyway. One down, three to go: Laos, Cambodia and South Vietnam. All North Vietnam needed was equipment and a little push, and China was sure that Russia could be persuaded to help with both of these also. First, to succeed this time rather than get personally involved with the United States. Pretend China had nothing to do with the fight and all the equipment was used Russian equipment that was not too hard to do. After all, gasoline, rice and food stuffs were not labeled unless the provider wanted to do so. Many supplies could come from anywhere and this must be presented as a civil war. All Indochina was one nation until the United Nations cut it up into four countries, so all of Indochina must be persuaded to become communist. It was not necessary for it to all happen together, it just had to happen. Almost all the Indochina people hated to be "owned" by foreigners, must less non-Asians. Basically they just wanted to be left alone and communist "teachers" had to be sent into all of Indochina to teach the people better. Many more people in Indochina were converted to communism with a gun to their heads.

Alex's department started getting information about an American patrol that had been sent to a village in the delta region. This patrol had been ambushed and killed to the last man though it had been sent to the village at the request of the local CIA in that area. As the internal affairs director, Alex requested more information about details. He was denied any information so Alex filled an official request for all activities and copies of their files of this local office for the last six months be forwarded immediately to Washington for review by internal affairs. The next week fourteen boxes of file copies were delivered. It was the worst paperwork mess Alex had ever seen in his life. The officials' files had handwritten notes made across them without names of the persons who wrote the notes. Many files had sections blacked out with black markers, this included names, places, dates etc.

effectively making the files useless. Alex took these files to directors' meeting the next day and complained. After a lot of discussion, several directors told Alex that the local operations needed the freedom to operate without interference from Washington. As mad as Alex got, he controlled his anger fairly well and said then there was no need for anyone to oversee anything—just send agents out with millions of dollars to do whatever they wanted! He was going to take this matter to the Congressional Oversight Committee for them to investigate the situation. Most of the CIA hated having an in-house internal affairs. When this happened, even walking in the halls was like walking around in a deep freeze. Few people would even speak to him and some of his staff transferred out while others just quit.

Still his maneuver resulted in action and in another two weeks Alex got more boxes of files without a black marker on a single sheet. However, this time there were a number of pages and even entire files that were in the first boxes yet were not included in the last shipment. Alex had his staff search out all these files that were missing and carefully go over each page to find out what was still being covered up. His decoding department had come up with a way of removing some of the black marker ink without removing all the print under it. This was hit or miss, but names and dates, plus a lot more was now exposed. Finally the story of how 22 American soldiers died came to light. Plus there was a lot more on other actions that had taken place in Vietnam.

The head man of a delta village finally had enough of how the Viet Cong was stealing his men and women, taking their rice and supplies. He had sent word to the Americans he wanted to help them to get the Viet Cong out of his area. Not only that, he had contacted several other villages and they'd all agreed to help. The local American adversary force asked the CIA for help in this matter. In a few days the CIA said they needed the advisory force to send their men into this village to consult with the head man. One CIA agent was to accompany them to make plans on how to work with these locals. Turned out that the CIA had asked one of their paid informants to find out about this head man.

A few days later the informant came back and told the CIA this was all good and they needed to send in an advisory force to make plans. The force was ambushed and all killed so the local CIA started an investigation. In the process, they found out that their informant was a double agent for the Viet Cong. The Viet Cong had gone into the nine local villages and raped the women and children in front of their husbands and fathers; then the V.C. killed every person and animal in that village. They moved on to the next and did the same until the first nine villages were totally destroyed. In every village that they destroyed they cut off the breast of every woman and the penis of every man in each village and took them as hostages. After the nine villages were destroyed a woman's breast or a man's penis was sent to every village in the entire delta to show what happened to any village that did not do exactly what the Viet Cong told them to do. The local CIA had made a major mistake so they covered it up and marked it down as just another ambush. Now Alex and his department went after everyone remotely connected with this mass atrocity. He was actually more interested in going after anyone involved in the cover up than the agents that let it happen.

Again he was blocked at every turn so he went back to the Congressional oversight committee and there he found help and men that wanted to make sure that such a thing never happened again. In spite of this, things were still moving slowly until the oversight committee cut off all funding to anyone that was uncooperative in the investigation. There were instant results, but there was no question that Alex and the entire I.A. was hated even to the point of death threats. Even the army said that this was war and bad things happened in war and nothing should have ever been done about it. This incident had set the American efforts to work in the delta back so far America was never again given any real help in the delta area and it became one of the hardest parts of Vietnam to work in. Nonetheless, in many men's minds, it was Alex and his internal affairs that had betrayed the CIA, not the men that had actually caused the problem. Some ex-CIA agents were sent to prison over this and many were reprimanded but in it all, the American public was never told anything except that an American patrol had been killed.

Intelligence is as important to any army, government, business or even individual person as breathing is to sustaining life. However when an intelligence source is attacked with a deadly infection it must be cured or the person will die. If the patient refuses to be helped, insisting there is nothing wrong with him, he will die. Many times people do not like the treatment necessary to cure them but if they will recognize the necessity, any thinking person will accept it. The old saying is still true, "A few rotten apples will spoil the whole barrel," but to get the rotten ones out one must go through the whole barrel and that is a big job. Trying to do this during the Vietnam War was close to impossible but necessary.

As things turned out, many of the paid informants in Vietnam were Viet Cong. Even more would go wherever the money was the best. Many were taking money from both sides and these double agents were much more afraid of the Viet Cong than they were of the Americans. The one group that Alex had trusted the least showed up in the long run as the most helpful, and that was the mercenaries. Most of the time they fought and died alongside the Americans, but even here there were some that would change sides at the drop of a few hundred dollars. As the number of American soldiers increased, so did the number that treated the Vietnam people as fellow humans. These young men did more to help the American cause than anything else that had been done.

This was very true in the river and delta region to the south that was super hardened against the Americans. When the French had owned the whole country, most all the productive lands were owned by the super rich and powerful French and local people.

Those that worked the land spent all their time just trying to survive, as the "owners" took everything else. When the French had little power during the WWII, the people had more to live on until the Japanese came and took anything they wanted. When the Japanese were driven out it was back to more for the poor. As things began to get better, the people organized new men with democratic ideas, started land reform, and basically gave the land to the people that worked it. A prosperity sprang up that these people had never known or even expected. In the 1700s an American by the name of Thomas Paine stood up and cried for American independence. In his Common Sense writings he declared that it is necessary for mankind to have government; even though all governments are evil, they are necessary. He said this because he knew that there is greed in mankind and when this greed is in the heart of those that govern, there are going to be real problems.

This happened in South Vietnam as a corrupt government took over. Why should the people have all that prosperity when a few rich and powerful wanted it? So they took the land away from the people and the people hated them for doing it. Then the V.C. comes along and tells these people that communism means that the land belongs to all the people in common. When they all become communist, everyone will own everything.

The big lie of communism is never exposed as in communism "all the people own it all." This really means that all, even the people, are owned by the government. Those at the top cannot be reached and they control everything. Yes, they spread things out a little, as slaves must be fed. If someone can convince them to work hard for communism, it makes them think that things will get better in time. When the South Vietnam government came and took most of what they produced, thousands turned to the V.C.–thinking it would help get their production and prosperity back. Now it was like being in the frying pan and jumping into the fire. In this part of the world water was everywhere and that water represented life and transportation. From the smallest boats to commercial boats, all life revolved around them and the vast waterways. As the Americans tried to come in, it was absolutely necessary for them to take and hold as many of these main rivers as possible.

The Navy and Coast Guard took and controlled the offshore coastlines. The thousands of miles of rivers and ten thousands of miles of river branches, creeks and canals was a whole different story. The army needed to know everything about this part of the country. The CIA was flooded with requests for everything knewn, but in truth they did not know that much except the place was a total hotbed of V.C. activity. Alex's division was asked to draw up a plan of operation concerning what was needed and how to approach the people and the V.C. in the very bottom part of South Vietnam. The only time Alex had ever faced fighting in water was when he'd first gone ashore at Utah Beach or crossing a river. Alex decided the best place to get information about what was going to be needed here was from the Coast Guard so he turned to them. The landing craft that had taken the 4th Division ashore at Utah Beach was controlled by the U.S. Coast Guard. They were experts with those small landing craft in every way possible. Now Alex knew he could learn much from them. Their first recommendation was that the army be equipped with small lightweight boats that could work in shallow trash-filled waters and still be heavily armed adequately to fight their way into and out of rough situations.

Looking at all known information, Alex and his staff had a pretty good idea what the American troops were going to be facing. Turning back in time, he recalled what his men had faced in the World War. He then immediately started putting together requests for any landing craft that the Marines had used to land on Japanese-held islands. These would work on Korean beaches if they might still be in working condition. Any boats at all like the PT boats of WWII or anything the army, navy or whoever had that was amphibious he wanted it for South Vietnam. Back to the Coast Guard, Alex asked them to recommend a boat designed to meet what they suggested. It did not take long for a response and they suggested a fiberglass boat from 30 to 35 feet long with a dual water jet system, to make it work in shallow water and still be highly maneuverable. In spite of its small size, it had to carry a large assortment of firepower to protect itself and soldiers. Even though Alex did not like it, this was recommended to carry very little armor as armor is so heavy it would limit the performance of the boat. It must rely on its firepower, speed, great maneuverability rather than armor. The Coast Guard said they would send men to help train army crews. In truth many of the Coast Guard sailors that went to Vietnam and into combat to teach and help the army ended up not only teaching but fighting alongside of those they taught, and many never survived the war.

These brave men of the Coast Guard and army took off in their small boats on the many hundreds of miles of rivers and streams. The navy used a number of larger boats such as the ASPB that were 50 foot long and armored yet could still operate in only 3.5 feet of water. Other than the small 31 or 32-foot riverboats of which about 250 frequented Vietnamese waters. The ATC [armored troop carrier] was modified into many forms. It accounted for about half of all the American armored watercraft in Vietnam for river use. It was 56.5 feet long and, as modified, carried nearly any weapons available. While originally intended to carry 40 fully equipped soldiers for shore landings, it was big and heavy and had to have five feet of water to operate. Some of these even had helicopter decks welded on top for evacuation of wounded. Before the Americans brought in the boats the Viet Cong used all the waterways as their private highways. They mostly used junks and sampans since getting large military watercraft into the south became impossible after American aircraft arrived in force. The V.C. also used very small boats on up to the sampans and mostly kept them closer to shore where they were easily hidden. Even a very small boat could carry a machine gun able to wreak a lot of damage.

The small 31 and 32-footers were small, light, and fast and still carried good firepower even if it was made of fiberglass. These were originally thought of as scout boats to scout out the rivers and smaller waters. This was truly their number one use, but was far from their only use. Including the sheer number of fights, they were surely the number one boat in Vietnam. From the first day they took to the waters in Nam. They were fired upon and they fought back. The bigger armed craft were called in to do the heavy fighting, but those little guys sure did their part. On many occasions when they received fire from shore they would turn right into the enemy and charge straight at them with their big twin fifties throwing so much lead into the shore that the V.C. soon decided it best to just hide when these little boats came by. Stopping to check out all the junks and many of the sampans, boat soldiers stopped a large amount of enemy supplies from reaching the V.C. Sometimes they got into a fight to capture the supplies and that meant that all the enemy fire only had to hit an area 10 feet wide and 30 feet long. This also meant the enemy almost always fired the first shots. Approaching a native boat did not mean it was an enemy boat.

Early one morning one of the American 32s approached a sampan of about 50 feet that appeared to be loaded with farm produce. As the Americans pulled alongside the produce suddenly started moving and three men with AK-47s started firing as the two boats were about to touch each other. At such a close distance the three AK's sprayed the 32 from end to end. The skipper of the 32 hit the throttle and darted forward. The back fifty caliber had a small steel armor plate to protect the rear gunner. The 32 had been swung away from all that AK fire leaving the back of the boat facing the sampan. The gunner opened fire and those big 50 caliber shells tore through that sampan like it was made out of paper. While four Americans were wounded, none were killed and while there were over 70 bullet holes in the 32 the ship was repairable.

One of the interesting things to happen in these first days of the operations of American boats on the rivers came about not by boat observation but by aircraft photo observation. An American pilot had been assigned to fly the river and take high speed photos. The navy studied these photos, looking for any sign of enemy activity as well as to learn and plot the river itself. The next week another set came in and the same navy man was studying them again. Nothing appeared suspicious until the photo observer thought something was different and received the prior week's photos and checked them again. A small island that had been on the left side of the river was now on the right side. An Assault Support Patrol Boat [ASPB] was sent to check this out. When it got to the moving island there it was but back on the left side of the river. As the ASPB approached, the small island came alive with rifle and machine gun fire. Well, the ASPBs are armored and rifle and machine gun fire just bounced off. As the ASPB returned fire the enemy fire soon came to a halt and the ASPB pulled up alongside and found a very strange movable island that the V.C. had constructed taking two large sampans and putting a lattice-like flooring across from one boat to the other. They had potted trees and all kinds of shrubs and vegetation aboard both boats and the lattice flooring. Under, around and beneath all this greenery, they were filling this movable island with men and supplies, moving it across the river by night and unloading it when there were no American aircraft flying over. Other than a few dead and wounded V.C. aboard and a lot of supplies, the "island" was empty. The Americans guessed that, seeing the American ASPB approaching, most had fled the island boat for the shore on the side hidden from the approaching ASPB.

When there were strong enemy camps spotted along the river the navy used the 56.5 foot armored troop carriers, carrying 40 soldiers each to land, however many men were needed. These boats totally protected the soldiers until they went ashore and gave them tremendous covering fire as they went ashore. They had to have five feet of water to land but with their front ramps they could get the soldiers close enough so all they had to do was get a little wet going ashore—sometimes they landed dry. As the war progressed, it turned out that these ATCs were about the best way the Americans had of getting their troops in and out of battlefields safely. The navy had several different classes and types of river boats that they used during the war. These were very successful to the point that the larger rivers were used less and less by the V.C. The opposite was true of the smaller rivers and streams and this greatly increased the effectiveness of V.C. ground troops against the smaller boats that had to be used in these smaller waterways.

As this part of the war progressed, Alex often wondered how men could be so brave as to head into known enemy-infested waters every day, knowing there was enemy on both sides of them with all types of equipment to kill. In a fiberglass boat a rifle shot could penetrate it while the enemy was hidden in riverbank jungle. To do that and get up and do it all over the next day was just beyond Alex's ability to grasp, even though he and his men had been in many tight spots in their war. Then again he thought the same thing about those men who climbed into a hunk of aluminum known as a Bell "Huey." In his own way, Alex helped fight this war but he never understood it. He well-comprehended trying to hold back communism, probably far better than most people. If only this war could have been fought like his war where his men fought an enemy face to face and took ground from him. Then they turned that ground back over to the people that had it taken away. He understood that kind of war, and even the Korean War he could understand to an extent, though he could never understand the politics that permeated it. Stopping communist aggression he well understood, but he thought that included a lot more than just an enemy body count.

As always, the Air Force was the big item in fighting the Viet Cong. This does not mean it was the most important; it was just the big hammer when needed. Like all wars from the first one ever fought, it was the troops on the ground or on the water that did most of the fighting and here the Americans were always outnumbered. Most

of Vietnam was jungle and one part was known as the iron triangle–
a huge area of Vietnam was owned and controlled almost entirely
by the Viet Cong. During the day parts were at least controlled by
groups of heavily-armed Americans. As night fell, the V.C. owned it all
except for those few small American campgrounds that were in reality a modern version of the Old West frontier forts with hostiles just
waiting outside. This was a war like no other. As stated, it was a war
Alex could never fully understand. The American military had only
one goal: body count, nothing else mattered. Yes, a reasonably safe
spot to eat and sleep was needed. But to take and hold ground had
no importance to the American brass except for these small fort locations and the larger cities. Maybe this started since the Americans
were always outnumbered, but as time passed it was all about how
many enemy were killed. As the "Iron Triangle" was full of the enemy, that was the place to go to kill the enemy. This was like during
WWII, but now the obstacles involved driving the enemy from jungle
where the very earth was a non-stop fortification. This placed the
Americans at a very distinct disadvantage. Here the defenders had
the fort and the Americans had to fight the Viet Cong and the fort.

Since I.A. had been involved in matters in Vietnam, Alex's office
was contacted in regard to getting information. Moving into this
Iron Triangle" meant that any information I.A. might have, or could
get was very important. Alex received a personal call from a general
on a secure line who introduced himself as General Fortland. He
said, "Colonel Vetov, when we were fighting in Korea our division
had received very good intelligence from your people that was of
great benefit. We respect your work and are needing information
on an area known as the Iron Triangle, and have received reports
from army intelligence and from the CIA. Now a report from your
office lands on my desk that varies greatly from both these other
reports. Your people claim more than double the number of V.C. in
the area and a large contingent of North Vietnam's regular army
troops as well. How come your reports are in contrast to the other
two?"

"We are a separate division that is primarily an analysts division," said Alex "We know that a great part of the men and supplies who have been coming down the Ho Chi Minh trail have entered the Iron Triangle. We know this includes large numbers of North Vietnamese regular army troops. This is a known fact not a guess, and where North Vietnamese regulars go, and when they cannot take in heavy weapons, they take large amounts of medium and light weapons. These are soldiers, not civil war fighters."

The general interrupted, "We have studied our air maps and even as thick as those woods are we see no sign at all of a large number of troops."

Alex answered, "That's because they are all underground. The Iron Triangle is the largest ant hill on earth—only it is full of troops, not ants."

The general came back, "We know the V.C. dig tunnels where they take cover, but they have never fought there. Explain your reason to believe they have."

"They were prepared for the French in the highlands before the French came to where they were. We know there have been vast amounts of hand tools for hand digging coming down the trail for years; now that has gone to the Iron Triangle—such things as oil lamps and large and small generators including many miles of electric lines with light sockets already installed on the wire. They have been preparing for the invasion of that area for a long time. These supplies will only be used in tunnels and miles of lighting wire means miles of tunnel. These lights would never be used above ground where they could be seen by night flying aircraft."

The general responded, "Well, we'll bomb it and that will be the end of their tunnels."

"No, general, it will not. Our navy and Air Force pounded Pacific islands for days with the heaviest battleship shell fire and bombs on earth and yet deep, well-prepared underground tunnels were never touched and many boys died trying to take those islands. Thousand pound blockbusters will not blast through the root growth of that jungle and their tunnels are below those roots.

The general thanked Alex but still was not convinced. Just the same, he kept what he'd heard in the back of his mind. Moving from the first shots between American and V.C. troops in the opening days of the war, a little bombing of the Ho Chi Minh trail started. This increased until the area became the most bombed ground on earth. In spite of this, the flow of men and supplies to the south never stopped except for quick repairs and even then, most of the time, the supplies just went around or on a trail extension. When the Americans started into the Iron Triangle with their armor, it was like trying to cross a river without a bridge. Cutting their way in was measured in yards, not miles. The V.C. was too smart to fight in strength all the time, it was just hit and miss. They'd give the American troops time to show themselves, kill a few VC and think there would be no retribution. Then when enough Americans did show themselves the V.C. killed them. The American high command said from the start the Iron Triangle was going to give America a high body count but never expected so much of it to be American bodies.

Then the unexpected happened, the VC attacked the Americans from behind their own lines. How did this happen? As Vitov had claimed, expertly concealed tunnel openings were discovered. The Americans would pull a cover off the mouth of a tunnel and toss in a hand grenade. While approaching the smoke coming from the hole, a rifle shot would ring out from a different hole and another American would die. This was exactly what the Americans had faced in the Pacific theater in WWII. There it was the Japanese fighting for their lives and their Emperor. Here it was a fight in which if American lives were traded one for one, the enemy would win. In fact, if one American died for every ten or even twenty enemy killed they would still win the war, and they did win the war. The American military could never understand this; they could never comprehend an enemy that was willing to give up everything and die trying rather than give up. Had the American military never learned anything from fighting the Japanese? This should have been understood as they'd just faced an enemy that had the same determination in fighting. If it had not been for the atomic bombs dropped on Japan, that nation would have fought just like it had done on Okinawa. Even if everything is lost, fight until all are dead; being dead is better than being defeated. Regardless, the American high command remained the same in purpose. Let us get a high body count, that's all that matters, and it will solve everything.

Some places in the Iron Triangle were like a New Mexico prairie dog town with holes everywhere, only these holes were well concealed. A V.C. would pop up and shoot an American and jump back down again. A hand grenade would go in but the V.C. were shooting more Americans than the Americans were getting V.C. This was not what high command wanted so high command called in the Air Force and napalmed the whole area. This burned the area out big time and when it cooled a few brave Americans went down into these holes. They looked around and came back out and told their officers what they'd found. There was very little if any damage below ground, only a few places in which the napalm had reached into the twisting tunnels and there were few V.C. bodies found below ground. The V.C. had simply done as the Japanese had done. They went elsewhere until things were clear. When the Americans tried to follow a tunnel, at least one American was killed by a booby trap so they pulled out. When there was a place that an armored personnel carrier could go, it ran over an anti-tank mine and was blown to pieces. The V.C. soldiers could walk right on top of these mines all day and never did one detonate. The weight of American armor always set them off. There were punji sticks everywhere and all types of devices to stop the troops, many of which were the type used for centuries in the past. This was just not according to plans at all and every Air Force plane that could be used was used to plaster everything in front of the American troops. All types of artillery were used to soften things up but as soon as the planes and choppers flew off and the artillery stopped, the V.C. came out of the ground like a bunch of ants that have had their nest disturbed.

Some soldiers started going into these tunnels with pistols to clear them out. The firing of a 45 or even a 9mm underground destroyed a man's hearing, not because of the noise but from the concussion in a small enclosed space. Men would plug their ears to save their hearing but they could no longer hear their enemy. This gave the enemy a great advantage until someone came up with a 22 caliber pistol. Even this small-caliber pistol was loud underground but did not create a strong concussion field around the shooter to ruin his hearing. Somehow there were suddenly a lot of these 22s showing up in Vietnam. These brave men become known as tunnel rats that cleared out miles of tunnels. In truth, a thousand Americans could never have cleared all the tunnels in Vietnam. Something new also started showing up, a new ear plug designed for indoor shooting ranges.

Many police departments used these ear plugs that blocked most concussion while still allowing the shooter to hear. The experienced tunnel rats taught new men the dangers faced in the tunnels. Hand grenades did not work but men with 22s not only cleared miles of tunnels but brought to the surface information beyond the wildest hopes of the Americans. The V.C. and the PAVN [the North Vietnam regular army] had never expected their secret plans and maps to fall into the hands of the Americans. These maps of their tunnels alone revealed untold miles of these tunnels that housed and stored the supplies for thousands of men. They also had many first aid stations and even a full hospital in the tunnels of the Iron Triangle alone. When it came to armament, it was far beyond what the Americans expected. This was armament stored for the final fight to totally conquer all of South Vietnam.

Maybe this information was what made the Americans turn to the idea of spraying these whole areas and killing all vegetation. A new product called Agent Orange was introduced and troops were assured it would kill plant life, not harm humans in any way, so it was used. This stuff was spread by the thousands of gallons, it couldn't be brought in fast enough to equip the huge transport planes that flew over Vietnam. The V.C. told all the people that it was poison to kill them all and when their rice fields began to die they believed it. When one village chief asked an American patrol about this, he was told it would not hurt him or his people as it only killed vegetation.

The old man looked at the American and said, "Would it not be better to just kill us now than kill our rice and cause us to die the horrible death of starvation?" Well Agent Orange did kill some of the jungle growth but not all by any means. When the leaves fell to the ground, the trees, vines, bushes still stood with just as much resistance to stop the passing armor and troops as before. It did do a great job of killing rice fields, other food crops, all fruit-bearing vines and trees. Whole villages had to be moved and fed to keep them from starving.

The big thing was troop mobility and that meant helicopters by the thousands. The American big brass only wanted to hold enough ground for their big bases. In one meeting with America's top military men, the CIA advisory committee and the Congressional committee on the progress of the war met to hold a discussion on the situation. President Johnson had promised the military whatever it needed to win this war. So now the military was asking for what it needed. The first report was made to all the members present and it was a report on how many V.C. and PAVN had been killed and what was needed to double that number and this required more men and equipment. The report ended with the statement, "If we hurt North Vietnam badly enough, if we kill enough of the V.C. and PAVN they will give up. We are the most powerful nation on earth; we cannot be beaten if we apply enough force."

Then he sat down and Alex stood up in front of everyone and asked if he might be permitted to ask this officer a question. "Sir, you sound sure that with enough pressure the communists will quit. May I remind you, sir, that King George of England stated, 'If we put enough force on those rebels in America—if we kill enough of them, they will quit. We English are the most powerful nation on the earth; we have to win.' Sir, we were being beaten everywhere we turned. We did not give up and, if we had, there would be no United States today. Can you answer my question, sir. How do you know these people will ever give up regardless of how much they suffer? The Japanese did not give up until we used the atomic bomb. Sir, are we going to use the atomic bomb on Vietnam?"

Things were very quiet for a long time so Alex finally sat back down. The chairman of the Congressional committee finally said, "I feel we should take a break and we will reconvene in fifteen minutes."

When they did reconvene, Alex's chair was empty as he has been asked not to return. He had simply been told that it was best for the good of a harmonious atmosphere that he not be there. When Alex returned to his office he wondered if he ought to start packing now or wait for the ax to fall. Maybe he'd send in his letter of resignation and retire. After all, he had put in many years and deserved to be able to retire and do something other than the intelligence work. He started off under Roosevelt and had served under a long line of presidents until now, Johnson. Maybe it was time to write that letter of resignation and retire. Margret might like being on their own. No, damn it all. He had always done his best. If they wanted him out, then they were going to have to fire him, and meanwhile Alexander Vetov was going to do his best to keep as many American boys alive as possible, just as he had done since 1943. As long as he sat in his chair he still had the power to do some good and he sure as hell was going to.

The Bell Huey helicopter had started showing up in large enough numbers to become the army's best known helicopter in 1961, and it had been extensively used from day one. Stepping back in time a little, when President Kennedy took over as the new president he had great plans and programs for the U.S.A. However he also had a tiger by the tail called Vietnam, and this he was not prepared to handle. It is very doubtful there was a single man on earth who could have handled that tiger with less than a WWIII. He did his best with the 1,000 advisers in Nam, and in short order it was changed to 16,000. By that time North Vietnam had over 100,000 doing the same job with the V.C.

The Kennedy years in the White House also saw the very first small parts of the CIA moving into their new home in Langley, Virginia. Alex and his division moved in December of '62, six months after Margret and the European division did. It was still well into '63 before things were totally up and running in Langley..

Alex thought Kennedy was the hardest working man he had ever seen. Alex had always worked long hours and it seemed to him that Kennedy used the late hours to work on the Vietnam problem. By the time he was killed in November 1964 and Johnson automatically became president, the build-up of troops that had been going on under Kennedy was continued until General Westmoreland asked Johnson for more troops in '65. Johnson had promised the American public he would do his best to finish what President Kennedy had started in order to win the war in Vietnam. It is doubtful that at the time he even imagined this promise was going to come back and bite him in the ass. Johnson was no military man either, so he left the war to the military. Johnson said on national television, "I have asked General Westmoreland what he needs and he has told me."

Then troops and helicopters flooded into Vietnam "to win this war." Johnson ordered in a total of 187,000 troops, tripling the number there.

A large number of these troops were sent into battle in Huey helicopters. How can you win a war by more than doubling the men and equipment to fight. You're begging to fail without superior intelligence to correctly provide information for the number you had before it was doubled or tripled. There were those that seemed to think, 'now we have enough and we can finish this. We will just go and hunt the enemy down and kill him and we will win.'

So "search and destroy" was the word of the day and little else counted. So what happened in only one instance where over 400 seventh cavalry men were loaded on Hueys and sent into the highlands close to the border? It was reported that the V.C. had been seen there so go get them. How many there were, exactly where they were, or how they were equipped never came up. Within minutes after the first flight of Hueys had touched down, the North Vietnam Army, not the V.C. opened fire on them. This happened before the second flight of Hueys could even bring in the second load of soldiers. When they did arrive, they had to fight while jumping off the helicopters.

How they held out no one knows other than the fact that they were brave troopers and very well led by quality officers. A captured N.V.A. told the American Lieutenant Colonel Hal Moore, commander on the ground, that this area was the headquarters of a contingent of 2,000 North Vietnamese soldiers and a few V.C. as well. The seventh at that time only had a few of its four hundred men in the fight. Every flight of Hueys received heavy fire while trying to bring more soldiers, ammunition, equipment and pick up the wounded and fly back out. They took fire from the moment they entered the area until they were out of it. There was a fire base close enough that artillery was able to provide heavy fire to help. That, along with air strikes kept the 7th alive. This was not a fight with time to recover. It was a time when the NVA applied their force in different spots, looking for a weak place, so the fight never really stopped. That night was even worse and, on occasion, men were fighting for their lives on the ground with knives. It was a trip back in time to the dark ages as men slaughtered each other en masse.

The second day of battle another group of air cavalry was landed a little over two miles away and moved overland to join Colonel More's men. They had to fight their way in and together they fought through another night and day, still greatly out-numbered but at least with enough men to keep most holes plugged up. Every hour of daylight the next day the Hueys kept coming, bringing ammunition, water, medical supplies and taking out wounded. Air power had been called in from far and wide and every branch of the services that had combat aircraft came. Air power gave the men on the ground a little time to take care of the wounded and redistribute men and ammunition even though the enemy had moved in so close air power could not help at ten yards. At one time it got too close and napalm bombs took out some American troopers—a terrible thing but so-called friendly fire has been a disaster in all wars. Night was still the worst time and it was combined with little rest and only a few minutes of sleep here and there for four days and three nights. But even with death staring men in their faces it was hard to react as needed.

Books have been written and at least one movie made on this story, but how this unit held out is still beyond what common sense would dictate. How many times this story was repeated in Vietnam with varying results is totally unknown. But facing an unknown enemy in number, equipment and even exact location and conditions is what Armstrong Custer did with his seventh Cavalry 200 years before and we all know what happened to him. The American public wanted a lot more than hearing the military claiming a body count of X-thousand V.C. and NVA. Also for the first time in history, American people watched their boys dying on the battlefield every night on television. As wonderful as the American people are, some began to say we should not fight, "Let's just bring our boys home, and who cares what happens in the rest of the world?" Of course, there is just something in Americans that says, "I know bad things happen but they cannot happen to me. When it does, I'll lock my doors and to hell with the rest of the world."

When Hal Moore, the commander of the battalion that was a part of the 7th Cavalry, was the last man that was a part of the battalion he commanded to leave landing Zone X-ray, he was considered a hero and he was. This was far from the end of that battle, even when it did change ground for a little over a mile it was not the last of the fight. The two support groups that had also come into the fight were ordered to pull out and travel overland and by helicopters to get out of the B-52s bombing area. When they had gotten a mile away flights of B-52s started pounding the whole place with heavy bombs. The first group out after Moore's part of the 7th only faced minor resistance retreating. [By the way General Forestland and the entire head of the American and South Vietnam armies never admitted it was a retreat. It was only a redeployment of American and South Vietnamese troops.

The second group, under Colonel McDades, headed in another direction and was mostly all on foot as they traveled through heavy jungle. They began to come into contact with NVA and harassing fire as soon as they started out. Traveling in deep jungle the Air Force did not know where to strike and as both forces were involved in this close contact, no one will ever know how many of those killed by American air power were NVA or American. While the LZ Albany was never actually overrun by the NVA they came right up to it and fought at long range. The Americans that fought from the LZ itself were continually firing into NVA soldiers that were moving around the edges of the non-cleared jungle. When the fight was over they found out these NVAs were moving around, killing Americans that were trying to get to the LZ, including many that had already been wounded. Over 50% of McDade's men were casualties before they were revealed.

American newspapers told the great story of how an outnumbered 7th Cavalry Battalion had fought and won a great battle in the highlands of Vietnam, just as they should have. This was a true story of how very brave men fought unbelievable odds. What these men did can never be praised enough. McDade's men were also brave. How many died? Some say 200, others say well over 400. In truth it will never be known, as the account of the whole battle of the entire Highlands episode was turned over to a South Vietnamese general to write the report as he saw fit.

Now billions of American dollars were suddenly flowing in support for the South Vietnamese army. Then we were supplying them with nearly anything they asked for in weapons and equipment. Plus a quarter million American soldiers were present to back them up. Thus for a time, things did start to look better in the fight to keep the Communists from winning. The NVA, however, just saw a long hard battle in front of them and one they had no intention of losing, regardless of hardship or time.

For the next two years while the American and South Vietnam military leaders were claiming progress in South Vietnam, Laos and Cambodia were totally lost to the Communists. Now only the small country of South Vietnam was the only hold-out. Alex never had a good report that declared everything was wonderful and the sun was shining bright when he communicated with the Commission. As this was not what they wanted to hear, after a while they paid little interest to what his staff had to say. While the news media was against what was going on, the military was saying they were not only holding their own but were making distinct progress.

In 1968 Vietnam exploded in the Tet Offensives which changed everything. The U.S. and ARVN lost over 50,000 men but that was a drop in the bucket compared to the loss of NRV and V.C. soldiers. As bad as it sounds, this was the first time in the war when American forces had ever fought on somewhat of a level playing field. The Americans were terribly outnumbered but once they got over the shock, they came back in typical American fighting style. They fought right back and advanced everywhere they fought. In spite of all the communists had, they did not have the ability to hold what they had gained. The American army fought their way back to the American Embassy and retook it. All over Vietnam, brave Americans took towns and villages back, house by house and brick by brick. However the "story" that we were winning in Asia was shattered. Johnson publicly declared "I will not run for another term and if I am elected I will not serve." For the rest of the year South Vietnam burned under the horror of hard warfare.

In 1969 President Richard Nixon, started the policy of "Vietnamization." This meant simply we were going to turn our equipment over to the South Vietnamese Army and gradually reduce our part in that war. Troops that had been going into Vietnam like a flood were reduced to a trickle, mostly just replacement troops. Then the pull-out started, reducing American troops steadily. The war continued but the communists were patient as they well knew if the Americans got out they could run right over the south. In '72 the U.S. started doing just that.

American troops felt they had been betrayed by their own government. However, that was nothing compared to the trauma when men that had given up so much for the United States returned home. Here they faced a hostile nation that blamed them for the whole thing. This was one of the worst times in American history: Americans had turned on their own heroes. The next year the world famous Paris Peace Accord was signed and the NVA promised to be good little boys and treat the south with respect and goodwill. They did the exact opposite, they rushed south, killing everyone that they even thought might have stood up to them. When Vietnamese tried rushing to the American Embassy for protection the Americans left untold numbers behind to be killed. Do not blame the few that got away, as there was nothing they could have done.

The Nixon years as president were not happy years for Alexander Vetov. Alex never said much one way or the other toward the president. He was no longer called to the White House for any reason. The last three presidents had called for his advice on providing intelligence. Nixon did not and this was fine with Alex, as presidents always had their own advisers. The nation was not in an open war at this time. However the need for intelligence continued to grow with each year. Alex's part in being director of internal affairs for the CIA had gotten harder in these years. Being in IA was worse than being an IRS agent and calling in to inspect someone's records was definitely not appreciated. Of course, with Alex this only made him work harder at digging into things.

In the first years of the Nixon administration, Alex thought that Nixon had done a pretty good job as president. Then he began observing Nixon using his office too much in pushing his personal agendas. Considering that every politician in Washington did the same thing on a daily basis, he guessed this was just the way Washington worked. In fact, he guessed that most politicians had always worked this way.

There were just too many times that this administration stepped over the line to get what they wanted. Now Alex began to get blocked by direct orders from the White House. Going directly to the chief director now did no good as the CIA director could not override an order from the president. What this did, however, was like taking a bone away from a dog. There were all kinds of bones showing up in the CIA, and Alex started digging up every one that showed up, that is, until he was ordered to stop, and this only made Alex wonder more about what was going on. The basic mandate for the CIA was as a foreign intelligence agency and the FBI handled matters inside the United States. More often now the two agencies worked hand in hand as, more than ever, too much was flowing back and forth without regard to borders. Alex had good friends with whom he'd worked for many years in the FBI.

In conversation with these friends, a pattern of conversation began to develop. Things had started developing inside the United States that raised questions in the FBI. When the White House and Congress set up roadblocks and stopped FBI investigations, the FBI was not happy either. From Alex's first day working in intelligence even back in WWII, he had come across times when politicians and other powerful people had wanted to use the intelligence service for their own purposes. This was a fact of life and not only did Alex not like it then, but as the years passed it got worse not better.

The worse it got, and the higher in rank Alex achieved, the harder he fought it. Alex was quick to admit that his doing this caused him a great deal of trouble throughout the years. This fact did not change his actions of fighting this wrong, other than make him fight harder. Both the CIA and the FBI had been hit up untold times for inside information on political opponents, business opponents, and even requests to check up on someone's spouse. Now things had climbed even higher, specifically in political circles. Now that both the CIA and the FBI were having their resources and agents pulled back, Alex did not like it one small bit.

16

THE LAST YEARS IN GOVERNMENT SERVICE

While things like this did make Alex sometimes want to quit, his very nature made him want to just fight harder. He was against the agencies being used for personal purposes. Now even an attempt to correct things brought pressure down on the ones trying to make things right. Now the ones doing the wrong thing were protected rather than punished or even corrected. Not long after Nixon was reelected things began getting much worse. Then you know what hit the fan. Watergate opened the doors of illegal activity and government agencies and employees committing illegal activities. After fighting back for a while, on August 9th Richard Nixon resigned from the presidency of the United States. Gerald Ford, the vice president, took office in his place. Alex wondered how this man was going to work out. In February Alex was called into the Oval Office and was introduced to President Ford. After being seated the new president said to him, "I have been reading reports from Eisenhower, Kennedy, and Johnson. They have all said that CIA agent Alexander Vetov helped them in obtaining valuable military information throughout our struggle in Vietnam. They also continued to say that you supplied many thing and information about Asian interests. On top of this, they also said most of your reports were different than other reports coming into this office and yet many times your reports proved to be the correct ones in the long run. I also check your service records for WWII and they are excellent.

Alexander, I am not a military man. I was not allowed to be very involved in the last administration. Even though I was the vice president, I was kept in the dark on most all issues. I inherited this chair without a proper knowledge and understanding of military issues and intelligence in our day. I now have access to all military records and information as they see it. The same is true for the FBI and other government agencies as they see it. That is not enough. In the past you and your office were always presenting alternate viewpoints to what others were saying. Alexander Vetov, will you and your people help me and this office get alternative viewpoints on what is going on now? In simple words, will your office supply me the same help you did for Eisenhower, Kennedy, and Johnson?"

"Mr. President, It would be my honor to do so," Alex said. They talked a little while longer shook hands and Alex left the Oval Office with a big smile on his face. He was going back to work again, not that he and his stall had ever stopped working, but now it was going to the president again and not into someone's trash basket.

Internal Affairs was back to being its old self again. It was still the "rat squad" that lived in the icebox. However now, in spite of everything, there was some of the old respect showing up. Alex's staff was working with a new zeal and increased performance. Regular reports went to the president and on occasion Alex was summoned to the White house. Alex referred to President Ford as a quiet but smart-thinking man who was a good president. He did not look or act like a president, but that did not stop him from being a good one. Ford did not get reelected and Jimmy Carter took over.

Alex's position remained the same with Carter, except Carter also said he was not a military man and left military matters up to the military and Congressional committees. Carter always read Alex's reports and often talked to Alex about some of his reports but still left military matters in the hands of the military and Congress. When Alex turned 53 he started thinking seriously about retiring and being with his wife and son full-time.

In 1974 the little island of Grenada was given its independence from the British Crown. Five years later the communists seized power and most of the world including the United States paid little attention.

Having seen what had happened in Cuba, the CIA along with some members of the military, sent up red flags. The current administration, however, said, "This is a small foreign matter in a very small place and things are going well right now, let's not rock the boat. The people of Grenada were never pleased with the communist government. Protests went on sometimes but the people of Grenada were easygoing people and said, "We're still allowed to vote so we'll wait for the next election. The elections never came in Grenada and America paid little attention to what was happening in such a small place. As President Carter still called him into the White House, Alex decided to wait and see if Jimmy Carter would be reelected in 1980. If Carter was reelected, Alex decided to give it a few months and then retire. Carter was not reelected—Ronald Reagan was, and he was the ninth president to be his commander-in-chief.

Reagan came in like his coattails were on fire, and the first week in February Alex was summoned to the White House. Alex liked Ronald Reagan from the first meeting. In some ways it started off a lot like his first meeting with Gerald Ford. The big difference was Ronald Reagan's personality was the opposite of Gerald Ford. Here he was sitting in the Oval Office all fired up to take on the whole world with the purpose of making things better for not only the United States but the whole world. As the years passed, Alex liked Reagan even more. In Alex's mind, no one would ever take the place of Kennedy as the number one president. Reagan was definitely number two in his opinion, but in many ways the two men were a lot alike. Very different in ways, yet still alike in drive and the determination to get the best for America. Even the appointment of his cabinet members showed clearly where he wanted to head. For example he chose CIA Director, William J. Casey, Ambassador to the United Nations, Jeane Kirkpatrick, national security adviser, and

William P. Clark Jr. who became the most important administration in foreign policy. All these were strong in mind and heart as to the future direction of America in the world. The next year George P. Shultz was added as the most outspoken of the lot.

This was where Alex and his staff fit in, so of course this occupied his greatest interest. This did not mean that Alex was not interested in all aspects of government; this was simply where he worked. On March 30th, after less than 100 days as president, Ronald Reagan was shot by John Hinckley Jr. Early reports declared the president was in critical condition, but later reports confirmed the president would recover. Two weeks later Ronald Reagan was released from the hospital. The American economy was in poor condition and therefore so was the government and all the aspects of the military. In July an emergency Economic Recovery Tax Act was passed to pull America out by her bootstraps. Next, the new president tore into government waste and needless spending. All this time the new government was working hard to get intelligence and other aspects of the government working to fight the big bad wolf, communism. This was done, of course, without fanfare or newspaper stories. This did have the CIA, including Alex and IA, working overtime. The next big item to be struck with the full force of the White House was crime in America.

Near the turn of the decade the Israeli war of '82 occurred, in which Israel invaded southern Lebanon. Much of the world cried foul and was against Israel for invading her neighbor country. The United States led by the Reagan administration, said Israel did not shoot first and cannot be blamed for protecting herself. This was the time that Muammar Gaddafi was sponsoring terrorism around the world. Again Reagan said no way and started after Gaddafi.

The CIA called Gaddafi of Libya, Leonid Brezhnev of the USSR, and Fidel Castro of Cuba the unholy trinity. At this point the CIA and all the help the U.S. could get was called upon to stop or at least hinder these three and others like them. This created a big problem for the new administration because it called for more money for defense while calling for the government to cut back on spending. Many Congressmen said their states needed new dams to conserve water or new bridges; and states' needs were more important than going after terrorists. However after the news media showed children, along with innocent adults, killed and dismembered by terrorist bombs worldwide the Congressmen were not as loud as before. Through the years Alex's staff had been chopped over and over until it was a skeleton organization. Now it began to grow again and still work piled up. While officially half of the work regarded the Far East, Internal Affairs covered all the CIA and therefore really covered every aspect of it. While terror might be planned in Libya or anywhere else, its actions sprang up in many locations all over the world.

The year 1983 brought many changes to the Reagan administration, including three very important ones. The Reagan Doctrine said in essence, "If you shoot at us or our allies we will hunt you down and shoot you and we do not care where you hide."

Second, was the Strategic Defense System also known as "star wars." Congress cried, "This will cost untold billions."

The public cried, "Who cares?

Some alarmists had dug bomb shelters and their children coming home from school had been asking "Mom, we had to hide under our desks at school in case of bombs. Are we all going to die from bombs?"

Then a new one hit that actually required boots on the ground again. The small group of communists that had seized power in the small island of Grenada were fighting among themselves. This was not a true civil war uprising but a small armed force that took over like a gang of bank robbers takes over a bank. Reagan said to CIA Director Casey, "I want every detail about what is going on down there. We need information as to who is who, what they are doing, and what they have to do it with, whatever it is they are doing. Last, if we need to go in we must know what we will be facing. Director

Casey called Alex and repeated every word the president had said. Alex gathered his staff and repeated everything. Next Alex went to several of the CIA Departments and again repeated the message.

Within two days his staff and other departments started coming in and all said the same thing. There was very little information about the island at all. One man spoke up and said, "It took me awhile to even find where it was. Then there it was—a hundred miles north of Venezuela. In truth that was about as good a piece of information as came in the first day. Slowly but surely information started coming in but little proved to be of much value. In fact, there were not even any recent maps. The best information maps delivered to Alex's offices were ones gained from a tourist agency. This little island was like it had never existed. Then the organization of Eastern Caribbean States called upon America to help settle the problems in Grenada. The United States had signed a treaty with this organization and this gave America more legal ground to get involved. On October 23 the Marine barracks in Beirut were blown up with the largest number of single day casualties since Vietnam. Then the French barracks was also blown up. All these men were stationed in Beirut as peace-keepers, but Islamic Jihad did not want peace they wanted war. First things first.

Reagan said, "We're going in. All those plans that have been made: I want them on my desk now." A few days earlier on the 16th, Bernard Coard had seized power in Grenada and put General Bishop under house arrest. When the word spread into the streets, a mass protest rushed to the house and released Bishop. Bishop returned to power for a few days but he was taken again and this time he was killed. This time even a Grenada General Paul Scoon secretly contacted the British and asked them to ask the Americans for help. He did not sign papers to this effect until after the start of the allied invasion, however. This made his papers invalid in the eyes of the world.

Another important fact was made known to the White House:

there was much "concern over 600 United States medical students at St. George's University on Grenada." This sparked fears of a repeat of the Iran Hostage Crisis. Congressional lawyers said America had the right to go in and rescue the American citizens. Several treaties with the Caribbean nations were legally binding for a collection of these countries to work together to protect their own interests. The green light was given and Navy seals were the first to go in. In very severe weather they had real problems in their small boats attempting to find the shore by the airport they were inspecting. It was impossible to land troops in landing craft. Maybe that was because of the very bad weather or other reasons [the information was never released].

The 75th Ranger Regiment was sent in, hoping to land on the Point Saline airport. While in flight the pilots were notified that heavy equipment had been parked on the runway and they could not land. Good preparation had sent the Rangers in with parachutes, so they parachuted in and captured the airport anyway. Jamaican and regional troops from the Regional Security system came in with the Rangers and the 82nd to fight in this brief war. The heavy equipment was moved to the side to allow the 82nd airborne to land on the runway. As soon as the airport was taken, the troops started spreading out to take the island.

The 8th Marine Regiment came in by helicopter and amphibious landings to capture the Pearls Airport on the north end of the island, giving the allies total possession and control of all aircraft traffic. This was the start of a three-day fight to take Grenada, rescue the medical students, and all other Americans on the island. While Grenada spanned only 133 square miles, that was still a lot of ground in attempt to wrest it from armed troops defending it. This was made much more difficult when there was little to no information as to what the men were going to be facing. St George's University was spread out in several campuses and American students were found at three different locations. It took all of three days to round them up. There were several places the allied troops were ambushed and some hard fighting took place. Compared to past warfare, the death total was light on both sides. The number of wounded was much higher, but even it was far less than it could have been. Cuban military hardware that was captured could have equipped a full army so it had to have been stored there to be spread into other South American countries. The 9,000-foot runway at the new airport was spacious enough to handle the largest airplanes of the Russian Air Force and storage facilities were the same. Even the huge fuel storage tanks would never have been needed for commercial aviation. They had to have been built for military use. Who knows what plans were made for this small island so close to America's gulf coast? American troops came in and overcame the Cubans that had been brought in to enforce the few communists that had taken over. We can only guess what plans the communists had. The people of Grenada were thrilled that the Americans had come and there was a new realization on the earth—this new America was not going to act like a whipped dog.

It is true that George Shultz had directed the president to remain unyielding while being more careful in his wording when he spoke to Russia. This lowered the temperature between the two nations some without reducing America's strong position at all. Russia was in bad financial shape at this point, in part because her main interest for decades had been in producing more and better weapons. When a country runs out of money, things begin to fall apart. Governments use money; they cannot make it. They can print it but it is valueless unless there is real monetary value to back it up. When Russia tried this, things started going to hell in Russia. This has been true in all of history and will always be true. Gorbachev was now using less threats and more of "let us all together and slow things down." It was now Russia expressing the possibility of a weapons freeze—and not only the Americans. Weapons or not, Russia could no longer afford to fight a nuclear war. America was now facing new enemies however. China, while waving the flag of friendship, was plotting a war of international finance and technology. A massive war of religion and radically different beliefs had come to light regarding how the world should be run. Above all, who in the world should be in control? Then there was also international crime with its control of worldwide drugs. Yes, America still had much it must fight to survive. This required a super update in high grade technology to even keep up. America must do more than anyone else to keep up, then America must excel.

Alex decided it was time to turn things over to younger minds that think more in modern terms. In February of 1984 Alex wrote out his letter requesting retirement. He also sent a copy to President Reagan along with a personal letter. "My dear President Ronald Reagan, I have enclosed a copy of my request for retirement. Dear sir, I want to tell you that of the nine presidents I have served my country under, I think you are the second best I have ever had. Yes, I think that John F. Kennedy was the best and I believe if he had been allowed to live he would have accomplished the goal he had in his heart for this great United States. You sir, have done much for our country and I have no doubt you will be reelected for another four years in which you will achieve even more. It has been my pleasure to have served under your administration. I am tired and long to spend a few years with my wife and son. Again sir, may I thank you for the privilege of being a part of our nation's great military service and then in the service of gathering worldwide intelligence for our wonderful country. Your servant and friend, Alexander Vetov."

Alex served another five months until he felt that things were all taken care of, then he and Margret moved to Kansas City where she still had family. Alex had lost both his father and mother many years previous. His brothers and sister had scattered and it had been a half century since he'd lived in his birthplace—New York City. They moved to a farm about twenty miles outside Kansas City. This was close enough to have all the advantages of a big city close by and still have the peace and quiet of country life. Both Alexander and Margret were definitely ready for some of that. Both began doing some writing. Margret wrote about her life in England and then Germany. She was very careful to avoid saying anything that might be harmful to anyone and especially the intelligence services. Alex did write some about his life in the 4th but mostly about his dogs and life in Kansas farm country. He never mentioned he had served under nine presidents and was a personal advisor to six of these presidents.

Lightning Source UK Ltd.
Milton Keynes UK
UKHW021139240520
363742UK00012B/532/J